Bridging the Silence

Blind Rebels book 1

amy kaybach

Keep rockin' + reading —

Amy Kaybach

Content and trigger warnings: This book contains adult subject matter and is intended for adult audiences. This book is not recommended for audiences who may be sensitive to discussions involving mass shooting, bodily injuries or death, anxiety and panic attacks.

Bridging the Silence- Blind Rebels book 1

Edited by: Editing Fox

Edited by: Nice Girl Naughty Edits

Cover: Emily Wittig Designs

Copyright © 2022 by Amy Kaybach

To my bestest,
Surprise! I kind of did a thing. -- A

Ƀ

To all the bands I've loved (past, present, and future),
Please don't stop. The world needs your music.
Rock on! -- Amy

Note To Readers

I know there are lots of ways you could be spending your time and money and I sincerely *thank you* for giving my book a chance! It means the world to me that you're willing to give these characters that have been living in my head a chance! I hope my book provides you with a momentary escape and most importantly I hope you love these Blind Rebel boys like I do.

When I started the Blind Rebels series my intention was to have four standalone books, each about a different band member in the series where the stories were not interconnected in any way and could be read in any order.

However, these Blind Rebels boys had something different in mind for me. The further I wrote into the series, the more interconnected the books got. Because of this, I do highly suggest you read this series in order (Bridging the Silence, Blending Chords, Reviving the Rhythm, Finding Harmony) and be sure to read the epilogues.

Note To Readers

I love to connect with readers. Check out the "About amy kaybach" in the back of the book for ways to reach out to me.

- Amy

Chapter 1

Kadence

I need to get my rear into gear. I promised Harden I'd be at his club in forty-five minutes. Shuffling through the stacks of filters on the desk in my makeshift office, I can't find my new star effect filter or my lens pen. I haven't had a chance to use either yet, and I think the darkness of the club with the stage lighting might make for some interesting shots to test them out.

A-ha! Of course, they're in my bathroom drawer, where I throw all my junk.

"Are you sure you're up for this, Kade?" My best friend slash roommate's voice filters down the hall. She's in helicopter mode again, and she's about to hover herself right into my room. My stomach tightens as the nerves hit me. She means well, but I don't need any more stress about this job. She's making it worse by reminding me I'm not quite as normal as I like to pretend I am. This job was all her idea. She suggested Harden put my name in before she even knew who it was for. I don't need her doubt piled on top of my own. I fire off a text to her—my only means of communication with anyone for the last two years.

Me: I got this. Step off.

I'm working for the freaking Blind Rebels! My heart stutters a little, and I get dizzy just thinking about it. I'm not one to get flustered at meeting someone famous, but it's insane that this photography gig is for *the* Blind Rebels. They were the hottest rock band of our age, until just over a year ago when the lead singer tackled the guitar player mid-show because he slept with his fiancée.

Even if the Blind Rebels reunite for these four weeks only, getting a job like this is next level for me. I haven't been at this photography thing that long. Harden has hired me to take pictures of other shows at his club, but no one of this magnitude has played Hard before since they are a new rock club here in Vegas. I've tried a couple of different hobbies, but this one stuck because it gives me the creative outlet that I yearn for. It's still not as satisfying as music, but that is something that I can't do anymore.

None of the other bands at Harden's club made me sign a non-disclosure agreement just to photograph them, but it's the Blind freakin' Rebels, so how could I say no? This is the kind of job that'll put *Photos by Kadence* on the map.

I tuck the lens pen in my back pocket and grab my brush since I'm in the bathroom. I brush my shoulder-length black hair behind my head and wrap a hair band around it because I hate it when my camera strap pulls on my hair when it's down.

"If I haven't told you lately, I'm so proud of you. This is big, Kade!" I draw a breath deep into my hollow-feeling chest and lift my eyes a bit in Hayleigh's direction with a subtle nod. Pulling on my black boots, I can't make direct eye contact with her right now, but I can see her blonde hair in the reflection of my bathroom mirror.

Hayleigh's been my best friend since we were eight. We met as kids on set of a very popular children's television show. She was the only person there for me two years ago when everything went sideways for me. Getting sucked into her mess of feelings will bring out my own. I can't afford to be lost, wallowing in my emotions. I'd rather keep them buried when I have a job to do, an important job, not just for me but our friend, Harden.

He and Hayleigh used to date, but that's before I came to Vegas two years ago, suddenly unable to communicate normally and very broken. He's always been here for Hayleigh and thus, for me too. I can't imagine a world without Hayleigh and Harden.

Thing is, I can't decide why Hayleigh is so proud. Is it because I'm doing this specific photo shoot or because I've started working in general? Or is she just proud I'm doing something with myself now? Maybe it doesn't matter why she's proud. At least not right now. The lump in my throat grows thick again, but I swallow it down. *Focus. Deep breath. Exhale.* I crack my neck. I need to get moving; I have to be at HARD in thirty-five minutes. That's what's important today.

My muscles involuntarily stiffen at the unexpected contact of Hayleigh's constricting hug. Memories of his arm barred across my neck as he used me as a shield play in my head. I scrunch my eyes shut and swallow hard, concentrating on being here in our apartment with Hayleigh and not back at the festival.

She means well, but I can't control my reaction. Two years later, and I'm still so messed up that I'm thrown by an innocent hug from my very best friend, the one who's been there through everything—good, bad, and quite ugly. Not to mention the no talking thing.

"Shit, sorry. I know better." She sighs and takes me gently by the shoulders, moving me so I stand directly in front of her. Her long, golden blonde hair frames her face as her blue eyes soften. "Hey, look at me."

She waits until I finally bring my green eyes to hers; it's the connection she's wanted since she came home, the one I've been actively avoiding in the name of getting ready. She may have been on Kangaroo Klub Houze with me when we were kids, but our career paths couldn't have diverged any differently. She ended up as the chief financial officer of the Black Mountain Casino group, and I'm starting over, yet again, giving this photography thing a go.

"You have this, Kady." She squeezes my shoulders to emphasize her point. "Harden wouldn't have hired you if he didn't love your work with the other bands, and shooting the Blind Rebels on stage at their first show since they broke up? This is beyond awesome. It could be a career changer." She slides her hands from my shoulders and runs them down my arms and back to my shoulders again in a soothing motion.

"But if something happens..." She stops mid-sentence, biting her lip. She's rephrasing her comment. We don't talk about the panic attacks, because talking about them is like throwing fertilizer on the ground for more of them.

"If you need me for anything, text me. I can be there in thirty, fifteen if it's an emergency." She squeezes my shoulders until I nod and look at her.

I grab my keys from the small flamingo-shaped dish by the table and flip my hand in a half-wave as I hit the door. I need to get out of here before I let myself think too much about what I'm about to do.

I pull up to the non-descript brick building on an industrial street to the west of Las Vegas Boulevard. From the parking lot, I can see the blue neon sign outside that says HARD. The head bouncer, Vic, pushes the door open and lets me in. He towers over me, with black tattoos running the length of his dark, rock-solid arms. His smile is wide. I like Vic a lot.

"Harden's expecting you." He nods his head towards the bar area running along the back wall of exposed brick.

Inside of the darkened club, Harden wears a simple black button-down shirt tucked into his black jeans. He waits for me in the empty club and takes the backpack from my shoulder as soon as I walk in.

"Kady, you look good. You good?" He lifts my backpack of camera gear onto his shoulder as if it weighs five pounds instead of thirty-two.

Grabbing my phone, I type out a message before sending him a text. Sliding the phone from his pocket, he turns towards me as he reads my message.

Me: Sorry I'm late. You look stressed out. Hope that wasn't because of me.

He shakes his head. "Not you. Putting the final touches together today has me a little haggard." His golden eyes crinkle on the outside, making him look slightly older than his thirty-two years. "The band's rider alone is ridiculous. Making sure everything is perfect has been—difficult."

I practically jog to keep up with his long strides on the way to his office by the backstage door. He sets my bag on the desk of his cramped but immaculate office and motions for me to sit in the only chair while he leans against the old metal desk. He takes a breath and runs a hand through his light brown hair. It's longer on the top than normal. He's been too busy getting everything perfect for this residency that he's forgone his usual trim. "My office will be unlocked if you need a place to chill or get away from the noise tonight. Feel free to come and go as you need. Vic's working security at the backstage door. He's been briefed to keep eyes on you as well as the crowd." I nod as he pauses. Would he be making these accommodations for just anyone? Or is it only because he knows about my panic attacks and my limits, since he's seen me at my worst?

Since I moved to Vegas almost two years ago, Harden's been the big brother I should have had, since the one I do have could care less about what's happened to me. I've only known Harden as Hayleigh's friendly ex, but he's always treated me like family, the same as he does her. I don't know when or why they broke up, but he's become a good friend to me. That's the kind of guy he is; he doesn't care that Hay's an ex. I just hope that he didn't tell Vic about the panic attacks.

"I know the band's PR person already talked with you, but they want pictures of the shows and candid shots from backstage. Grab me a few shots for the web page and social media, too. Maybe get some crowd shots, shots from and of the bar. Hell, you know this kind of thing better than I do."

It's still weird to me that people will pay me for taking pictures. According to Harden's web person, being a local, relatively unknown photographer gave me a leg up on some of the other bids to shoot these shows. I'm still surprised a band the caliber of the Blind Rebels doesn't have their own resident photographer. Maybe that's because they have been apart for the last year?

Me: Do I give the shots to you or to the band?

He scans his phone, quickly reading my message.

"To me." Harden looks like he needs sleep. His golden eyes have bags forming under them. "Get the pictures for the first three shows to me by Monday afternoon and I'll get them to the label rep."

He blows out a breath. "Kady, these shows can put HARD in the black, well into next year since we aren't on-strip. Every detail has to be on point." He runs a hand through his hair again. I have to do this for him, get the kind of pictures they are expecting.

"The band brought their own security, so you'll need to wear this at all times." He hands me a 'Blind Rebels' backstage pass with the word 'photo' scrawled across it in black marker. "If you run into any trouble, text me or Vic and we'll come sort it out. Got it?"

I nod. In my old life, back when I was known as Kandi, I hated the nosy concert photographers hired to follow me

6

around at shows. Now, here I am doing exactly what I used to loathe. Funny how life changes.

"I'll let you get to it." He pushes off the desk and looks down at me in the chair. "Don't be shy about asking for something to drink or eat. I don't need you passing out from dehydration, kiddo." I inwardly cringe and type into my phone.

Me: I'll ask for what I need. Don't worry about me. Worry about this first show! And don't call me kiddo just because you're old.

He grins at my text. He's not that much older, seven years. I mean, he used to date Hayleigh, but it doesn't stop either of us from rubbing it in sometimes.

"You're a kiddo to me."

I roll my eyes, and he chuckles before rubbing his hand over his lightly stubbled jaw. He heads towards the door with a chin lift. This is the kind of show Harden has been praying for. Vegas doesn't hurt for live entertainment, so drawing the masses to a new, off-strip venue like HARD is key to its survival. Maybe I should have told him about the line that's already forming outside.

I wander through the club with my camera. I warm up, taking shots of the mostly empty club. The colorful bottles of high-end liquor lined up on glass shelves against the exposed brick wall makes for a great picture for Harden's website. *Click.* Opposite the bar is a row of empty high-top tables that line the edge of the area that will soon be packed full of music fans. *Click.* Just beyond the tables is the expansive black floor before the stage. HARD isn't a flashy night club like those on the strip. When there isn't a concert going on, the floor is filled with more tables for the bar. Harden tries to book as many shows as he can in the hard rock, heavy metal, and punk genres. Now he's landed a four-week residency by one of the premiere rock bands in the country, or at least they used to be before they broke up.

It takes me a few tries to get a shot of the stage and the

Blind Rebel's bright red logo backdrop without one of the crew members running in to my shot. *Click. Click. Click.*

I eventually slip outside and take a few shots of the growing line out front. Fans clamor for my attention when they see the backstage pass emblazoned with the Blind Rebels insignia hanging around my neck. The attention causes my throat to constrict a little bit. *Click. Click. Click.*

Standing back in the safety of the darkened hall backstage, I adjust the settings on my camera for the indoor lighting. Crew members with matching black Road Crew shirts scurry around me. Some are pushing large black road cases, while others carry rolls of wire or tape. Harden buzzes by, holding out a bottle of water to me.

He still thinks I can't take care of myself. When he first met me, that might have been the case, but I can take care of myself now. I already have a couple of bottles stashed in his office, but I make a show of opening this one and drinking half of it in his presence to appease him, while the crew members dash around us, organizing and setting up.

"Getting what you need so far?" I give him a thumbs up while I drink down the rest of the bottle. That should make him happy. I crinkle the bottle and toss it in the recycling bin nearby, nearly getting run-down by a crewmember pushing a case marked 'DRUMS' back towards the back door.

Harden nods at what used to be a storage room. "I hope they aren't trashing my dressing room." His eyes dash towards the door and back to me. "If the rumors are true, today is the first time they've been in the same room with each other in a little over a year. You know, since the singer tackled the guitarist on stage at the Garden and started waylaying him mid-show." Harden glances at the door, the creases in his forehead growing deeper. "Difficult to tell with the door shut like that."

Me: I'm steering clear of the dressing room until after the show.

Harden nods after reading my text. "Good idea." He winks at me.

"WatermelonX goes on in ninety minutes." He checks his silver watch. "Have one of the waitresses bring you something to eat to my office," he says as he pushes off the wall to go about his checks for the show tonight. He's constantly trying to feed me. I try not to take it too personally since he does it with Hayleigh as well and she's not messed up like I am. I nod to show I hear him, but I make no move from my current spot. It's more important for me that I get the settings on my camera right for the lighting back here.

"Bring an order of nachos and a diet coke to my office. If no one's in there, just leave it on the desk and shut the door. Over," Harden calls on his walkie-talkie. I shake my head at him. I can't believe he just did that.

Me: I'm not hungry right now.

"I know you eat nachos, Kay. Humor me." He chuckles as he heads off to put out whatever fire's next on his list. I shrug, not letting him off the hook. I'm an adult and I can feed myself.

I don't need Harden concerned about me when he has this residency to worry about. Heck, the next several weeks are going to be crazy, but I think once Harden has the first show or two under his belt, he won't be so on edge and bossy. Between Hayleigh and Harden, sometimes I wonder who is worse with the constant hovering and doting. Helicopter friends are a real thing, I should know.

Chapter 2

Mavrick

The best I can figure is this dressing room used to be some sort of large storage room. The windowless, concrete room is painted bright white and has four small, ready-to-assemble desks, one in each corner of the room and two single bathrooms on the far end. Each bathroom has your usual toilet and sink, but each is also fitted with a small shower stall. There's one dressing table for each member of the band. Each has a mirror, a small set of drawers, and a welcome basket on top. It all looks like cheap IKEA shit, which isn't surprising since Darren, our label rep, mentioned this club hasn't been around that long.

I claim the dressing area farthest from the door. If I'm sitting too close, the temptation to just say 'fuck it' and walk right out and drive straight back to L.A. would be huge. Instead, I flop down into the chair. I'm here for Sammy, and to get Monument Records off our collective backs. Sammy will be wrecked financially if we get sued for breach of fucking contract. Fuck the twins; they can take care of themselves. I'm here to keep Sammy from financial ruin.

It isn't hard to believe it's been just over a year since we've even been in the same room together. These guys, my band-mates, they used to be my brothers. There was a time I'd lay down my life for each of them, and I knew they'd do the same for me. These days, I'm not so sure. I shift around in this already uncomfortable chair like I have ants in my black leather pants. I survey the others as they filter in and pick a dressing table. We all keep to ourselves at our self-assigned desks.

The last time we were together was at Sammy's condo, a place picked for its neutrality, but honestly, not the best place for any of us to go, especially Sam. He's owned it for years and rarely sets foot in it, preferring to stick with staying with me or one of the twins. It was a week after I tackled Callum on stage in a hot, burning rage at the Garden. Yes, that Garden, as in Madison Square. Sammy begged us to come together and figure out how to put the hard feelings to bed. I don't remember much about that day, because I was crocked by the time I got dropped off. All I remember is it ended in me sitting on top of Callum, pounding him while his twin Killian tried to pull me off.

Cal always wanted what he didn't have, including my fiancée at the time. The fucker may have won that war, but I'm pretty sure I kicked his ass that day. What I remember of it, anyway.

Damn, I think I still owe Sammy for busting his coffee table. I stretch my hand in reflex, remembering the pain in it the next day. I glare at him from the side of my eye as he plays with his phone over in his corner. The asshole better stay over there.

I look away quickly. I promised Sam I'd behave. It just burns that I've known Cal the longest of all of these assholes. We had a couple of classes together and got into trouble together. Even before I knew he had a twin, we were best friends, ever since we were stupid kids in detention together at Fernando Valley High.

Now when I look at him, all I see are his pants around his knees, as he's pounding into my fiancée in a white bathroom at some venue. All I hear is Becka begging him to tell me about the baby they made. Then everything turns red, even after a year. I blink, trying to clear the anger out. This is not the place for that shit.

A wadded-up piece of paper hits the side of my head and I flinch in a delayed reaction. Looking in the direction it was thrown, Sammy grins at me. His long, curly blonde hair bounces against his shoulders. He's in his usual shorts and a rock band t-shirt. Today, it's one of ours, but tomorrow, who knows. He's like a damn kid. An easy-going kid. I pick up the balled-up paper and toss it back at him but miss. He heads over to me.

"Hey, dumbass, how about we go over the set list together... as a band?" He gives me a once over, like he's trying to assess my mood, then motions to the couches facing each other in the center of the room. I give him my death stare, but he's fucking Sammy and immune to my shit. I remain cemented to my chair. Fuck them.

"Someone has to make the first move, Mav. Come on, be that someone." Sammy's voice is low, so only I hear him. Fucking Sammy, he knows I can't say no to him. I don't think anyone can. I get up and flop on the end of one of the couches.

"Band meeting," he announces as he settles on the other end of the same couch.

Callum and Killian look up simultaneously from their phones; the twin thing they share has always freaked me out just a little. Kill is the first to get up. He may be Cal's identical twin, but Killian's done everything he can to make himself look different. Kill's tufty hair is just past his ears and dyed jet black, that color that's so black it's almost blue. His brow and lip are pierced with simple silver hoops, as well as his ear. He almost always wears all-black. I think even his damn swim trunks are black.

Cal, on the other hand, has the longest hair of everyone in the band. His natural dark brown hair is nearly stick straight and well past his shoulders. He tends to wear jeans and whatever t-shirt he can find. They both share the same dark blue eyes that reflect their moods.

Killian sits across from me but stays on the edge of the black couch cushion, like at any moment he'll need to jump between me and Cal again, and he's right, he just might. A year ago, during our brawl at Sammy's, I mistakenly landed a punch square on Killian's jaw and nearly knocked him out. I don't remember doing it. Sammy told me about it the next day. I heard he sported a bruise for nearly a month. I still feel bad about that one, it was meant for Cal. I have no beef with Kill.

"Cal, come on. Sit." Killian urges his brother over to us. The trepidation on Cal's face can't be mistaken, but he sits on the couch with his brother across from Sammy.

"This set list," Sammy starts as he sets it down on the table in front of us, shaking his head. "We kind of discussed this during rehearsals, but since we weren't all there"—he looks pointedly in my direction— "we should go back over it."

I phoned it in. Literally. FaceTime meant not having to worry about breaking my hand over Cal's head.

"This needs to be changed. I'm telling you, closing with 'Hollywood Dolls' is a mistake. We need to end with a ball-buster. Maybe swap 'Dolls' with 'Burn It.' We've always ended with 'Burn It,' why change what works?" Sammy looks over at me and then at the twins, then leans back against the couch.

I'm about to say something when Cal jumps in before me. "Leave them wanting more. Solid idea, Sammy. I'm in, and maybe we should use 'When It Rains' for the encore.' Kill nods in agreement.

"We also need to change the song we cover at mid-show."

Sammy's starting to get excited as we delve into the set list. I don't care. Give me the list and play the music. I'll sing the fucking songs.

"Instead of AC/DC, like we've always done, we need to do 'Back in the Saddle' by Aerosmith. Mav crushes the vocals on that track. Plus, it says something about us, right?" I give it to Sammy, he's thought this shit out. Kill and Cal nod along again and all three turn their stares at me.

"Whatever," I give them flippantly. I wholeheartedly agree with Sammy, but like fuck am I saying that. I'm sick of being the one that gives all the shits in this band. Plus, Callum agreed first, so I'm not giving them the satisfaction of thinking I agree with that cheating motherfucker.

Disappointment clouds Sammy's face. He gives me a pleading look and mouths, "try?" I don't know what he expects. Just being here is me trying. Especially considering I want to beat the shit out of Callum just for being in the same fucking room right now.

Sammy makes a show of gathering the set lists and marking the changes on each one in big black marker. He gives them to our road manager, Jeff, before closing the door to our dressing room.

"Okay," he blows out, running his hand through his curly hair. "I'm going there because someone has to," Sammy says as he paces behind the couch nearest the door. He looks to me and then Cal. "You. Two. Need. To. Settle. Your. Shit." His light blue eyes annihilate me. It's not like Sammy to be so aggressive. *Go with the flow Sammy* is what we're all used to. I see Cal fidget out of the corner of my eye. Right now, Sammy has all of our attention.

"Whether we're a band after these shows or not, the shit between you two needs to be dealt with." He runs a hand through his curly mop, but this time, when he speaks again, his voice wavers. "I'll be the first to say that I hope there is a Blind

Rebels at the end of it. This band is my life. You guys, you're all my fucking family. This discord, this limbo, it fucking sucks. Being stuck in the fucking middle sucks." Sammy's voice breaks like he's about to cry. No, Sammy, we're family, but we don't cry in front of each other.

"Mav talks to me, but not you two." He motions at Cal and Kill, his voice rising. "You two talk to me, but not to each other or Mav. You're my only family now, and I'm stuck in the damn middle here, and there is no fucking winning! No winning." He whispers the last sentence, his breath hitching as he struggles to rein himself in.

He tugs his hair and then looks up directly at me. "This..." He motions between me and Cal. "It's killing me. Legit killing me." His voice is quiet and destitute. "I'm done being the monkey in the middle." He looks more lost than I've ever seen him, not even when we helped him bury his sister. "I can't take this shit anymore." He crosses the room to the door and stops just shy of it. "Figure it out before we go on tonight. For me." He slams the door so hard the noise echoes off the painted concrete walls.

We all stare at the plain white door Sammy just vacated through. Fuck. This isn't going to work. I knew better than to say yes to these shows. Sammy's having a fucking meltdown.

My gut threatens to eject the whiskey I downed when I got here. The silence between the three of us weighs a metric ton. I had no idea this was so bad for Sammy. I didn't think of him at all, which makes me a complete asshole. Putting him between us has been killing him slowly, but he didn't say a damn word all year, until today.

I've poured an entire year into loathing Callum without a single damn thought of what I was doing to Sammy. The youngest, newest, and most tenderhearted of the four of us, when we found him, he fit with us, and not just musically. He was the missing piece of our dysfunctional, self-assembled

15

family. He's everyone's little brother and a damn good drummer, one that needs us as much as we need him.

All this hate I've been holding onto has been poisoning Sammy the most when I thought it was aimed squarely at Callum. Sammy's been my one connection through this year of animosity, the one grounding me. I scrub my hands down my face and look up at the twins. I don't say anything because, this time, I'm at a loss for words.

"He's right," Killian says softly, the first of us to break the silence. "I don't belong in here either. You two have to be the ones to fix what's broken, but I'm afraid to leave you two alone for fear that one of you will kill the other, like you almost did a year ago." He glares at me.

Killian stands and nods at the door. "But it needs to be done. By you two." He motions between me and Cal. "Tonight, before we go onstage." He glares at Callum and communicates again with that weird twin thing that they do, with no words, just a look. "I'm going to go find Sam." He slips out the door.

The silence between Cal and I seems to stretch for hours, but I doubt it lasts even minutes.

"Look, Mav..." Callum pauses to clear his throat, sitting up a little straighter. "It wasn't... I didn't... I mean, I did, but it's not..." He stops and breathes a heavy sigh, giving up his attempt at what? An apology? An explanation?

"Maybe I should just quit the band." He blows it out quickly and then looks down at his feet.

My head snaps up and I just stare at my bandmate. I haven't seen him since I beat the shit out of him on Sammy's living room floor a year ago. He looks different, not just the difference of a year older. As he looks at his boots, his posture is slumped, tired, and defeated, words I've never used to describe Cal before. Ever.

"Is that what *you* want?" The chill in my voice surprises me as much as the question. Why would I care what he wants when he didn't give me a choice with Becka? But leaving the band, that's the end. It's not just of the Blind Rebels, but of my cherry-picked family. Cal has always been the glue that held us together as a band. I may be the fucking lead singer, but Cal is the rock 'n' roll soul of the Blind Rebels and always has been. He's the ultimate rock God on stage, but it's his diligence and energy that has driven this band to the fame and success we have now. It's Cal that got a label to even look at us. It's Cal that got us our first recording contract. It's Cal that's always the first person to pick you up when you fall.

Putting my animosity aside for the greater good is a lot to fucking ask. Can I forgive him for what went down between us? I've spent the last year resenting, no, hating, the fucker in front of me with every beat of my damn heart. He betrayed me the way no other has. Not only did he fuck my fiancée, but he stole her, and the family I've always wanted. Then he wasn't even man enough to tell me. I had to find out through a viral fucking video.

Cal runs a hand over his stubbled face. "Want? No." He barks a humorless chuckle, his face chiseled with deep lines of worry that weren't there before. Not even when we were four dumb kids living together, struggling to make both rent and music. Or maybe they've always been there, and I never needed to notice before.

"The thing with Becka?" I wince at him saying her name because it's like my best friend punched me in the gut with a fiery fist. Actually, that probably would have felt better than this gut churning constant ache because I lost the girl and my brother at the same time.

"The video? How everything went down? I regret all of it, Mav. All of it. I was fucking wasted most of that tour." He shakes his head. "It got to me. The fame, the constant touring, writing, and recording. I don't know what I was thinking hooking up with her, man." His sigh is heavy as he looks back up at me.

"The only thing I don't regret from that time is Gibson. He saved me. I've changed for him, because of him." He stares off behind me.

His son. It dawns on me I haven't even heard the name of my best friend's kid. Fuck me, but Gibson is a perfect name for his kid. Callum looks back over at me. "How you found out? That was beyond shitty. I should have told you way before it broke. I..."

"Damn right you should have," I roar, causing him to jump slightly. The bite in my words is raw and icy as I nod vehemently in agreement with him.

Cal looks at me with pleading eyes. "I'm not asking for your forgiveness anymore. What's done is done. I can't change it." He stands with the finality of his statement. He turns and moves to stand behind the couch.

"Mav, music's always been my focus, but this band has always been more than just music to me. It's been my life. Kill's life." He sighs and his tired eyes hold mine with honesty. "Yes, I miss the music, but that's not what I miss most. I miss our misfit family. Kill misses it. He blames this whole last year on me." He pauses as the shock of his last statement must show on my face. Kill blames him? A rift between the twins? It's the first I've heard of it. Something hard for me to fathom with as close as they were.

"It's my fault. If I quit, you guys can go on at least. Finding a new guitarist should be easy. What is it you used to say when you were mad at me? Guitarists are a dime a dozen?" He looks at the door like it's beckoning him to walk through it. When I say nothing, he starts towards it. "I'll stay on through the shows, unless you find someone before then."

"Is that what you want?" I repeat, my tone different this

18

time, softer. I turn towards the door where he's standing, his hand on the knob, about to open it.

He shakes his head slowly and turns back towards me. "I've never wanted that, Mav. Man, the Blind Rebels..."

"Wouldn't be the Blind Rebels without you, Callum." I finish his sentence, solemn in its truth. He's not bragging. If Cal walks, the band as it stands is officially done. There will be no replacing him. Killian would leave shortly after, I have no doubt. Years of our lives would be wasted because I couldn't forgive him for not keeping his dick in his pants.

Can I let go of the anger enough to make this work? That's the question. Cal's head turns first when my words hit his ears, his eyes wide. He releases the knob and turns slowly, leaning against the door behind him.

"What are you saying?" His eyes look almost hopeful at my revelation. It's an excellent question. What the fuck am I saying? I have to figure out how to release this fiery ball of anger I've held in my gut for over a year, or we'll just go down in another blaze of glory at some point over the next four weeks. If that happens, we won't come back from it, not together anyway, and what would that do to Sammy? If we get sued by Monument Records, he'll go bankrupt.

"I'm saying that maybe we can, no, maybe *I* can work on putting this behind me." I love the band more than the music too. I miss the four of us staying up all night writing. Playing and writing alone, sure, I tried it, but it wasn't the same.

Callum bends at the waist, still leaning against the door, and releases a feral noise that's part cry of relief, part agony.

"Mav, you have to know, Becka and..."

"Woah!" I hold my hand up, stopping him, probably a little too forcefully. His head snaps up. "For this to work, Cal, I don't want to hear about Becka. I can't. I don't want to see Becka. I know it's not fair to ban her, but if there is any chance we're going to work through this, I need this one thing."

19

He nods at me and blinks like he's realizing something for the first time. "Okay, deal." He steps towards me and holds out his hand in a handshake.

I take it and pull him towards me in a hug instead. "Deal. It's not going to be easy, brother. I'll do my best to make this work." He pulls away and nods.

"Me too, whatever I can. I need this to work, us to work" He looks me directly in the eye. He means it. "I better go find Sam and Kill."

"You know the assholes are probably standing outside the door with their hands cupped to their ears, waiting to see if we're going to throw down again." He snorts in a semi-laugh at my comment.

"Probably."

Chapter 3

Mavrick

After Callum and I talk, we rehearse as a band on stage. This is more than our typical sound check, as it's our first time playing together in a year. We've never taken a break since we broke on to the scene. The music part is like riding a bike, but we need to get reacquainted with working in each other's spaces and remember how to cue off each other. Most of the failure is on me. I bump into Callum, not paying attention to where I am on stage. He rolls with it, but I need to get my shit together for the show. The fans didn't pay to see me fumble around onstage like a jackass. I turn towards Sammy on his drum riser as Cal practices a guitar solo. He nods at me with a little grin. We're getting there, knocking off the rust. If we're truly going to make another go at this as a band, then I need to give it my full attention; anything less would be using them to pay my bills. Tonight, we might be a little rough. How can we not be after not playing together in so long? I'll be on the ball.

After hearing fans have been lined up for over an hour, I can't resist going out there to see them. How can they possibly still be excited for us after a year of nothing? Especially when there is so much music out there. Sammy and I slip out the back door of the small club and head around the corner to see the line for ourselves. There are at least a hundred, maybe a hundred and fifty, fans out here already, all primed for the show, wearing Blind Rebels shirts. Standing peacefully in line, they chat amongst themselves.

Sammy slips me a few Sharpies with a huge grin. "Come on, let's make them some memories." He flips his chin towards the calm line. Someone sees us approaching and what was once a calm becomes chaotic.

They clamor for our attention. "Sammy! Mavrick! Over here. Oh my gosh, they're coming!"

Sammy approaches the line first, with me not far behind.

"Mav! Can I get your autograph?"

"Sammy, will you take a selfie with me?"

Then there's the girl in front of me. Her cheeks redden as I approach her with a genuine smile on my face for the first time in a long time. She's not reaching for either of us or shouting demands for our attention, instead she holds her phone tightly in one hand as she looks at me with wide eyes.

"Hi, sweetheart." Her cheeks get even redder, and she averts her eyes down a bit, looking at the pens in my hand, at my boots, anywhere but my face.

"Um, hi." She clears her throat. "Hi." She looks back up and I smile encouragingly at her. I don't want her to regret her shyness, regret being this close and not getting an autograph and a few words, a photo maybe.

"'Bring It!' Good taste. It's my favorite album of ours." I nod at her shirt with the 'Bring It' album cover on it. "Do you want me to sign it?"

She gulps and nods. "Um, yeah, yes. Please." I uncap the gold Sharpie with my mouth while my hand pulls an area of the shirt between her shoulder and her breast taut. She trembles slightly as I scrawl the large *M* and *S* with a line between that makes my signature.

"Do you want a selfie to show your friends what they're missing?" She nods and holds up her phone, unlocking it with her face. I take it from her, lean in next to her, and take a few quick shots.

"Thanks for coming to our first show at HARD." I squeeze her shoulder slightly with one hand as I hand her phone back. Her lips gape at my 'thank you.'

"Thanks to you. I mean, thank you too. For, you know, the selfie. And autograph." She stammers and takes a step back as the pushy blonde next to her horns in to make sure she gets her moment too.

"Ohmigod, Mavrick. I just love 'When It Rains.' Can I take a selfie with you? Please?!" The blonde fumbles with her phone with shaky hands. I take it from her. If I don't, I'll end up spending hours out here while they try to get a picture that isn't blurry as fuck from the shaking.

Even though I'm standing in front of them, these fans don't see me. They see Mavrick from the Blind Rebels. Maybe that's all I am anymore. I file that thought into the back of my mind to revisit another day.

"Here, let me." I lean back next to her and snap two shots and hand her phone. I scrawl my name on the shoulder of her Blind Rebels t-shirt, despite the fact that she shoves her large breasts at me. She doesn't come out and say it but she's wishing the autograph was just a little lower. It's a double-edged sword. If I sign her breast, I'm sexualizing her, accosting her, whatever. If I don't sign there, I'm not being friendly enough.

A few feet from me, Sammy leans in and smacks a chaste kiss on a fan's cheek while her friend takes their picture. That's going online within the minute. I roll my eyes at Sammy. He catches me watching and throws a smirk my way as she whispers in his ear. In turn, he slips her one of the backstage passes in his pocket. He keeps them at the ready for the willing. Sammy hasn't changed, immersing himself in the sex of the rock 'n' roll lifestyle. Can't we just do the rock 'n' roll without the sex and drugs blurring the lines? I got royally fucked over by that last time. I guess I can't blame him for sowing his oats or whatever, but it's a tired game for me and has been for quite some time. It's why I was trying to settle down with Becka. Lot of good that did me.

When we return to the dressing room, everyone is in their own little world, doing their own thing instead of talking to each other like we used to. Fuck this. I head to the side of the stage to watch our opener, WatermelonX, play a few songs. The crowd is starting to fill out the club and some show mild interest in the band onstage, except for the handful of diehards up at the front that know all the songs.

From the darkness at the side of the stage, I can see a sliver of the audience as the room starts to fill up. The fans are wearing *our* shirts. That shit never gets old, seeing them displaying their love for us on their person. More than one fan in line showed us their Blind Rebels tats. It's crazy knowing they love us enough to put it on their bodies permanently.

I can't wait to hit the stage tonight. I miss the fans almost as much as I miss the band. These are our people. I have no reason to be nervous, but it doesn't stop my heart from picking up speed because I want to give them the best show we can. I guess it isn't dead after all.

Back in the dressing room, we wait for WatermelonX's crew to finish their breakdown and our crew to put down the final touches on our set-up. Sammy twirls his sticks and beats out the rhythms in his head on imaginary drums, his hair bouncing along with his movement while his eyes are closed in concentration. Cal quietly uses his phone, his favorite guitar lying silently across his lap. Kill meets my eyes with a soft smile, fingering chords on his bass.

There's a weird vibration in the room, a nervous undertow that keeps us all in our own little worlds. It almost feels like this is our one chance to get back to being us. Almost like that gig in San Antonio, when we found out that Darren Scoffield from Monument Records was in the audience. I was so nervous that day, I threw up ten minutes before we hit the stage. Killian handed me a bottle of water before we went on and said, "We got this. Let's crush it." He nods at me as if he remembers too, but he just continues fingering chords on his bass as he rocks back and forth.

The club owner sticks his head in. "You're up."

We move to the side of the stage where techs help the twins get their instruments on and settled. Cal slides his pick across the strings of his guitar, and the audience comes alive as the sound of his warmup vibrates through the speakers out front. They can't even fucking see us yet, and their excitement ricochets through me as their cheers echo past us at the side of the stage. Cal nods. That was exactly the response he was looking for.

This is music, the pouring of our collective souls into the audience here to receive it. I need to move, so I bounce on the balls of my feet and swing my arms around to loosen up. I close my eyes and concentrate on the buzzing their excitement brings. *Fuck yeah, let's do this.*

The lights dip down, my stomach drops and then lifts as if I am on a roller coaster. That familiar flutter of nerves mixes with the speeding shot of adrenaline as the crowd reacts again. I close my eyes to receive their energy. It's what will get me through this exchange of souls, their eager energy.

They want this. They want *us*. It's not lost on me that if this was a solo show, just me up here, like Darren offered six months ago, it wouldn't be the same. His words swirl in my mind. 'You're the fucking lead singer.' That I damn well am, but it's all of us that makes us a band, *this* band.

25

"They're so ready, man, I can taste it!" Sam hops a few times, expending his built-up energy so that he can concentrate when he slips behind his kit.

"Let's crush this motherfucker!" Killian slaps Sam and me on the back before he steps forward, taking his place behind his microphone.

I push out into the darkness that covers the stage. The first several rows can probably see my silhouette, but nothing more. I grip the mic, holding it close while waiting to feel Sammy set the pace of my heart with his kick drum. *Boom. Baboom. Boom. Baboom.* Kill and Cal join in and the sounds melt into the music. *Like riding a bike.* I can't hear the crowd anymore, only my breath and my heart as it picks up Sammy's rhythm. When the lights illuminate me from behind, I let out the raw, screeching yell and our fans respond in kind, screaming with me. We launch into our set like a mostly well-oiled machine.

Just two songs in and the crowd vibrates in time with the music. It's like they are one big, living, breathing entity that's eating up our songs out there. The ones I can see up front, they sing along, knowing every single word as if they wrote them because they've lived these words in some tiny way. They jump in time to Sam's kick drum, fists waving in the air.

"How ya doing, Vegas?" I hear them scream their response during this short interlude between songs while I banter with them.

"It sure feels good to be back onstage with you all." I look back at Sammy as the house lights go on. He nods his head, stands from his seat and holds a stick in the air as a salute to the fans. This place must be at capacity because all I see is a blur of people beyond the stage. They push up against the barricade, squeezed together tighter than a virgin's pussy. They are hot and sweaty and living the music we are breathing into them. They are here for *us*.

"I see you out there singing every word and I fucking love it. Keep that shit up!" I encourage them as they scream.

We are one with them tonight. I'd almost forgotten this on top of the world, invincible feeling they offer to me as their master of ceremonies for the communing of our souls with theirs. The music that feeds their souls, feeds ours.

With the way they cheer, bob their heads, pump their arms, it's like we never left the spotlight. Thank fuck.

I catch Callum's eye and give him a look that says, 'Can you believe this shit? They still want us, even after everything.' He nods at me subtly and wipes the sweat from his forehead on his wristband.

I scan the sweaty bodies pushed together in the room, as close to the stage as they can get. A girl at stage right a few rows back sits on her boyfriend's shoulders as she pulls up her shirt and flashes Cal. He nods at her, not missing a note, and then turns to me with a smirk. He's pleased they still want him. He's even more cocky than normal now.

A guy in the middle of the first row yells out, "Fuck yeah, you rock!" I lean out and slap his hand, thankful he's here with us tonight, because this is about them. And Sammy. And us. But there would be no us, if there were no fans. I realize this now.

My eyes are drawn to a girl with a black ponytail in the pit between the crowd and the stage. She has her back to me, facing the crowd, but when she moves, my eyes follow her like she's a magnet. There's a professional camera in her hand. She must be the photographer the club owner hooked us up with. I thought we'd see more of her in the dressing room, but right now, she has her camera turned towards the fans.

"Smile, front row! Looks like you're on candid-fucking-camera!" I kick out my leg and start the next song, and when I do, the photographer swings her camera back towards us and I put my leg up on one of the amps. I do something of a lunge, leaning in towards the audience and the photographer.

They sing the lyrics back to us all fucking night. It's this interaction and adulation that I've been missing over the last year. I'm in the middle of a show and already so inspired to write I want to run offstage and jot shit down, so I don't forget some of the lines coming to me while we play, but I don't. Instead, I throw everything I have at them, and into these songs, the songs I was worried I'd never be able to play live again. Not like this, where the four of us are in synch and just on it.

R

FUCK, I'm out of stage shape. Sweat runs from my head and down my back. I work out almost every day, but there's just a different level of fitness required to perform onstage for over two hours straight with the unrelenting energy expected by the fans. I may have been dragging a little at the end. I hope they didn't notice too much. I'll get that fitness back.

I towel off my head and flop onto my chair as the rest of the band piles into the stark white dressing room behind me. Kill gives me a high-five as he walks by and grabs a fresh towel from his area. Within minutes, our dressing room fills with people, mostly leggy women looking to bag a rocker.

One of the security guys stands at the door with Jax, checking the passes as ladies continue to file into the room. Our head of security, Jax, has been with us since the beginning. He towers over all of us. He must be six-five, maybe six-six. He's former military and looks the part. His light hair is closely buzzed to his head. His arms are bigger than my thigh and his blue eyes can turn to ice when he's intimidating someone. He's a straight shooter, always concerned about our safety, always six steps ahead of everything and everyone.

The scantily clad female fans circle the edges of the room, trying to decide who to approach first like they're sharks, and we're being sized up as dinner. Who'll give it up easiest? It's a tired game I don't think I want to play anymore. They are looking for a fantasy I just can't fulfill anymore.

It's not long before two women have Sammy sandwiched between them on one of the couches. One of his new friends has her hand near his crotch and the other is whispering in his ear. His eyes glaze over lustfully at whatever she says. He notices me watching, smiles and lifts his chin lazily at me while twirling his ever-present stick. It's just a matter of which he'll be losing himself in tonight. I look away. I can't do this part anymore. I glance around, hoping for an out, but the door is blocked with the steady stream of incoming new sharks ready to party.

Some of the WatermelonX members filter in with even more women in tow. Callum strums his guitar in his corner, a bottle-blonde sitting on the table next to him, looking like she is ready to eat him. It doesn't seem right that he's entertaining, but what do I care who he fucks?

Maybe I need to loosen up and follow suit; it's been too long since I just let go. I could find a woman to lose myself in, and it's not using her if I go into it straight forward about it being only for the night. I haven't been in such a target-rich environment in over a year. It somehow feels wrong, but I scan the room, looking for someone interesting to talk to when Darren approaches me. His short black hair is slicked back, and his beady, dark eyes seem to be wandering all over, but it's clear the little weasel's coming towards me. I'm just shy of six feet, and I tower over Darren. Despite his inherent sliminess, he's always worked well with and for us. This time is no exception. He worked with Sammy to get us these shows so that we don't get our asses sued by Monument for breach of contract and end up owing the label a metric ton of money. Darren doesn't need to care, since he'd get paid either way, but he cares about us to an extent that he's loyal. Us being in good standing with the label makes him a load of money, so of course he'd be loyal.

"Mavrick, awesome show. Awesome! How did it feel to be back at it?" he oozes, overly chummy, as he surveys the group gathering in the room. He's not fooling me. He's here for a quick lay, and to rope us into more music. Finish the tour. Finish an album. It's all dollar signs and side pieces for him.

"Like it's been too fucking long, Dare." He slaps my back at that answer as I take my whiskey neat from the waitress. Part of the rider, I probably should have forgone, but I thought I might need some liquid courage to get through these shows.

"Tell me you used the hiatus to write?" Hiatus? Ha. Subtle, Darren, subtle.

"I have some stuff, but the guys haven't seen it yet." I shrug.

"Let me know if you want me to book a space somewhere here, local. You guys can get together and write or lay tracks. There are a few studios open here in Vegas." He nods at the blonde passing by. She's caught his eye, so he'll be trailing after her soon, using our fame to get him ass and a cut of our profits, but would we be where we are without him? Probably not.

"We'll see, Dare. Baby steps, man, okay?" He nods and moves along as I set my sights on a redhead in a tight, faux snakeskin pleather skirt, leaning against the wall playing with the straw in her drink. Fuck, I may as well give in. I'm obviously not the marrying kind.

There's a reason sex comes first in sex, drugs, and rock 'n' roll. It's part of the expectation. The girls want to bag a rocker and the rocker just wants to get his rocks off. I can feel the guys are watching my actions, waiting, hoping I'll lose myself in the lifestyle like I did before Becka.

I make eye contact with the girl in pleather, then move to the couch across from Sammy. Like a charm, the redhead sidles up to me.

"Is this seat taken?" She smiles coyly, fiddling with her straw again like she's nervous, but she's just playing the game. She sets her drink on the table, making sure to press her assets into me as she does.

"By you, I hope." I wink at her as she wraps an arm across my shoulders and starts to play with my sweaty hair as it curls against my neck.

"I'm Heather, by the way," she purrs. "You're so amazing, baby." She flicks her tongue in my ear. Isn't this how I met Becka, at a random after party, in a room not unlike this filled with booze, drugs, and women?

These girls are all the same, including Heather, and apparently Becka. Heather wants bragging rights, to say she was with a member of the Blind Rebels. It doesn't mean she won't end up getting exactly what she wants from me.

But I'm not stupid. I know her motives. I'll get exactly what I want from her, a means to scratch an itch. It's all I'm good for now. I'm not stupid enough to let emotions and shit get in the way this time, like I did with Becka.

Heather rubs my thigh and starts working her way up to my crotch while kissing my neck. For the first time since I've been in this god-forsaken desert, the knot that's been constant between my shoulders loosens as a distant but familiar warmth spreads through me. Between her and the whiskey, I might enjoy this evening after all.

It's only a slight surprise to me that the bottle-blonde has moved from sitting on the dressing table to Callum's lap. What would Becka think of her baby daddy moving on? Pfft. I don't care about Becka. Who Callum fucks is not my business.

Killian's got one wrapped around him in the corner, with her leg hitched over his hip and her arms around his back. Sammy's still between the two girls on the couch across from me, not even bothering to make a choice. I return my attention to Heather and stick my tongue down her throat. This causes her to moan and throw a leg over my lap, so she straddles me between her strong thighs. Looks like Heather is a take-charge kind of girl. I grin and lift my hips into hers, my eyes closing briefly at the sensation.

I'm trying to concentrate on Heather and the feeling of her rubbing against me when a phone catches my eye. Wait, a fucking cell phone pointing our way from the door? I squeeze my eyes shut, trying to get the images of Becka and Callum screwing against a bathroom room wall out of my head. I look up again.

Oh, fuck no! This is how it starts. There's a woman standing in the doorway fucking filming us, but all I see is her damn phone.

I inadvertently knock Heather to the floor as I jettison myself across the room in a hot fury.

I have to stop this before it happens again.

"What the fuck are you doing?" I rip the cell phone out of her hand and throw it across the room in one solid motion. The phone crashes against the wall hard enough to leave a mark. It bounces off the concrete floor, the sound echoing through the silent room. Her moss-green eyes widen, her wordless lips gaped in shock.

"Get the fuck outta here," I roar as my eyes widen. Stomping right up to her, she cowers when I look down on her, so close I can feel her hot breath on my face. She glances towards the door because I have her trapped against the wall.

"No cellphones." I seethe as my spit lands on the side of her face. She blinks rapidly at me but says nothing, just keeps blinking her wide, green eyes. The club's bouncer steps between us and she all but disappears behind him.

"We were crystal clear, no phones back here!" I erupt. Fuck, this is exactly why I didn't want to do this. There's no privacy anymore. Everything we fucking do is on the damn internet.

"It's not like that. She wasn't recording or taking pictures," the bouncer starts with his hands up between us, a wall between me and the girl. Typical bouncer move. This guy is big, but Jax is bigger and always ready to back me up. Trustworthy to the core, he moves in behind me.

"I don't give a flying fuck. We were crystal clear, no phones back here," he growls again at the bouncer. No doubt she already has buyers lined up for her little video. "It's in the fucking contract we signed with the club."

Jax positions himself even closer, ready to grab the bouncer should he try to throw down with me. "Eighty-six her for the rest of the shows. And this guy too." I bark at Jax while motioning my head towards the bouncer. "They're in on it together. Her phone's over there. Wipe it." I motion behind me, where the phone sits.

Jax maneuvers the bouncer out the door. The room that was in full-on party mode minutes ago is now funeral silent. The only movement is Heather stroking her arm. Shit, I hope I didn't hurt her when I knocked her off of me.

"She was filming. Fuck this place. They promised no cameras!" I shout at no one in particular, as I pace the short loop around the center of the room. I'm out of control. I feel it vibrating through me, the anger, the fury. Snippets of the video of Becka and Cal play in my head, and I can't get them to stop.

"This is how it starts. First, it's innocent videos of everyone having fun, and the next thing you know, it's a video of your guitarist fucking your fiancée!"

Everyone's eyes are on me, except for Cal's. He looks down at his feet, his long hair hiding his face. We can't heal as a band, and get past this shit, if I keep throwing it in his face. We can't have people back here filming because someone's going to fuck up and that will get sold to the highest bidder. We have to protect ourselves and each other.

Out in the hall, Jax towers over the shrinking shadow of what I assume is the girl. "You obviously knew that there were no phones allowed. It's clearly marked. Your friend at the door told everyone who came in. I heard him. I was standing right there while he was telling people." His voice is loud and authoritative.

I can't see or hear her reaction. Despite Jax's stature, the club owner doesn't think twice about jumping between him and the girl. "She needs that phone to communicate. She's non-verbal, asshole. Without that"—the club owner points to the phone Jax holds— "she has no way of communicating. With anyone. This is the photographer the label hired to shoot this shit show."

The girl in the shadows, with her back to the wall, inches her way past both of them and flees down the hall with a door slamming in the distance. Jax and the club owner continue talking, their words muffled now that someone closed the door to the dressing room.

"Mav, calm down." Sammy's voice is gentle as he heads towards me.

"Calm down?! We couldn't have made it clearer. No cell phone use back here. Sure, nothing is going down right now, but if we are going to make a go of this... I mean..." I lose my steam as Sammy lays a calming hand on my shoulder. I stop my raving, but my stomach still roils. Fucking hell. I run my hand through my hair. *Non-verbal? What the fuck does that even mean?*

Sammy pushes me gently back towards the couch. I flop onto it harder than I mean to and cross my legs with a scowl. I'm acting like a petulant teenager now, and I fucking know it.

Callum turns and grabs his guitar from the corner by his little desk and strums a few chords. Slowly, the room relaxes back into the party atmosphere, but I'm having trouble following along with them.

"You caught it, man. Sit." Sammy hands me another whiskey. "Have another drink and celebrate the reuniting of the Rebels. Jax'll take care of that."

I jerk the whiskey from his hand and slam back half of it in one go. The cool liquid does nothing to calm me. I feel almost suffocated by the anger that I promised Callum hours ago I would work to put behind me, and here it is in all its fucking glory. The throbbing at my temple increases the more I think about it, the more I ruminate on the video of Becka and Cal, and the girl's wide terrified green eyes.

Non-verbal. Shit, I really fucked up this time.

Heather sits down beside me and tentatively places a hand on my thigh.

"Are you okay?" I ask. What the fuck was I thinking? Her hand caresses my thigh lightly as she nods. I release a breath.

"I know how to get you to relax, Mav." Her voice is thick with seduction and alcohol as her caresses turn to a squeeze.

Chapter 4

Kadence

Hot, too hot. I swing my legs out from under the suffocating bedding. Ugh, my tongue is all cottony and dry. It begs for water, no doubt thanks to the Ativan I took last night. I'll be foggy all morning, and I need to get work done. I imagine this is what being stoned is like. Everything is just less important.

I hate the disconnect the drug causes, but by the time I got back last night, my arms were so stiff I could hardly bend them. My breathing was so constricted it felt like trying to breathe through a cocktail straw while running a marathon. It would've been smarter to call Hayleigh to come get me or ask Harden to bring me home. Thank God I made it home before the panic locked me up completely. As it was, I laid there last night on my bed, stiff, waiting for the drugs to relax me enough to pull me under into sleep.

I rub my hand over my face, trying to wake myself up. My arm and thigh muscles ache from last night's panic attack as I roll over to grab my phone. Shit, I left it at the club, not that it would be any use. I'm sure it's toast with the way it bounced off the concrete after Mavrick Slater threw it across the room.

My stomach rolls with protest as I sit up. I need some juice or something, but I stop in the bathroom first to splash warm water on my face and brush my teeth, hoping it will quell the dryness. I don't bother to brush out the tangled nest in my hair.

Trudging into the living room, I flop onto the couch, pulling my legs up under me, and gaze out the floor-to-ceiling windows. The hustle of Las Vegas Boulevard is in full motion as tourists wander between casinos and the lights flash the newest shows, but I sit here in the quiet apartment. Dammit, I forgot my juice, but now that I'm curled up here, I don't want to get up. Instead, I lose myself out the window, focusing on nothing in particular, as life on the Vegas strip goes on as usual.

"Oh, hey, you're up." Hayleigh sits on the table in front of me. I slide my eyes towards her. The concern knitting between her eyebrows makes my stomach roil. My abdomen tightens, and my chest starts to follow suit. Shit, not another attack.

Deep breath. *I'm here and I'm fine.* I work through my grounding exercises. I see the television that isn't on. I see the magazines stacked on the table. I see the hands on the clock; it's 11:04 am. I see the flowers on the counter from Hayleigh's date two days ago. Deep breath.

Hayleigh puts a hand on my knee, and I concentrate on the warmth of her palm on my leg. "Harden came by about an hour ago. He left your camera bag." She nods at my backpack by the door, but I just concentrate on the concern in her voice as she squeezes my knee.

"He's upset, Kay. When I told him you were still sleeping, he said he'd come back this afternoon. Be prepared, he'll probably bring pizza and force feed it to you, you know how he fixates on food." Her effort to distract me falls short as the fog doesn't let it compute.

I smell Hayleigh's rose bergamot perfume. I smell...

"I'll make you some tea." She squeezes my knee again and gets up.

I close my eyes and let my head drop to the back of the couch. Breathe in two, three, four. Breathe out two, three, four. Lather, rinse, repeat.

Hayleigh slips a warm mug into my hand. The peppermint tickles my nostrils before I take a sip. Shit, that's hot! My throat closes, warning my mouth to expel the scalding liquid, but I force myself to keep it in my mouth and revel in the scorch.

"Here." She holds my laptop out to me with her perfectly polished fingers. She wants to talk. "Harden told me your phone's broken."

I flip open my computer and launch the chat app.

Me: I'm fine.

Hayleigh reads my words on her phone. "I call bullshit, Kay. Harden was in full-on panic mode when he finally got in touch with me last night. His voice, I wish you could have heard it. By the time I got here to check on you, you were already out like a light." Her voice is quieter than normal.

Me: I took an ati.

"I figured." She sighs. "A whole one?" I nod again. "Then you're not fine, Kay. When was the last time you had to take a whole one, or even half of one?" I shrug.

Almost six months. I can feel her looking at me, and I feel the burn of shame in my cheeks. I hate that I'm weak and have to resort to medication to deal sometimes. Still, I don't want to be this weak person anymore. I thought I had the panic attacks under control, but they were there to prove me wrong, again.

She pauses and starts again in a soothing, low tone.

"Want to talk about it?"

Me: No.

She purses her pink glossy lips as she reads my reply. "Do you want me to call Dr. Murphy?"

Me: NO.

"Kay..."

Me: I'm fine. Just foggy from the meds.

She continues her hard gaze. I can feel Hayleigh's disappointment in me. As much as she wants me to acknowledge the panic attack, I'm not giving her more. I just can't do it. I'm done with this conversation.

Me: Can you bring me my camera bag? I'm going to work on the pictures so I can give them to Harden if he comes back. I'm not going back to the club. I don't care if it ruins my chance to make something of Photos by Kadance.

She sighs as she reads my message, but grabs my camera bag and deposits it on the table. I curl up in my favorite chair, headphones on, and try to focus my flighty concentration on processing pictures through my digital lightroom software. It's taking me twice as long to process each picture as my brain struggles to remember the difference between white balance and contrast. I should know this stuff. I *do* know it, but the after-effects of the pill don't always let me remember.

It takes a bit before I'm in the zone, but I get to that point where I'm tweaking white balance, contrast, and brightness in my pictures until they have the feel I'm looking for. Any background activity and noise fades away, until I get to the first picture of Mavrick Slater on stage.

My stomach clenches, reminding me of the ache that's already there from last night's full-blown episode.

Mav leans toward the crowd with his microphone stand, mouth open in song, brown hair falling forward, creating a halo of darkness around his head. The quintessential rock star pose. I gaze at his face. I can't deny that he has a certain something. This is not the man who was backstage, though.

The anger that rolled off him last night when he ripped my phone out of my hand nearly knocked me off my feet. My stomach drops as the memory plays through my head and reminds me of another time I felt someone's anger so strongly.

That ended spectacularly badly, and not just for me. His breath was so hot on my face, his angry words sticking spittle to my check, just like Jerrod at the festival. I remember my shoulder blade hitting the jamb as I tried to flee, his cold dark eyes accusing, and the vehemence and power of his words as he yelled at me. I release the breath I didn't even realize I was holding and focus on the photos. One picture at a time.

I lose myself in the groove of post-processing. It's not so much about the content of the pictures, it's more about manipulating the images so they display the emotion I want to convey. The light in the room has shifted. I've been working on these pictures longer than I thought. I've only processed about five hundred of the eight hundred pictures, but that's plenty. If they find raw ones they want processed, they can hire someone else to do it. I stretch my arms above my head and move to sit up in the chair, adjusting from my curled-up position.

I save the photos to a thumb drive, then remove the SD card from my camera. I've never had a band ask me for the raw materials before, but it's what I promised and it's what they'll get. I put the card and the thumb drive in an envelope and write HARDEN on it. I slip a check for most of the deposit for the residency back into the envelope. I scrawl on it that I'm keeping $60 for the SD card and thumb drive.

Backing out of the deal to shoot all the shows feels shitty, really shitty. I can't build a business by backing out of jobs, but I won't put myself in that position again. Being trapped against the wall was bad enough, but the anger, the yelling, no. I leave the envelope on the table in the living room and take my laptop back to my room. It's time to figure out how to make a claim for my cell phone on my insurance. Urg. I'll need the damaged phone. I wonder if Harden has it?

Even though I'm in my room, I hear the knock on the front door. It's got to be Harden since the phone didn't ring and he's the only one the doorman lets through unannounced. Hayleigh can deal with him. I slip in between the covers of my bed. I'm sleepy and I don't want to face disappointing Harden when I refuse to go back to his club.

Hayleigh was right. I smell food, but it isn't pizza. It's tacos from Charritos. Damn it, he knows I can't resist them. They're talking, but I can't make out what they are saying, and I really don't want to. I put my headphones back on and snuggle further into my bed. I'm just plain exhausted, which is typical after a panic attack like the one last night, one where I need medication.

Hayleigh enters my room a few minutes later and sits softly on the edge of my bed. She slips my headphones off and brushes the hair out from my eyes.

"Harden brought us tacos." She smiles softly in an I-told-you-so manner. I shake my head at her, and she frowns. "I know you're tired, but he's still worried about you. Don't be mean. The panic attack isn't his fault. Come out and let him see you're okay. Please, for me?"

She's right, it's not his fault. It's not mine either, and there are tacos out there with my name on them. I grab my notebook off the nightstand and follow Hayleigh out.

Harden stands in the living room. His usually impeccably styled hair looks like he's been running his hand through it repeatedly since yesterday. His eyes droop with exhaustion, and I think he's still wearing the same clothes from last night. I try to remember, but it's all hazy right now.

"Kady!" His eyes scan over me quickly and I don't miss his mouth turning down. "I came this morning, but you were asleep." I nod and motion towards Hayleigh, so he knows she told me.

"Fuck, I was so worried, kiddo. You took off before I could help you, Kay. When I couldn't get a hold of you after you ran off, I was worried you didn't make it home. You didn't even answer the house phone." We have a secret code, Harden and me. If he calls the house phone and I answer, I press numbers on the dial pad. A quick tap is yes, and a long press is no.

Fear flickers through his light brown eyes and I'm reminded of the first time I had a panic attack in front of him. I remember his panicked pitch when he noticed something was wrong with me, his side of the call to 9-1-1, him repeating he didn't know what to do.

"I got ahold of Hayleigh, so she'd come see if you were here." He looks me over again. I feel a little bad that he had to call Hayleigh away from her date to come check on me.

"Fuck, Kay. I had visions of you stuck on the side of the road somewhere in the dark, panicking, having trouble breathing." He closes his eyes and releases a long breath. He holds his arms out, clear about making sure I know he wants a hug. I walk into them, and he envelopes me in a gentle embrace. His muscles release the tension they're holding as he rocks me slowly. This embrace is just as important for him as it is for me.

"I'd have driven you home." My throat clogs when he gets like this. Harden's witnessed a couple of my panic attacks, but they've affected him deeply. I pull away.

I smell tacos. I scrawl the words in my notebook and hold it up for him to read.

"Charritos, your favorite. But first..." He takes my notebook from my hands and sets it on the back of the couch and exchanges it for a gift bag. I peek in beyond the crumpled tissue paper and see an iPhone box. Not just any iPhone, but the newest top-of-the-line model. Shit. He didn't need to buy me a phone. I have insurance. My old one wasn't top-of-the-line when it was new.

I grab my notebook and shake my head vehemently as I scribble. *Too much $. I have insurance, just get my old phone so I can claim it.*

Harden chuckles, but there is a coolness to it. "Trust me, I didn't pay for this. I billed Monument Records at their insistence after I ripped that greaseball Darren a new one last night. He's just lucky I didn't see that fuckin' singer."

Wait, what? Why would he risk these shows? They'll put HARD on the map. My eyes well with tears I refuse to let flow. He reaches towards me deliberately to ruffle my hair. "Come on, no one wants soggy tacos." He makes a gagging face that makes me smile a little.

After our tacos are consumed and we've moved back into the living room and settled on the couch, I glance at the envelope with Harden's name on it. It's already been opened. He catches me looking at it.

"I assume that means you aren't coming back?" His eyes are a little sad, but mostly they are filled with an understanding I don't deserve, not for backing out of a job. I guess it's back to doing high school proms and engagement pictures for Photos by Kadence.

I shake my head.

"Ever?" His eyes widen.

I grab my notepad since I still haven't activated the new phone. *Not while they're playing. I've been eighty-sixed, remember. Maybe I'll come back for a different band.* I push the notebook towards Harden.

These things have a way of getting out. I'll be labeled the photographer that couldn't buck up and finish the job because some self-entitled musician broke her phone. No one will want to work with me.

Harden's shoulders slump slightly. "All a misunderstanding, and I'm pretty sure it's cleared up, but I understand. I wouldn't want to go back after I'd been assaulted either. If you did come back, I'd probably spend the whole time worrying–"

"Hold up. Did you say assaulted?" Hayleigh stands, hands on her hips, looking between the two of us, her face scrunched up. "What the fuck happened, Harden? I thought she had a panic attack and ran off? No one said anything about assault!"

I grab my pen off the table. *You tell her. It's too much to write.* I shove my notepad at Harden.

"I wasn't there. So, if I say something wrong, correct me." He waits for my nod before continuing. "Kady was using her phone to talk with Vic by the door to the dressing room. Apparently, the singer saw her phone and flipped the fuck out on Kady, knocking the phone out of her hand."

I flip my hand up and quickly scribble, *GRABBED & THREW, not knocked.* I underline 'grabbed' twice and show it to him.

"Sorry. Grabbed and threw her phone. Vic said the singer got in Kady's face while screaming at her." He looks over at me to see if he got that part right, and I nod with exaggeration. "Vic stepped in between them and that got their security guy involved. I rounded the corner to Kady cowering in a corner being yelled at by their huge-ass bodyguard. I got between Kady and their security. When I did, Kady bolted out the back door before I could make sure she was okay." He looks at me again.

I nod.

"Jesus Kay, you should have called." Hayleigh wraps her arm around my shoulder. "And you want her around them?" She glares at Harden like he's crazy. "Like hell." They talk as though I'm not even here and able to make my own decisions.

Harden flinches. "In their defense, and there is no defense for his behavior, they do have a contract item stipulating no cell phone usage in the dressing room. He thought Kady was filming or taking pictures. He didn't realize she needed it to communicate."

I'm not going back. Return their deposit. Thanks for the tacos. I'm beat, I scrawl out. I drop the notebook face up on the table, take my new phone, then head back to my side of the apartment. If they want to talk about me like I'm not here, then I'm going to bed.

I can still hear Hayleigh and Harden talking as I go. "I can't believe you think she should still work with them. This could set her back months."

Chapter 5

Mavrick

I add another coffee pod into the machine, hoping this variety is stronger than the last. Leaning against the counter while the machine heats the water, I survey my rental. It's roomy and airy with lots of windows, yet plenty of privacy. From the outside, it looks like a large Spanish villa. The inside of the house is decorated in earthy tones, right down to the oversized leather couches in the living room. It's decorated in that generic Airbnb kind of way. Nothing too personal or expensive. Darren, or whoever picked it out, did an amazing job. It's in a gated community with a pool and a walking path right to the lake. No garish casino suites with a new girl every night for me. No tempting gaming tables downstairs.

I've been slammed with shit to do since I got to Vegas four days ago. This is my first real day off and I'm going to enjoy it. I grab my cup and make my way out to the lanai and sit. It's bright as fuck out and I left my sunglasses inside. I need something to get me going. Ahh, this *is* better coffee.

It's kind of serene here. Hot as fuck, but peaceful, a totally different vibe than LA. The lawn is fake but looks realistic for artificial turf. Some sort of flowers grow on a trellis by the back gate. Just beyond the gate is a paved path that leads right down to the lake. Most of all, it's quiet here. The only thing I hear is the noise of the pool's filtration system humming. The neighbors are far enough away that I can't hear them, but even out here, it's not peaceful in my head. A pair of terrified green eyes haunt me whenever I close my eyes.

The terror in those eyes is because of me. Fuck. I'm not like him. I'm not. I set my coffee cup down a little harder than I mean to and coffee slops over the side. I remember the look on my father's face as he grabbed my mom by the hair and pulled her off the couch. Shit, I am not like that.

She was just using her phone to talk to the bouncer until I intimidated her so hard she fled. How fucked up is that? I hold my head in my hands. Who does that? Someone who loses control, that's who. I refuse to be like him. I won't intimidate a woman.

My phone rings. It's Darren returning my call from yesterday. "Mav, you called?"

"I want to apologize personally to the photographer and ask her to come back. Maybe offer her more money or something."

"Not a good idea." He's being short with me. He must be getting his ass chewed by the label. Has it leaked? The room was full of people.

"But..."

"If you piss her off, she could go to the press. Or worse, sue the label. You don't need that." He sighs and I hear the squeak of his chair as he leans back in his office. "Look, Mav, Monument Records is already unhappy with you. They see your attack on your own guitarist as a liability, and the year of radio silence as a breach of contract. The ice you are skating on is already thin. This will not help things. If she so much as breathes a word about it, Monument will be wanting out of their contract with you. You've already given them plenty of reason to do just that."

I run my hands down my face. Fuck, she could sue us. That's all we need.

"Just let it be." He hangs up.

Still, I have this overwhelming need to apologize face to face. I want her to see that's not me, to set my wrongs right. I never used to give two fucks what anyone thought of me, so I'm not exactly sure when I grew this conscious. It doesn't matter, though, since she didn't show back up at the club for the next two shows.

I flip through the proofs of her photos again. Her stage shots are spot on. We could use these to put together a reunion photo book to go with the new album Monument is pressing us to release, maybe even use some for the CD booklet.

I didn't know she caught photos of Sammy and me outside signing autographs for the fans in line. How did she do that without us realizing? The guys will dig these photos just as much as I do. My favorite is one of Sammy behind his drums. The way she captured the blue stage lights on his curly blonde mop gives him an ethereal quality you'd never get, even from Sammy.

Sammy: You up fucker?

Me: Yeah. Whatsup?

Sammy: Bored as shit.

Me: I got an idea. Invite the twins, it'll be family friendly. Come to my place, I know just the thing. I'll call a few of the crew.

Sammy: Cya soon.

A little over an hour later, me, Sammy, Cal, and Gibson board a totally decked-out rental boat on Lake Las Vegas, along with some of our regular road crew. Tunes flow through the speakers as we take turns wakeboarding off the back of the boat in the blue waters of the lake. It's a great way to blow off steam in the heat. Too bad Kill refused to come. I don't know if that's because Cal was coming, or he had other plans or what. I think he could use the release as much as Cal and I could.

Cal is out on the wakeboard, flipping around the back of the boat while Gibson sleeps in this bouncy seat thing under the awning, not far from me. It's a nice day out here and surprisingly, there aren't many people out taking advantage of the dark blue water. It's still hot as fuck, but it is cooler out here on the water, and under the boat's canopy. Sam flops down next to me on the blue and white bench seat, water dripping from his board shorts.

"What's going on with you?" He eyes me with a knowing look.

"Not sure what you mean." There's a bite to my words that I don't necessarily mean.

"You rented us this awesome boat, and you're out here with us, but you're also a million miles away. Is it because of Gibson?" He motions toward the sleeping baby.

"No. He's cool." I gaze down at the sleeping kid. I can't put the sins of his parents on him. He may have been born from a fucked-up situation, but it's not his fault. Even I know that. Being this close to him, I can't decide if he looks more like Cal or Becka.

"I'm surprised Cal brought him and didn't make a stink about not bringing Becka. Hell, I'm surprised Becka let them come without making a huge thing about not being included. I guess for all I know, she did." I don't know much about Cal's life lately. It's another thing I need to fix.

Sammy remains quiet next to me for a few minutes before he speaks. "Becka took off after Gibson was born. I don't think she lasted two weeks. Cal woke up to Gibs crying and a note from Becka and all her shit gone." He says it quietly, like maybe Cal's ashamed for people to know she's gone.

I'm the one who told Cal I didn't want to even hear her name. He was trying to tell me in the dressing room that first day and I shut him down. I should have asked about her. I can't imagine caring for a kid alone. Cal must be scared shitless. I sure the fuck would be.

"Shit." I drop my head and Sam pats my shoulder.

"Don't feel bad. Cal knew you didn't want to hear about Becka, so he didn't say anything. I should've mentioned it." He pauses. "If it's not Gibs, though, then what's up? You're a space cadet today. That's not like you."

"Truth? The girl with the phone." I look over at him. "You know, from the dressing room the first night. I treated her like shit." Finding out she has a disability or something wrong with her makes my stomach turn sour. Fuck. "I went overboard."

"Way overboard. But how were you to know?" He shrugs it off in typical Sammy fashion.

"I can't get her terrified eyes out of my head," I admit.

"So go apologize or whatever." He says it like it's so damn simple, but that's Sammy. Everything seems easy to Sammy, but that's what he wants people to think.

"How? She quit the photo job. Plus, Darren specifically told me to let it go. Contacting her could make matters worse for the band. He's worried she'll run to the press." I'm pretty sure that if she was really going to do that, it'd be all over the fucking rags by now.

Sam looks at me, incredulous. "Since when do you listen to that dick?" He makes a face, even going so far as to stick out his tongue. "Jax can find out anything, man. Tell him you need her address, and he'll get it. He loves putting all his special forces recon shit to use." He pats my back.

I shrug him off but pull out my phone and shoot Jax a text. Sammy's right. Jax has his ways of getting information. I don't ask and he doesn't tell. It's just how it works with him.

Gibson starts moving his hands and looking around. Not seeing Callum, he starts to whimper and screws his face in a knot.

"Uh-oh, someone's unhappy." Sammy stands to try to motion for Callum's attention.

"Leave him out there. He needs to blow off steam more than we do. I got him." Sammy's jaw drops slightly as I lean over, then pull him out of his little seat and bring him to my shoulder, careful to keep my hand behind his head. Never having touched a baby in my life, I'm running totally on instinct. His warm, soft head rubs against my cheek as I move us back to relax against the bench seat. He's got the softest blonde hair covering his little head. I sit in silence, watching his dad flipping around on the waves generated by the boat, his small body snuggled up next to mine. The little dude's warm body against my shoulder calms me in an unexpected way. It relaxes me. It's unexpected, and I kind of like it.

Sammy watches every move I make like a hawk or maybe more like a momma bird, so unlike his usual laidback, anything goes persona. He's just as protective of this little shit as Cal. Then it hits me. What Gib's has is what we had as a band. What we are rebuilding slowly. Family. His mom may have walked away, but he's got two pseudo-uncles who would do anything for him, and his real uncle probably would too, despite whatever shit is going on between the twins. I know I'll be right there in the mix after holding him for only three minutes.

I'd be a shit father judging by my role model, but I'll be a kickass uncle for this little guy. We're starting to get back to being us. It started right before the first show, with the olive branch between Cal and me. Brothers for life, like we promised all those years ago under the watchful eye of a pissed off librarian while in detention.

"Have you ever even held a baby before, man?" Sammy eyes me, holding his hands out to me as if to take him. Fuck that, this little dude and I are bonding. He puts his clenched fist in his mouth and relaxes against me. He doesn't even know me, and he already trusts me.

"Nope, not once in my life." I switch shoulders so Gibson is farther away from Sammy. The little dude exudes an inner peace that envelopes me. I don't understand it, but like hell am I giving him up to Sammy. Gibson runs his warm, moist hand along my stubbled jaw.

"I'm good. He seems to like me." I straighten my neck to look at him. He stares back at me intently, then blows some sort of spit bubble.

"Dude! He does like you!" Sammy's eyes go wide with his soft gasp.

"Don't sound so surprised." I try to shoot him a glare of irritation, but it's hard to be mad at Sammy and he knows it.

"You don't get it. Gibson doesn't like to be held by anyone but Callum. Sometimes he tolerates me. He doesn't even like their Aunt Sandy, and you know how cool Sandy is." The twin's Aunt Sandy is a cool lady. They are damn lucky to have her, and they know it.

Sammy sits with his lips gaped in awe as Gibs cracks a gummy smile at me and rubs his hand along my jaw again.

"What can I say? I have the touch. Gibs knows Uncle Mav's the coolest of the Rebels. Right, buddy?" I pat him reassuringly on his back and he makes some sort of baby noise. I look at Sammy. "I think he just said 'yeah.'"

Sammy snorts. "He can't talk yet! He's way too little. He's just making noise because you are." He rolls his eyes at me, but I sense he's jealous that the little dude is so taken with me already.

Gibs fists the chain around my neck and shoves it in his mouth. I pry his small, slobbery fingers off my chain, remove it from my neck and shove it in my pocket.

"I think he's hungry. Maybe I should give him a bottle?" Sammy rummages through the camo purse that Cal had with him. I guess it's full of Gib's gear, good to know, because I was wondering when the hell Cal had taken to using a purse.

Sammy pulls a bottle out and shakes it up. He then holds his hands out to take Gibs again. Why does he keep trying to take him from me?

I reach with my free hand and snag the bottle from him. I glance at Sammy for guidance. This was a mistake because Gibs sees the bottle and starts freaking out. He tenses his body and starts waving his arms around and grunting.

"Tip it towards his mouth, asshole, you're teasing him." Sammy reaches over and tips the bottle in my hand down towards Gibs's mouth. He sucks in the nipple and within a few seconds his eyes hood as he relaxes into my arms, one hand against the side of his bottle.

"Hold his head a little higher." I adjust my hold on Gibs and Sammy nods at me. "There you go."

Sam watches me for a few moments and shakes his head. "I gotta get a pic of this." He snaps a few pictures with his phone. "Mav feeding a baby. Man! The internet would eat this shit up." His eyes go big immediately after he says it. "I didn't mean it, uh, I'm just saying it. I'm not posting it or anything."

"I know what you meant, Sammy." I let him off the hook. Behind him, Callum wipes out on the wakeboard. The boat slows to pick him up and set up for the next person to go out for his turn.

Cal climbs onto the rear of the boat, shakes the water from his long hair, grabs a towel and starts rubbing his head vigorously. He glances at Gibs's empty seat and then in our direction. He freezes momentarily as he notices his son in my arms. Is he about to lose his shit because I have his kid? He blinks at me a few times and continues to dry off without a word, eventually tying his hair back. He then joins us under the shade of the boat's canopy.

He says nothing as he sits in the swivel chair across from me and watches me feed his son. When I look up, Cal's teary and almost looks relieved. If I mention his display of emotion, though, I know he'll just blame it on irritation from the lake water or some stupid shit like that.

I look down at Gibson. This little shit makes me feel all warm and soft inside. What must Cal feel like as his dad? The little guy exudes all this love and trust and doesn't care who he gives it to. Sam wanders off towards the rear of the boat to give us privacy.

"You want me to take him?" Cal holds his hands out, but I really don't. I want to keep this unfamiliar contentment that feeding his kid gives me for just a while longer.

"I'm good. Gibs is happy. Why mess with him?" Cal nods his head a few times and settles back, watching us again. He swallows loudly and swivels around to rummage through the cooler behind him for a beer.

When he turns back, he takes a long, slow drink from it. "Thanks man." His voice is weighted down with unspoken emotion so thick that I can't bring myself to look over at him. This is uncomfortable territory for me. For us. We might be chosen brothers, but feelings and shit are not something we wear well.

"I didn't know about Becka bailing, man. I found out from Sammy twenty minutes ago." I have to break the emotion-laden silence between us. "I'm sorry."

He won the girl, my fucking girl, but Gibson doesn't deserve his mother walking away from him. I had no clue Cal was doing this alone. I wish someone would have told me, but what could I have done? I don't know shit about kids. It's my own fault I didn't know. I pulled away from everyone except Sammy.

Cal stares out over my shoulder. "I didn't think Sammy had mentioned it." He sips his beer again. When I look at him, I can tell he's okay with this. With me holding, feeding Gibs. He's more than okay with it. It's like all the animosity between us just melted away all because of Gibs. He's a pint-sized miracle worker, this kid.

"I don't know how she could leave like that, Mav." Cal's rasp is quiet. "I had to have Jax track her ass down so I could get her to sign the paperwork." He swallows air and then locks eyes with me. "She signed away her fucking rights. Didn't put up the slightest argument. How does a mom do that shit to her own kid, man?"

I don't know and I don't know what to tell him, but we both know it happens because it's happened to everyone in this band in some form or another. It's why we're so solid in our brotherhood.

I've known Cal the longest, so when his betrayal came to light, it was so damn easy to hate him. He seemed to hate me right back, but maybe I built that up in my head. I put all the hate on Cal, when Becka deserved to bear at least some of that load, but now, Cal seems so broken. It's not something I'd ever expect to see in my brother.

"I love Gibson more than I've ever loved anything or anybody. From the moment I held him at the hospital, it's only been him for me. It's like nothing I've ever experienced or known before." His voice is soft but steady. Cal's eyes drift off over the lake, looking for answers it won't give him. "I'd give up music for him, Mav." Cal gasps, stunned at his own revelation. "Yet his mom just walked the fuck away from him." He hangs his head and shakes it slightly.

"I'd understand if she didn't want to be with me." He pats his chest. "We weren't good together. We didn't connect, even though I truly tried." He looks over at Gibson. "But him? He's perfect, still fresh. The world hasn't touched him with its bullshit yet."

Gibs releases the nipple of the bottle with a sigh on his bow-shaped lips. I think I'm supposed to burp him or some shit. I set the bottle down and put him back on my shoulder and start patting his back gently.

"Is this right?" I softly ask Cal. He nods and looks back over the bow of the boat, past the lake and beyond. Gibs lays his head against my shoulder and relaxes while I continue to pat.

I take the opportunity to really look at Cal. He looks different, older than his twenty-nine years, or tired maybe. His posture is more rounded, and his head hangs slightly. His forehead now sports deep creases that I've never seen before. Smaller creases edge the corners of his eyes and pursed lips.

"You know how you've been pissed at me for a whole year?" Not sure where he is going by rehashing this shit, I nod. My brother pauses, struggling to find the right words. "I understand that level of anger now. That deep, heavy ball of hate that sits right here." He hits his stomach with his balled fist.

"I didn't understand it at first. I didn't understand why or even how you could be pissed *at me* when it was Becka who strayed, who made her choice." He shrugs.

"But I get it now, Mav. I've been so fucking pissed at Becka, but not for me, for him." He nods at Gibson on my shoulder. "He deserves all the shit a mom can do that I can't." He sets his beer down next to him with a sour look. "Fuck. It's chewing a hole in my damn gut."

"Don't get me wrong, I fucking love Gibson. I'd lay down my life for him. But..." He stops, his eyes wide as terror visibly rips through him so hard that I feel it in my gut. "Fuck, Mav. How can I do this? Play with the Rebels, raise a fucking kid, keep him alive and safe? Show him the love I never got as a kid while touring and writing music? I mean, fuck. I just don't know how to make it work." He hunches over, elbows on his knees, rubbing both hands over his face before leaving them there for a few minutes. His shoulders hitch a few times before he sits back up, revealing his moist face.

Gibs belches in my ear and relaxes his whole weight on me with a heavy sigh. I don't know the answer for Cal. I wish I did, but he needs to trust us, like the little dude trusts me.

I hand him his drowsy son. I've never seen doubt weigh so

heavily on my friend, my brother. I lay my hand on Cal's shoulder and squeeze.

"We'll find you a kickass nanny or something, and he already has three awesome uncles." I look down at him. "We all have your back, Cal. Always." He relaxes a bit but doesn't quite look relieved. "And now his."

I set my hand on the warm back of his son and nod at Cal before walking to the back of the boat.

"All right, fuckers, my turn."

Chapter 6

Kadence

J errod, my boyfriend of the last eighteen months, sits across from me at our table in the exclusive new Sunset Strip restaurant. He's dressed nicely in a white button-down shirt and dark black slacks, and I'm in my favorite long-sleeved dress, so that the bruises from last night are well covered.

I brought us here to do this publicly because he's gotten more aggressive and physical with me lately, and I can't deal with it anymore. I am not a naïve little girl who will continue to be his punching-bag. I know he won't do it here, not in public. At least, I think he won't.

"I'm done. I don't want to see you anymore." I say it clearly and firmly, looking him directly in his blue eyes.

He stands, moving from his side of the table into the seat next to mine. He grabs my wrist tightly, nearly cutting off my circulation, the veins in my hand beginning to pop as they try to wriggle out of my skin. He leans in closely, his face an inch away from my ear. To anyone watching in the restaurant, it probably looks like lovers having an intimate moment. They have no idea the words he is whispering to me.

"You're more stupid than I thought, you bitch," he snarls in my ear with undertones of loathing that I'm becoming more familiar with by the day. "You should count yourself lucky that I'm even with you."

I wriggle, trying to get out of his grip, but it only tightens on my wrist.

"Get up," he grits out, his teeth clenched. He thinks he's being quiet, but he's not. Heads turn behind him to gawk. Tears burn my eyes as I struggle not to let them escape. "Do not make a scene. You hear me? Honestly, I don't know why you're like this. Why do you have to push me this far?"

With his firm grip on my wrist, he drags me towards the exit. Jerrod loves this place because it's where you go if you want to be recognized and he loves to be seen with me on his arm.

We pass tables of people, his grip making fingers go numb. Most diners refuse to make eye contact with me, but those that risk it look sad. Maybe they're sad that I let him treat me like this, or maybe they're embarrassed for me. He doesn't love me; he loves what I do for his image. But real love doesn't bruise.

He swipes at the few strands of his blonde hair that have fallen against his forehead from his carefully slicked and gelled hair, trying to get them back into place. He never wants anything out of place in front of the press. He thinks that marching me out the front door past the gathered paparazzi will keep me compliant.

I can't take being around him anymore. I might not know what real love is anymore, but it's not bruises and feeling like I'm always doing something wrong.

"You know I love you. Why can't you just accept it?" His teeth clench together behind his thin, pulled back lips. His eyes slightly bulge in anger.

He takes his free hand and grabs my chin, pulling my face close to his. I need to just go along with him for now. I will not let this be my undoing.

59

"If you leave me, I swear to fuck, you're going to regret it." His eyes grow glassy with tears, and he drops to his knees in the lobby. The hostess, mistaking his gesture, thinks he's proposing to me and clutches her hand against her heart. Panicked, I bend down and pull him back up to his feet. He looks deep into my eyes and starts sobbing. "I'm sorry. I just love you so much. Don't you understand? Don't you understand the lengths I would go to to make sure that you're mine forever?" I take a deep breath. I close my eyes and repeat my mantra: I just have to make it until Hawaii.

We step outside and the media erupts at us. I search the crowd for someone I know, anyone that I have a semblance of trust with. I see her. I step towards Charlotte Michaels from Entertainment L.A. Because we're in public, as much as Jerrod hates to let me go, he does.

The scene morphs and I am no longer at the restaurant with Jerrod but in the VIP guest tent at the festival. I'm squatted down, chatting with a pair of girls, both eight. With big eyes and matching innocent laughs, they tell me about how much they love Kangaroo Klub Houze and sing me their favorite Kandi Matthews song.

Two firecrackers go off near the tent, causing both girls to jump. I stand and turn towards the noise. My blood runs cold when I see it's not firecrackers at all. It's Jerrod, and he's got a gun. A woman I don't know is lying on the ground in front of him. I grab the girls' hands and rush to the corner of the tent and pull it away from the pole as far as I can.

"Run!" I scream as I push their little bodies through the tight opening, not thinking about their parents, who're probably still behind me. I stand back up and turn towards Jerrod just in time to watch him shoot my manager Claude.

Claude drops to his knees after the first shot. His blood hits my white pants as he falls forward onto the cement with the second and third shots. I can't look at him. This isn't happening. I focus on his blood spattering against my white jeans.

"Kady!"

"No, no, no, no, no," I cry and hold my hands up as he advances towards me, gun pointed straight at me. First it burns. Then I smell the coppery scent of my blood as it seeps out of my chest slowly.

"I told you, you'd regret it." Two more bangs and I fall to the floor, the cement unforgiving against my knees. My hip is on fire and my chest hurts. Am I having a heart attack? Did he shoot me in the heart? My breath comes in pants as my vision goes fuzzy and dark around the edges.

Jerrod grabs me around the neck and pulls me up against him, his arm a strong bar across my neck. He smells of cigarettes and body odor, making me gag. "I told you. This is all your fault. This is all because of you." His hot breath moistens my ear.

He drags me to the front of the tent, and I kick my legs out, trying to get away. He shoots Claude again. My manager lies lifeless on the concrete floor at an unnatural angle, his light blue eyes open but not seeing anymore. I feel so tired and cold. I don't know which is worse. I just want to go to sleep.

"Kady! Come on. Wake up, honey."

Hayleigh? She's not supposed to be here until tomorrow morning so we can fly to Hawaii together. I've been so looking forward to spending two weeks with just my best friend, far away from everything. Just us, the sand, and the sun. We haven't vacationed together ever, now finally we will.

Jerrod's arm tightens across my neck, and I try to grab at it, to loosen it, but he continues to pull me towards the back corner of the tent. My feet try to keep up, but my hip hurts so much. He swings the gun back and forth, looking for his next target. His arm against my neck is getting tighter, so much tighter I can hardly breathe.

"Kady! Wake up! Come on, Kadykat, please. Wake up!"

The gun goes off with another loud, resounding bang. This one is so close to my head. So close I can smell the metallic smell of the fired gun.

Gasping, all I see and taste is blood. I can't breathe. I can't breathe. It's dark and I can't help but wonder if I'm dead until my shadowed room slowly comes into focus, and I pant as if I've been running. I'm sitting up in my bed and don't even remember doing it.

I'm in Vegas. I'm not in L.A. This is my room. I'm not at the festival grounds. These are my things. I'm in my house. I am here. I'm okay. I'm okay. I'm okay. I try to catch my breath.

"Oh, Kady." Hayleigh's words crack and break with emotion as she pets my hair gently. "You're okay, honey. You're okay." I finally focus on her face, and tears run down her cheeks as she continues to murmur to me. My nightmares mess her up just as much as me.

She pulls back my bedding and I scoot over to give her more room. This is the third night in a row that Hayleigh's ended up in my bed. I haven't had back-to-back nightmares like this in nearly eight months.

Snuggling down under the blankets, I lay on my side to face Hayleigh and she mimics my position so she's facing me. She reaches out slowly and tucks my black and purple hair behind my ear.

"I should have known something wasn't right between you and Jerrod." Her voice wavers as she scoots closer to me. "I should have known when you begged me to go to Hawaii with you that something was going on." A fresh round of tears flow from her eyes as I shake my head and fumble for my phone on the bedside table behind me.

It's times like this that the pang of not being able to talk is more of a curse than usual. I type out a note quickly.

Me: I couldn't tell you. I was too embarrassed that I let myself believe the awful things he said about me, that I let it get that far. I thought the restraining order would work, that he'd leave me alone.

Me: I was going to tell you in Hawaii, I swear.

She scans my message and then looks over my phone at my face.

"You're my best friend. I should have listened to my gut."

For the third night in a row, Hayleigh falls asleep next to me while I watch the white ceiling fan for hours, afraid that if I close my eyes again, Jerrod will still be there.

Chapter 7

Mavrick

Could this cranky fuck of a doorman be any slower? My fingers tap on the cool marble counter while he dials whomever the hell he's calling. He's too old to even know who the fuck I am, but if he keeps me standing at this desk any longer, he's bound to find out. I pull my hat farther down as three people amble out of the elevator. All these people in the lobby are going to figure out who I am and cause a scene, which is exactly what I don't need. Just let me upstairs to give my apologies and then I'm out.

"Okay, follow me, young man." I follow the old-as-fuck doorman as he escorts me to a different elevator and pushes the fifteenth floor. "The door on the left." He steps out and the doors close. It lifts off so quickly it leaves my stomach downstairs, or maybe it's the whiskey from last night. Trying to drown those terrified eyes out of my dreams doesn't work, hence why I am here. That, and she's got real talent as a photographer. I want her to continue to work with us.

When the doors open, I step onto the white and gray marble floors of a foyer that doesn't look unlike the lobby from downstairs. The top floor has been divided into two large units.

64

The only color in here is a bouquet of purple and blue flowers gracing the small table next to a stylish but uncomfortable-looking wingback chair. Except for the flowers, it's almost clinical, fancier than my place in Malibu. Someone must have laid out some serious dough for this place. Why haven't I heard of this photographer before if she's this loaded?

As I lift my hand to knock, the door flies open. A blonde wearing a navy skirt suit and matching heels steps out, pulling the heavy-looking white door mostly shut behind her. Her red lipstick is perfect until it pulls down into a frown. Between her makeup and dress, she must be a businesswoman of some sort. Am I even at the right address? This might be the first time that Jax has gotten something wrong.

"What the fuck do you want with Kady?" Miss Blue Skirt has her hands on her waist, one hip cocked while her eyes narrow. She takes in my tight black jeans and black t-shirt. Judging by the curl of her lip, I'm not her type, but at least I know the address is right.

"I'm Mavrick..."

"I know exactly who you are, Mavrick Slater." She spits my name out like it's the worst tasting thing ever, while she stabs her pointed fingernail into my chest. Fuck, that hurts. "What do you want?"

"I'm here to see Kadence." She stares at me blankly. "Um... please?" This chick's so pissed that her face is scrunched like she just stepped in shit.

She must know what I did to Kadence. This perfectly polished talon of hers could be considered a weapon. It digs into my chest again. Who is this chick with the talons of death? I rub at the sore spot on my pec. "And you are?"

"Hayleigh. Kady's roommate." She squints at me again. "Kady can't talk to you. Not that she should want to." She huffs at me and grabs at the door like she's getting ready to slam it.

"I deserve your anger, and hers." I've got to get her friend on my side. Maybe she can help me convince Kadence to come back and work for us.

I step towards the door, trying to peek around it. I need to see her. To fix this. "I've felt terrible all week. I just want to make sure she's okay and say I'm, uh, sorry?" It comes out more of a question, which makes me sound like even more of a dick. *Shit.* I just need to see that Kadence is okay and get those eyes out of my dreams so I can sleep. This isn't going how I planned.

"This is all about making yourself feel better, huh, Mr. Rockstar? You aren't worried about how Kady feels. You're worried about your image." She shakes her head as she answers her own question. "Why should you care about Kady or her nightmares?" Nightmares? Shit, I *am* the biggest asshole. Hayleigh steps forward again with that poking fingernail. "You. Are. An. Egotistical. Dick." Her other, non-poking hand tenses on the door. "Go!"

"Shouldn't your roommate be the one telling me off and not you?" I give her my best glare. This chick needs to back the fuck off. I'm not leaving before I see Kadence. I step forward again, close enough that I can stick my boot in should she try to slam the door. "I'm just here to speak with Kadence."

"I already told you, Kady can't talk to you." Her face begs me to challenge her.

"Look, I know she's, uh, disabled? She can't speak or whatever…" Saying the words out loud makes my already churning stomach sour even more. I rub my eyes. "Why don't we let her decide if she wants my apology?"

Hayleigh's eyes narrow at me again. "Disabled? She is most certainly not disabled! You really are a dick." She says it like she expected otherwise. Maybe she doesn't know me as well as she thought. "I can't let you come in here and wreak even more havoc on her life."

"I am not that guy. I am here to make amends. Set things right." *Come on, Blue Suit, let me in.* "I won't make it worse. I promise." That was Darren's fear, but he's an ass and doesn't belong in our personal matters. This is between Kadence and me. Not him, and definitely not Monument Records.

Finally, her arm on the door relaxes, and she opens it wider before turning on her heel and holding the door open to me.

I follow her lead. Unlike the clinical foyer, the apartment's decorated in shades of gray and pink, giving it a warm and welcoming but feminine feel. Walking through the entrance, I pass an open concept kitchen to the left and then enter the living room, which has an amazing view of the Las Vegas Strip from the wall of windows. I bet it's a gorgeous sight at night.

Hayleigh motions toward the seating options and I take a seat on the couch. She sits in a gray chair and looks me over again. Her scrutiny makes me uncomfortable in a way I haven't been in a long time. She clearly knows who I am, but it's a question of how much of a disadvantage this puts me in.

"So, uh, is Kadence here?" I shift on the couch. Hayleigh knows how to intimidate for sure. She must be used to busting balls in whatever boardroom she walks into.

"There's a lot you don't know about Kady." She breathes out softly. "And most of it isn't my story to tell." She crosses her legs and regards me with a cool aloofness I am not used to from women. I nod, not sure where this is going. I just want to apologize to Kadence, get her to agree to fulfill her contract, and get back to the band to work on some new music.

"She's gone through a lot of shit the last couple of years." She blows out a long breath. "So, you'll find I'm overprotective of her." She leans forward. "I get that you're used to getting your way, being a rock god or whatever." She glances at me, her nose curling with derision at whoever she thinks I am. "When you thought she was breaking your rules, you didn't think before acting. Kady deserves your apology. But for her. Not to make you feel better."

So, Hayleigh considers herself Kadence's keeper. Interesting.

Hayleigh looks to her right to take in the cityscape outside. "Most people assume Kady's deaf. She's not. Don't raise your voice or slow your speech when you talk to her." She sweeps her eyes back to mine. "It reminds her that she's different now. But she's not, not in any way that matters. Her only 'disability', as you put it, is that she can't respond using her voice, so she uses a cell phone. Which is what she was doing that night with Vic." She gives me a pointed glance. I nod, not about to admit I had assumed that she was deaf. I even googled 'I'm sorry' in sign language and practiced it all morning.

Hayleigh stands. "I'll tell her you're here. It's up to her if she'll see you." The clicking of her heels fades as she moves down the hall.

Not able to sit still, I take in the bustling Vegas strip from the windows. People walk down the walkways and over the pedestrian bridge at the intersection, looking like ants from way up here. Tourists encounter hustlers every few feet. They are inundating the tourists with everything from advertisements for the legal prostitution in the next county, to hawking generic bottles of water at twice what they paid for them. My favorites are the street performers. Everything from musicians busking, to magicians performing sleight of hand, and let's not forget the mimes and other performers, all vying for a spare dollar or two on the sidewalks and walkways between casinos that run from grandiose to garish.

There's an unfamiliar heaviness deep in my stomach, along with the need to move around, to pace, but the living room doesn't provide me the space to really move around like I need to expend the nervous energy building in me. I'm not used to someone who might not want to see me. Usually, women want to see me, to touch me. Having all this up in the air is unsettling in a way I'm not used to.

Hayleigh returns and doesn't look happy. "She'll be out in a second. I'll be right over there." She points to the kitchen area. "Don't make me regret letting you in, Slater." She takes a seat at the bar with her back to me and I return to the couch and wait.

I hear Kadence's soft shuffling getting louder as she comes towards me. She shoots a worried look at Hayleigh as she passes through the kitchen. She wears a loose t-shirt with a turtle on it and black yoga pants. She's barefoot, with her phone clutched to her chest. Kadence hands it to me as I stand when she enters the living room.

Kadence: Hayleigh said you wanted to see me.

I hand the phone back and nod. She continues to hold the phone with a death grip. She's probably worried I'll bust this one too. Her shoulder-length black hair has the last two or three inches of the ends dyed vivid purple and now that she's close to me, I spy dark marks under her soft but tired green eyes. She's not sleeping well because of the nightmares Hayleigh was talking about, ones that I no doubt star in, front and center.

Fuck, those dark circles are all my fault. Kadence perches on the edge of the gray chair her friend was just seated in, like at any moment she'll run out of the room.

"I wanted, um. I'm here, uh..." Shit, I sound like a babbling fool. I pause to collect my thoughts. I didn't think this far in advance. "I wanted to say, in person, I'm so sorry for the way I treated you. There's no excuse for it." I pull the stupid baseball cap off my head and run my hand through my hair. "That's not me. I don't intimidate women."

But didn't I do just that? I treated her the way my dad treated my mom. Shit. I am just like him. My stomach clenches as I fight with myself.

Kadence stares stoically at me, not giving anything away. I can't tell if she's buying what I'm selling. Fuck, she won't give me a break.

"I scared you..." Shit, that's fucking hard to admit. "I wanted to make sure you're really okay."

She taps quickly on her device and then hands it to me. She leans back in the chair, watching me scan her short message.

Kadence: I'm fine.

She's not giving me much to work with. I shift on the couch and run a hand through my hair again. I can't make this right.

"I'm not as big of an asshole as I came off that night." She shrugs at me, her face telling me she's over it and couldn't care less I'm here. She just wants to move on, but why can't I let her?

For the first time ever, I need *this* girl's approval. To know that she's not only physically okay, but that she understands that I'm not a guy that abuses women. I may be cavalier with my relationships, but I do not cause harm.

"You're not going to make this easy on me, are you?" She shakes her head slightly, then gives me a frustratingly blank expression, not a smirk like I expect. She doesn't make a move to type into her phone. I'm irritated with her purposeful lack of communication until I see a slight upturn of her lips ghost across her mouth. She's enjoying my frustration. She's playing me.

"Is this you giving me the silent treatment, Kadence?" Her eyes widen momentarily as she realizes I have figured out her little game, but at least she's tapping into her phone again.

Kadence: We've established I'm fine & you want me to think you aren't an asshole. Is there a reason you're still here?

Ouch. Her eyebrow is raised to me in challenge. Challenge accepted, babe.

"Come back as our photographer? Document the band's reunification? I promise we won't bite. Especially me."

She shakes her head vigorously as her fingers move quickly across the screen. She shoves it back at me, suspicion pulling her lips taut.

Kadence: No. Did Harden put you up to this?

"The club owner? He doesn't know I'm here. I'm pretty sure he told our label rep that he'd disembowel him if any of us dared to breathe the same air as you. Is he your boyfriend?"

She snorts and grabs her phone from my hand and continues her rapid typing, then shoves the phone at me when she's done.

Kadence: Not my boyfriend. Did he really say he'd disembowel you?

"Not me, our label rep, Darren." I chuckle. "He's one of those slimy record label types, so I don't blame him." My joke lands flat between us on the floor with a flop. She isn't the slightest bit amused by me. My charms don't seem to work on her.

She sits back against her chair, watching me watch her. I'm struck by this silent woman in front of me. She may not be able to talk, but she's expressive in so many other ways. I'm pulled towards her; she's so full of sass and silence.

"So, I can't talk you into coming back to the club for our next show? Even if I promise to stay away from you? Or give you hazard pay or something?" I can't believe I offered her even more money to photograph the band; Darren will have my ass for that one. Her eyebrows shoot up at the offer of more money. She pauses to consider my offer, then slowly shakes her head with a soft smile. Maybe I should just give up on mentioning the photos for now, but then that means this conversation is over and it's time for me to go.

"We all really like your photos. We want more. Please reconsider." She continues to shake her head at me, but I'm not ready to let her go yet.

"Have dinner with me tomorrow, Kadence." The words just come out without me thinking about them first. Her eyes widen as she shakes her head even harder. She's as surprised as I am by the offer.

I have to see her again, then maybe I can talk her into

working with us after she gets to know us a as regular guys. "It's just dinner."

Hesitation works across her face, clouding her eyes. "Have Hayleigh come," I encourage, nodding towards her friend who's now facing us from her stool in the kitchen as she watches our exchange closely.

She still shakes her head, this time holding her phone out. *Kadence: No.*

My stomach sinks. She's steadfast in not coming. Her face is a combination of panic and resolution. Is it because she's intimidated about us being the Blind Rebels or because she's afraid of me?

"Bring your boyfriend if you have one. Or that club owner guy. Heck, bring them all. I know I can get Sammy to come for sure. I can't guarantee the twins can make it, but I'll try to get them there too." I can't believe I'm practically begging this chick to go on a group dinner date with me. How much more desperate do I have to sound? I haven't had to work so hard to get a girl to go out with me since high school. I've gone from apologetic to desperate, and I don't like it one bit. Mavrick Slater does not beg for a woman's attention, but here I am, doing just that.

"Not many people can say they've had dinner with members of the Blind Rebels." I dangle the only leverage I have in front of her like a carrot and top it off with my megawatt, charmer smile. *Please say yes.*

Kadence swings her gaze toward the right at her friend with a question on her face, and I'm worried this is it. She's going to shut me down completely, demand that I leave and not come back. Surprisingly, Hayleigh doesn't interject an opinion one way or the other, but her silence hints at disapproval.

Kadence doesn't appear to need guidance or caretaking. She seems like a perfectly healthy, capable woman who happens to not be able to talk. Hayleigh made it sound like

Kadence has only been this way for a couple years. What happened that caused her to suddenly become non-verbal?

She looks back at me but still hasn't agreed to go. More importantly, she hasn't declined either.

"So, you'll come, then?" I ignore the wild look in her wide green eyes, but it's better than the terrified one.

"It's settled." I can feel the panic rolling off her as I stand. "I'll send a car for you and however many friends you'll bring tomorrow night at, say... seven?" Kadence looks down at the phone in her lap but doesn't pick it up.

"Give me your phone." She hands it to me reluctantly, and I can't help the chuckle that escapes me. I add myself to the contacts in her phone.

"Now you have my number should you need anything or just want to say 'hi.'" I hand her the phone back. My phone dings from my pocket with the text I just sent myself from her phone. I smile. "And now I have yours." I stand and move toward the entryway. "I'll see you ladies tomorrow evening."

Chapter 8

Kadence

Hayleigh's gaze bores a hot hole into the side of my head. "Did you really just agree to have dinner with the Blind Rebels?"

I guess I kind of did. When Hayleigh came to tell me Mavrick Slater was here to see me, I didn't want to come out at first. It's easier to make him out to be the bad guy, to push my issues onto him. The incident at the club freaked me out, but not just because of what Mavrick did, although there is really no excuse for him to treat me like that.

It was also because of how strong the panic attack was, and how quickly it came on. I thought I'd gotten a handle on them. I could feel them coming and worked through them with my breathing before they struck, but not that panic attack. That one was just an ugly reminder that they'll rear their head whenever they damn well please. Control over them is a false reality.

At least it had only been the one. There was no call in to Dr. Murphy, no emergency therapy sessions. The next morning, I was still on edge, but that eventually waned as the fog from the medication dissipated.

Hayleigh didn't push me to come out of my room the way she did when Harden showed up. I was under the distinct suspicion she hoped I'd say I didn't want to see him, so she could kick Mavrick out. Something in the pit of my stomach told me to come out, and I'm glad I did.

I didn't say yes, but I didn't say no either, I repeat in my text response to Hayleigh.

"He seems to have taken it as a yes. He's sending a car, Kady." She looks at me like I'm nuts. "I assume you'll text him and tell him you've decided against this dinner?"

Her reluctance only makes me want to go even more. As much as I love her, I also love pushing against her overprotectiveness of me. I need to rebel a little. She took over when I needed her to, but I'm better now. I can deal with my own shit, most of the time anyway. I can make my own decisions. I know she wants to protect me, but I'm not made of glass, and I don't need to be coddled.

Kady: Dinner might be fun.

"Really, Kay?" She gives me her best 'I'm the boss of you' look. She should know well enough by now that this only makes me want to do it even more.

Kady: If you don't want to go, I'll go alone.

I shrug as I send my text and give her my best blank look, like I don't care. It's the stoic mask I've perfected over the last several years, even before the incident at the festival, but in my gut, I'd feel so much more comfortable if she went with me. She's my security blanket, and I hate that I feel that way, that I need her as my buffer in new situations.

Kady: Or I can ask Harden.

I know he'd go with me. Harden's just that kind of guy. Even if he disagreed with me going, he'd go with me if I asked. I know he would.

Her eyes narrow. "You seriously want to do this?"

Kady: Who wouldn't want to have dinner with rock stars?

I head back to my suite in the apartment we share. She can stew about it for a while, but I know Hayleigh better than she knows herself. She'll come. She'll use me as an excuse, but she wants to have dinner with rock stars.

My phone vibrates in my hand. That didn't take her long, but then I see the text is from Mav Slater.

Mav: Are you girls still arguing about me?

Me: Are you standing outside the door listening to Hayleigh's side?

Mav: Nope.

Me: Then how'd you know we were arguing about you?

Mav: I didn't, you just confirmed it. See you tomorrow, Kadence.

Me: Call me Kady.

Mav: See you tomorrow, Kady. ;-)

I haven't looked forward to a social event like this in forever. I really want this dinner to mingle with new people. I don't know what is more pathetic, that I don't mingle with new people, or that I am this excited to do it.

Even before losing my voice, I lived in a void of my own making. I never let people too close, despite being surrounded by a large entourage when I was Kandi. I didn't realize how massive that void had become until I woke up alone in a hospital, unable to talk. I may not go out much, but the life I live now is more real than anything I lived as Kandi.

The fame in my old life got me enough money that I don't need to work if I don't want to, but that life wasn't real. Living here with Hayleigh, working to get my footing in a world that forgot me, regards me as different, as damaged, that's real life. In my real life right now, the excitement of having dinner with rock stars has my stomach filled with butterflies and my mind is already going through all the possible scenarios that I could be faced with at this dinner. Even though Hayleigh tries to appear aloof and inconvenienced, I know that deep down she's excited too.

R

MAV: *Expect a town car at 6:30 pm.*

Mav: *I hope you are looking forward to dinner as much as I am.*

I'm about to respond to Mavrick when I get a text from Hayleigh, who's in her wing of our condo.

Hayleigh: *I have a closet full of clothes and nothing to wear. What does one wear when having dinner with rock stars?*

It cracks me up that Hayleigh's texting me from her side of the apartment while I'm over here in my room. It didn't take me long to decide what to wear. I just threw on my favorite jeans and paired it with my favorite shirt and voila. The old me would have bought something new and very expensive for a dinner like this.

Me: *You have more clothes than I do, and I was finished 15 mins ago.*

Hayleigh: *Not helping. Get your ass over here.*

I cross our condo, which we purchased specifically for the separate wings. The common areas of the living room and kitchen are in the middle. Each wing includes a large master bedroom with an en-suite bathroom and a walk-in closet. There is also a sitting room I use for an office, with a huge balcony. I use the smaller bedroom of my wing for storage. Hayleigh's wing is an exact copy. She uses her sitting room as intended, and the spare bedroom on her side is used as a guest room.

The separate wings give us each privacy, so when Hayleigh has a date over, I'm not forced to hear their dalliances. I don't need that kind of privacy, but I do like having my own spaces to escape to and disconnect.

When I walk into her bedroom, Hayleigh's got a heap of clothes on her pink and gray bedspread that's growing by the minute.

Me: You are overcomplicating this. It's only dinner.

"Easy for you to say. You thrive on blending in, but I want to stand out." She snaps her head in my direction as soon as the words leave her lips, a frown pulling down on her mouth. "You know what I mean."

She's not wrong. I used to live to stand out too. Now I prefer to blend into the background. It's easier to do that now since I don't have a voice, and I prefer to do my blending while dressed comfortably.

Me: Wear your fave. That's what I did.

"But what if we go somewhere with a fancy dress code." I'm horrified by her words. Fancy is not in my vocabulary anymore, so I never thought to ask.

Me: Shit.

"Yeah, shit."

I send a quick text to Mav.

Me: Hayleigh needs to know if we are going somewhere with a 'fancy dress code.'

He responds almost immediately.

Mav: Do YOU want to go somewhere with a fancy dress code?

Me: Just wherever you planned is fine. She needs to know for clothing reasons. I'm already dressed.

I don't tell him that depending on his answer, I may be running across the apartment on my own mission to change clothes.

Mav: No dress code. Wear what's comfortable.

Me: Thanks.

I return to my texts to Hayleigh.

Me: Mav says no dress code.

"You call him Mav now?" She looks over at me. I pull up his contact and point to the name to illustrate that's how he refers to himself. He added the contact himself; she saw him do it. She goes back to pulling out shirts. I nudge her out of the way and grab her favorite top and a pair of nice jeans and hand them to her.

"This isn't too casual?" She holds out my choices between us. I point at myself so she can see that I'm wearing a similar outfit; jeans and a favorite top. She still adds several layers of bangles to her arm, and huge silver hoop earrings to jazz up her ensemble.

I lounge on her clothing covered bed while she dresses and goes over her makeup, again. I don't wear much makeup anymore, just some mascara. If I am feeling extra fancy, I'll put on some foundation and maybe eye shadow, but that's not today. The intercom chimes as she returns from her bathroom. She presses the button as we head to the foyer.

Our car is here.

The evening doorman escorts us to the front of the building, where a large limo sits just beyond the doors of the lobby.

I was expecting a town car, but this is a freaking stretched limo and it's drawing the attention of residents making their way through the lobby. My stomach clenches. What have I gotten myself into?

"This was your idea, KadyKat." Hayleigh senses my apprehension and touches my arm gently. The driver opens the door, and she slides in first. "Get in here, Kay." She jerks her head toward the inside of the limo, and I slide in next to her.

Mav: The driver knows where to go. Text me when you arrive.

Me: Ok.

Instead of heading toward the strip or even the upscale Summerlin area to the north of Las Vegas, as I expected, the limo heads more towards the suburb of Henderson, and continues through to the gated community at Lake Las Vegas. I've been to the lake, but not the gated community. We eventually turn down a cul-de-sac, stopping at the last house at the end of the short street.

Me: I think we're here? By the lake?

The driver opens the door and helps us out.

"Woah," Hayleigh says for the both of us as we stand in front of the large Spanish hacienda style home.

The door opens and Mavrick lopes down the walkway toward us.

"Hello, ladies. Good to see you again." He grins and pulls Hayleigh in for a friendly hug. He starts to reach for me, and I stiffen in anticipation of the contact. Mav somehow senses my hesitation and pulls back. I don't think that anyone, except maybe Hayleigh, has ever stopped to consider that I might not want to be hugged.

"Follow me, ladies." He places a light hand on the small of my back as he walks us up to the house, but nothing happens at the contact.

"Your home is beautiful." Hayleigh looks around at the immaculate and open home. She's not wrong. The walls are a cream color, topped with earthy open beam ceilings. The furniture is all in rich, leathery browns. It's the kind of place that invites you to come and sit for a spell. It's obviously a short-term rental, though, because, while the colors and the furniture are quite inviting, the décor isn't personalized.

"Well, not mine, but it'll work while I'm in town. The rest of the guys are staying at the Wynn, but Sammy ends up here more than there." He looks us over. "Can I take your bags?" We hand over our purses and he puts them in a closet near the door.

I hand him my phone.

Me: I thought we'd be eating at a restaurant.

He smiles at me. When I'm this close, I notice how his eyes are the color of chocolate, but with flecks of a lighter, almost coppery, color around the edges. "A chef is preparing most of the food, but Cal will be barbecuing the chicken and steak. At most restaurants, we'd be dealing with constant interruptions and travel with a security team. We won't be interrupted here.

We're free to be ourselves." He eyes me. "Trust me, this'll be much better." He pauses like he's waiting for my reaction, like he expects me to complain. I won't. I prefer this to a fancy strip restaurant, no matter whom I'm eating with.

"So, come on in. Meet the guys. I was able to get the entire band here after all." We follow Mavrick into the rear of the home. The whole back of the house opens up to a partially covered patio that faces the lake behind the house, its silvery blue patches reflecting light over the brick wall. The covered part of the patio attached to the house keeps the outdoor area cooler, but the heat from off the lake still blows in hot and contrasts with the rest of the air-conditioned house. The rest of The Blind Rebels lounge in various spots around the large living room that the kitchen looks into.

"Hayleigh and Kadence, meet the rest of the Blind Rebels. This is Sammy, our drummer." Mav puts a hand on the shoulder of an impish looking blonde with a mop of bouncy blonde curls. He looks up and smiles at us. I start to wave, but that seems lame, especially since I just did that a minute ago. I should make flashcards for times like this, where I can just hold up words like 'hi!' or common phrases like 'nice to meet you,' but that seems stupid too. I'm the epitome of awkward.

"The rogue with the adorable kid on the end of the couch is our guitarist extraordinaire, Callum. His son's name is Gibson. Yes, as in the guitar." Callum nods at us, his long dark hair pulled back into a low ponytail.

Mav moves over to him and takes the boy from his lap and brings him over to us. "Gibs, these lovely ladies are Hayleigh and Kadence." The baby grins a gummy smile at us and then goes right for the necklace Mav's wearing. "Nope, sorry, little buddy." He peels his hand off the thick long chain and hands the baby over to Sammy. "Gibs has an affinity for jewelry, just to warn you. Trust me, you'll end up holding him. He's a total lady killer already." Mav winks at us.

"And lastly, the surly shit over there is Callum's twin, Killian, and on his lap is his new friend. Uh, sorry, what was your name again?"

Killian's hair is shorter and darker than Callum's and he has a piercing above his left eye and in his lip, but you'd have to be blind not to notice the resemblance. The blonde on his lap shows more skin than not. I'd be surprised if she bothered to put on underwear.

"Veronica, but most people call me Roni." She gives us both a very noticeable once over, then centers her attention back on Killian. He looks at us both over her shoulder for the briefest of seconds before sticking his tongue in her mouth. Nice welcome there.

"Guys, this is Hayleigh." Mav makes a gesture towards her.

She waves and smiles brightly.

"And this lovely creature is Kadence. But she goes by Kady." I wave like a dork again and Hayleigh talks for me. "Kady can't talk, but she can hear fine. She uses her phone to respond instead of her voice." I wave my phone in a lame illustration. This doesn't seem to be news to the group except for Roni, who curls her lip at me. She probably doesn't even realize she's doing it. She likely thinks I'm some sort of freak. I feel my shoulders slump. I'm always the freak now. *No one sees me, Kady.* I'm just the weirdo who can't talk. She's soon disregarding me, rewrapping her tentacles around Killian's neck.

"Please make yourselves at home. Can I get either of you something to drink?" Mav looks at Hayleigh and me.

Hayleigh asks for a beer for herself and water for me. Mav looks directly at me. "Are you sure you want water? Besides a full bar, I have most sodas in regular and diet, iced tea, hot tea, coffee?"

I smile and mouth 'water' at him.

"I have sparkling lemon-lime, peach, and some sort of berry, or just regular water."

Hayleigh sits on the couch across from Sammy. "She likes regular ol' water."

Mav tears his deep brown eyes from mine to look at Hayleigh, his voice laced with irritation. "You don't have to speak for Kadence."

Hayleigh looks up at Mav, her eyes big, her cheeks rapidly reddening. I've never seen her look so mortified. "It's not, uh, like that. I just know what she likes. Sometimes it's just easier."

She looks embarrassed, like when I catch her eating the brownies she's made for Harden, but Mav's expectant eyes are already back on me.

Me: The "some sort of berry," please.

Mav grins at me. "Kady, you're a gambler. Some sort of berry it is." He glances at Hayleigh before heading over to the sizable wet bar. He pulls out a beer for Hayleigh and what ends up being a blackberry-flavored water for me.

Chapter 9

Mavrick

I join Cal at the pit while he pokes at the steaks, but I'm distracted by Kady. I can't tell if she's having a good time relaxing, or if she's uncomfortable here with us, with me.

She's sitting cross-legged on one of the lounge chairs, watching Hayleigh as she holds Gibson while Sammy entertains him. I knew that kid would end up on one of their laps eventually.

Killian and Roni peeled themselves apart long enough to join us out on the patio, but are now reclined in a lounge chair on the far side of the pool practically dry humping. I don't know what is up with him lately. I'm all about the ladies, but he seems to need to have someone on him at all times. At this rate, he'll be the next Blind Rebel with a kid.

Kady's supple lips pull on the straw as she sips her berry water, and it has me thinking of things I shouldn't be thinking about, not at a barbecue with a child present. Not about her. Not when I'm trying to convince her to come back and work with us. I shake my head.

"Mav?" Cal is looking at me expectantly.

"Sorry, what did you say?" I tear my eyes away from Kady and bring them back to Cal, standing there in board shorts and a t-shirt, meat tongs in one hand, beer in the other.

"I know she can't talk and all, but she seems pretty quiet over there." Cal nods towards Kady, who's still sitting in her chair, observing everybody. I've noticed it too. This isn't the sassy girl back at the apartment, the one I texted with this afternoon.

"She wasn't like this yesterday." When I finally catch her gaze, she smiles softly at me then returns to watching Gibs, who lets out a happy shriek when Sammy hands him a drumstick from his back pocket. It immediately goes into Gibs's gummy, drooly mouth.

"She was in her own domain there. It's probably intimidating being around us. You know, for someone who isn't us." He grins cockily and turns back to the meat. "Plus, chewing out her friend ten minutes after they arrived probably didn't help."

"Kady doesn't need someone to speak for her." I don't understand my sudden need to defend Kady, but the weird protectiveness buzzes just under the surface of my skin. She has her own thoughts and opinions, and I want to know what Kady wants, not what Hayleigh thinks she wants. Something about her makes me want that closeness with her.

"Still..." He turns towards me. "You went off on her at the club. You go off on her friend here." A serious look crosses his face. "You have anger issues. They have classes to help you get over that."

Shit, maybe he has a point. I'm coming off as an angry ass. "I don't have anger issues, you dick," I deny and push his shoulder while he laughs at me. I won't take it any further, because those tongs in his hand are hot.

"Why's she here anyway? I thought you made your amends." Callum scrutinizes me. Fuck if I know. I had to see her again, but I don't want to tell him that. Even with her here right now, I already want to see more of her, but the version I met back at the apartment.

"I'm trying to talk her into coming back to work with us. Plus, she fascinates me for a reason I can't put my finger on." He looks at me, wanting more, but I just shrug. I've already said too much. "I can't explain it. It's like she's hardened but innocent. There's more to her than the quiet girl who blends into the background." I think about the somewhat sassy Kady at her house and how she's almost shy here. "I just want to know her."

Callum clears his throat and looks over my shoulder briefly, then turns back around to the meat on the grill. Kady approaches with her phone in hand.

Kady: Can I help?

"Help me set the table? I thought we'd eat out here. It's not too hot if we eat under the shade." I motion to the table, and she nods, heading toward it. I hand her a stack of paper plates and follow her around, placing flatware next to each setting. She shakes her head hard and takes a small stack of the napkins, folds one for each place setting, and picks up the flatware and lays them on the napkin. Her brow knits at me and she flashes me her phone.

Kady: Who taught you to set a table? Barbarians? Napkins UNDER the flatware.

A chuckle slips out of me. This is the Kadence from her apartment. She smiles at me for the first time. It's not a big smile, but it reaches her green eyes, making them sparkle like gems. There's my girl. *My girl?* How can I call her *my girl?* Even if I like the sound of it. I definitely want to make her smile like this all the time.

"Mav, watch the meat. I'm going to give Gibs a bottle and try to put him down before we eat." Cal nods towards the pit as he walks back into the house with a fussy Gibs in his arms.

I turn back to Kady. "Steak or chicken?"

Kady: *Steak!*

Gotta love a girl who's not afraid to eat.

R

As our dinner seems to be wrapping up, Sammy pushes back his plate. "Ugh, so full." He rubs his stomach and tips his chair back on two legs. This kid is always hungry, so I am sure that his fullness is only temporary.

"For twenty minutes maybe." Killian cracks, echoing my thoughts, and throws his napkin at him. "You're a bottomless pit, man. The rest of us have been done for fifteen minutes."

Sammy laughs. "It's my metabolism. It's super high because of the drumming. It's scientific or something like that." He throws the napkin back at Killian.

Roni comes back from the bathroom and slides herself back onto Kill's lap. Sammy's face falls momentarily, until he looks across at Kady sitting next to me.

"So, Kady, why can't you talk?" The only sounds after Sammy's question are the soft snores of Gibson coming through the baby monitor next to Cal. He's asked the one question everyone wants to know but didn't have the balls to ask, and he did it so casually, like he's talking about the weather. All eyes are on Kady. Her back straightens to an almost unnatural posture, and then her shoulders slump forward and she pulls in on herself, looking smaller than she did just minutes ago.

I love Sammy, but I want to punch him in the face right now. Kady shrinks in on herself, like she wishes she were invisible. It's not that we all don't want to know, we do, but asking a question that feels so personal and intimate in such a spur-of-the-moment way seems almost flippant. I know that's not how he meant it, that he's just being Sammy, but that's not how it comes off.

I try to smile at her, to encourage her when she glances over at me, but she doesn't seem to see me, or really anyone, like we aren't even here. She leans hard against the back of her chair and pulls her phone into her lap, staring at the screen, but her fingers are immobile.

The stillness of her thumbs and fingers only signals her increasing discomfort. A grimace spreads across her face as her downcast eyes well with shiny, unshed tears.

I kick Sammy hard under the table. He jumps with the contact and mouths 'what?' I nod at Kady. He's upset her, the dumbass. I'm trying to get her to feel comfortable with being around us, not make her want to run away. I shake my head at him and narrow my eyes. Surely, he understands he's made her feel bad.

Hayleigh reaches down slowly to Kady's knee, gives it a squeeze, and then takes her phone from her hands and sets it back on the table. "Do you want me to explain?" Kady nods so slightly I almost don't catch the movement. Her eyes never leave her lap.

Hayleigh straightens in her chair, and she looks down the length of the table at everyone. "Kady has adult-onset selective mutism." She makes eye contact, first with Sammy, and then with me.

Kady's gaze at her hands doesn't change at Hayleigh's words. She doesn't even try to make eye contact with anyone, not even her friend.

"Selective mutism is more common in children and young teenagers and its causes are varied. Sometimes there is no cause. Kady's is caused by a traumatic event." Sadness weighs down the corners of Hayleigh's lips as she glances at her friend before locking eyes with me. "There are different levels of functionality with selective mutism. Kady's is one of the more severe forms because she's unable to talk at all. Some people can speak in certain circumstances or only to specific people."

I quickly glance at the rest of the table, and judging by their expressions, they're just as surprised and gutted as I am.

"The name sucks." Hayleigh brings a hand up to her face to swipe at a tear. "It makes it sound like Kady *chooses* not to talk." She looks at me, the worry she must usually hide causing deep creases in her face. It's like I can feel her pain for her friend in my stomach.

"It's not her choice; she'd much rather talk. Right, Kady?" At her name, Kady looks up and nods, but doesn't make eye contact with anyone.

"Will she ever talk? Is there a treatment or medication or something?" Sammy's low voice mirrors his serious face. He looks like my gut feels; stricken, cold, sad.

Hayleigh sighs, glancing sideways at her friend. "None of the medications she's tried have helped, and a few caused some fairly gnarly side-effects. She's seen a few therapists and a specialist in the field of selective mutism, but for right now, Kady's decided to take a break."

Kady snatches her phone from the table and types quickly, then shoves her phone at Hayleigh's chest. Hayleigh swallows hard. "'From being a lab rat,' is what she says."

"You're not a lab rat," Hayleigh says, so only Kady and I can hear.

Kady grabs the phone back from Hayleigh to a chorus of uncomfortable chuckles while she types out her next message.

"Kady says she was tired of being treated like someone's broken toy," Hayleigh relays, her eyes welling with tears for her friend. The emotion and sadness affects everyone at the table. Callum shifts uncomfortably, glancing at the baby monitor, probably wishing Gibs awake so that he has an excuse to get away from the feelings overload. Even Veronica drops her arms from around a frozen Killian for a few minutes.

Kady rips strips from her napkin and piles them in stacks of five on her plate. I wish she'd look at me instead of her damn plate. I want her to know I don't see a broken toy. I see a warrior hiding behind a curtain of black and purple hair, gripping her phone like a shield.

Chapter 10

Kadence

Sammy's question was innocent enough. I should have expected it and not let it knock me for a loop. I didn't anticipate it, which proves exactly why I shouldn't do things spontaneously. I know better.

I'd been lulled into a false sense of security when Mav seemingly ignored the fact that I used a phone to communicate when he came to the apartment. Here, everyone seems friendly enough. Well, except for Killian, who seemed to want nothing to do with anyone except Roni. I felt accepted for who I am, or maybe I had just hoped I was.

I should have known it was going to come up somehow. So, now everyone sits in an uncomfortable silence, absorbing the information that Hayleigh gave them. Here I am, the freak at a sideshow, while everyone talks about me like I'm not sitting right the fuck here.

Hayleigh must have expected it with the way she squeezed my knee. Sometimes I forget that I've been so sheltered these last two years. I was stupid to think there wouldn't be some curiosity about my lack of a voice around new people. Until Sammy asked the question, I hadn't realized I've only surrounded myself with people who already know my story, people who won't bring it up unless I do, which is pretty much never.

Now that Hayleigh's explained it without going too in-depth, there's a stiff awkwardness around the table that's preventing them from asking the real question I know is on their minds. The looming elephant of 'traumatic event' is now sitting prominently in the middle of the table. Everyone knows it's there and wants to ask about it, but they don't dare upset the freak.

No one except Mav even looks at me now. They look at their plates or fidget with their forks. Nobody talks, not even amongst themselves.

When I finally look over at Sammy, he looks like he's been kicked in the stomach. He's the first besides Mav to finally make eye contact, and when he does, his is face full of regret and something that looks like pity. I glance away quickly before the anger starts.

I can't stand the pity. It makes me feel weak, like a failure. Feeling reduced makes me angry; really fucking angry. I've spent too much time working on myself to go back to seeing myself as weak. I don't want to go back to being angry with myself for being a headcase. Something in my psyche prevents me from talking, no matter how much I try.

Mav drapes an arm across my shoulders and squeezes lightly a couple of times. The sudden, unexpected pressure of his arm and the squeezing of his fingers should send me skittering away from him, but my body does the opposite. My muscles don't go rigid, I don't lean away or push up out of the chair.

Instead of pushing him away, I lean slightly towards him, feeling the comfort and warmth in his touch. There isn't even the slightest tightening in the pit of my stomach, like when

Hayleigh grabs me without thinking. Hayleigh, whom I've known since we were kids.

"Want to help me get dessert while these fools throw their plates away?" His voice is low, his mouth close to my ear. Even if he's just providing me with an escape, I'll take any excuse to get away from the weighted blanket of awkward that is encompassing the table. I nod and rise from my chair while Mav instructs everyone what to do with their paper plates. I follow him through the door to the kitchen.

The counters are filled with desserts of every kind. There are trays of cookies, cupcakes, and brownies. There are pies, some fruit tarts, fancy mousse in small edible chocolate cups, and even a bowl of mini candy bars. If it's sweet, it's here.

Is he trying to sugar up an entire army? I go to type it out and realize I've left my phone outside by my plate, so I look at him, hoping to convey a 'what the heck is with all the desserts' look.

He must understand because his cheeks tinge ever so slightly red, a look I wouldn't expect on a rock star of his caliber. It's adorable. "I didn't know what you liked, so I had my chef put together a bunch of different desserts. The guys will eat anything that doesn't eat them first; especially Sammy, as he proved during dinner." Mav chuckles.

Shaking my head slowly at him, I can't believe the variety of the spread in front of me. It's more extensive than the dessert trays at the fanciest Vegas buffets I've been to.

"Everyone likes dessert. Surely, there's something here you like." I survey the spread closely, zeroing in on the tray of delicately decorated cupcakes. They are all so beautiful. I point to a perfectly iced cupcake on a tray containing more than a dozen, each cake decorated slightly differently. He carefully lifts the exact iced treat I pointed at and not just any random cupcake from the tray and hands it to me.

"Better get it now. Killian's right about Sammy's appetite.

He'll wipe out a third of this spread tonight by himself." He winks at me and hops up to sit on the kitchen island behind him while I contemplate the seamlessly perfect lavender rosette on top of the cupcake he just handed me.

"Go on. Dig in." I glance at the path from the patio to the kitchen. "They'll wait."

These cupcakes aren't your standard grocery store cupcakes. They are iced with the care of an artist, this particular one with purple ribbons of icing making a perfect rose on top. It looks so beautiful I almost don't want to eat it.

As somewhat of a cupcake connoisseur, I've found the general rule is that the prettier they are, the worst they taste. It's like either the baker puts all their care into making the batter just right and the icing is just a tasteless mess, or the cupcake is exquisitely decorated but the cake itself is terribly dry, or even worse, bland. I slip my poker face on to not show how bad this cupcake will likely be. He's taken a lot of time to consider what I might like, and I don't want to hurt his or his chef's feelings.

I gently peel the paper away from the golden cake and take a good-sized bite, making sure to get equal amounts of cake and icing. Vanilla and sugar dance in my mouth and as I chew, just a hint of something spicy and curious is revealed. It's not enough to distract from the cake, but enough to be pleasant and unexpected.

I lick my lips clear of any frosting and go back in for another bite, closing my eyes this time. This cupcake is so freaking good. It's the unicorn of cupcakes. The cake is moist and not overly sweet. The unusual spice to it adds an enjoyable twist when paired with the smoothest, sweetest frosting I've ever had. I can't help but take a third bite, my eyes rolling in enjoyment.

As I finish my little cake, Mav groans and my eyes snap to his. I almost forgot he was watching me devour this little masterpiece. I was way too into that cupcake, and he witnessed it, and the very thought of that has my cheeks warming.

Mav doesn't seem notice. His brown eyes look almost black as they dilate and focus in on my lips as I lick the residual frosting off.

"Fuck, that was probably the sexiest thing I've ever seen." He slips off the island and leans against it. He bends down slightly so we're face-to-face. "Oh, you have a little frosting on your nose." He cups my face and gently rubs it away with his thumb.

Again, my body doesn't go rigid. There's no burning in my stomach, no uncontrollable urge to get away from him or out of the kitchen. It surprises me when I lean into him without even thinking about it. He's warm and hard and smells like leather and the smoke from the barbecue, with a hint of sweet underneath.

He sticks his thumb, the one that rubbed the frosting away, into his mouth.

"Mmmm, so sweet." He pulls it back out, his eyes partially closed.

It's sexy and almost kind of naughty, and yet I'm surprised by how much I like it. I wish I had frosting somewhere else. My face flushes red hot.

"Was it good?" His eyes lock back on my mouth. I lick my lips, then pretend to dab frosting off with a napkin as I nod slowly.

"Glad you enjoyed it." He blinks like he's suddenly reminded that we're supposed to deliver the trays of confectionary delights. "Let's take these trays out, then."

He grabs three trays while I grab the other two. He winks as he deftly arranges the trays along his corded, tattooed arm.

"I used to pick up server jobs before we hit it big. I could carry all five if I needed to." He grins at me.

The heavy awkwardness is gone when we return to the

table. Now, Cal is telling an animated story involving Mav, a San Diego County Sheriff's Deputy, and a stolen car.

"It wasn't stolen. I had permission," Mav mumbles as we set the trays down the length of the table.

"Permission? Permission, he says!" Callum laughs. "He was supposed to run to the store. Not joyride to San Diego."

"Are there not stores in San Diego? I was just appreciating the car. A car like that needed to be tested out on the highway." Mav leans back on two legs of his chair and pops a bite of brownie in his mouth. Killian snorts as he reaches for a cookie.

Stripper Barbie doesn't seem to care about the desserts, as she has her arm wrapped around Killian. He either has his tongue halfway down her throat or is ignoring her completely. I almost feel sorry for her. She's wrapped her existence around what little attention he gives her. Part of me understands Killian's aloofness, probably more than he does. A couple of years in therapy will do that.

I watch the band banter around like family and feel almost like I'm part of it, but not quite. Cal's like the father of the band, interestingly enough since he is a father. Sammy is like everyone's little brother. He's adorable and funny and loves to make everyone laugh. Killian's the dark one. I'm uncomfortable with him. The way he stares at me is almost like he sees who I used to be. The ugliness of Kandi.

Mav is different, though. He's charismatic, that's for sure, which isn't a shock since most singers have some sort of charm about them. With Mav, I'm drawn to him like he's the other half of my magnet. My eyes always seem to settle on him, and my stomach warms as well as my cheeks when our eyes lock, which is often.

Hayleigh's face has been filled with questions and concerns since we've returned with the desserts. I know she's watching me, but I give her nothing in my return gaze. Keeping my emotions to myself helps me process them in my own time. It drives Hayleigh crazy. For a while, I did it out of necessity as a way of keeping people, even my best friend, at arm's length. It was necessary when the thought of being touched or coddled hurt nearly as much as what was happening on the inside.

Now, I reach for my mask out of habit. Part of me hates that I'm sick of Hayleigh being up in my business all the time. I know she means well, and she's always been there for me, but I'm not even sure how I feel right now. Not about having added to the group of people who know what is up with me, or about these weird flutters I get when Mav looks at me. I don't want to be hashing this out with her right now in front of people I barely know.

After everyone's done eating, Mav and Callum start a fire in the pit on the other side of the pool area nearest the lake. They pull chairs and loungers around the firepit and then grab guitars and start messing around, playing a melody down by the fire. Soon, everyone has migrated to the fire pit area. I sit on the end of the semi-circle next to Sammy, who's fetched some hand drums. Mav and Callum sit in the center of our semicircle. They start with some standard classic rock songs and soon everyone is humming or singing along. Even Hayleigh and Stripper Barbie are swaying and singing along.

As much as I'm loving being here, I'm disconnected from what's going on and everyone else that's here as the music progresses. Not being able to participate makes me empty. Music used to be my life, my livelihood, my dream. Now, I'm exiled to the outskirts of it, forced to sit on the fringe and only listen. I tap out the beat with my foot when I want to be right there in the middle of the circle, my fingers working along the frets. I try to sneak a note or two, but my vocal cords remain frozen.

I'm glad for the low light, because I feel the wetness of a big, fat tear as it rolls uninvited down my cheek. I brush it away quickly, praying it goes unnoticed. Luckily, everyone else is into the music; even Killian, who's joined in with another guitar. It's ironic because I just want to be in their world, instead of stuck on the outside, silent and lonely.

As the first few songs draw to a close, Sammy springs to his feet. "Hold up. Wait for me, I'll be right back." He jogs back into the house.

Everyone sips their drinks and murmurs amongst themselves. Killian tunes his guitar, not happy with its sound. It was a little off, like maybe he hasn't played this particular guitar lately.

I pull my legs onto the lounger and shift to face the water. It's still so warm out here. Probably something I'll never get used to. It was warm in L.A., but not like this. It's at least 8:30 or 9:00 p.m. but it feels like sitting under one of those salon hair dryers, even the breeze carrying over the lake is warm. I lose myself in the blackness of the lake.

"Here." Sammy holds out a tambourine with a shy smile and shakes it at me, so it makes its shimmery noise. "You've got rhythm." I look up at him and he recognizes the question on my face. "Your feet gave you away."

He pauses and extends the instrument until it touches my knee. "Come on, just do what comes naturally." He smiles when I take it and returns to his hand drums next to me.

"Follow my lead." He starts to pound out a simple 3/4 beat time signature on his hand drum and encourages me to follow along. Liking what he hears, Sammy nods vigorously and picks up the tempo and again, I match it. His grin grows and soon Callum joins in on guitar and the familiar opening of 'Back in Black' starts. Mav comes in on vocals and it draws a faint "hell yeah" from somewhere beyond the fenced yard.

Jamming on rock standards mostly, we continue to make music. For a while they seem to be playing stump the tambourine player, but I keep up, even when they switch things up to more poppy music or slow things down to country. At first, I concentrate on Sammy and the beat, but eventually, I let myself go. Sammy seems to really like that and encourages me. "You got it. You're a natural." Something stirs inside me, something I haven't felt in what seems like forever. Sammy slings an arm across my shoulders and gives me a brief hug.

Chapter 11

Mavrick

Across the pool from me, Kady hugs her knees to her chest while listening to Sammy talk. They've been there since the firepit jam session broke up. I flex my clenched hands, enjoying the tightness of my fist. The skin on my knuckles pulls taut, matching the tightness in my chest. I love Sammy, but I don't love him scamming on Kady.

As Kady nods, and Sammy continues to blabber on, I grind my teeth. Is he into her, or is he just trying to reassure himself she isn't upset with him for making her uncomfortable after dinner? Fuck. I don't need him making this worse.

I haven't been able to pull her aside yet and ask her if she'll come back and fulfill her contract to take our pictures. As much as I want her to say yes, I hesitate. If she says yes, it might make getting to know her more difficult. Since the cupcake incident, her mouth has been starring in some indecent daydreams. I run my hand through my hair to keep it from re-fisting.

Sammy cuffs Kady's shoulder and she shirks away from him. I jump up. Is he fucking bothering her? He's done that to me a thousand times. It's his way of connecting. She leans away slightly, and Sammy's hand drops as his brow creases in concern. Maybe I should intervene.

"She flinches with everyone, even me sometimes," Hayleigh says when she notices me watching their interaction.

I glance at Hayleigh, and she continues. "It's especially bad when she's nervous or caught off-guard. Sometimes, she'll jump like she's startled or her whole body will tense up and get so tight you can noticeably feel it, like she's guarding herself." Hayleigh pauses, and her voice lowers slightly. "But not with you." She doesn't even turn her blue eyes to look at me. Her voice is laced with something that sounds a lot like jealousy. "Your touch hasn't made her flinch once tonight. Not even after the deal at dinner. What is it about you?"

Trying to gauge if that was meant for me to answer or if she's just musing, I look at Hayleigh. She gives nothing away, just continues to watch her friend, ever on guard. I suddenly get that this is Hayleigh's life; always worrying about and protecting her friend. I have a feeling this is due to the traumatic event. It makes me want to ask.

I want to ask what the hell happened to her that made her like this.

"I can't give you more of her story, Mav. That's Kady's to share when and if she feels comfortable." She eyes me wearily in a way that tells me she wants to say something, but for whatever reason, she can't. Or won't. "Kady doesn't share much with people who aren't in her inner circle. And that inner circle consists of two people right now."

I don't just want to know why. I want to know everything about Kady. The light that shines from her, the darkness that shadows through her eyes when she thinks no one is watching. I want all of it and everything in between. I admire Hayleigh for being so protective of her friend, but it just makes me even more curious about Kadence.

What does Kadence's voice sound like? Is it breathy and

sensual? Light and airy? In my head, it has a lyrical quality that can't be described. I sigh, following Hayleigh's line-of-sight back to Kady, who's still enraptured with all that is Sammy.

Hayleigh shifts. "Thanks for inviting us." She pauses and takes a quick breath. "But also, for bringing back a little piece of Kady I thought was lost." She looks at me with unshed tears glossing her eyes.

"Seeing her while you guys were jamming? With that free-ness? It's something I never thought I'd see again." She pats me with almost a blessing of sorts. "I do have to work tomorrow, so we should go. I'll have a rideshare pick us up."

"Don't be ridiculous. I'll drive you." Her eyes widen, but she's no more surprised than I am with my offer. If it'd been Becka, I'd have let her Uber.

"But your party?" Hayleigh looks around at the guys scattered around the living room doing their own thing.

"Don't worry about them. These assholes know if they break it, they buy it," I say loud enough for them to hear while I wink at her. I ask Sammy for his keys, which he tosses to me without question.

Kadence's eyes light up at the sight of Sammy's lifted, shiny black Jeep in the driveway, despite the darkness outside. She hands me her phone.

Kady: Can we ride with the top off?

Dammit, I don't know how to remove the fuckin' top. The Beast is Sammy's baby and if I fuck it up, Sammy would blow his top. Okay, knowing Sammy, he probably wouldn't blow his top, but I don't want to find out.

"Maybe next time?"

I help her into the backseat of the large vehicle. I was hoping she'd pick the front seat, but Hayleigh already staked that claim.

The minute I turn the Beast over, Motley Crue comes

roaring out of the speakers, the bass thumping so hard the rearview mirror vibrates in time with the music. I flail my arms, scrambling to find the volume button on the damn radio so we don't disturb everyone within a five-block radius. This neighborhood is quiet, and I have a feeling this could cause complaints.

"This isn't my car. It's Sammy's. Apparently, we need to get his hearing checked." I make eye contact with Kady as I adjust the rearview mirror. She smiles back at my reflection. In the low lighting of the back seat, she looks beautiful. I can't help myself, so I wink at her.

She bites the corner of her lip. She has no idea what that does to me. Fuck, she's sexy, but not in that in-your-face way that I'm used to. It's almost like she doesn't even realize how attractive she is. It was everything I could do not to kiss her in the kitchen when she was eating that damn lucky cupcake.

Her eyes tell me she's interested, but she's not obvious in her attraction, and that in itself is such a breath of fresh air. Having women throw themselves across my lap gets tiresome. Kady is so much more that I'm willing to work for it, and she doesn't even realize how big of a turn-on it is.

"Why are we taking Sammy's car? You have a driver's license, right?" Hayleigh pipes up from the front seat, making me break my connection with Kady in the backseat, but not before I see her roll her eyes at her friend's questions.

I face Hayleigh in the passenger seat. "I have a valid California driver's license. The car I brought to Vegas only seats two. But even if it sat more, it's in the garage and Sammy's blocking me in. Taking the Jeep was logical. Sammy doesn't care about stuff like that." Mostly. She just stares at me.

I preempt her next question because I know it's coming. "I've had one whiskey at least three and a half hours ago, well before dinner. The rest of the night I drank soda or water. I'm fine to drive." Hayleigh lets out a little 'hmph' and turns to look out the windshield. I catch Kadence's amused look in the rearview before I pull out of the driveway.

Traffic's fairly light until we hit Las Vegas Boulevard. I don't know how they live so close to this traffic and noise. I get enough of it when I am heading in and out of L.A. from Malibu. Each time I glance up into the rearview mirror, I catch Kady's eyes watching me. This last time, her tongue darts out of her mouth and licks her lips quickly. It makes me squirm in my seat. It's a good thing that she's in the backseat after all. If she were in the front seat, I wouldn't see so much of her face. I love her mesmerizing green eyes so much more than her terrified ones.

I cross over the famed boulevard and am soon pulling up to the door of their apartment complex. Not caring about the red curb or the looks from the doorman, I rush over and open Kady's door and guide her descent from the Jeep.

When Kady's feet hit the ground, I touch her arm lightly to stop her from leaving. She preempts my speech by handing me her phone.

Kady: *Thank you. I had A LOT of fun.*

"Thank you for joining us. We had fun too." I want to discover more of Kady; what makes her tick, what makes her smile, what her favorite foods are, why the black and purple hair? Just everything.

"Before you go, I want you to seriously consider coming back to work with us." Her eyes get tense at my request. "Kadence, your photos are amazing. I'm thinking a photo book of just your photos to go along with the next album. I'd be a partnership of sorts."

Kady: *Can I think about it?*

I lean in to whisper in her ear and catch hold of her subtle tropical smell. Is that coconut? It's something that reminds me of a refreshing island breeze. No, it's pineapple. I close my eyes and take in another breath. This girl's driving me wild by not doing anything at all.

"While you're thinking about it, I want to see you again, without your warden next time." I fight the urge to kiss and nibble her ear as my lips brush against it. My breath against her ear intensifies her warm pineapple fragrance in my nose.

My pulse jumps erratically when an unexpected sound bubbles from her lips. Kady is laughing. It's slightly deeper, throatier than I expected, but it's one of the sweetest pieces of music I've ever heard, delicate yet deep and complex. I could write entire songs about it.

A quick glance at Hayleigh's stunned face tells me this wasn't something that happens often, or maybe even at all. Hayleigh's surprise gives way to something that looks a lot like jealousy. Not because she wants me or anything like that. I think it's because Kady laughed at something I said. I want to make her laugh again and again just to surround myself with the sound.

Kady pulls away and glances over at Hayleigh with round eyes. It was as unexpected to Kady as it was to Hayleigh and me.

"I'll call you tomorrow. We'll make plans to take Sammy's Jeep out topless. You'll love it."

Kady: Don't call.

She holds her phone out to me.

She doesn't want to see me again? Talk about mixed signals. She smiles and her eyes twinkle in the light from the overhead awning. She's kidding. She snatches her phone back to input something quickly before holding it to me again.

Kady: Text. Phone calls are always one-sided ;-)

A joke. My Kady made a joke at my expense.

My Kady? Shit, she's getting under my skin. I already can't wait to see her again. This could be so bad. I've never been so captivated so quickly as I've been with Kady. Is it one of the reasons I want her to come back and work for us? If I'm honest, yes. I don't want to let her go yet. I glance at Hayleigh, then to the doorman, wishing like hell we didn't have this audience.

"Text, then."

Kady's black and purple hair swishes slightly from side to side as she and Hayleigh stroll inside the lobby of their building and disappear behind the elevator's closing door. I'm left here, standing outside under the glaring eye of the doorman because I'm still parked in the red, wishing like hell I had kissed her in my kitchen when I had the chance.

Chapter 12

Kadence

Since I lost my voice, I've never made a noise as deliberate or complete as a laugh. I usually hate the odd noises I do make, like an occasional grunt when it's just Hayleigh and me. Speech therapy had me trying to make more of these grunts on purpose, but they don't even sound human half the time. I sound like a wounded animal, not a person.

Hayleigh was jealous that Mav got me to laugh. It wasn't anything he specifically did. I mean, what Mav said was funny. He called Hayleigh my warden, and he's not completely wrong. Sometimes it feels like that to me, especially lately. It's not Hayleigh's fault. I needed her help so much in the beginning. I was dealt a triple blow. First, the festival shooting and having that guilt, knowing it was my fault. Then the injuries I sustained and lastly, not being able to talk or sing. Jerrod took so many things away from me that day, but the one thing that hurt me the most was losing my ability to express myself. The darkness after was all-encompassing and my ability to function was at an incredibly low point. It was easier to just be and let Hayleigh deal with everything. She was so good at taking over and taking care of me, but I don't need that level of support anymore.

There's no need for her to be jealous of Mav. I couldn't help what happened at his words. I still can't believe I laughed. Out. Freaking. Loud.

Hayleigh wants to say something. Her body vibrates as she holds it in. She had to hear me laugh; it was so loud in my own ears there is no way she couldn't.

I try to force myself to talk to Hayleigh while we ride up to our floor.

Say something, I command my mouth and tongue. Just say her name, anything, but my vocal cords betray me. Just a fluke. I knew it.

As soon as we walk into our apartment, Hayleigh gets right to preparing for work tomorrow. First, she gathers all the fixings to make her lunch without even a glance my way.

She continues to ignore me. I just laughed while we were downstairs and she's totally ignoring me now. Burning tears form in my eyes, making it hard to text her from my perch on the couch.

Me: Why are you ignoring me?

As she checks her message, her head dips down for a moment as she takes a breath. When she looks back up, I can see the glassiness of her eyes from across the room.

She stalks into the living room and grabs my face with both of her hands, pulling me close to her. My body tightens momentarily. Her breath is hot and the tears in her eyes make my own start to spill.

"I am *so* not ignoring you." She shakes her head. "What I'm trying to do is *not* make a big deal out of this, when I want to scream about it from the freaking roof! Your speech therapist told me not to make a big stink when little breakthroughs happen." Her breath hitches slightly.

"But this is such a huge fucking deal. That wasn't some

random, non-committal noise. You freakin' full-out laughed, Kady." Her breath catches as tears start rolling down her cheeks. "And it was so damn beautiful. I'd forgotten what it sounds like."

I can't help the shuddering sob that erupts from her words. She hugs me tightly to her and rocks me hard from side to side.

"Oh, KadyKat, you laughed. You laughed!" She laughs even though tears pour down both our faces. She pulls me back into a tight hug. I curse the involuntary tensing of my back at the contact. Either she doesn't notice it, or she doesn't care, since she offers none of her usual apologies. She just rocks me.

"I've missed it so much. I miss you so much." Her voice is soft like we're in a library and her breath moves the hair by my ears.

I want to tell her I miss me too. I sigh, and she pulls back and runs her hands over my shoulders and upper arms.

"I thank God every single night that you're still here, that you made it out. I've been waiting 22 months for just a small piece of you, the person *I know*, not Kandi, that's been stuck inside here." She taps on my head. "That laugh was *everything* I've been waiting and praying for. *Everything.*"

What if I can't do it next time? Hayleigh is taking this as a breakthrough instead of the fluke that it actually is. She's setting me up to disappoint her.

Me: I tried to talk in the elevator. Didn't work.

"It's a first step, Kady." I can't stand that hope in her eyes. It's full of pressure and dreams that I know won't happen, that I don't deserve to happen.

Me: Or a fluke.

"Baby steps, hon. Baby steps." Hayleigh squeezes me into a hug again, but I'm expecting it this time.

It hurts too much that she's so positive. I just can't believe in it like she can. It constricts my chest. I stopped speech therapy and psychotherapy for a reason. It wasn't helping. I've accepted

I'll never talk again, that it's the price I'll pay for the innocent lives lost that day. But Hayleigh is so determined I don't give up. I head to bed, leaving her on the couch with her hope.

R

THE VIBRATION of my phone against my nightstand keeps pulling me back out of the haze of sleep. Dammit, I wanted a few more minutes. Grabbing my phone off my nightstand, I roll to sit up.

Hayleigh: *Dinner out tonight. Just you and me.*

Harden: *Need to talk to you. Pick you up at noon.*

Mav: *You. Me. Sammy's Jeep. Tomorrow. Pick you up at 8:30 am? Bring your camera.*

Hayleigh: *You up yet?*

I should've known better than to try sleeping in. I shoot off a text to Harden, letting him know I'll be ready and then send a similar one to Mav.

Hayleigh won't like me going off with Mav in Sammy's Jeep tomorrow, and I feel a little guilty about not telling her, but I know if I do tell her, she'll try to convince me not to go. I need to slowly break my dependence on her. I need to show her I can function on my own now, that I can make my own decisions.

I love her and all that she's done and continues to do for me, but I'm starting to understand that I need to deal with my life myself, starting with deciding who I hang out with and when.

Last night she said she missed the old me, but probably not as much as I miss the old her. She's not the carefree Hayleigh she used to be, the one with the bright smile and the devil-may-care attitude. That changed because of me, because of what happened to me. Now she worries too much for a twenty-five-year-old. She worries, not just for my wellbeing, although that's a big part of it, but I think what happened at the festival changed her outlook on the world around her. I know it did for me. We both lost our security and footing in the world. Me, because I was there, I saw it, I heard it, I felt it. Her, because she saw what happened to me after. Instinctively, I pulled away from the world, but she did too in her own way. I'm not convinced that she didn't break it off with Harden because of me and what happened. By the time I came to Vegas, they weren't together anymore. She holds onto the heaviness that surrounds me and it's creased her face since she showed up at the hospital. She wants me to be happy, but I want carefree Hayleigh again too.

As promised, Harden arrives at noon but won't talk to me until we're at the restaurant so that he can get my reactions. He chooses the Player's Locker in Summerlin, an upscale area near the practice rink for our local professional hockey team. This isn't a place we frequent, which immediately makes me suspicious of Harden's motives. We enter the restaurant together, greeted by floor to ceiling temperature-controlled glass lockers with stored bottles of liquor. The ones for specific hockey players on the Las Vegas team are labeled. There are a few that aren't labeled either, and I wonder who they're for. The hostess leads us to a small booth at the back of the main dining room. As soon as we are seated, I text him.

Me: What's up?

He glances at his phone resting next to the menu he's perusing and chuckles at me. "Why does something have to be up?"

Me: You said you wanted to talk. What's up, Harden?

We're interrupted by the waiter taking our drink order. Harden orders me my favorite Perrier and himself a cola. As the waiter leaves, I continue my steely gaze, so he knows I mean business.

"The Blind Rebels have added an additional two weeks to their residency." He leans back against the booth and doesn't look as happy as he should, considering the added shows can only bolster HARD. I overheard him tell Hayleigh the shows have been at capacity each night. Additional shows should be a good thing.

"I've heard they're courting you to come back as their photographer, and that they want that to include day shoots too. I assume they're offering a very generous amount, but I don't know that I'm comfortable with you hanging out with them outside of the club, Kade. At least at the club I'm there if something happens."

I shake my head. Harden's guilt is over the top. He blames himself for not watching over me that night. I knew it. I shake my head and go back to my phone.

Me: It's not about the money.

Money is not what my photography is about. I've got plenty of money. For me, it's having something that's mine again, a way to express myself like I did with music.

Harden eyes me after reading my text. He's one of the very few people who know I used to be Kandi Matthews, former child actor and pop princess.

"Does Hayleigh know you're seriously considering this?" Harden fiddles with his menu, not meeting my eyes.

I shake my head.

He sighs. "I can see you doing it at the club. I'm there, Vic is there. We'll have your back. But following them around as they do whatever the hell they do before they get to the club? Or on their off days?" He shakes his head. "I'm not comfortable with that. I don't care how apologetic they are about what happened. I think that Mavrick guy is a little off. You're the one in control here, Kady, so tell them you'll do the shows as originally stipu-lated. Fuck the rest. I don't want you hanging out with these guys outside of the club, Kade. Don't do this just for the exposure."

Me: I don't want exposure. I want purpose.

Harden purses his lips as he reads my reply.

"What do you want? From the menu. I'm having the burger."

I point to the quesadilla, and he nods. When the waiter returns with our drinks, Harden orders our food and then goes quiet on me. His face is somber. I hate disappointing him when he's been nothing but supportive of me, but if I decide I want to take pictures of the band, I will.

"You and Hayleigh are like the little sisters I never wanted but love to death. I know you two are close, and I also know it must be hard sometimes. I see the way she takes over. It's time you put your wings back on and fly for yourself, and I'm all for that. I really am, Kady. But don't put yourself at risk to do it."

Me: I haven't told Hayleigh yet. If I even decide to do it.

"And you think she'd be okay with you being alone with them? You're smarter than that."

His last words echo in my head, reminding me of Jerrod belittling me again. *"I thought you were smarter than that, Kay."* He'd use it to belittle, to gaslight me, to make me feel small. The ghost of my past haunts me, even from Vegas.

Harden's words sting as if he slapped me across the face himself. I always thought he was on my side, but now he seems to be almost as bad as Hayleigh. Where and who I take pictures of is not his business; it's mine, quite literally.

My eyes sting with tears threatening to pour, but I won't let Harden know his words hurt me. I love that he cares, but I can make my own decisions now.

"Kady," he starts, his voice soft.

Me: It's my decision, Harden. For both me and my business.

He doesn't think that I can do this on my own, that much is obvious. Why do he and Hayleigh interfere in what I want to do? I love them both for everything they've done for me. If Hayleigh hadn't offered to bring me back to her place in Vegas,

I would very likely be shut into my former home in Los Angeles, refusing to leave the house.

He reaches across the table to touch my hand after reading my text, but I pull them off the table and onto my lap. "You're taking what I am saying wrong, Kade..."

I can't hear his words anymore. I slide out of the booth without looking at him. Walking straight out of the restaurant, I order a rideshare. Luckily, there's one not too far from where I am and within minutes, I am slipping into the back of the car.

Harden: Our food's here.

Harden: Come out of the bathroom.

When I don't reply right away, he texts again.

Harden: I'm sorry. Don't make me embarrass myself by coming into the women's room to get you.

I shouldn't let him know I left, let him barge into the women's restroom and embarrass himself. But I text him back.

Me: I'm halfway home. I think you're forgetting I'm an adult who can make my own decisions. Because I am, Harden.

R

I DON'T KNOW how long I have until Harden will show up at the door of our apartment, because I have no doubt that he will, likely with my lunch wrapped up tidily in a to-go box. I pull my hair into a ponytail that I feed through the back of my Vegas Golden Knights baseball hat, then grab my camera. I leave on foot to head to The Strip. Being alone with my camera, to wander around in the tourist mecca, is exactly what I need.

Out here, I don't have to worry about being mistaken for Kandi Matthews. Walking around in just jeans and a t-shirt, with no makeup and black and purple hair, I don't look much Kandi these days, no sky-high heels, perfect hair, and nails, no entourage, no bodyguards. Kandi's been out of the limelight for over two years now. In L.A. time, that's like 20 years. No one would expect to find someone like Kandi Matthews wandering around the Vegas Strip midday with a camera in hand. Kandi wouldn't dare look so plain or do something so banal. I purposely dye my hair, so I look different.

Today, I'm just one of the tourists. Blending in, I absorb the wind that is so warm it's what I imagine walking through the insides of a blow-dryer must be like, and make my way onto the boulevard of lights. Pausing to take a few snaps of the street performer in caked silver paint, I wonder how long it takes him to dress for the day. That used to be me as Kandi, the hours of preparation for work, but without all the struggle. I like to imagine he's got a family and works hard out here hustling to bring home whatever he can to them. Unlike Kandi. She was hustling through life because it was a big void. She had no larger purpose.

I've taken this particular performer's picture before and he's not really what I am feeling for subject matter today, so I press on after just a few snaps. I know just the place I need to go.

I continue over the pedestrian bridge, ignoring the street vendors trying to earn a few bucks by hawking water out of a cooler and the porn pushers trying to hand out their cards as I make my way to my destination.

I can't believe how much it's changed since the last time I was in here. I breathe in the damp air in the glass domed conservatory at the Bellagio. The displays give life to scenes from Dr. Seuss books done up with fanciful floral flair. I wonder how long they will be here until they switch over to a more fall-like feel. I almost missed these. The flowered sculptures are as lighthearted and colorful as the children's books they represent. I wander around the path, enjoying scenes from The Lorax, Horton Hears a Who, and Fox in Socks. The big display at the very back is from The Places You Will Go. It reminds me of being snuggled in bed with Mom and my brother in a dimly lit bedroom. Crap, can I really be remembering something from when I was five or six?

A little girl, probably about seven, gazes at the 'Cat In The Hat' floral sculpture with huge eyes, one hand outstretched as she points to something. When she looks up at her mom, I'm hit with an overwhelming sense of loss. I miss my mom, even now.

The sun streaming in through the glass overhead makes the little girl's eyes sparkle, and imagination runs loose on her face. The lighting around them is perfect. Her mom looks down at her with love in her eyes. I snap a few pictures of them together. This moment is everything for this little girl, basking in her mother's love. I grab my notebook out of my backpack and I scratch out a note on a page of my notebook to hand to her mom.

Hi. My name is Kadence. I'm a professional photographer here in Vegas. Excuse this note, but I can't speak. Your daughter is enjoying the display so much I had to snap a picture of her. Here is my cellphone number: 702-555-5239. I want to email you a copy of the picture when I get home tonight. No charge, no strings. It was a moment in time I had to capture. Text me your email address if you'd like it. – Kadence

The woman almost brushes me off when I hand her the note. She makes sure to stand between me and her daughter the way a good, caring mother should. I hold up my camera so she can see the LCD with the picture of her and her daughter. I put on my friendliest smile and encourage her to look back at the note, hoping she doesn't think I'm too creepy. It's happened before, so whenever kids are involved, I try to be cautious.

"Oh, that's a great picture. I'd love it. Thank you!" The woman texts me her email address right away and I smile and carry on through the conservatory taking pictures. As I leave, I stop in the lobby to take pictures of the huge colorful glass flowers coming out of the ceiling. I know it's one of the most photographed places in Vegas, but I can't help myself.

Back out on the Strip, I continue taking pictures of anything and everything that catches my eye. Street performers are dressed in outrageous costumes, trying to entertain for a couple of bucks, and tourists are interacting with the street performers or admiring the fountain show; it's all in the mix.

My phone vibrates in my pocket. That better not be Harden.

Hayleigh: I'm home. Where are you? Are we doing dinner?

Shit, I've been out here longer than I realized. Luckily, I haven't strayed too far from home.

Me: OMW- I got caught up taking pix at the Bellagio.

I hoof it home. Hayleigh's already changed from her work clothes when I get in. I hit send on my text to her as I walk by with a nod.

Me: Putting my camera away and changing my shirt. BRB.

I go right to my office and set my camera on the small desk and plug it into my laptop to start the download of pictures into my digital light room program. When I return to my bedroom to change, Hayleigh's sitting on my bed.

"Wanna tell me why Harden was sitting in the foyer with a to-go box when I got home?"

I shake my head while I pull my shirt off and head into my walk-in. It's not her business why I'm not speaking with Harden. I'm tired of being the center of everybody else's business. Hayleigh follows me and leans against the door.

"You know I'll get it out of him eventually." She tries to taunt it out of me.

I don't care. I'm not talking about this with her. I slide each t-shirt on the rod with a violent flick of my wrist and refuse to even look at her. Finding the one I want, I yank it from its hanger and tug it on.

Me: If we are going out, let's go-I have pictures to process.

Hayleigh rolls her eyes and mutters, "This should be fun," as she reads my text.

No. I'm officially done with everyone's attitude today. I tap my words hard into my phone and hit send while shooting her a glare.

Me: I'll stay home.

Me: You & Harden should have dinner together.

Me: WITHOUT ME. Leave me alone. Both of you.

The minute I hit send, I regret it. While I wouldn't even put it past her to have Harden show up wherever we are going, I could have been nicer, but I'm allowed to be angry. With him, with her, with whomever I want. I rip my shirt back off, throwing it into the corner, not even bothering to put it away. I put on my pjs for the night. Hayleigh watches my display, a slight upturn on her lips like she's amused. That just sets me off even more. I don't know if they are in on this together or if it's just both of them managing to piss me off today. Without giving Hayleigh a second glance, I head back into my office.

"I don't know what crawled up your ass today, Kay, but don't take it out on me," she hollers from the other room, not realizing I'm flipping her off.

Fuck this. I wish I could go back two years and warn myself what was about to happen, keep from ruining so many lives, and go back to just being empty Kandi Matthews. Sometimes it's easier not to feel, then the guilt starts seeping in and I feel bad for standing up for myself when Hayleigh's probably the only reason I function as well as I do.

I should just take an Ativan and force myself to relax off into nothingness, into not caring about what Hayleigh and Harden think of me. I'm tired of wanting to please them because they've been there since the beginning. But I'm mad at them too, mad at them for being too much, for not letting me live my life the way I want to, for always making the decisions, and not giving me any leeway. I may have needed that right after the shooting, but not now. I can make my own decisions.

I know that's how you become addicted. Dr. Murphy warned me that I need to only use them when I'm in the middle of the kind of panic attack where I can't breathe.

So, I sit in my office and go through my photos instead. I concentrate on the pictures and their emotions, not my own.

Chapter 13

Mavrick

Stopping in the fire lane in front of Kadence's building, I jump out of the jeep at 8:30am on the dot. I haven't even had my coffee yet because I didn't want to be late. I give the doorman a sneer as he tries to tell me I can't park here. The Jeep's top is off and stowed in the garage at the lake Las Vegas home I'm staying in. Sammy and Cal are already on route to the dunes towing Sammy's new sand rail with Cal's Suburban since I commandeered the Beast. Without seeing the off-road sand vehicle, Kady will have no idea where we'll be going. I hope she'll think it's fun and not boring. I'm surprised she said yes to coming out with me without her friend Hayleigh.

She's already walking toward the Jeep before I've even entered the lobby. She must be as excited as I am. I rush to greet her, but she jumps up and hurls herself into the Beast.

"Anxious to feel the wind in your hair, huh?" She answers me with a little shrug and glances at me from the corner of her eye. When I get in, she hands me her phone.

Kady: Why did you tell me to wear clothes I didn't care about?

"You're an inquisitive one today." I smile. She's wearing a

well-worn, faded black band t-shirt for Bent, and is looking hot without meaning to be.

She hesitates and presses her lips together. I should probably at least warn her about the drive.

"We're going on a little day trip, and when we get to where we are going, there is a chance you might get dirty, so I didn't want you wearing anything you loved."

Kady: Where are we going?

"That's the surprise. Sammy and Cal are probably nearly halfway there, so we should get a move on. We'll stop for a coffee and snack on the way out of town."

Kady: I don't drink coffee.

Ugh, who doesn't drink coffee this early in the morning? "Well, I do and this early I need it. I'm not usually up before eleven. I'm sure you eat snacks, right?"

Kady: Should I be worried about you driving if you're usually in bed right now?

Hayleigh is rubbing off on her. I chuckle. "No. You should worry about where we are going." Her eyes widen slightly, and she shifts up straighter in her seat.

After we stop for fuel, coffee, and snacks, I head to Highway 15.

"This has nothing to do with where we are going or what we are doing, but I wanted to talk to you about your new contract offer for working with us," I holler over the wind as I glance at her. She shifts to face me in her seat.

"We want you back, Kady. All of us. We've all seen the shots you took the first night. They're amazing. I have this vision of putting together an entire photo book of your pictures that we can market with the album. Also, we want to have some for the album booklet and maybe even the cover." I shouldn't be doing this on the highway because I want her full expression, not just to gauge her reactions by glancing at her. I have no connection with her this way. There's too much traffic on this windy part through the high desert to not give it my full attention. I want her to know that I'm not just one of those guys, the ones who give her platitudes.

Her answer comes over the Bluetooth speakers, voiced. She looks startled as Siri gives voice to her words.

Kady: We'll see. I'm still considering my options.

I nod, keeping my eyes on the road.

"It's not an excuse, but there are reasons I overreacted the way I did. I thought you were filming us. It was a total mistake, Kadence. It won't happen again."

When we hit the state line, Kady grabs my jean clad leg and squeezes. She points to the 'Welcome To California' sign. Her nails pressing into my jeans shoot a flash of heat straight to my groin. Damn, this girl does it for me and I hardly know her, but I want to know everything.

Between the wind whipping through the cabin and the music that's a little too loud, she wouldn't be able to hear me even if I answered, so I smile and keep going.

I love that her black and purple hair is whipping all over the cabin. She'd probably be mortified if she realized what the wind is doing to her hair, but I love the wildness of it. It suits her somehow. Mostly, Kady watches the scenery going by and fiddles with the hairbands on her left wrist.

We stop in the little desert town of Baker, if you can even call it a town. The main drag is three gas stations, a Starbucks, a diner, a fast-food burger joint and a beef jerky place that looks like aliens landed on it, complete with a flying saucer. I top off on gas, mostly to give Kady a chance to use the facilities. When she returns from the restroom, her hair is in a ponytail and she's missing one of the hairbands from her wrist.

Kady: We aren't going to L.A., are we?

She holds her phone out to me.

"No. Definitely not L.A. We're almost there, actually. Only another 30 minutes or so."

Her forehead wrinkles in the most adorable way as she looks around. There aren't really any signs visible from here that would give away where we are going, but I have a feeling that is what she is looking for. I smile at her, and she purses her lips and puts her hands on her hips.

"Come on, let's go. I bought you some Red Vines while you were in the bathroom." I hand her the package and we head off to the Dumont sand dunes.

Pulling up behind Cal's rented Suburban, I put the Jeep in park. Cal's found us the perfect spot at the dunes. The area we're in is flat, so we can set things up as a base camp. We're close enough so we can see the hills of golden sand that stretch out before us as far as the eye can see, starting out close and small, gaining in size and steepness the further out they get. Before I hop out, I glance at Kadence. Her eyes are locked onto the blue and black sand rail zipping around in the sand just beyond our camp.

"We all have a penchant for anything fast, whether it be guitars or cars." I point to the vehicle zipping by that has all her attention. "That is a sand rail. It's kind of like a dune buggy, but rails are built specifically for the sand. They're basically roll-cages with engines and seats. You'll notice no windows or doors or fenders. That's because they are made to be super light so they can go fast and not get stuck in the sand like a traditional dune buggy or 4-wheel drive vehicle." Her eyes zero in on Sammy flying up the first small dune and then watches him jump off it. He's just getting a feel for it. Knowing Sammy's love of the dunes, he'll be flying that sucker off the biggest dune he can find by the end of this.

"See why you might get a little dirty?" I ask as Sam comes driving back into our area, a rooster tail of sand following him. Kady nods as she digs her camera out of her backpack and slips the strap around her neck.

"We've all done this lots of times. As a matter of fact, we all have rails, we just didn't bring them with us. Sammy's just bought this one. Point being, you're safe with us. We even brought a helmet for you," I assure her as we walk towards the Suburban. I conveniently leave out the part about Sammy being something of a daredevil.

Cal emerges from a green and white pop-up tent set up on the far side of his vehicle. "Gibs just went down for a nap. If one of you will keep an ear out for him, I get dibs on the next ride with Sam."

Kady shakes her head, but I can't tell if it's because she thinks it's crazy to race around on the dunes or that she won't be listening for Gibs because she's going to be the one in the sand rail.

"What do you think?" I ask her quietly so only she hears. I don't want to embarrass her in front of Cal if she's freaked out about off-roading in the dunes. My phone alerts a text as she answers me.

Kady: *Cal might have to thumb wrestle me over who gets first ride.*

I can't help the deep laugh she pulls out of me. I think Kady might have a little adrenaline junkie in her, just like the rest of us. Her lips pull up into a grin and there's a twinkle in her green eyes that lets me know she's all in.

Callum's brow creases at our interaction, so I show him her message. He chuckles and pretends to stretch his thumb out for the challenge she's offered. It's not a surprise to me that when Sammy pulls out for the next ride, it's Kady in the passenger seat and not Cal. He even helped her get the extra helmet we brought and tightened on her chin.

Sammy takes off with Kady, sand blowing up into the air behind them as he speeds across the flats and right up the nearest dune. I can hear Kady squeal with delight from the flats when he takes her over a jump on the first little dune. He's just warming up, but she's having a blast out there.

Sand is still in the air when they return from their first outing and Cal jumps into the passenger seat Kady's just vacated as Sammy races off again.

The grin on her face shines brightly even though there's a sandy dust cloud around her.

"Did you have fun?"

She nods emphatically, her smile getting even bigger.

"Would you let me drive you around the dunes?"

Again, she nods, her grin growing even wider. I was a little worried she'd be put off by the all the sand and grit in the air, but judging by the sparkle in her eyes, she's having a great time already and she's only been out once so far.

When she's not riding in the sand rail, Kady's got her camera to her eye as she frames the next picture she's going to take, and there is nothing that she doesn't take pictures of. She takes them of us, Gibson, the sand rail from all angles and in all manner of operation, the pattern of the ridges in sand caused by the wind and even a feather she's found in the sand close to base camp. If she's not taking pictures, she's begging to go back out with each change of driver, and she usually gets her way.

By lunch time, we've all taken turns racing Kady around the dunes. She and Sammy are sliding around the dunes one last time before lunch, so Cal feeds Gibs in the tent to keep the sand off him. I start going through the coolers in his SUV to set out the food. I'm impressed with Cal's fathering. He knew to bring a tent to protect Gibson from the sun, sand, and heat. Fuck if I'd have known to do that kind of thing. He's spent just as much time in the tent occupying Gibson, as he's spent goofing off with us. I still sense he's got a lot of doubts about being a good father, even when all I see is him killing it.

"She seems to be having a lot of fun." Cal side-eyes me as he joins me in setting out the food on the wooden picnic table in our little area. "You like her, huh?"

His simple question has me tightening up, and I stretch my

hand to try to get over the urge to grab him by the yoke of his shirt.

He catches my reaction. "Cool it, Mav," he says, his hands up between us and his voice low and calm. "I deserve that, but it's not like that, honest. She just doesn't seem like your typical fair." I don't answer him because I've been struggling with my attraction to Kady. I like her so much that I want to make sure that I don't destroy her like I've done in every other relationship I've ever had. I also want her to work for us. I don't want to fuck that up, either. I sigh, not knowing how to express this to Cal without sounding like a pussy.

"Is it because you feel sorry for her?"

Dammit, he had to go there. I'm disgusted by what he's insinuating.

"I'm not fucking her. She's a friend. You aren't fucking her either. Nor will you ever fuck her. She's a *friend*." I elongate the last word, so that he gets it. "When I drove her home the other night, she got excited when she saw Sammy's Jeep, so I thought she'd like joining us."

Cal's eyes are hard as he assesses me. He looks into me the way no one else can. Kill might be his actual twin, but Cal may as well be *my* twin because he knows me better than any human on this earth.

"That might be your excuse, but you like her." He shifts from foot to foot. "Mav, I've known you longer than I haven't, brother. I don't know why you don't want to admit it, but you definitely like her."

He's not wrong, but there is a very small part of me that worries that the minute I show interest in Kady, he'll be waiting in the wings to get in her pants. Kady is mine.

This possessiveness of her, of anyone, is unfamiliar. I didn't have it with Becka. Is it because Cal and Becka ended up getting together or is it because Kady already means more to me in the handful of days I've known her?

Cal sits on the tailgate with a loud, exaggerated sigh. "We have trust issues, you and me." His legs swing gently, and his head hangs down slightly as he watches his feet. "No one blames you for that, Mav. Especially me. What I did..." He goes quiet as he thinks about how to word his thoughts. *That's a Callum thing I didn't even realize I missed from the year we were apart.*

"It was fucking low." His words are rough and gravelly. Cal looks over at me, his long dark hair obscuring part of his face. "It won't happen again. That I can fucking guarantee." The bite in his voice tells me he's angry, but not with me. Most likely it's with himself.

"I've learned my lesson. Family above chicks, always. And definitely no taking chicks from my brothers." He pauses. "I'm not after any woman, yours or otherwise. Not until Gibs is eighteen. Hell, maybe even twenty-one." He shakes his head and releases a deep sigh.

"I barely keep my head above water most days. I love Gibson, but it's also fucking hard. I don't need all the drama that comes with chicks on top of everything else I'm dealing with. Get me?" When he looks over at me, Cal's truth is in the deep creases in his face.

I nod and remind myself that we need to find him a regular, trustworthy, live-in nanny as soon as possible. Not his aunt Sandy or some stranger that the label pays to watch his kid while he's onstage, but someone he gets to know and trusts implicitly. He loves his Aunt Sandy, hell, we all do, but she is just not cutting it and he needs help.

"I only bring up Kady because for whatever reason, that girl is special to you," Cal says pointing at the sand rail zipping by. "Not just because you feel bad for treating her like shit, and not because of whatever fucked up thing made her go silent, but because there is something about her you connect with. Here." He points to my chest, then tilts his head. "And you've never connected with anyone there. Ever. Not like this. Not counting us, of course."

"I saw it at the barbecue, man. You defended her against her best friend, Mav. You fucking cared about what kind of *water* she wanted. You didn't treat Becka, the supposed love of your life, like that. I've never seen this in you before. It's... refreshing." Cal's chest puffs out like he's proud of me. Is he proud of me for lusting after our photographer? Because that's all this is. Some sort of strange lust. It has to be.

He studies me and then pushes out of the cargo area and reaches to grab a bag. "Look, Becka knew what she was doing to you, man. She wasn't staying with you, with me, or with him." He jerks his head towards the tent where Gibson sleeps.

He hops off the tailgate. He's right. If Becka wouldn't stay for her own son, why would she have stayed for me? If it hadn't been Cal, she'd probably have fucked around with someone else. But Kady, I don't know about Kady. I don't know if I should try to figure out what's going on between us. Not if she's working for us. That can only be a recipe for disaster.

"All I'm saying is, don't treat Kady like a fuckin' groupie. Be sure what you want before you start it with her, because if you start something and then you treat her like she's disposable," Cal pauses and shakes his head and thinks for a minute, "I don't think she'll recover from that, and you may not either." He pats my shoulder as the noise of the sand rail pulling up gets our attention. "Come on, lunchtime."

Lunch is full of laughs, with Kady holding a very content Gibson in some sort of pack thing while we all eat. And he's not the only one that loves Kady. Cal and Sammy love her too. She and Sammy are already best friends, and she loves getting Cal to tell some of our craziest road stories.

"I promised Kady she could drive the rail." Sammy grabs his helmet and reaches to grab the helmet Kady's been using.

I look at Kady. "Have you driven in sand before?" The thought of her driving that death trap has goose bumps popping up on my arms. We know what we're doing, but it could be dangerous if you've never done it before. I get that she wants to drive, to harness the speed of the rail is not just freeing but invigorating, but I don't know that Sammy's the one to teach her.

Behind her, Cal gives me a smug, satisfied look like I just proved his fucking point or some shit.

She shakes her head.

Sammy looks between us, his eyes resting on Kady. "Don't worry, Mav. She wants to. Right, Kady?" Her head bobs vigorously. "I was showing her how it works before lunch."

"It's not like driving a car." I grab her helmet from Sammy. "I'll go with you."

Sammy knows the dunes and the sand rail like the back of his hand, but I need to be the one out there teaching her. It's weird to need to be in control like that. I've never felt this before. I trust Sammy with my life, but not with Kady's, apparently.

He doesn't put up a fight. He shrugs and drops down next to Cal. "Cool. Have fun."

Kady sits behind the wheel of the rail and starts buckling herself in. She looks so damn cute with that helmet on her head. When she pulls the googles down over her eyes, they somehow make them look bigger and greener.

"Hand me your phone." I hold up her phone to snap a picture in the driver's seat, the smile that's been on her face all day radiating in the photo.

The smile makes her eyes twinkle and come alive. It isn't just beautiful, because she's always beautiful. Even that day I came groveling to her condo. The way her eyes sparkle with her natural grin, it brings a new life to them, like she's enjoying something for the first time. It's breathtaking, and I want to coax more of them out of her. "That's profile picture material right there."

She takes her phone and shows me the picture as she is about to post it to Instagram. She raises an eyebrow in question. She wants to know if she can post it.

"Sure, if you can find signal out here."

I spend the next forty minutes or so teaching her to drive the rail, and the smile never leaves her face. When she takes her first tentative jump off the dune, she turns and grins at me when we stop at the bottom. This is a triumphant grin, one I haven't seen before. Even without her telling me, I can tell she's thinking, 'I did it!'

I unlatch my seat belt so I can lean in to kiss her the way I've wanted to since the cupcake incident at the barbecue. She clicks her belt too and presses across the rail at me, her green eyes turning almost a forest color through her goggles as her lips part in anticipation, until our helmeted foreheads crash into each other with a resounding bonk. She giggles out loud and my face stretches with a grin, causing my heart to flutter when it turns into a full-bodied laugh. My mission for today is accomplished. I might have messed up this first kiss, but she laughed again and that's even better. I want to kiss her even more now.

I gently remove her goggles and then release the snap of her helmet under her chin and lift it from her head. Her hair is plastered to her head thanks to the helmet, except a few strands standing straight up thanks to the static from the desert. Pink tinges her cheeks from the sun exposure and her lips are slightly chapped from the wind. She'd likely be horrified, but she couldn't look more alluring to me.

Her eyes darken as I weave my fingers in her hair and gently bring her towards me. She leans across the rail to me again, her pink tongue darting to wet her lips right before I bring mine to hers.

Her lips are as soft and warm as I imagined, and she tastes like vanilla and red vines. Her eyes flutter closed as our lips make full contact. She brings her hand up to my face and slips her fingers around the back of my head, rubbing her thumb over my jaw.

I press in towards her while simultaneously keeping a steady hand on the back of her head. My heart beats erratically and the crotch of my jeans tightens. She tastes smooth and sweet, even better than my most expensive whiskey. The kiss isn't over yet, and I already want more.

I sweep my tongue against her lips, begging her to let me in. And she does. Our tongues co-exist as we learn each other's taste. This only deepens the urgency in me.

She sighs and I pull back from that kiss, her eyes open and wide.

"Yeah, I felt it too." I smile and gently tug her helmet back on, clipping it under her chin.

Chapter 14

Kadence

H ole-lee-shit. *That.* Kiss.

Chapter 15

Mavrick

She drives each of us around the dunes, getting more confident with each pass, each jump. After she's had enough, Cal and I head out for one more run before we pack it in. Kady spends most of her time holding Gibson and walking him around our area while we all get ready to leave.

Sammy comes to me with his hand out for his keys. "Hey, I'll take the Jeep back since Cal won't let me drive his Suburban. I got shit to do when we get back."

He turns to Kady, who's swaying back and forth with Gibson. "Do you want to ride with me or with Cal and Mav?" He grins at her, and I swear he's trying to flirt with her. I grind my teeth into a smile as she looks between the two of us.

She juggles Gibs and her phone, eventually handing it to Sammy. "Dammit. I lost out to Gibs. He's not even one, and he's already stealing babes out from under me." Sam winks at her and heads off to secure the trailer to his Jeep.

Kady leans Gibson and herself into the Jeep to get her backpack she left in the passenger seat.

"Let me help you." I take her backpack and stow it in the back seat of the Suburban.

Sammy waves as he pulls away slowly, trying to not throw up sand at us. I help Cal get the coolers and other stuff loaded back into the Suburban. Kady watches us, her lips to Gibs's head as she sways back and forth with him slowly while shielding his face from the sand. While half in the cargo area, I hear a hum, so soft it's hardly audible. It's definitely some sort of tune. It takes me a minute to realize Kady's humming to Gibs as she sways back and forth with him. She doesn't seem to realize she's doing it.

I hold myself back because I really want to pick Kady up, swing her around and celebrate that she's humming. Plus, she's holding Gibs, and I don't want her to drop him or give him baby whiplash in my exuberance of twirling her.

Cal catches my eye, then gives a quick glance to Kady. He hears her too. We wordlessly continue to slide things around the cargo area in the name of reorganizing to prolong this moment. I glance up at her again, my heart swelling with pride.

Is humming new to her too? I want to ask, but won't risk it. I don't want her to feel uncomfortable like she did at the barbecue. Cal finally slides out of the cargo area, since we can only move stuff around in the back of his rig for so long.

Kady presses a soft kiss onto the baby's bald head before handing him over to Cal so he can settle him in his car seat. Kady settles into the seat next to Gibs. I go to climb in the back on the other side of Gibs.

"Really, Mav? You're making me feel like a damn chauffeur," Cal mumbles. Kady starts to get up like she is going to sit in the front with Cal, but I reach out to stop her. "I want to sit with Kady. Kady wants to sit with Gibs."

Cal grumbles and leans into the back seat and goes through the rigmarole of moving Gibs's seat, so it's stationed behind the driver's side instead of in the middle. "Better?" He glares at me as Kady scoots into the middle seat so she's closest to Gibs.

"Thanks." I slide in next to her.

Gibs fusses as we get underway. Kady entertains him with some soft toys leashed to the car seat. Eventually, he nods off.

Kady starts slapping her hands on her pants like she's looking for something. Her eyes grow big when they meet mine.

"What's wrong?" She shakes her head, continuing to slap her pants and then checks the pockets in her backpack and even the crease in the bench seat behind her. She finally holds up her hand like she's holding her phone. Shit, she must have left her phone in the sand rail. Her eyes well with tears.

"It's probably in the rail." She nods. "Sammy keeps it at my place since he's staying at the Wynn. We'll swing by and get it before I take you home. No harm, no foul." She nods and squeezes my knee. Electricity runs straight to my groin again. I shift slightly.

"Here." I hand her my phone. "You can use mine. The unlock code is 201420." She looks at me like I've just given her the pin number to my ATM card. "It's just a phone, Kady."

She unlocks and opens the text app.

Kady: I'm so stupid. Thank you. For everything. The fun day.

"You're not stupid. And you're most welcome, beautiful." Her face pinks up, and she scrunches her nose at the word 'beautiful.'

Kady: Beautiful? I probably have helmet hair.

"Oh, you definitely have helmet hair," I joke as I rub my hand in her soft hair. "But you're still beautiful." I can't help but chuckle as she runs her hands over her hair, trying to smooth it. She fiddles with the hairbands on her wrist like maybe she's going to throw her hair up into another ponytail like she had before we got to the dunes, but instead she pulls at them like they are too tight on her wrist.

I shift my arm so it's across the back of the bench seat, like I'm in freaking high school trying to slip my arm around my lab partner in science class as we watch a film about proto-fucking-zoas.

Kady's warm body nestles into my side, her head on my shoulder. The tropical smell of her sunscreen surrounds us as she settles into my side.

Not long after, her breathing settles into long, even breaths of sleep, just like her little buddy Gibs. Cal's eyebrows shoot up in the rearview mirror when he notices Kady's head on my shoulder, and I just smile smugly back. This is going to be the best hour and a half I've had in a while.

When Cal pulls up to my place, Sammy's already maneuvering the trailer with the rail into the garage. I shake Kady gently.

"Kady? We're here." She lifts her head and then her eyes grow big as she looks at me and she picks up my phone.

Kady: You let me sleep. On you.

"There are much worse ways to spend a few hours." She blushes, the pink reaching the tip of her cute nose again. I grab her backpack and we slip out of the Suburban, careful to shut the door quietly as to not wake Gibson. I give Cal a chin lift as we pass. He smirks and waves as he pulls away. I know that bastard will be calling me later.

"Sammy, Kady left her phone in the rail." Kady and I approach him as he chocks the tires of the low open trailer the sand rail sits on.

"No, it's on the front seat of the Jeep. I didn't see it until I'd already hit the highway. It's been vibrating pretty regular most of the ride. I think someone's worried about you."

Kady grimaces as she leans into the Jeep for her phone.

Glancing at her screen before she unlocks it, it looks like Sammy's right. Even with my quick glance, I could see a multitude of texts on her screen. I bet they're all from Hayleigh and Harden. She opens her phone, but instead of responding to her messages, she sends one to me.

Kady: Today was the most fun I've had in a super long time.

Kady: Thanx for letting me tag along. Tell Sammy and Cal, too.

"I will. Do you want to come in, have something to drink? We could get some dinner later?" I don't want this day to end, but her phone vibrates yet again, and she shakes her head, her cute lips pulling downward into a frown as she glances at the screen again.

"Another time. Let's get you home." I hope she can't hear my disappointment. Or maybe, I hope she does. I didn't want our time together to end so soon. I've got to get her alone again. This time, just the two of us.

Sammy pipes up. "I can drive her. It's on my way."

I shoot him a like-hell-you-will look, and he cringes slightly.

"Oh wait, I'm supposed to meet Killian soon." He looks at his wrist like he's looking at a watch. The idiot doesn't wear one.

"I'll take her. No worries, Sam." I pat him on the back, letting him know that his terrible cover job was appreciated.

Kady: Finally! I get to ride in YOUR car!

Her gorgeous grin is wide as she eyes my red corvette in the garage. It might be a rock star cliché, but I love my cars fast and Stella's just one of my babies. I open her door and she slides down into the bucket seat and smiles up at me and mouths, 'thank you.'

She grips her cell phone tight on her lap during the drive to her place. It occasionally buzzes, announcing the arrival of yet another text. She stares straight out the windshield. The fun girl from the sand dunes earlier today is locked somewhere inside the sad girl in my car.

I press down gently on the brake to stop for a red light. "So, have you decided if you'll return as our photographer yet?"

She nods, and it feels as if a large barbell has been lifted off my shoulders. I'm so light that I might float right out of my 'vette.

"You've made my day, Kady. You have no idea."

She smiles at my declaration. I do too, because it means I'll be seeing more of her. A lot more since she's agreed to take pictures of us outside of the shows too.

I pull into a guest parking spot at her building instead of the curb outside the door. She turns toward me in her seat with a furrowed brow.

"I'm walking you in."

She shakes her head and moves to get out of the car.

I put my hand on her knee and reiterate. "I'm walking you in." I say it a little too firmly, but no way is she facing whatever firing squad that is awaiting her alone.

She firmly taps out her message, and I wait for it on my phone.

Kady: Hayleigh and Hard are worried. I don't want you stuck in the middle.

If I let her face them alone, I run the risk of them convincing her not to take the job, not to hang out with me, that I'm bad news. Even though she's going to work for us, I want more. I want to take her on a real date, just her and me, with no band members, and no best friends. That won't happen if Hayleigh and Harden convince her otherwise.

"All the more reason for me to escort you."

She's curled into the bucket seat, no longer the confident girl she was in the sand dunes. It kills me to see her upset like this.

The old doorman has been replaced by a younger, muscular dude who already has the elevator door open for Kady when we approach. He greets her by name. She gives him a short nod as we get in.

Hayleigh and Harden jump up from the couch simultaneously as we walk into the apartment. Both sets of eyes fall on me, both narrowing.

My stomach drops and clenches, and I'm not the one they are even focused on. Part of me is thankful for that little reprieve, but I know now I was right to come up here. I steel myself to prepare for what's to come.

Hayleigh focuses in on Kady to begin her onslaught. "What the hell, Kady? I was so worried! Especially when I see your phone is in the middle of the desert in California?"

I place a supportive hand on the small of Kady's back. Just enough to show her I'm here, that I have her.

Hayleigh's face is red, and her eyes are puffy. Her forehead is creased as she stomps around the couch. She's truly concerned for her friend. My stomach sinks at the thought of causing Hayleigh worry, but then again, I'm not Kady's keeper and under no obligation to report when I'm seeing her to anyone.

"You couldn't shoot either of us a text? For hours?" Harden steps up to stand tall behind Hayleigh, his jaw ticking. I can't tell if he's pissed at Kady or me.

Hayleigh flexes her hand. Shit, I don't want her to start poking my chest again with that talon of hers. I try to placate the situation and take the blame before she starts in with the poking. "I invited her to go off-roading with us at the Dumont Dunes."

Hayleigh's text alert goes off. Her face turns even redder after reading it, which I didn't think was possible. She looks like she's ready to explode.

"Of course, I tracked your phone. I was worried. You never ignore my messages."

"She wasn't ignoring you. Signal at the dunes is spotty at best. Then she was separated from her phone on the drive back because we switched vehicles with Sammy."

Kady shakes her head and her whole body tenses up as she takes a small step back and crosses her arms over her chest.

Instinctively, I rub her back lightly, trying to ease the tension she's holding there and remind her I'm here. I'm on her side.

Hayleigh eyeballs my hand, my connection with her friend, and her eyes narrow in on me. Shit. I know that look. My chest flexes in preparation for the poke.

"This is your fault. I told you to leave Kady alone." Hayleigh fires at me, her fingernail hitting the same damn spot as last time.

Here it comes, the 'Mav isn't trustworthy, and you shouldn't hang out with him' speech. I could have scripted this scene out. The rocker's never good enough.

"Kady can decide who she hangs with and when." I stand up straighter when Harden takes a step towards us, his posture constricted.

Kady steps out of my grip and stomps her foot repeatedly until we all look at her. She shoves out her phone so we can all see.

Kady: I'm an adult! I don't have to run my whereabouts through anyone.

Kady: And I can also speak for myself, Mav.

Her disappointment in all of us sounds off in the stomps of her boots down the hall, slamming a door hard behind her. Well, she just schooled us.

I can't believe I just did what I accused Hayleigh of during the party. Speaking on her behalf like she's a child. I just hated witnessing her being yelled at and judged because of who I am.

Hayleigh lunges towards me, getting up in my face. Not expecting it, I step back.

"This is all your fault. She was fine before you, and now she acts like a cantankerous teenager. Get out of my house." Her voice is so venomous that even Harden's eyes widen at the bite in her tone. He puts his hand on her shoulder and gently pulls her away from me.

I'd hoped to smooth this out for Kady, but I've just fucked it up even worse. I drop my head and step farther back, hands in the air, giving up this fight for now. But I'm not giving up Kady. No way is that happening. "I'll leave. But I won't stop hanging out with her. I like her."

Harden's intimidating posture softens at my white flag, and he steps around Hayleigh towards me. "I'll ride down with you."

We stand in silence, waiting for the elevator just outside the apartment door. He crosses his arms across his wide, puffed-out chest. As the door slides open, he says, "what are you doing here? What is your end game with Kady?"

"There isn't any game. I like hanging out with her. She had fun at the dunes. A great time, actually. Until she got home." I look at Harden, hoping to convey that they are the ones that took the joy out of the day.

"I'll be the first to admit, Hayleigh's too overprotective of Kade, but think about what you're doing, man." He blows out a breath and turns to face me in the elevator. "You're only here for, what, another month? And then you're off to live your rockstar life. Kady's life is here, and she's fought damn hard for it over the last couple of years."

As much as he has a point, I already know I won't be able to leave her alone. Cal was right, there is something about that girl. The elevator doors slide open, and we stand it the area just outside the penthouse elevators.

"Can I ask you something? About Kady?" I change my tactic.

Harden grimaces at my question. "I won't tell you her story." He frowns.

I'm not going there, and I didn't expect he'd betray her

confidence anyway. I'd hope he wouldn't if he's really her friend.

"You've known her longer than me. Does she ever laugh?"

He looks at me like he doesn't understand my question. "Do you mean, is she happy?" He tilts his head slightly at me when I shake my head.

"No. I mean, have you ever heard her laugh out loud. Where you could audibly hear it?"

Harden shakes his head.

As I thought. Too bad because her laugh at the barbecue is probably my favorite sound. Or her humming. I can't decide which I like best. I want to hear both again and again.

"What about humming?"

He shakes his head again, his brow creasing as he tries to figure out where I'm going.

"Too bad. Because I've had the pleasure of hearing both now. You're really missing out."

Harden's mouth gapes slightly as his eyebrows shoot up at my statement.

I stroll out of the lobby of the apartment building as I feel him continue to stare at the back of my head. I just left the best proverbial mic drop in my wake, and love that I was able to rub it in just a little bit that Kady's already given me small parts of herself that she hasn't given to anyone else.

Chapter 16

Kadence

My stomach rumbles with hunger. I should've taken Mav up on his offer of dinner before bringing me home. Now I'm stuck in my room because, like hell, am I going out there right now.

I can't even relax in my own room, I'm so amped up and frustrated. I can't believe she tracked my phone just because I didn't answer a text right away. It's ridiculous. I could understand if I'd been missing overnight or something. Was she going to call the police next?

Hayleigh was yelling at Mav a while ago and then the front door shut and now it's just quiet. Too quiet. I'm worried about Mav. I didn't hear a scuffle, but that doesn't mean Harden didn't escort him to the elevator or outside and then hit him. Harden's stepped in unnecessarily on my behalf before, so I wouldn't put it past him. I hope Mav is not laying out in the parking lot bleeding or something while I'm stuck up here in my ivory tower, too pissed off to even go get myself a snack.

I warned Mav that coming up was a bad idea.

Me: Sorry about that. Are you ok?

Mav: I'm fine. I'm sorry for answering for you.

Me: I get it. It's easy to do. Just ask Hayleigh.

Mav: It was hard to see them so angry at you. Are YOU okay?

Me: I'm fine. Hungry. But I refuse to go out there. Hayleigh treats me like a child.

Mav: If you could eat anything in the world right now, what would it be?

Me: A couple of shredded beef tacos and a cheese quesadilla from El Charritos.

Mav: That's very specific.

Me: They're my favorite. Well, them and pizza, but I don't feel like pizza.

Mav: Where is this El Charritos place?

Me: Why?

Mav: Maybe I want some.

Me: So you can tease me? I never pictured you as cruel.

Mav: Humor me.

Me: Two blocks down Industrial from HARD, but on the opposite side of the street.

Since Mav hasn't texted anything in a few minutes, I decide to take a shower. The grit of the sand scrapes against my scalp as I shampoo. Damn, I really did get dirty. The shower feels so good, but does nothing to fix my rumbling tummy. I throw on a t-shirt and some sweats so I can brave the kitchen for food when my cell phone vibrates against my dresser.

It's a photo from Mav of bags from El Charrito on the seat of his corvette. He *is* mean. I'm just about to tell him so when I get another message.

Mav: I'm in the lobby. Can I come up?

Me: Yes, if you bring that food with you. The doorman will let you up.

I send a text to Patrick, the evening doorman, telling him to let Mav up. I wait a few minutes and then start quietly down the hall. Hayleigh and Harden are talking in hushed tones in the living room, their voices low enough so I can't hear the words, just the murmur of their voices. I stop before they see me and wait until Mav knocks. The rap on the door startles them since Patrick didn't call to announce him. I speed past them to the door and fling it open.

"Taco delivery." Mav holds up the bags of food in his hand. I grab his free hand and interlace my fingers with his, and pull him past Hayleigh and Harden on the couch. I drag him straight through the kitchen, down my hall and into my office, and then out onto the balcony.

"Wow. You have quite the view out here." Mav sets the food on the table. The sun is behind the building on its way to slip behind the mountains and out of sight so it's starting to cool from raging inferno hot to acceptably warm. I help him unpack the bag of food.

Me: Do you want something to drink?

Me: We have regular water. Coke regular and diet. Diet Root beer. Milk. Coffee. Several varieties of tea. And possibly some Guinness, unless Harden drank it all.

Me: Oh, and vanilla creamer, but who drinks straight creamer?

"I thought you didn't drink coffee?" Mav looks at me, his eyebrows pulling closer to his eyes.

Me: I don't. Hayleigh does.

Mav smiles at me with a spark in his eye. He stands. "Let me get it. It's in the kitchen, right?"

I nod.

"Water for you?"

I nod again.

Mav strolls through my office with purpose and returns a few long minutes later. "I was in luck. There's still some beer left." He chuckles. "Boy, was I getting eyeballed in your kitchen, though." I can only imagine. Harden probably wasn't too pleased to see Mav leaving with one of his beers.

My stomach lets out a loud rumble, and my cheeks instantly heat.

Mav's chuckle reverberates deep in his chest. "Let's feed that growling tiger you swallowed."

I chuckle too. Out loud. Again.

He seems to be the only one who makes me laugh. That's good on his behalf, but kind of sad. I never thought I was unhappy. Just not happy enough to laugh, I guess.

Mav doesn't say anything, but I know he heard it because he's grinning widely as he unpacks the bags of food. He has quite the variety of Mexican food in there, including all the items I mentioned in my text, mixed in with lots of others.

"Dig in," he says as he grabs a burrito. I go for the tacos first, so they don't get soggy.

"Crispy was the right choice, then?" His mouth pulls up slightly at the corners into a small smile.

I nod as I bite down on the crispy goodness of corn tortilla, shredded beef, lettuce, and cheese.

Me: Best in town.

I roll my eyes with the next bite to get my point across.

"And I thought you eating that cupcake was sexy." He watches as I take another bite and licks his lips. "I had no clue the key to your heart was tacos." He chews a bite of his burrito. "There's a lot I don't know about you, Kadence. A lot I'd like to know."

I freeze mid-reach. *Shit.* I just want to eat my tacos, not go back to that time and place. I'm suddenly not hungry anymore. I wince at the thought of having to expose all the skeletons in my closet to Mav. I tentatively reach for my phone.

"Relax. I don't want your bank account information, just more about you. What makes Kady, Kady? Favorite color? Favorite movie? Hobbies? Why photography?" He pauses to take another big bite of his burrito but doesn't take his eyes off mine. I finally look down at my phone so I can answer.

Me: Purple. Almost Famous. Photography, duh. Oh, and I read-a lot.

Me: Why photography? I'm good at it and it lets me be creative in a way that's satisfying.

Me: Photography lets others see things through my eyes.

I chew a piece of cheese quesadilla while I watch him read my answers.

"Well, purple explains the tips of your hair." He winks at me, his brown hair falling messily into his eyes as he sets down his burrito. "Almost Famous. Interesting choice for a favorite movie. I find it somewhat depressing, that band is so dysfunctional. But then again... pot, meet kettle, I guess. So, what does Kady like to read? What does Kady do for fun?" He tips back in his chair and waits for my response.

Me: Kady reads for fun. ;-)

Me: Mostly Thrillers, mysteries, and angsty romance. What I read usually depends on my mood. I also have a soft spot for classics.

He smiles. "Are you a Jane Austen girl, Kady?"

I shake my head.

Me: I've read her, but she's not a favorite. I like the grittier classics.

Me: All Quiet On The Western Front, Animal Farm, Fahrenheit 451. Johnny Got His Gun. Shakespearean tragedies like Macbeth. Things like that. What about you? Favorite books? Colors? Hobbies?

His eyes widen as he reads my list of books. "That's a hardcore list. Cal's the bookworm in the band, although I do like Fahrenheit 451. But I haven't read many of the other books you mentioned. My favorite color is black, but I also like purple now. My hobby and biggest love is music, of course. As you know, I also have a penchant for fast cars. Stella, the 'vette, is my everyday driver. I also have a Ferrari, a Lambo, and I just purchased a Shelby after going through the tour at the heritage garage here the other day."

He had me at fast cars. There's nothing like the feeling of some horses vibrating the pedal under your foot.

Me: Harden has a contact at the racetrack.

Me: If I were talking to him, I'd have him set us up one of those racing experiences.

Me: I've always wanted to do one.

Mav tips his head at me and smiles. "You love fast cars too? I thought you might. You lit up when you saw my 'vette. What do you drive?"

Me: A purple scion. I know-oh so sexy.

I roll my eyes to accentuate my sarcasm, and he chuckles for a moment, then his face turns serious again.

"So, how long have you lived in this place? You got great views." He looks over the railing out at the mountains.

Me: 16 months or so? Hayleigh and I went 50/50 on it.

"It's nice." He nods and stares out towards the city and chews on his bottom lip, then he gazes at me. I get the feeling he wants to ask something.

Me: Just ask.

"Why do you let Hayleigh steamroll you?" He waves his hands up like he's giving up, then shakes his head slightly. "I mean, it's not my business, I guess." He leans back in his chair, gazing into the city beyond my balcony, still chewing on that bottom lip.

I don't want to get into the gritty details with him right now. The hows and whys; that's a place I keep locked away. Hayleigh is my best friend, and after I got out of the hospital, she was my lifeline when the world was so overwhelming and scary that I couldn't function. How can I explain that I was so lost for a time that I needed that kind of help?

Me: She doesn't do it on purpose.

Me: But I'm starting to see how much she influences my decisions.

Me: It comes from a place of love and caring. But ...

I don't know how to finish so I send it as it is.

He frowns and looks up at me, but says nothing.

I slouch back into my chair, drawing my shoulders towards my chest. Hayleigh does so much for me, but how do I explain it to Mav without revealing too much, letting him see the part of my life I keep locked solidly behind a big metal door in my brain. It's embarrassing that I was so drawn into myself and under a blanket of depression that I needed her to make decisions for me. But Harden's right, I let her make choices now because it's easier than disagreeing with her.

Me: Harden said yesterday I need to get back to flying with my own wings instead of riding on her back.

Me: It's kind of true. And I see it. It's just... not that easy.

He nods his agreement like he knows who I am. Who I was.

His knee hops up and down and he changes his position a few times. He's uncomfortable. Whether that's because he doesn't imagine being in a place where you are so messed up that it's hard for you to decide what you want to drink with your dinner, or because he wants to ask more questions, but doesn't feel like it's his place, I'm not sure.

The silence between us drags on a little too long, and I can't come up with something to say, something to bring us back to our lighthearted conversation.

His brow momentarily creases in concern as he looks around him then smiles. He reaches behind him to the balcony floor.

"Churro?" He holds up the other, smaller brown bag he brought with him.

Me: HELL YES!

He laughs and hands me the cinnamon-sugar covered doughy treat. He got me churros.

Me: How did you know I heart churros?

"Who doesn't?" He shrugs.

149

R

MAV FLIPS THROUGH MY PORTFOLIO, scrutinizing each photo wordlessly. He stops at each one, examining them closely, lips pursed. His eyes scan each photo like he's afraid he's missing something. When he's finally content that he's seen the picture, he'll flip the page to the next one and then start the whole process again.

My stomach clenches, waiting for him to say something. Anything. Having someone outside of Harden and Hayleigh examine my photos, my art, is like having my soul on out on a table, waiting to see if there are any takers. The fear of rejection or dismissal is high, and it churns the acid in my stomach. It's killing me to not know what he's thinking, but I can't read his face as being anything other than contemplative.

I can't take the silence anymore, so I pace my small office, burning the nervous energy thrumming through me.

He continues to flip through it, oblivious to my movements, examining each image as if it's hanging on the wall at the Getty or something. It's like he doesn't have what's left of my creative soul sitting on top of his jean-clad legs. I wait for the inevitable.

"Kady, these pictures!" Mav's lips are parted slightly as he finally looks up from the book. He stops for a second to make eye contact with me. "They're amazing."

I release the breath I didn't know I was holding. He gets the depth I was going for. He gets my art. My whole body relaxes, my nervousness from before completely dissipates at his praise. Sure, Hayleigh and Harden have told me they're good, but Mav's the only person who doesn't have a reason to lie. Giddiness lightens me.

"Actually, no, amazing isn't the right word, but it's the only one I have right now. These are even better than the ones you took of us that first show."

My cheeks strain with the widest smile, and there is a sudden ease with which my breath comes. These pictures weren't commissioned shots like the ones of the concert. These pictures are more how I view the world around me. I'm capturing the emotions I was hoping to if he is this moved by them.

He stops and ponders one of my favorites, a closeup of the silver painted street performer. The thick, caked make-up evident in every crease of his street-weathered face seems to emphasize a life that was anything but easy.

"There is something about this one. It's lonely, no, haunting." He looks up at me. "Now I understand why you love photography. Your talent. It's like you said, I feel through your lens." He shakes his head again. "Amazing. It's like I'm learning more about how you work on the inside, Kady."

Me: I took a cool picture yesterday, but I haven't printed it out yet. Want to see it?

When he nods, my heart skips around my chest as I fire up my MacBook. He wants to see more. He's not patronizing me as he looks at my work.

I join him on the small couch in my office, our knees touching, and I try not to think about our kiss earlier today. It seems like so long ago already. I want another one, but maybe he doesn't.

I pull up one of the pictures of the mother and daughter in the Bellagio's Conservatory and tilt the screen so he can see it. He looks at the little girl, hand in her mother's, as she looks at the display.

He takes the laptop and gazes at it. An unnamed expression settles on his face, almost wistful, but that doesn't seem quite right. His mouth is a tight line, and his eyes are unfocused, like he's thinking of something from the past. Then, just as quickly, he shakes it away. "This is great, Kady." He closes the computer abruptly and sets it on the floor gently beside the couch. He draws in a deep breath and then blows it out slowly.

"I need a favor." His chocolate eyes are like warm hot cocoa, but his expression is strained. The lines on his forehead deepen as he looks away and out the small window in my sitting room. Is the favor going to be kissing him again? Because I couldn't say no to that.

"Cal's, well, Gibs, uh, shit. How do I say this?" He pauses and rubs a hand over his face. "Will you take some pictures of Cal and Gibs together for me? I'll pay whatever you ask to free-lance or whatever it's called, to work on the side for me."

I'm not sure what he's asking. I already work for the band. How is this any different from what I'm already doing? I want to ask, but he continues before I can wiggle my phone out of my pocket.

"The twins' birthday is coming up. I already know what I'm getting Killian, but I've been struggling with what to get Cal. Seeing these pictures, I think he'd enjoy having some profes-sional shots of Gibson and him together. He needs to see himself with Gibs from an outsider's perspective. As the apt, capable, and loving father that he is." He pauses. "Cal's been struggling with single fatherhood. He has a lot of doubt, and he's the surest person I've ever known. I want him to see what I see; that he's rocking fatherhood without realizing it."

My gut instinct is to balk, to say no. It takes me hundreds of pictures sometimes to get that one good one. Plus, I don't work with kids. Not babies, anyway. But what kind of photographer would I be if I didn't try to stretch myself and my craft?

Mav's thoughtfulness about Cal is touching. The relation-ship between them fascinates me. If I believed the tabloids, I'd think they never speak and were on the verge of choking each other to unconsciousness when they find themselves together, but that hasn't been my experience. The more I hang out with them, the more they seem like brothers who are working back toward a closeness they once shared, a closeness I wish I shared with my own brother.

Me: I'd be happy to.

I reach over and squeeze his forearm with a smile. It's a thoughtful gift to want to capture moments of a father and son in a light that illustrates his strengths. He's a true friend to Cal, and I am happy to try my best to get him what he's after.

Mav smiles. "How much do you need? Should I give you a sitting fee now, or how does this work?"

Me: We'll work out the cost later.

Me: The pictures will be more natural if you invite me to a function like the barbecue.

Me: Where they're both there but don't know I'm photographing them specifically.

Me: People get weirdly uncomfortable sitting for formal portraits.

"You realize we've all worked with professional photographers for many years, right?" Mav smiles and winks. "We are rockstars after all. Pictures come with the territory."

Me: Yes, but that's his guitar player persona.

Me: You didn't ask for headshots, you asked for pictures that show him as a father.

Me: The best pictures are taken when the subjects don't realize they're being photographed. Like the ones of the street performer or the little girl.

Me: Trust the professional on this ;-) Let Cal be Cal and Gibson be his adorable little self, and I'll take care of the rest.

He bites his lip as he thinks about my response. "You're the pro. We'll be writing and jamming tomorrow afternoon at my place. You think that'd work?"

Like I'd turn down witnessing the Blind Rebels jam. Silly Mav. I nod.

"Seriously, though, how much do you think this surreptitious photoshoot will run me? Ballpark?" He smiles.

Me: Let's see how it goes. I'll let you know after I get a chance to look at the photos.

He surprises me by pulling my body closer to his until he finally grabs my hips and drags me onto his lap. "There."

He leans in, his lips close to my face, his breath warming my cheek. "There's something I've been wanting to try again." His voice is raspy and low. He leans in so close, I breathe in his spicy scent.

Mav pulls my face to his, kissing me, his hand on my cheek holding me still. Almost melting into him, my hand moves to the back of his neck, his hair tickling my wrist. He holds my lower lip hostage between his teeth and then releases it and attempts to part my lips with his tongue. I shift so that I'm facing him. We lean in and start the kiss together this time. He gently nips my lower lip and again tries to get me to open my mouth. Relenting, our tongues do a warm dance that increases the depth of our kiss until my knees clench tight on the outside of his thighs as I tentatively rub against his hardness through his jeans.

The pressure in the room changes as the door to my office opens.

"Kady, I... Oh. Shit." Hayleigh's voice stutters through my small office. I feel like a kid caught sneaking a cookie before dinner.

But not Mav. He takes his time, pulling back slowly from our kiss with a sexy smirk. His eyes blaze, holding onto mine. I can't bear to tear myself away from his smoldering gaze to look back over at Hayleigh.

"Uh, we'll, uh, talk. Maybe later. Yeah. Okay." She pulls the door to my office closed.

As soon as she's gone, I leap off his lap, my brain catching up to being caught making out like a teenager in my office. For some reason, I feel like I've been caught doing something wrong, but God, there was nothing wrong with that kiss. That kiss was everything the kiss at the dunes was, and more.

His cocky, lopsided grin makes my stomach flutter as he stands, facing me. One hand runs down my spine, resting where my butt meets my thigh, pulling me against his hard body. My hand on his stomach, I feel the firm ridges of his abdomen through his soft t-shirt.

His tongue darts out of his mouth and wets his bottom lip. "Sexy as fuck. Just as I suspected."

Chapter 17

Kadence

Sexy as fuck. No way am I sexy. I'm a wreck. My face gets hot as Mav takes my hand from his stomach and lifts it to his mouth, then kisses each of my fingers with soft, sweet kisses I wouldn't expect from this virile rockstar in front of me.

"Yes, Kady. You're sexy as fuck." His eyes burn into mine, his words are hard as fact, like he can read my mind. He chuckles. "I'm getting better at reading your body language, for the most part." He shrugs at his acknowledgement, not realizing that just doing that is a feat most people don't bother with. They don't take the time to get to know *me*, but for some reason, Mav wants to know me. Me. Not my issues, or he'd be badgering me about them when he hasn't so much as asked. No, he wants to know me. The real me. The person I am now.

"I don't want to mess up you working with us. I'm very serious about putting together a photo book for the album, but there is something about you. I'm drawn to you, and shit, that kiss on the dunes." He shakes his head and runs a hand through his dark hair, and his eyes dilate when they connect with mine. "And then this one. I'm not going to be able to just walk away from kisses like that."

He's quiet for a few seconds as he stares into my eyes. "It's against my better judgement. As you likely know, my last relationship, well, it went spectacularly bad in a very public way. It broke up the band for a year. We're just starting to get back to being us." He sighs, looks over my shoulder, and gazes out the window. He has no way of knowing that my last relationship also went spectacularly bad in a very public way too, a way that cost others their lives. "But I can't help it, I'm drawn to you."

He laces his fingers through mine. "Walk me out?" I nod slightly, still woozy from that kiss and his confession. He tugs me, leading me towards the door by our joined hands.

"Thank you for having dinner with me, for letting me learn more about you and showing me your amazing photos." He says it with emphasis as a pointed comment to Hayleigh as we breeze past her on the couch. I feel her gaze on me as we walk out.

He tugs me through the door to where the elevator is.

"Didn't want an audience for our goodbye." Using his foot, he closes the apartment door behind us but doesn't push the elevator call button. He walks me backwards until the knob digs into my hip. Standing between my feet, he's so close, his body heat emanates off him and into me, those chocolate eyes of his assessing me as his head tilts slightly.

He leans in and covers my mouth with his again, his hands on the door, caging me this time. My body should be revolting, stiffening at feeling trapped, looking for a way out. Instead, it recognizes it's his mouth that's warm and soft against mine. His body, firm yet giving, lightly pressing me to the door. His spicy leather scent intoxicates me, even after he pulls his lips from mine.

I want more. More kisses. Just more Mav.

"You."

I don't understand what he means, but I already miss his lips against mine. Suddenly, I'm flushed. I can't even remember the last time my body reacted to a man like this. Maybe I never have. Not like this, with this intensity. It seems too much and not enough at the same time.

"Hey." I raise my gaze to his when he calls me out of my head. "Don't get caught up in what's going on in here." He kisses my temple sweetly.

"Concentrate on what's going on in here." He puts his hand where my heart pounds erratically in my chest. Can he feel that? Does he know that he's doing that to me? "Okay?"

My nod gets lost in a barrage of his sweet, tiny kisses behind my ear.

He backs up and reaches behind him, pressing the call button. "I'll text you about the jam session." I give him a small thumbs up because my head's spinning, still leaning against the door because that kiss made me dizzy, like I forgot to breathe for a second.

My chest heaves as if I've just run a marathon. He backs into the elevator, a beautiful half-grin pulling up one corner of his mouth. He never looks away from me, not until the door closes completely between us.

After he's gone, his scent still circles me as I pull in a deep breath, trying to calm my racing heart. I should've panicked, the way he caged me to the door, but the usual claustrophobia never set in. No tightening of my limbs and restricted breathing, nothing but Mav in the moment. I don't understand the how, but I like it. A lot.

I shake those thoughts away and turn to the door. I don't really want to go back inside and ruin this moment.

Hayleigh will jump me about Mav and wreck this small, perfect span of time with him. She'll tell me not to let him 'take advantage' of me. She'll try to convince me of what's right for me.

I don't want lectures. I want my friend. The one who stayed up all night with me when we were eleven and giggled with me about the cute older boys who filmed on the next set over from our show Kangaroo Klub Houze. Not the one who tells me what's best for me.

Hayleigh will pull me out of my Mav induced fog. She'll bring me back to the point in time when I lost my voice, back to when she stopped being my best friend and became my caretaker. I wanted and needed that for a short bit, but now I don't. I don't want to argue with her because I love her for helping me, but I just want to live in the warm haze with Mav. It makes me forget, just for a second, who I was and reminds me of who I am right now.

All I want right now is more. More kisses. More Mav. But what I want even more is to flop on the couch and talk about those kisses with my best friend. I want to tell her about Mav and how his eyes make me feel warm and gushy on the inside, instead of the void I've felt for years. I want to tell her about how my stomach flip-flops when we are in the same room together and I'm not sure how to separate these feelings because we kind of work together.

Might as well face Hayleigh and get it over with. I straighten my back and start back into our apartment, walking straight to my office for my phone, then back into the living room where Hayleigh is. I sit next to her and type out a text to her on my phone.

Me: You wanted to talk?

She pulls her legs up onto the couch to sit cross-legged and faces me. Her face is soft, and she shrugs.

"Sorry I interrupted you before. I should've knocked." She looks down at her hands. "That was rude. I'm not about getting in your personal space." She peeks up at me.

Now that it's over, her walking in on us was kind of funny.

She knew I had a guest. She got the awkward eyeful she deserved for that. All I give her, though, is a shrug.

"I need to apologize." She looks up at me, her face serious but not with that concerned wrinkle between her eyes that is usually there.

I raise an eyebrow. Again? She must sense my confusion, because she smiles at me with sadness in her eyes.

"Uh, Harden said some things before he left, while you were eating with Mav. I realize..." She pauses as she struggles to find the right words. "I've been, uh, what's the word that he used? Overbearing." Agreeing with him, I nod vigorously.

Hayleigh glances out the window as the lights from the strip become more prominent as the sun fully sets. She turns back to face me.

"It's just, so hard for me, Kade." She takes in a fortifying breath and looks back out at the colorful lights. "When I finally got to L.A., I was terrified for you. I knew by then what had happened, what most of your injuries were."

We've never talked about this. Most of that is a weird mishmash of time. Specific things stand out. The back of my throat burns like it did at the hospital, and I feel the tears building and wanting to spill. I close my eyes and I remember the stupid white clock on the wall. It was stuck on 10:47 and didn't move the whole time I was at the hospital.

She turns back to look at me, her eyes brimming with memories she's never voiced in almost two years since. "Sitting by your side, waiting for you to open your eyes, I knew you'd heal physically; the doctors assured me of that. I was more worried about how your heart, how the Kade *I knew*, would survive, could survive, without being tainted or bitter. But look at you."

She shakes her head and I slam my eyes shut tight. That sanitized hospital smell comes rushing back as if I were there. It still reminds me of a recently cleaned swimming pool. The constant noise, the beeps and blips of equipment, the constant, faint chatter at the desk outside my room, of needing and wanting to sleep but not being able to for more than ten, fifteen minutes at a time.

Her coarse whisper continues. "Then we discovered you couldn't talk, and I took over. I used that, turned into the fixer I needed to be, so I felt like I was helping when I knew nothing could fix what you saw, heard, or felt that day. Doing something calmed my fears and I just can't seem to let that go, even now that you're fine."

Tears leak from the corners of her eyes, and I reach forward and grab her hands. I need the connection with her. I need her to hold me in the present, so I don't go spiraling back into the past.

My heart thumps in my ears. Hayleigh's giving me what I want, but why does it suddenly seem like I'm drowning?

"Harden is right. My protectiveness is holding you back." My stomach drops and the panic rushes up, gripping my neck tighter, making it hard to breathe. I shut my eyes tightly so it can't get in.

"No, Kay, Listen. He's right. You can make your own decisions. You don't need me."

I shake my head. No, no, no. I'll always need Hayleigh. She's my safety net, my security blanket. I fumble for my phone. I have to fix this. Now.

Hayleigh puts her hand on my phone. "Let me finish. You don't need me making your decisions. Whether it's what to drink or who to kiss." She looks up at me and my cheeks instantly heat. I'm not used to having to lock doors. It was my own fault she walked in on that, but maybe she needed to see I'm not the broken girl from the hospital anymore.

"It's not my decision if you want to continue therapy or not. I know I've been giving you a hard time about that one. I'll stop. These are decisions *you* need to make, not me. And I'll support you, whatever your decisions are, because that's what's best for you, Kade." She squeezes my knee.

"As much as I hate to admit it, Harden is right. Letting you rely on me too much is only hindering your progress." She sighs heavily. "I'm really going to try to stop making decisions for you, and stop speaking for you, unless you ask me to."

Me: I'll always need your advice. You're my BFF.

She smiles and takes my hand, but I pull it back, needing to use it because I am not done.

Me: I've never thanked you.

Me: For being here for me when no one else was.

Me: For helping me when I couldn't help myself.

"But that's just it, Kay, you can and do help yourself. I see it every single day. You've come so far. I'm too focused on *my* worries for you. About you backsliding, about you retreating into yourself, into the dark again." Her face blanches. "Why it took Harden, of all people, to make me see this..." She shakes her head, looks up at me and smiles and pulls me into a hug.

"I am proud of who you are right now. And I promise to let go as much as I can, as much as you need," she whispers into my hair as her tears clog her throat. "But I'll never stop being here for you."

Me: I'll always need my best friend.

"And I'll always need mine."

R

MY PURPLE SCION looks ridiculously out of place in the driveway of Mav's Airbnb. It looks even shittier, dwarfed by Sammy's massive, but uber cool black Jeep. The Blind Rebels allowing me into their personal space to watch them write and play their music, see where their passion is made, it makes my head spin. Especially since Mav's confession.

Approaching the door, it hits me. I miss my music.

Watching them at the firepit the other night made my soul a little lighter. Hopefully watching them today will stoke my muse's fire a little more, ignite the creativity I've held down.

But this is work, twice over, since I'm now working on Operation Cal on the sly. Drawing in a deep breath, I repeat my mantra. This is work. Ignore the warm tingling in my stomach that the very sight of Mav has given me lately. Yep, like that'll be easy.

I knock on the front door, my camera backpack drooping heavily across my shoulders. I probably brought too much gear, but I'm not sure if we'll be inside or not, so I brought my good flash with me in case lighting is an issue. I also brought a second camera and a few different lenses.

The door swings open, and Mav stands there in a plain white t-shirt and tight dark jeans. He's fresh from the shower, and a soapy, slightly spicy clean smell greets me. His hair is still damp yet artfully askew and his feet are bare. He hooks his head toward the inside.

"You probably saw Sam's already here. The twins should be here soon. Make yourself comfortable." I tuck my backpack under a side table, so no one trips over it. When I stand up, Mav pulls me into his hips and bends down to kiss me. My knees weaken, just like they do in the novels I read. That's a real thing. Who knew?

"I've wanted to do that since I left last night." I melt into his side. When I'm with Mav, I'm comfortable in my own skin. I'm unburdened by my past, like I'm meant to be here just as I am.

"So," Mav starts, brushing my bangs out of my eyes, "everything's good between you and Hayleigh?" I nod at him. He texted last night, asking if I survived the firing squad after seeing him off, and I'd explained our heart-to-heart conversation.

He kisses the top of my head. It's a simple, tender gesture that makes me tingle deliciously all the way to my toes. "Good."

"Hey, Kady." Sam gives me a wave as he appears from the nearby staircase, then drops onto one of the couches.

"Mav, the twins will be here in about five." His grin grows as he looks between the two of us. "She looks good on you, Mav."

Sam sends me a wink and Mav gives him a look that would make most men cringe. Not Sammy. He just smiles at us like it's the most natural thing in the world. I wish we were that straightforward, that we were just two people dating, but it's so much more complicated than that. I honestly think Mav and the rest of the rebels have no idea that I used to be known as Kandi Matthews, the former child star turned pop sensation. Granted, I don't look or act anything like Kandi these days, but it's still hard to imagine that being this close to these guys multiple times now has not gotten me recognized.

"Let me show you the fridge." Mav leads me to the kitchen, our fingers entwined. He opens the fridge door as a barrier between us and Sam, who's still sitting in the living room area.

"Feel free to help yourself. While you're here, you're family, and family help themselves." He lowers his voice. "The guys know you're here to take pictures of us working. I reminded them all so it wouldn't seem odd to Cal."

I bob my head with understanding. It's the perfect ruse, being here for work. Like taking pictures of everyone would be a hardship. I can probably get pictures that will help with both the photo book and Operation Cal.

"Hey, Kade, bring me a beer on your way back, would ya?" Sammy calls over his shoulder from the couch.

I reach for a beer, but Mav gently slaps my hand away.

"Get it yourself, Sammy. She's a guest, not your maid." Mav scowls at Sammy around the door. Sammy mutters to himself, but joins us near the fridge to grab his own beer.

"She's right here anyway. Family helps other family members, too," Sammy mutters as he eyeballs Mav, who scowls

164

right back at him. If you didn't know them, you would probably think they were mortal enemies.

Their faux standoff is interrupted when the door swings open without warning. "We're here, fuckers." Killian stops dead in his tracks when his eyes land on me as he enters the living room.

"Kill, seriously, can you stop with the cursing when my kid's awake at least? Please." Callum enters behind him, nearly running into his back. Kill looks between the three of us like we're conspiring to throw him out of the band.

"You didn't say we were having company." Kill's glare is like a death ray.

"I emailed everyone that Kady's here to work today. Surely Cal told you she signed the new photography contract." Mav steps around me and grabs Gibs's carrier from Cal.

"Where's her camera, then?" Kill challenges.

Is he always this much of an asshole, or is it just with me? I've been nothing but polite and friendly with him, but he seems to loathe my presence so much he can't even bother to be civil.

"It's in her backpack. Quit being such a dickweed." Sammy flops back onto the couch without spilling a drop of his beer. "She just got here a freaking minute ago."

I hand Mav my phone, then squat to unpack my camera as the band settles into the living room area. "Kady says to just pretend she's not here. She'll get better shots that way."

"That'll be easy," Killian mutters to himself. I try to ignore his comment, but it cuts just a little.

Sitting on the floor gives me a good angle as they sit around the room in a semicircle. The great lighting means I won't need a flash.

I work quietly, trying to blend into the background as I snap shots while the band settles in with their instruments. The more invisible I am, the more the band will be themselves.

Cal holds Gibs in his lap while Mav messes around with a guitar. I snap a few shots of Mav first. I then work my way over to Killian, but he shoots me another glare, so I skip over him, and I move on to Cal. Gibs is all smiles right now as he leans back against his dad, enjoying the view of the band and the soft music that comes from their instruments. These shots will be gold for Operation Cal.

As much as I want to fangirl over the music and their writing process, I'm here to work. It's hard, but I have to purposely tune out the melodies and concentrate on the photos I'm taking. Even Killian seems to forget my presence eventually. After a couple of hours, Cal puts Gibs down for a nap. He frowns at me, his brow pinched as I follow him into a small bedroom on the first floor that's filled with baby stuff. I snap pictures of him soothing his son to sleep. I even stay to get a few of Gibs as he sleeps. This kid is going to be a heartbreaker, there is no doubt about it.

I return to the living room and retake my spot on the floor in the corner as they start working through a song I haven't heard before. Their creative process fascinates me, and I try my hardest to capture its collaborative spirit as the members comment on certain parts of the song or try to come up with ideas to help each other. Cal has his guitar on his lap instead of his son and is fully involved in the session now. They work through the song together, stopping when something's not right and starting over.

They run through several unfamiliar songs that seem mostly solidified, but then Mav starts working with one that the guys don't seem to know as well. They work out the actual music quickly while Sammy records a rough cut on his iPad. It's fascinating to watch them work through their songwriting.

"Again." The band picks up at the chorus and then moves into the bridge again while Mav paces as he hums the lyrics to himself. "Dammit."

He tosses his notebook onto the couch and grips his hair. It's the transition back to the second verse that's giving him fits. I hear it when Mav tries to force his lyrics into the music, but I also hear a possible resolution in my head.

My heart flutters wildly in my chest. This is the first time in over two years that I've worked a song out in my head like this. It feels so freaking good. I want to give Mav my suggestion, but how can I? They have no idea I used to be a musician. Even if they even knew who Kandi was, it's not like Kandi and the Blind Rebels ran in the same circles. Physically, I don't look anything like her anymore. My hair is different, I don't wear makeup, my clothes are far more casual, and I don't act like a pretentious bitch.

"We need a break. Let's order some food." Mav gives in. His frustration with the song and himself is evident in the way his rigid shoulders pull up close to his ears. He waves his arms back and forth in a stretch.

The former musician in me yearns to help them fix the song, but I'm an outsider, and rusty with my songwriting. Rock is definitely not in my wheelhouse. Not that I've never written any, but Monument Records told me that it would be easier to market Kandi in the pop realm. Not to mention, I haven't even touched an instrument in two years.

Sammy gathers a list of what everyone wants from the Burger Shack, and I go with him to keep him company. "They'll probably have it worked out before we even get back. Mav or Cal will write something and then we come in and alter it a bit for the sake of the song and then the lyrics need to be fixed. Or sometimes the lyrics are perfect, but the song needs to be tweaked. It's a whole process," he explains, not realizing it's a process I'm intimately familiar with. And for a split second, I see my opening to fess up to who I am. Who I was.

Sammy explaining songwriting to me, though, that makes me feel like a fraud, like I'm lying. It's because I genuinely care about all these guys. Even the one that doesn't seem to like me too much. Somehow, I've become one of them and now I feel bad that I am lying by omission about who I am.

"They'll figure it out. They always do." Sammy drums his fingers against the steering wheel in time with the music while we wait in the drive-thru for our massively large order. These guys can eat.

Besides Mav, I'm closest to Sammy. There is no awkwardness with him, even after the barbecue. He gives his friendship easily. He's so unguarded and carefree, and I wish it was like that for me. Maybe it can be, someday. I gravitate towards him when Mav's busy.

I trail Sammy into the house with a heavy bag of takeout. "Food's here. Figure it out yet?"

Cal responds with a slight shake of the head.

Soon, we're all sitting out on the patio devouring food, while the instruments lay abandoned inside.

I excuse myself for a few minutes to take some pictures of the guitars propped against the couch. There is just something about the way they lay that's begging me to take their picture. I move around to get a few shots from different angles. Cal walks through a few minutes later and glances over at me hovering over Killian's bass, doing the same thing I was just doing with his guitar. I'm loving these close-ups of the strings and the fretboard. I shrug at him as the baby monitor in his hand squawks. Gibs has woken up.

When Cal strides back through with Gibs in tow, I hold my hands out to him in the universal offer of taking the child.

"Are you sure? You don't have to hold him." Cal doesn't seem to understand I really want to. It gives me a warm feeling when Gibs comes to me willingly. I think he remembers me from the dunes.

I hold him on my lap as he plays with his small fabric toy against my chest. Mostly he gums it, but when the guys bring their acoustic instruments outside, he pounds it against my chest in time with the music. This little guy already has music in his blood, in his soul. How could he not, since it probably surrounds him constantly?

I cuddle him into my side and use one hand to type out a message to Mav and then slide my phone over to him.

My stomach clenches tight. I'm outing myself as a former musician and interrupting their creative flow. Songwriting is so deeply personal and my intruding on that process could be very unwelcome. It's not like I'm in their inner circle or anything. Then again, it could be just the push they need. It's the not knowing how they'll react, specifically how Mav will react, that has me reaching back across the table to rescind my suggestion.

I'm too late. Mav snatches my phone up and reads it before I have the chance to get it back. He tilts his head, glances up at me and then back at the phone. He closes his eyes as if he's trying to hear my suggestions in his head. He stands abruptly and goes inside, returning with a keyboard he lays on his lap.

He runs through the song on the piano, with Cal accompanying him on the guitar. They go through it the original way, where Mav's words don't fit. He motions for Cal to stop and runs through it again alone and this time he shifts the music downward, slowing it just a bit to fit the lyrics, and then ramps it back up into the second verse. It flows better and keeps his original lyrics fairly un-tweaked. Giving into the sudden softness of the lyrical quality, followed by the building back up of the strong melody, shifts the song to what I heard in my head.

"Shit, Mav, that's it." Sammy grabs his iPad and hits record. "Do that again, this time with Cal." The music starts again. Killian narrows his eyes at me as the pair runs through the song. Either he doesn't like it, or he doesn't like that I butted into their creative process. He feels I've stepped on toes.

I stand with Gibs after they play through the end of the

song a second time and point to his diaper, which has gotten considerably heavier in the last several minutes. Callum motions to take him away, and I use my free hand to let him know I got it. While I don't relish changing the diaper, I need to leave the patio, and not intrude any more in their creative process than I already have.

After changing him, I lay Gibs on a blanket on the floor of the nursery. I scatter his toys around us, and we both lay on our stomachs, me with a camera. I try to get his attention long enough to snap pictures. Down here on the floor, I can see Cal in him, especially when he wrinkles his brow in concentration while stretching to reach a toy or my camera strap. Cal does that when he's playing his guitar, except Cal's tongue is usually between his teeth.

I pull my now moistened camera strap out of Gibs's wet fist. Wrangling a baby and a camera isn't easy and is probably why most portrait photographers have assistants. I love him, but working to get pictures of him alone isn't something I'm excelling at.

I startle when I notice legs in the doorway. I roll halfway up, finding Mav standing propped against the jamb of the door, watching us with an unreadable expression. I sit up from my awkward belly-down position and wait for him to speak.

"Just wondering where you got off to." He watches Gibs on the blanket before turning his eyes on me. "Are you getting some good shots?"

I nod, feeling naked without my phone. I should have grabbed it from the table before I left with Gibs. Now I have to gesture to get my point across and hope he understands.

"The guys are taking a pool break. Cal wants me to bring Gibs out to the pool. He loves water."

I saw swim diapers in his bag, so I reach for one and change him again, then slather him up with a good layer of sunblock before getting up with him.

"Sammy has a floatie thing already blown up and waiting for him," Mav tells me as we walk out to the patio. "I should've told you to bring a suit, so you could join 'em."

I'm fine that he didn't. I'm not much of a swimmer. I'm more of a lying under the umbrella with a book kind of girl.

Cal and Sammy are both in the pool when the three of us enter the patio. Sam swims up to the side to take Gibs from me.

"Look what your favorite uncle bought you, buddy." Sam fishes Gibson's chubby legs through the seat holes to allow him to float upright. Sammy sets some of the water toys on the tray as Cal gently sets him afloat in the pool.

Mav sits in one of the double loungers. He sets my phone on the one next to him. It must be his subtle way of telling me he wants to talk. I sit in the seat, squinting from bright sun.

"Here, let me fix the shade." He wrestles the canopy over our lounges, then disappears into the house.

Killian sits across the pool from me, on a barstool near the built-in barbecue. He seems to be scrolling on his phone under the shaded part of the patio near the table. I stare, trying to figure out why he's always scowling at me. He rarely says more than two words to me, and they usually aren't kind ones when he does speak. His intensity makes me uncomfortable. As if he senses my scrutiny, he looks up and grimaces at me again.

Mav returns, offering me a bubbly blackberry water complete with a straw, like at the barbecue the other night, and I accept with a smile.

We face each other, sitting on the sides of our respective loungers, knee-to-knee.

"You fixed our song." It's not a question, but a quiet statement. His chocolate brown eyes gauge me. I can't tell if he's surprised, confused, or angry. He gives nothing away. I squirm and fidget with my phone. How much should I give him? How much can I give him without losing myself all over again?

Chapter 18

Mavrick

"You are like one of those presents wrapped in a bazillion layers of gift paper. Every layer is something new, and I never know what I am going to discover behind the next layer, but I can't wait to see what's inside." Being with her is like a gift. I love how she fits in with us. She and Sammy are already close, and Cal obviously trusts her with his son. Kill's more stand-offish with her, but I think that's because he's suspicious. He's worrying about her motives when it comes to hanging out with us and having a relationship with us.

Kady reddens and won't make eye contact as she concentrates on her phone. Her thumbs hover as she contemplates what she wants to say. This beautiful, silent, yet musical creature sitting across from me doesn't even realize the effect she has on those around her, on me especially.

I noticed her trying to take the phone back after sliding it across the table at me earlier, second guessing herself. Her approach to our song was so different. I could have worked on it for a year and never come up with the solution for it that she did.

This song is different from previous Blind Rebels songs, more personal, more intimate, and a slightly different sound. Her idea of a shift in the dynamic of the song was exactly what it needed. Not sure why I didn't think of it. And she gave it to us freely.

Kady remains silent.

"We appreciate the help." Her gaze shoots over to Killian briefly before gracing me with a soft smile.

Kady: You're welcome.

"Do you play?" I broach the subject cautiously, straddling that fine line between my need to know more and pushing her too far, too fast.

Kady: Piano since I was 6. Some guitar. A little drum. The last two are self-taught. Mostly, I sang.

Kady: Until the afternoon the music died.

Kady pulls her legs up under her chin on the lounger and sits in a ball, another layer added to the fortress walls that surround her heart. It kills me that she's distancing herself from me when all I want to do is hold her to me and give her the reassurance she probably craves, kiss away the pain swimming in her eyes. Mostly, I want to demolish the walls she keeps up, not help her fortify them. So, I don't make my move. Not yet.

Sammy cannonballs into the pool, the cool water from his huge splash spraying over both Kady and me. She wipes her phone off on a dry spot of her mostly soaked shirt.

"Shit. Sorry, Kady. Not sorry about you, though, Mav." Sammy smirks at me from the pool and then swims away, the little shit. The waves from Sammy's entrance into the pool make Gibs cackle as he rides them out, which causes a soft smile on Kady's face.

Kady: Music hasn't been in me, in my head, since I lost my voice.

Kady: Until today, that is.

173

"You listen to music." There's no way she hasn't. She works as a concert photographer at a rock club.

Kady: Listen, yes.

Kady: But listening isn't the same as when it's in me.

Kady: In my body.

Kady: When I live in it. I'm not explaining this right.

Kady: I shouldn't have butted into your songwriting process.

"I know what you mean when you say, 'it lives in you.' You're a musician, so music is the fiber that makes us who we are. It's how we express ourselves, how we relate to our world. I had no idea you're a musician." I watch Gibson drifting around in the pool, never more than an arm's length from a watchful Cal.

"We've been trying to fix that song for three days and hadn't gotten anywhere. You fixed it after hearing it only a few times. Your suggestion fixed it." She glances at me out of the side of her eye. "You fixed it, Kady. You did that."

Understanding lights her face, and I see hope striving to peek through the cracks in those freaking walls she keeps herself behind.

Hope. I can give her even more of that.

"You're wrong, though, Kady. The music was in you before today. I saw it at the dunes."

She turns her head to face me, her full lips parted, eyes glossy and wide. "When you were holding Gibson while Cal and I loaded the SUV. You were humming to him."

She moves her hand to her chest in a wordless, 'me?'

I nod. "Cal and I rearranged his cargo area for an extra twenty minutes just to keep you holding him, to keep you humming. So, your music's there." I squeeze her leg as the tears in her eyes begin to fall.

"It's still in you, still part of you. It might be in hibernation, but it's not dead." *What the hell happened to this girl two years ago to make her go silent?*

Kady tucks her head behind her knees and lets out an audible, ragged sob as she rocks herself slightly.

Cal, Sammy, and even Killian all turn our way, Cal's alarmed expression asking me, 'what the fuck did you do?' while Sammy starts to get out of the pool to help fix whatever made her cry. I pin him to the pool with a glare as I move to sit next to Kady. Killian stays on the far side of the pool, his eyes narrowed in suspicion at our interaction.

I don't know how to take away her pain, so I do the only thing I can think to comfort her. I rub her back in light, soft circles, feeling it quake under my hand with the now silent tears she cries. I can't help but pull her into me. She reaches over and wraps her arms around my waist, burying her head into my side as her tears dampen my t-shirt.

I rock her slowly and glance across the pool where Killian still assesses us. I don't understand what his deal is with her, but he's very suspicious of her and has been since the start. He turns and goes back to scrolling through his phone when he notices me watching him.

Her sobs ebb, and she pulls away, wiping her hands under her eyes. She grabs her phone to send me a quick message.

Kady: *I'm going to use the restroom.*

She stands and walks into the house. It's all I can do not to follow her, but she needs some space.

Sammy pulls himself out of the pool and sits on the edge. "She okay?"

"She's okay. She just needs a moment." I reassure him so he doesn't go bounding after her.

Killian joins us. "I don't trust her."

"Why the hell not? What's she done to make you not trust her?" I don't understand his attitude towards Kady at all.

"There's something off about her. First, she's a photographer and now suddenly she's a musician, too? And helping us write songs? My gut says there is something not right here."

Killian crosses his arms over his chest. "She wants something from us."

"She doesn't want anything from us, Kill. You don't know her like I do."

He gives me a curt nod and goes back to the other side of the pool and back to his phone.

Chapter 19

Kadence

he music didn't die, Kady. It's still with you, still part of you.

Mav's words have been on repeat in my head since yesterday. Hayleigh wasn't thrilled with me not telling her the specifics of what had me so quiet when I got home. How could I explain it to her when I'm still working through it myself? I don't remember humming with Gibson in the desert, but it's not something that Mav would have reason to lie about.

I remember holding Gibs, swaying with him while watching them pack up. It was completely unconscious. I had no idea I was doing it. Not then. Not now. The speech therapist would have a field day with that if I were still seeing her.

I stretch out in my bed and think about what to do with my day today. No doubt Hayleigh will want to know what happened at my last session with the band. As I finally sit up on the edge of my bed, my phone dings.

Mav: Wanna go out?

Me: Where?

Mav: Guitar shop and then ...

Mav: *Come with me.*
Me: *Ok.*

I get dressed and head down to the lobby. Mav is just pulling up outside in Sammy's Jeep as I stroll out the lobby door.

He rushes over and opens my door, then guides me up into the massive vehicle. We drive to a local guitar shop in an upper end shopping area not far from the airport.

It's been forever since I've been in a music shop. While Mav talks to the salesman who seemed to be expecting him, I peruse the wall of guitars for sale. There's a drum kit in the corner, some violins, and a cello.

What really draws my attention is an upright piano in the corner with a sign that it's on consignment. It's older but in good condition. The price isn't bad. It might be nice to have access to a piano that isn't down in our very public lobby. Getting it into the apartment would probably be a fiasco. It's one of the two things I miss about my place in LA, my baby grand and the proximity to the ocean.

I sit at the upright and run some scales to see how it sounds. It could stand to be tuned. A salesman comes over to me. Mav looks over and says, "She's with me." The salesman wanders away. I play a Bach piece I've had memorized since I was thirteen. That's what rote practice will do. When I play some Blind Rebels, Mav glances over at me with a smile while talking to the salesman.

He grabs a guitar from the wall and tunes it quickly and joins me over at the upright.

"Shall we give them a show?" I'm not sure why I didn't notice the store is way more crowded than when we strolled in. I shrug and wait for Mav to take the lead. He starts off with some Blind Rebels stuff. It's easy to play along; I know their music and can play it by ear.

The more we play, the bigger the group inside gets until it spills outside. This is crazy. We play through some rock standards and then Mav leans in.

"Play the Bach again. I'll follow along."

I mouth, "Are you sure?" I've been playing the piece for over a decade, so I know it like the back of my hand. He obviously recognizes it as Bach, so maybe he knows it too, but on an electric guitar?

Somehow, he makes it work. It sounds good, like we've played together for years. I don't think that the crowd knows what to think of it. As we finish it, he uses the opportunity to do a wailing guitar solo. I watch his deft fingers work over the fretboard at a manic pace.

He finishes up and faces the crowd with his showman's mask on.

"Bet you didn't know I could shred a guitar solo just as good as Cal, did ya?" The crowd claps. "One more and then we've got to go."

He leans into me. "Can you play 'Imagine' by The Beatles?" I nod and start us off. He plays and sings along. The group cheers when it's over.

"Thanks, you guys. It's been fun." Mav holds his hand up to applause then puts the guitar away.

The salesman Mav was working with prior to the impromptu show comes over and thanks him. They talk shop a bit and we leave with a bag of guitar strings and the promise to have the bass he just ordered delivered as soon as it arrives.

Mav grabs my hand with his free one. "Come on, I'm starving. Let's get lunch. Well, it'll be brunch for me." He winks at me, and we head out the door. There is a fairly large crowd lingering as we exit the store and we're immediately encompassed by fans.

"I'll sign and take selfies for a few minutes, but then I have to go, okay, guys?" They swamp Mav and I let go of his hand. He gives them most of his attention, a smile, an autograph, a selfie with a few kind words. Every so often he pulls his eyes from whomever is in front of him to make sure I'm still within his view. Each time his eyes connect with mine, my heart beats a little faster, knowing that he's looking for me.

"I hate to do it, guys, but I have somewhere I need to be. Thanks for your support. Love you guys!" He moves through the swarm to me. Most of them are respectful of his wish to leave and part a path for him to walk through.

He grabs my hand and leads me to Sammy's Jeep. "Thanks for humoring me. Them." He shoots me an unsure smile. This is who he is, so why would I complain about that?

Me: They're your fans. I understand they all want their little piece of you.

He grimaces. "That's true. But when I am out with someone, I want it to be about us and not them. But that's not what I was talking about. I meant in the shop. Thanks for playing the impromptu concert."

Me: Again, didn't mind. They're there for you, I was just background music.

He gives me a funny look after reading my text and shakes his head. He pilots us out of the shopping center. "For lunch I thought we'd have burgers if that's okay?"

I nod.

He takes us to a local hamburger joint and we sit in a booth at the far end of the restaurant, his hat pulled far down on his head.

"Any weird proclivities I should know about?" he asks after our waiter walks away to put in our order.

Me: None that I can think of.

He reads my text and then eyes me for a second. "Come on, Kady, everyone has them. What are yours?" His tone is a light, teasing one. I just shrug.

"I've noticed one. You always have a hairband around your wrist, always prepared to put your hair up and get to work."

I shrug. That's what it probably comes off as. He has no idea that the real reason I wear a hairband around my wrist is as a talisman of sorts. Initially, it was a way to keep myself grounded when I noticed I was spiraling, but now it feels wrong not to have them on.

"I couldn't help but notice. You fiddle with them sometimes." He grins, pleased with himself for noticing the small detail about me. I need to refocus this conversation on him, get it off of me and the hairbands.

Me: What are yours?

"I take a small notebook with me most places." He leans over and pulls the small notebook from his back pocket. "It's just in case I get inspired and want to jot down a snippet of conversation or something. I don't drink as much as I used to, but when I do drink, it's usually whiskey." He shrugs. "I'm not as scandalous as the press makes me out to be." His mouth pulls down at the corners when he says it.

Me: No?

He shakes his head after he reads my retort. "I'm a regular, one sock at a time guy. I see the shit that's written about me, about the band. Sure, when we were first hitting it big, I drank a little too much. Hell, we all did. We trashed a hotel room or two in our day. We learned really quick that the moment of attention didn't beget the large bill at the end of the tour." He shrugs.

I nod.

"It was bad, the things that came out after the sex video. Looking back now, I'm pretty sure that Cal sleeping with Becka was a good thing."

I couldn't have heard that right.

He chuckles at my expression. "Sounds weird to say, I know. But I can see it for what it was now. In the moment, I thought I loved Becka, and she loved me. But the more I've thought about it, our relationship was more about comfort than love. I was comfortable with her and didn't see her for the fame whore she truly was. I don't know why I didn't see it then. But looking back, I can certainly see it now."

My eyes must be round with surprise, but it doesn't stop him from continuing to bear his soul. He's giving me pieces of him he doesn't share. He's trying to prove to me that he's a safe place.

"She left Callum and Gibson. I didn't know until recently because of our big blow up. Sammy told me she just took off one night. Gibs was like, two weeks old." Mav shakes his head. "I'm disappointed in myself that I wasted so much energy hating Cal."

"And now I learn he's stressed, like really struggling with being a dad, a mom, and a rock star." He shakes his head. "No one knows any of this, or that he nearly quit the band."

I blink. Shit, Cal almost left the band? He's sharing stuff with me that he's never told anyone. Yet here I sit across from him and can't even bring myself to tell him my old name, who I used to be. I don't want to be judged because of what I did in the past.

Me: I won't tell a soul.

He nods at my text. "I know. I wouldn't have told you if I thought you'd tell. What I'm trying to say is that we all have our issues." He fiddles with his napkin in a very un-Mavrick way. "My stage persona is a cocky, larger-than-life asshole, right? But that guy? He only lives for 90 to 120 minutes a night. He's not the real me." He stares at me.

Me: I've found that out. But I like both Mavs.

He looks up from his phone, and a deep hearty chuckle erupts from his lips. "You do, huh?"

I nod.

"Well, good to know."

Maybe I shouldn't have said that, but I love the cocky rock god who feeds off the crowd. He's a talented showman and musician, but I also like regular Mav, the one who brings me tacos and has a thing for driving fast cars, the one who apologizes when he makes a mistake.

"Enough about me. I want to know more about Kady." He laughs as our food is set in front of us. "So far, I know your favorite color, that you're a reader and that you love Mexican food. I want to know something about Kady that nobody knows. Not even Hayleigh." He grabs the ketchup and taps some out on his plate.

Me: That won't be easy. I've known Hayleigh since we were 8. She knows me better than anyone.

He nods, but still has that expectant look when he peers up at me. I try to find something I can give him that will feel like enough.

Me: I have a brother. I mean, Hayleigh knows that, but most people don't.

His eyes light up. "A brother? You've never mentioned him."

I shrug at him again. I don't talk about Allen much because I'm embarrassed. Not of him. I'm ashamed that we don't have a relationship and that's mostly on me. How can I explain to Mav that the only living relative I have won't give me the time of day because I let money get in the way of that relationship?

Me: He's six years older than me. We're estranged. I haven't seen him in a really long time.

Mav's eyebrows lift in surprise, but he looks kind of pissed otherwise. "How long is a really long time?"

Me: Eight years or so.

He stiffens in his seat as he reads my message. His jaw clenches so tight the muscle in his cheek tics. "You haven't seen your brother in eight years?"

I shake my head.

"So, he doesn't know that you can't talk?" His voice is low and gravelly.

Me: He knows. Hayleigh got ahold of him when it happened.

Me: He didn't want to see me.

I look down, trying to get the sting out of my eyes. I can't tell Mav the truth. Allen didn't want to see me because he thought I got what I deserved at the time. It's easier pretending I don't have any family, easier than admitting that my own brother wants nothing to do with me.

Caught up in the glitz and glamor of being Kandi Matthews, I was so young. I didn't understand what was really going on around me. Estranged by my brother and loathed by my only other living relative, an aunt who tried to steal from me, I was abandoned when I tried to stand up for myself.

Her words still echo in my head from the last time I saw her. "You are just a lost little girl no one loves, Kadence. I'm the only reason Kandi Matthews exists. Without me, you'll be nothing." That was the afternoon the judge granted my emancipation.

Mav reaches across the table and squeezes my hand. "He's the obvious loser. You're an amazing person. Your photos are breathtaking, and you're a talented musician. I'm so glad I met you, Kadence. You're a woman of many talents." He squeezes my hand again.

I give him a weak smile and turn my attention back to my lunch.

After he settles the bill, Mav takes my hand, and we leave Hamburger Haven to walk to the car.

A group of brightly colored lowriders drive by. The first one in the procession uses his hydraulics to show off for his friends that follow. The third car in the cluster is so low it scrapes along the roadway, a grinding noise that throws sparks out from the car's undercarriage.

My vision goes wavy around the edges as my heart speeds up. *Oh no. Not now. Please not now.*

I reach out for anything to hold on to, but there's nothing. My leg muscles tighten until I'm frozen in place. I can't draw in enough air, like I'm trying to breathe through a cocktail straw. I focus on slowing my breathing, which is coming in short, rapid pants. *Concentrate on walking.* I try to emphasize being normal because I'm with Mav, but my feet won't move, and I can't get enough air. I clutch the collar of my shirt with one hand as pain radiates from my tight chest and breathing gets even more difficult.

So much for normal. Every time I relax and start believing in myself, my ability or anything positive in my life, a panic attack cuts me off at the knees, proving I'll never be normal again.

It's bad enough this is happening on a public street, but it's with Mav. He's going to think I'm nuts. He'll know just how damaged I really am.

I'm completely frozen. I need to go home, now. Back to the apartment. Back to my room. *I. Can't. Breathe.* My breath comes in gasping wheezes that rattle. My chest starts burning. My shirt and bra feel too tight.

"Kady?" Mav is standing in front of me, hands on my shoulders, looking me up and down. He's trying to figure out what's going on, but I can't get my phone out to explain because one hand is still gripping my shirt and the other is balled up at my side.

"Kady, are you okay?" I try to shake my head, but dizziness threatens to take me down as the world starts sliding together in a colorful blur. I grip his arms as they rest on my shoulders. Everything shifts and tilts every time I move my eyes, like the world around us is melting into a moving haziness. I can't focus on anything.

Mav grips my shoulders, his firm hold keeping me from going down. His eyes continually scan me.

My lip trembles, but I force myself not to cry. I've got to get home first. I try to drag in a deep breath. That's what I'm supposed to do, but I can't. I can't breathe.

Mav releases my shoulders. *No! Don't let me go. God, please don't leave me alone like this.* That'll be a one-way ticket to a medicated ride to the hospital.

In a swift motion, he swoops me up into his arms. "I've got you. Hold on." He walks us quickly towards Sammy's Jeep.

Relax! You're okay. Don't do this. Not here. Not with Mav.

My arms and legs are so stiff I don't think I'll be able to fit in the Jeep, but somehow, he is able to maneuver me in.

He hustles around the hood and jumps into the driver's seat. A phone rings. Not mine. I try to reach for my phone to text Hayleigh, but if I do, I'll slide off the seat. I still can't breathe. My chest continues to tighten. Maybe this isn't a panic attack. Maybe I'm having a heart attack. I'm only twenty-five, I can't be having a heart attack.

Every movement makes the world smear and spin. Every gasp I take seems to slow down time, making it harder for me to get air in, get air out. Why is this taking so long?

"Mav?" Hayleigh's voice comes over the speakers in the car. I try to talk, but all that happens is a terrified gasp.

"Something's wrong with Kady. She's frozen and breathing funny. She won't make eye contact. I'm not sure where the nearest hospital is. I'm by Hamburger Haven, kind of by HARD."

"She's okay, Mav. It's a panic attack. Bring her home."

Hayleigh knows. She'll help. Hayleigh's voice comes through the speakers directed at me. "Kady? You're okay. Feel your feet, Kady." I can't feel my feet. They are numb. Not even a tingle.

"She needs a hospital." Mav's voice is tight and panicked. *Not the hospital. They'll drug me. Home. Hayleigh.* I shake my head, trying to make Mav understand.

"Bring her home. She'll be okay. I promise."

The scenery smears together and I feel like I'm spinning again. My heart races like it'll come out of my chest. Leaning against the passenger window, my breath fogs it with each pant as the city goes by in one continuous blur.

Mav and Hayleigh are talking, but I can't focus on them, the dizziness so bad I close my eyes. Then I'm floating inside the lobby. Almost home. Almost home. Almost home. Then I feel the whoosh of my stomach dropping in the elevator.

Mav's lips whisper into my hair, my hand fisted in his soft t-shirt, his spicy leathery smell in my nose. "You're going to be okay, Kady." His voice is soft and shaky, like he doesn't quite believe himself.

"Set her on the couch." I hear Hayleigh's voice.

He lowers me as if I'm made of precious glass that may shatter at any moment, when in reality, I shattered two years ago. He gently pries my fingers from his shirt because I can't release them. "In the freezer, Mav. Get the bag of peas in the door."

She grips my hands hard, squeezing my fingers, trying to ground me to here and now. "Kady. You're okay. Breathe in-two-three-four. Hold-two-three-four. Out-two-three-four-five-six." I want to breathe with her, but I can't control it. "Come on. Breathe with me, or we'll have to call the ambulance. They'll medicate you. You hate that."

I nod. *Come on lungs. In, two three four.* My breath won't behave, and my heart continues to race like it's about to explode.

Hayleigh cups my hands over something. My fingers are getting so cold they hurt.

I blink hard, the cold jerking me out of my head.

"There she is." Her hand softly moves my bangs from my face. I focus on her and follow her breathing. Hayleigh's voice is soft, like she's in a library. "In-two-three-four. Hold-two-three-

187

four. Out-two-three-four-five-six." She strokes my hair. "You're safe. You're okay."

Breathe in with Hayleigh. Hold my breath with Hayleigh. Blow out with Hayleigh. The tight hold of my muscles gradually starts to loosen.

In the background, Mav paces in the space between the kitchen and the living room, his hand running through the long locks of his dark hair. He looks totally wrecked, his face a mixture of fear, concern, and helplessness.

This happened in front of Mav. And cue the tears. As if having a full-blown panic attack in front of a rock star wasn't bad enough, now I'm bawling. Just another reaction I can't control. He won't understand. No one does. *Hayleigh and Harden, they understand.*

Hayleigh hugs me gently, careful not to hold on too tight or long. "Hey, you're okay, Kadycat. You're okay." She smooths her hands over my hair, the motion soothing me as my eyes well even more, then release.

"Maybe I should get you half an Ativan?" I shake my head no and swipe the hot tears on my cheeks. *Fuck crying. I'm done crying over this shit.* I don't know what's worse, having my own brain betray me by throwing me into a panic attack in front of Mav, or crying in the aftermath, also in front of him.

Her brow creases at me. "You sure? That was kind of a bad one."

I shake my head. I mouth, "I'm okay. Water?"

"I'll get you some water." She squeezes my shoulder as she gets up. When Hayleigh passes Mav, she lays a hand on his arm. "She's okay. Sit with her. She needs to see you're still here."

Mav sits on the edge of the coffee table across from me, his eyes searching my face. I try to slip on my mask so he can't see the real me. I'm not successful, but it doesn't really matter. He's seen me in all my fucked-up glory now, so why bother to hide it?

I refuse to make the eye contact he tries to establish because I don't want to see what he's feeling. Doing that would acknowledge he's seeing this broken, fucked up part of me. I stare out the window over his shoulder as my body starts to feel heavy.

Mav takes one of my cold hands off the peas and pulls it up to his lips to kiss it, then warms it between his hands. He removes the peas from my lap and does the same with the other hand. The gesture is so intimate and caring it makes my unwanted tears flow harder.

Hayleigh sets my water on the table next to Mav and whispers, "I'll be in the kitchen if you need me." He nods slightly at her, but never breaks his gaze from me. She takes the peas with her.

"Fuck, Kady, you scared the shit out of me." His voice is low, and his posture is much less rigid than it was when he was pacing.

"I didn't know what to do, what was happening." He drops his head to my shoulder. His breath is heaving as he collects himself. "I'm glad you're okay."

I nod and take my hands back from him. I grab my phone.

Me: I'm sorry.

He shakes his head at me, not accepting the apology he's just read.

Me: They're better than they used to be, but I'll probably never be completely free of them.

He nods. "Are they because of what happened, what caused you to lose your voice?"

I nod.

"What do they feel like? I know what they look like, but what does it feel like for you?"

No one's ever asked me to explain that aspect before. He sits patiently while I tap it out, squeezing my knee repeatedly, reminding me he's here. I'm here. I'm okay.

Me: When they're bad, I can't move. My muscles go rigid, and I can't walk. My heart beats really fast, scary fast.

Me: It feels like I can't draw in enough air. Almost like trying to breathe through a swizzle stick.

Me: I get dizzy. My hands and feet tingle. Sometimes, like today, I can't feel my feet at all.

Me: But I want to run away. I have an intense need to get home, but it's like I am cemented to the floor.

Me: Thank you for bringing me home. I'll be fine.

He looks at me like I've lost my marbles right along with my dignity. "You aren't getting rid of me that easy."

Me: You don't want to be around a freak like me.

He clucks his tongue against his cheek. "You are not a freak, Kady."

I shrug and look over at Hayleigh, who's busying herself in the kitchen. He can't want to be around someone who stops functioning like a normal person without warning.

"I'm not going anywhere." His voice is soft but insistent.

Me: I won't be much fun. I'll probably fall asleep soon anyway.

He nods in agreement and squeezes my leg. "It's an adrenaline dump. You're so full of adrenaline and then poof, it's gone. You need to let your body recover. Sleep if it wants sleep. Just relax with me."

He moves, so he's sitting next to me on the couch and pulls me into him. He's so warm and welcoming, I soften into him because when we're close like this, I feel safe. Somehow, this rock star comforts my soul in a way it has never been before. He lays his head on mine. He doesn't say anything, just holds me to him. His leather and spice scent envelopes me as my eyes start to get heavy. I move my thumbs across the screen of my phone.

Me: I'm sorry. This is so embarrassing. You can go. I understand.

He slips my phone from my hand and slides it on the table. "I told you, I'm not going anywhere." He slips his shoes off and moves to lie on the couch, bringing me down with him.

"I got you, Kady," he murmurs softly. "All of you. Let's just relax for a while."

He takes a deep breath, and my head falls naturally to his chest and the weight of his arms around me is comforting and not constricting. His heart beats a steady, solid rhythm in my ear, and it's so comforting my eyes slowly shut.

Chapter 20

Kadence

The Blind Rebels are the hottest ticket in Vegas right now. The entire five-week residency has been sold out since they released the rest of the tickets on day three and then announced the extension of the residency a week later and the sixth week sold out too. Harden's got to be thrilled. Not just for the attendance but for the exposure it's brought his small club. I am so proud of him.

The fans lining up outside of HARD shoot daggers at me as I walk past them straight to the front door. I've been taking pictures every night, but tonight, even though I have my camera with me, I'm not on the clock. I'm here to watch the show instead of work it. I'm so excited to not have to worry about camera settings and lighting angles. I have my camera with me, because I almost always have it with me, but tonight, it's more about the show than what I capture.

"Get to the rear of the line," someone shouts as I tap three times on the door.

Harden sticks his head out as more people start to grumble their disapproval at my bypassing the line.

"Hey, kiddo, come on in." He holds the door open for me wide and I have to suppress the urge to look back at those in line and send a smirk their way.

"Mavrick's expecting you." He says it in his loud booming voice. It's enough that the crowd behind me doesn't taunt me for cutting in front of them anymore.

Stepping into the dimly lit club, Harden grasps me in a hug. I gasp and my muscles stiffen at the unexpected contact. "Sorry, not sorry." He rocks me in his brotherly embrace until my muscles start to relax with the realization that I have nothing to fear.

"You look good. You good?" I nod at Harden. He looks much calmer than he did on the first night. He tousles my hair. The other times I've been shooting the band, he's been too busy to pay me much attention and honestly, I worked better because of it.

"Mavrick said you'd be coming early." He hooks his head towards the bar, and I follow him.

"Water?" He watches me as I shake my head and point to the Diet Cokes he has in bottles behind the bar for staff.

"You got it." He heads behind the bar and slides me a bottle.

I smile and hold it up and mouth, "Thank you."

"Just go ahead to the dressing room. Sally is on her way there with some drinks if you want to follow her back."

He reaches out and touches my arm lightly as I'm about to go. "Kade, if you need me tonight, text me. For anything." Harden's brow wrinkles despite the thumbs up I give him. I head to the dressing room.

"Kady!" Sammy bounds over to me and grips me in a hug that has my gut tightening again. "Mav said you were coming early to hang with us! We're so glad you are here. Right, guys?" Sammy ushers me into the room, arm over my shoulder. I love Sammy.

"Hey, Kady." Cal greets me from the corner with Gibs on his lap, and an older woman with a sweet smile is standing next to him. "This is my Aunt Sandy. She is Gibs's babysitter tonight."

I wave to her, and she smiles at me in a matronly way. "It's nice to meet you, dear."

Killian snickers but doesn't look up from his phone.

"Don't be so effin' rude, Kill." Cal kicks him while shaking his head. Killian scoots out of Cal's reach, ignoring his brother for his phone.

I squat in front of Cal, so I'm eye level with Gibson. The tot smiles at me and reaches for my face with his wet fist. I offer to take him, and Cal gladly gives him up to me. I've quickly learned that Gibs's snuggles are the best. I breathe in his unique scent of baby powder and lavender, with an undertone of something masculine that I assume comes from Cal. I bounce him softly as we walk over to the couch and sit.

Gibs reaches for my camera, so Sammy takes it and places it on Mav's dressing table. "Out of sight, out of mind," he says to me with a wink.

"Mav's doing a radio interview in the club owner's office. He'll be back soon."

Sammy pulls a drumstick from his back pocket and hands it to Gibs, who squeals in delight and shoves it into his drooly mouth. I wonder if he's teething. He's so dang slobbery, but it only adds to his cuteness quotient.

Sharp pain radiates through my temple as I struggle to keep my grip on Gibson, so I don't drop him. My eyes instantly well with tears as the pain rushes around the perimeter of my head like a lightning bolt and my vision goes fuzzy.

"Shit. Sorry." Sammy sounds far away. Gibson's weight is lifted from my arms as I blink a few times, my sight coming back into focus.

"Are you okay? Kady?" Sammy's concerned face is up close

to mine as I focus on him. "He walloped you good. Dammit. I'm sorry. This'll help."

He holds a towel with ice to my head.

"I'm okay," I mouth and move my hand to hold the icepack to my head myself. Sammy doesn't seem to believe me, and hovers around me like Hayleigh would do.

"Give her some space, Sammy," Cal instructs.

"Hey, is Kad—" Mav freezes the moment he notices the icepack I'm holding to the side of my head.

"What the fuck happened?" Mav squats in front of me, shooting pissed off looks between Sammy and Cal then focuses back on me. He cradles his large hand over mine to help me hold the ice pack to my head.

"She's okay." Sammy's voice is a little shaky, like he's trying to convince himself just as much as he is Mav.

"Gibson used her skull as a snare drum." Killian chuckles, bouncing his nephew on a knee.

Mav, in turn, shoots him a cold, murderous glare.

Killian shrugs. "What? He had good form is all I'm saying. He obviously takes after Sammy. It was fuckin' awesome."

"Drumsticks aren't toys, Sammy. And language when you're holding Gibson, Kill. I don't want his first word to be the F word." Cal chastises his brother as he takes a seat on the short table across from me. He scrutinizes my face, just like Mav does.

"He likes them." Sammy's voice trails off to a whisper.

Cal keeps glancing back and forth between my eyes like he expects to find something wrong. Mav takes control of the ice pack and moves it away from the side of my head to inspect the damage. He runs his fingers through my hair.

"Uhhhwah." The guttural noise escapes my lips when he hits a spot that sends another lightning bolt of pain around the back of my head again. My eyes slam shut, needing to block out the light until the lightning turns back into a dull throb. When I open them, Mav is wincing at me.

"You've got a little knot forming. Sammy, make her another ice pack."

Soon Mav is holding a new ice pack to my head with one hand and handing me my phone with another.

"You know where you are?" I nod, but he pushes my phone towards me. "Use your words."

Me: Hard.

"You know my name?" Another expectant look.

Me: Mavrick Slater, I'm fine.

He purses his lips. "How old are you?"

Rolling my eyes this time, I answer.

Me: Twenty-five. I'm okay. Just caught me off guard.

He leans forwards to inspect my eyes, as if he's a doctor and knows what he's looking for. Then his low whisper hits my ears. "I really want to kiss you right now."

Cal groans and shoves off the table. "Mav, she probably has a headache. She doesn't need to choke on your tongue. And we don't need to see that anyway."

Mav shoots Cal the finger and pulls me onto his lap sideways. I giggle a little.

"Let me." He takes control of the icepack again, encouraging me to lay my head against his defined chest, which I won't say no to. I may have a headache, but I still have enough of my wits about me that I'm not going to give up the chance to cuddle with Mavrick Slater.

I relax into his warmth, lulled by the rhythmic, steady beat of his heart. I'm so glad he's wearing his stage shirt, so it's open most of the way down. The sound of his heart soothes me more than anything, and I nestle into his spicy, leathery scent.

Being snuggled up to Mav is warm and comfortable and I like it here. The band and people come and go from the room, but I'm disconnected from the goings on. This must be what being completely comfortable is like. Something I haven't felt most of my life.

"Still doing okay, angel?" Mav whispers into the top of my head. *Angel*. He called me angel. My heart speeds up at the nickname from back then, and Jerrod flashes across my mind. Oh no.

My arms tense, as do my legs. No, no, not again. Not here. Please God, no, not in front of everyone. I'm happy here. Mav is safe. Please not now. I take in a deep breath and his spicy, yet earthy scent relaxes me a little bit. I glance at the door, making sure my path is clear just in case I need to bolt as my stomach starts to clench deep inside. I try to breathe. In, two, three, four. Hold, two, three, four.

As if he senses my mounting inner panic, he squeezes me to him tighter as I exhale. "Kade, you okay?"

I nod hesitantly. "That's my girl." He kisses the top of my head and rocks me slightly as he moves to discard the damp towel on the table and lightly runs his fingers through my cold hair. Cal strums his guitar in the corner, a familiar tune. He smiles at me, and I feel myself relax a bit more. This close, the sound of his fingers sliding along the fretboard is oddly comforting when usually noises make the panic worse. The couch shifts. Sammy. He's still close. I can't see him, but it has to be him. I'm okay and my body listens to me this time and slowly relaxes my legs.

"Fifteen minutes." Harden's voice rings out from the area by the door. "Um, is everything okay?" I turn my head towards the door, and he's looking directly at me while I'm cradled on Mav's lap.

Harden's brow creases as he looks me over. I try to slip my stoic mask on so that he doesn't suspect I could be minutes, seconds away from bolting out of here.

But no. I won't ruin this. I'm excited to be here. I want to see the show. I breathe in Mav, reveling in his scent that's all spice and leather and body wash and him. I am okay. My arms start to relax a little.

I nod at Harden.

"She took a drumstick to the head a bit ago. From Gibson, not Sammy," Cal quickly clarifies as Harden levels a steely gaze at Sammy. "Think she's okay, though. Right?"

I nod and reluctantly pull away from Mav to reach for my phone to text Harden.

Me: I'm fine. Got any Advil?

Harden reads my text and nods. I knew he'd have some. "But you're sure you're okay?"

I nod and gulp from the water bottle Sammy brought me earlier.

"Probably more like ten minutes now, guys." Harden knocks on the open door twice and leaves. The guys start to gather by the door.

"You can stay in here if you want? Relax on the couch." Mav's still worried about my head. He has no idea I was seconds from running out the door and it had nothing to do with getting hit in the head. I shake my head and pull out my phone.

Me: I'm good. I want to watch the show.

He reads my text. "Okay, but if you get tired or something, come in here. We're having a VIP meet and greet with some fans out in the pit after the show. It should be quiet in here, though. We'll be in as soon as we're done."

Me: How do I get to be a VIP? Will you sign my breast?

I shimmy my shoulders at him with a wink after I send the text.

He growls in my direction as he leaves the room and Cal looks between us with a humored expression before following his bandmate.

Harden pokes his head in as I'm about to head to the side of the stage. He holds his hand out to me. "Here's the Advil. You sure you're okay?"

I nod and take the pills, grateful to have something that will at least dull the ache in my head. Not the way I wanted to spend the first part of tonight. Although being held by Mav was definitely something I didn't mind. At all.

Harden walks me to the side of the stage. "You want some tacos or something from the bar?" I shake my head and he heads off. I hope that he doesn't bring me nachos again. Or anything. I don't need to be coddled like that. I wish I could make him understand, but Harden has something about not wanting people to be hungry. I don't understand it and I don't think Hayleigh does either, because we've discussed this. It's something he keeps close to the vest.

I could eat, but I'm waiting until after the show. Mav mentioned a late dinner. I step up to the small area at the side of the stage. There's a stool here. I don't remember it from the other nights I shot the shows, so it must be there for me, but it's not where I want to be. I want to be in the pit at the front of the stage. I text Harden to see if he has an extra pass since I didn't bring my working photographer badge. I want to be front and center, so it's worth a try anyway.

I stand in front of the stool and take a few pictures of Sammy. From this angle, the stage lighting illuminates his wavy blonde hair, making it look like a bluish halo as it moves in the stage light's beam. These will be awesome shots of him. I stand as close to the side of the stage as I can get without being seen by the audience and squat to take a few pictures of Killian.

His eyes close, tongue held fast between his teeth, foot stomping in time with Sammy as he strums his bass. It's amazing how much he looks like Callum in this moment despite the shorter, darker hair. They've never looked more alike to me until just this minute.

I scoot closer to the front of the stage, trying to get a better picture of him with this new revelation. I want to capture their alikeness here. Almost as if he knew what I was trying to do, Killian turns toward me slightly and I get the exact shot I was looking for. His eyes fly open, and he sneers at me, his lip curling up in a snarl. The audience probably wonders why the hell he's making such a mean face.

My stomach drops as I grip my camera hard and jump back to the safety of the stage curtain. In the process, I end up on my ass and tangled in the bottom of the curtain. Killian's lips turn up at the corner, and he nods with an amused look before turning away from me. I gave him exactly the reaction he was hoping for.

A hand catches me under my arm and helps haul me up. My heart speeds, blood whooshing through my ears as my body starts its tensing game again.

"Geez, Kady, you okay?" Harden. I release the breath I was holding and remind myself that it's just Harden. He looks me in the eye. "You're okay?" I nod, shakily.

"You sure?" I nod again. His lips pinch down into a hard, thin line. He doesn't believe me. "You wanted this."

He slips my original Blind Rebels photo pass over my head. "It's Vic and Tanner and that Jax asshole from their security down there tonight. Try to stick closer to Vic or Tanner. I don't trust that Jax guy as far as I can throw him." I nod. I remember Jax yelling at me. He's not someone I want to tangle with. "Text if you need me. For anything." He tousles my hair again and rushes off. Darn it. Now I have to redo my ponytail.

I sit on the stool for a few minutes. My desire to photograph the band from the pit is waning. I don't want to be in Killian's direct line of sight. Plus, I don't really want to be around that Jax guy. I rub my elbow as I remember him dragging me away from the dressing room that first night. He was shouting and demanding that I answer him. When I couldn't, he got so close his breath was on my face and I couldn't breathe anymore.

During a transition between songs, Mav catches sight of me on the stool and throws a quick wink at me as he joins Killian on the drum riser, hitting the occasional cymbal with his hand while Cal does his not-so-impromptu guitar solo intro to the next song.

I finally work my way to the floor, to where Vic is standing at the metal barricade that separates the stage from the audience. I flash my pass at him and smile and he bends down to hug me and talk in my ear. "Kady! Arms up." He wraps his big arms around me and easily lifts me over the temporary metal barrier and sets me on my feet on the other side. He just likes showing off for the groupies that he's strong. Besides equipment and some cabling taped to the floor, it's empty in the pit except for Tanner at center stage and that Jax guy at stage right.

I lean against the metal barrier and lift my camera up and take some pictures of the band as a whole before zeroing in on Mav and taking a few shots of just him. I do the same with Sammy. I shoot a couple of Callum from afar, not comfortable enough to go over to his side of the stage. Then I put the camera down and just watch the show.

Their energy is contagious. The crowd behind me feeds off them and they, in turn, feed off the exuberance of the crowd. I've never realized the exchange that can happen during a live show. Sad, since I've done my share of them.

It was never like this for me, never so close to the fans, never so intimate. My live shows were a big production, which made them a colossal chore. Most shows I felt like an unfeeling puppet on stage, dressed in clothes I didn't choose, singing songs I didn't write. Dancing routines I didn't want to dance. All a necessary evil to make music.

I should have pressed more to do my own music, but I didn't want to be dropped from Monument's pop side or be branded as difficult to work with. I didn't feel a vibe with my audience like these guys do. There was never a connection like the Rebels have with their fans.

I feel it in the way the guys interact with each other, the insider smiles they shoot each other, the way they move on stage around each other but not choreographed. I see it with the way they all interact with the audience in their own way. It's an eye opener. I snap a few more shots and head back to the side stage to watch the last few songs of the set. I assume they'll do at least one encore song. Maybe two. This crowd will want as much as they can get from the band.

I return to my stool and consider going back to the dressing room for the last couple of songs. But I don't. I snap a few pictures from my seated position, but mostly I just enjoy the show.

"Thank you again, Las Vegas. We're the Blind Rebels!" Mav waves a hand, and the stage lights go down. The house lights come on as the guys leave the stage, filing toward me.

Mav throws a sweaty arm over my shoulder. "Stay for the encore. Please." He kisses my temple and returns to the band as they huddle. I watch them. They seem to be discussing something intensely, I assume the encore song, but this looks heated.

Cal steps between Mav and Killian, his hands on his brother's chest. I can't hear what they're saying because the crowd is now stomping along with their cheers, calling the band back to the stage.

Mav grabs a tech running by and says something while motioning to the stage and the tech nods and scurries off in the other direction. He returns a few minutes later with a keyboard and sets it up in front of Sammy's drum riser in the dark, just a little flashlight held in his mouth for light. This is different from the previous shows I've photographed.

The house lights go dark again, and the crowd goes crazy knowing that the band is on their way back out. First Sammy slips behind the drums. Then Kill and Cal walk out. Mav comes over to me.

"Trust me," he rasps in my ear as he squeezes my shoulder before he lopes onto center stage.

I don't know what he is up to, but when someone says trust me and has that kind of sparkle in their eye, it can't be a good thing. What the hell does he have up his sleeve?

When Mav hits the stage, the lights come on with him in the spotlight.

"You want a little more, Vegas? Is that right?" He puts his hand to his ear as if he's listening and the crowd grows even louder.

"You've been an amazing audience. So, we're going to do something a little different tonight." Again, the crowd responds with deafening cheers.

"We've been working on some new material. We'd like to perform one of the new songs we've been working on for you tonight. You want to hear something new?"

Oh shit. Oh shit. *Oh. Shit.*

Please don't be doing what I think you are about to do, Mav. Please.

The crowd is probably going crazy, but all I hear is the rushing of the blood in my ears as my heart pounds away, thumping so hard it might beat clear out of my chest.

"Anyway, we've only played this song live one other time, but not with piano. To play it right, we need a little help. I'd like you all to welcome Kadence to the stage. Kady, come on out here and play the keyboard for *our* song." Mav looks at the side of the stage to where I stand frozen and waves me out with his hand. The rest of the band looks over at me. Sammy also beckons me with a jerk of his head.

Oh, hell no! I shake my head. No way am I going out on that stage. I stay rooted in place, feet refusing to move. Harden is next to me. "Kady, go. You can do this." He puts a hand on the small of my back and tries to push me out toward Mav. I lean back on my heels, resisting Harden's little push.

I can't go out there! Why the hell is Harden encouraging this?! I need the fuck out of here, but Harden's hand is firm on my back. I look for something to grab onto so he can't force me out there. Something I can anchor myself to. There is nothing. I can't even reach the freaking stage curtain and I'm too far from the lighting trellis to be able to use it.

"Kady's a little shy. Let's see if I can convince her to come out." Mav clips his mic back into the stand and heads over to me as the cheering of the fans grows louder. His eyes are soft and his expression welcoming as he reaches me and puts his arms around my shoulder. Harden's hand still pushes firmly at the small of my back.

Mav's warm breath is against my ear. "It's just a little piano. You know this song. You won't see the crowd. I promise. It'll just be us and you on piano. Let them hear our song the way you hear it in your head, Kady." I shake my head, tears welling in my eyes. I can't do this. He doesn't understand. I can't. My stomach gives an acidy churn.

"Look at Cal and Sammy. They're waiting for you to take your seat at the keyboard. It's all set up. Just watch Cal the whole time. It's you and Cal and me. And Sammy. And Kill." He nods at Harden and replaces Harden's arm with his own around my waist. "Let's go, Kady. The guys are waiting."

A tech runs up to me and sets me up with a set of monitors in my ears. "You'll only hear the piano, Mav, and Cal in here. Okay? They feel okay?" I nod as he tucks the receiver pack into the back of my pants. Out of the corner of my eye, I see him give Mav a nod.

"All set. Let's do this, Kady. One song." Mav takes a step forward and my traitorous feet actually follow him. Don't they know that this will be a disaster? I've only played this song a couple of times. It's a full house out there.

Mav leans in as we approach the keyboard. "It's just us. Eyes on Cal till you're comfortable. You got this, Kady." Mav escorts me to the bench in front of the keyboard and waits as I sit and settle in. I look up at Cal, who faces me at the keyboard instead of the audience. His eyes hold mine as my heart roars in my ears. He approaches and stands close to the keyboard. In-two-three-four. Hold-two-three-four. Out-two-three-four-five-six. Cal seems to notice my breathing and nods, eyes still holding mine. He mouths, "You got this."

"Hell yeah, Kady!" Sammy yells from my left, his voice muffled by the monitors in my ears, but I can still hear his excitement.

"Okay, Vegas, this is called 'Star Chaser.' Let us know what you think." Mav's voice is clear in my monitors.

"Two, three, four" He counts softly for my benefit, I am sure. Being so close to Sammy, I feel the rhythmic vibrations of him bringing in the drums more than I hear it. I close my eyes and my fingers just take over the song. Cal joins at just the right spot and Mav comes in perfectly as I play, his words laying over my piano. "Star chaser, heartbreaker. You tore me open and made me bleed..." His rasp in my ear melts into my piano and Cal's guitar. Mav's right, it *is* just like I hear it in my head.

My fingers play the song automatically, like I've been practicing it for years, just like my go-to Bach piece. After the first couple of lines, I open my eyes. Cal's still standing in front of me. He looks at me and nods and lifts his lips in a brief, encouraging smile. I *can* do this. I am doing this. I nod at Cal, letting him know I've got it. That I'm okay.

He turns to the crowd and moves up to the front of the stage to join Mav and Kill. We're approaching the part that was giving them trouble. Mav sits on the edge of the bench, his back to my side, so he faces the audience. I hear him in my monitors and feel him leaning against me as he slows down the lyrics. "Star chaser, star chaser, what happened? Did you forget my love? Star chaser, why me? Why me?" He jumps up and I imagine him kicking his leg toward the audience as Sammy picks the tempo back up, the bass drum thumping with my heart, encouraging my fingers to speed up as well, until the song wraps up.

Holy shit! I just did that. I look down at my hands on the keys. They shake slightly even though I played the song perfectly.

I just played piano onstage with the Blind Rebels in front of however many people are crammed in here. I breathe in and out slowly through my nose.

"So, Vegas, did you like it?" I pull my earpieces out in time to hear the crowd go completely wild.

I turn to look at Mav, silhouetted by the spotlight on him, darkening the inside of HARD so much I can't see it.

"Maybe it will end up on our new album, then." Mav nods, egging on the crowd. They go crazy again.

"Love ya, Vegas. See ya next time!"

Sammy comes out from behind the drums with some drumsticks in his hand. He stops at the bench and leans down to speak in my ear.

"That was freaking awesome, Kady. Stand with us at the front." He offers his empty hand and I take it.

He walks me up to the stage, positioning me between him and Mav. With Cal on Mav's other side and Kill on the other side of Sammy, we bow as the house lights come on, revealing a totally packed house. Harden is filming and Jax is clapping as they stand in the pit. The fans beyond the pit are cheering, yelling, and clapping. The chances of any of them recognizing me are probably pretty slim, but it's still a possibility.

Sammy lightly tosses his sticks out over their heads to the audience, while both Kill and Cal toss out some picks.

Mav puts his arm across my shoulder and leans into my temple. "I knew you could do it, Kady. That was amazing."

He plants a soft kiss before we file offstage, with Mav's arm still across my shoulder. A tech runs up and takes the guitars from Cal and Killian, and another walks by removing our monitors.

I still can't believe I just did that. I shake my head. That was *me* playing piano on stage with the Blind Rebels, playing in front of that crazy audience.

I feel light and giddy now that it's over, like I might float away if I jump.

We head into the dressing room. Everyone moves to their dressing tables and towels off. Cal and Mav opt to change shirts.

"We gotta meet the VIP fans, but there are only seventy-five of them tonight in the VIP, so we won't be long, okay?" Mav leans over me on the couch and plants a kiss on my head. "Don't disappear on me. Dinner after, right?" I nod.

It dawns on me that I have no idea where my phone and camera are. I look around the dressing room. Not here. I don't remember what I did with them when I was suddenly foisted onstage. Maybe by the stool?

I get up to see if I left them on the stool when Harden sticks his head in.

"You were so awesome, kiddo." He approaches me for a hug, arms open in front of him. "You really helped them write that?" I shake my head no, but without my phone, I can't explain.

"No?" He looks at me for an explanation I can't give. "Oh shit. Your phone and camera. I put them in my office on my way to get my phone to film that."

I follow Harden to the office. He hands me my phone, and I see that Hayleigh has left three messages. I don't look at them.

Me: I didn't help write it. I helped transition the music, so it fit the lyrics better.

I shrug it off as I hit send. It's not like I wrote the music or the lyrics. It was just a slight rearranging of what they already had. It was no big deal, but holy crap, I was onstage performing it with the Blind Rebels.

"Well, it was a great song, whatever you did." I look at Harden. "It was. I'm not just saying it because it was you up there."

He blows out a breath and looks away from me. "Don't be mad, but I recorded it and sent it to Hayleigh."

I shake my head to let Harden know I'm not mad.

"Did you know they were planning this?"

I shake my head vehemently and Harden chuckles that deep chuckle of his.

"I didn't think so." He pats my shoulder. "I knew you could do it. I would have helped him carry you out there. Just saying." Harden shrugs an arm at me.

"You heading out?"

Me: Mav wants me to wait. We're getting dinner.

Harden nods as he reads my message as if it's a common occurrence that I play a show to a packed house and then go off to dinner with the lead singer of the Blind Rebels afterwards. "Well, have a good time. I gotta get back out there."

"Good song." He pats my shoulder as he goes by.

Ɍ

MAV SLIDES into a red vinyl bench seat opposite of me in the booth of the nearest greasy spoon. I'm starving and so glad we're here instead of some overpriced casino restaurant.

Me: They have great breakfasts here.

Mav smiles at my text and scans the standard diner fare on the menu quickly before looking at me. "What are you having?"

Me: Usually, I get the bacon omelet, but today I want the straw- berry Belgian waffle with two scrambled eggs and a side of bacon.

"I'm sensing a trend here. Fan of bacon, I take it?" He chuckles.

Me: I never used to like it, but within the last year or so I can't get enough. Weird, huh?

His eyes sparkle at my answer. He's about to respond when the waitress comes to take our order. She barely glances at me, her eyes glued to Mav as he orders for us both. If she's not careful, she'll drool into the soda she just set down in front of him.

I shake my head slightly and just watch the show. It's blatantly obvious she knows exactly who Mav is. When she finally leaves, I text him.

Me: Do you get tired of being fawned over like you're the most amazing thing ever?

He smiles, but not his eyes, as they are slightly weary. "It gets tiresome, but I try to remember the reason why I'm in this position, because of the fans. But, yeah, on dates and stuff, it can be a pain."

It makes perfect sense to me. Back in the day, I used to live off being fawned over. I loved the attention of being Kandi, being different, being special. Now I'd rather fade into the background, but being onstage with the Rebels tonight felt good. Nerve-wracking, but good. I can't even fathom a world where performing could feel that exciting, but it so was.

"Penny for your thoughts, Kady." Mav pushes a penny across the table at me with a wink.

Me: How was I onstage tonight? Honestly.

The minute I hit send, I grimace internally. Do I really want to know? What if he thinks my performance was terrible, or that calling me to the stage was a mistake? He had to spring it on me though, because if he'd asked me in advance, I wouldn't have done it. I wouldn't have even shown up despite desperately wanting to see him.

"Your playing was flawless. It added such depth to the song live. It's probably hard for you to tell with the monitors in, but it was much better than when we played it a few nights ago without piano. It was well received from the VIP fans we spoke with after the show too, and a few had been to both shows. They had nothing but nice things to say about your performance." I sense a *but* coming, and my stomach gets acidy.

"Your stage presence could be improved, but that was mostly nerves. I did surprise you, after all." He pats my hand. "I just hope you're not mad at me for dragging you on stage."

Me: Furious.

"Yeah, you look it." He fiddles with his straw. "Would you do it again? Play with us on stage?" I look up at him, thinking he's joking. His chocolate brown eyes stare at me with an intense sincerity. He's not messing with me. He means it.

Me: Maybe.

He smiles and rubs his hands together as our food is delivered. We enjoy our breakfast, until he tries to steal a piece of my bacon. I slap his hand away and shove the piece in my mouth practically whole. He laughs so loud the noise turns the heads of the only other table of customers. As we finish up our late-night meals, he tells me stories from the band's early days, and I feel like I know each of the members a little better.

As I'm eating my last bites of English muffin, I consider telling him about who I was. I'm surprised he hasn't had questions. He carte blanche accepted my musical abilities. I feel like a fraud with him not realizing that I used to be pop sensation Kandi Matthews. I'm just about to type out an explanation when he throws a handsome tip on the table and settles our bill at the cash register.

"How tired are you?" He grabs my hand and leads me out to his Corvette.

Me: Not at all. Weird cuz I've been up since 7. You'd think I would be.

He grins after reading my message. "I was hoping you'd say that. You're probably still wired from being on stage. It's the best feeling in the world. A total rush. There's nothing like that feeling. At least not for me. I live for it. It's my favorite part of being a musician."

He opens my door and deposits me in the passenger seat. "I want to show you something." He heads off towards his house by Lake Las Vegas.

I watch the lights of the city go by as he speeds through the streets. He holds my hand and rubs his thumb over it occasionally when he's not shifting. It's comforting when he does little things like this and warms my insides in a way I'm not familiar with.

When we get to his house, we enter through the mudroom. He immediately takes his shoes off. I follow his lead and pull my Chucks off and set them next to his boots.

"Make yourself comfortable. Grab a beverage from the fridge if you want. I'll be right back." He bounds up the stairs two at a time while I settle on one of the overstuffed leather couches. About a minute later, he comes back down looking relaxed, having changed from his leather pants into heather gray sweats. He holds a pair of headphones and an iPad.

He hands me the headphones. "This is the song we played tonight, as I recorded it out on the patio when you first made your suggestion. You had taken Gibson to change him, remember?"

I nod, and he plays the song. It sounds great for a rough recording on an outdoor patio.

"Okay. Now this one is the one our sound tech recorded of our encore tonight. He texted it to me. Really listen to it." He switches the recording and plays the encore song from hours ago.

I played it a little different than Mav did when he was on the keys. We're both playing by ear, and I'm sure that's the real difference. I motion for him to go back to the first recording and then back to the one from tonight so I can hear them again.

The differences are subtle. Neither recording is wrong, just slightly different.

"Which version do you like better? Don't take into account the shoddy recording qualities. They're both just rough cuts." He looks at me, then his iPad, waiting for my answer.

Me: Mine.

I am not being conceited or smug. I just prefer the way I played it. The sounds blend better with his voice and the guitar.

"Me too. Can you read music?"

Me: Piano since I was a kid, remember.

"Will you write it down for me? I want to record it like you did it tonight. No! Wait. Even better. Come to the studio tomorrow and lay the track down yourself. You'll get royalties from the song for helping." He immediately starts texting someone.

Me: The studio?

He nods. "Darren booked us some time in a studio here in Vegas. We've been rough cutting songs as we write them, so there is less to do at the label's studio when we get back to L.A. The label sorts through the roughs and decides which ones we'll record for the album. I mean, we get a say too. They want the new Blind Rebels album to come out as soon as possible."

Makes sense that the label would want to strike while the iron is hot with these shows they are doing in Vegas. It would be stupid not to consider how popular these shows have been, but that just means Mav's leaving and I don't want to think about that yet.

Me: I don't need the royalties, but I'd be happy to come to the studio tomorrow.

His smile lights up his face, including that sparkle in his eye. "Great. I'll pick you up about 4:00? We don't have a show, so we'll start recording around 5:30 or so. We'll grab a bite to eat, and the lawyer will meet us at the studio. You'll have to sign a release for us to use your version."

My eyes must widen at the mention of the lawyer. "Don't worry, it'll all be on the up and up, I'll make sure. If you want someone to come read over the contract first, you are more than welcome."

Me: I'll scan it and if there is something I don't like, I'll ask. I'm pretty adept at reading legalese.

His grin is wide again, almost like it was the day of the barbecue.

"Now I have another favor to ask." I lift my eyebrows at him as if to say *what now?*

"There is another song I'd like your take on. I'll send you the rough mp3 from when Sammy and I worked it out one night at the studio. I want you to play with it and see what you bring back. Can you do that? Do you want to borrow a guitar or something to play on?"

Me: I'll do it. I have a guitar. And if I need a piano, there's the one in the lobby.

"This is going to be so awesome. It's something only Sammy has seen so far. I played guitar, and he played drums and the studio tech played bass on the rough."

He texts the song to me. When I go to play it, he puts his hand over mine. "Not yet. When you go home." Mavrick Slater's cheeks turn pink. The lyrical mastermind behind one of the most famous rock bands in this era is embarrassed by his own rough draft.

I nod my agreement and put my phone on the table because the temptation to listen is overwhelming, especially now that he's told me he doesn't want me listening until he's out of my sight.

He pulls me onto his lap. "Thank you."

As he plants a soft kiss on the end of my nose, I lean into him, lightly running my lips against the underside of his stubbled jaw. I shift, so I am straddling his legs between mine like we did in my office. He's warm and I have to keep myself from running my hands underneath the back of his soft t-shirt. Instead, I press my front against his and nuzzle into his neck, peppering it with kisses.

He groans in appreciation.

The solidness of his chest feels good against mine, firm and steady. It's almost comforting, but also stirring up an intense and unfamiliar yearning. I want him. I want him to help me remember and forget at the same time.

I want to feel him, all of him.

Chapter 21

Mavrick

I'm not sure if Kady wants me because she needs to expend the pent-up energy left from being on stage or if she really has feelings for me, but there is no mistaking she wants me as much as I want her in this moment. She pushes herself against me and wraps her arms around my neck to give herself better leverage as she grinds herself against me. It's a clear indication of where this night is going.

I shouldn't want this, not with Kady. It could blur too many lines, but the feel of her against me is consuming. I don't just want her, but I need her. And I'm a man who needs nothing.

Her fingers worm around at the top of my sweatpants until she works my shirt out so she can run her hand up my abdomen. Her warm, soft touch about does me in. When I feel her lips smile against my neck, I can't help the growl that escapes right before she surprises me with a fiery, all-consuming kiss. She's trying to tell me she's all in, but not here. Not on a freaking leather couch in a rental house.

I clutch her ass to me and stand. She makes a surprised squeak, but wraps her legs around my waist, locking them at the small of my back. Her arms go around my neck.

"Not here."

Somewhere on the stairs, I lose my shirt completely thanks to her deft fingers. For someone who can't talk, Kady's making it very clear what she wants.

She hooks her arms under mine and sucks my neck. Her nipples pebble through her shirt as they rub against my chest. The friction sends a jolt right to my balls.

I kick my partially closed bedroom door open. As much as I want to just toss her on the bed, I take care to set her gently on the end of it. She leans back on her elbows, legs dangling over the edge of the bed. Her skin is flushed, her dilated eyes fix on me.

She licks those luscious lips of hers. Sitting up, she bends to pull off her socks when I move to stand between her legs at the end of the bed. She looks up at me, sock forgotten, and wraps her arms around my waist and plants soft kisses on my abs. They tighten as my cock begs to be freed so it can join the party.

She looks up at me, resting her chin above the band of my sweats. She's so trusting.

Fuck, this is killing me. It's like I'm a damn teenager again. If I'm not careful, this will end in my pants before we've done anything.

Finger under her chin, I lift her face up so our eyes can meet, her green to my brown. "Before we go any further, I need to know you're absolutely, completely sure." I gaze directly into her eyes.

She locks her green eyes to mine and nods a slow, deliberate nod. She's sure. Thank fuck.

Bending, I pull her face to mine and kiss her slowly as we lie back on the bed, with me hovering over her. I cage her head between my hands and pepper her smooth jaw with kisses.

She wraps her legs around my thighs and pulls me towards her. We have entirely too many clothes on. Her eyes roam my chest as she pulls her lower lip between her teeth. I stand to slide my sweatpants down.

She smiles.

I grab her hips and pull her towards me so that her ass sits on the very edge. I remove a sock, depositing a kiss on the arch of her foot. I repeat it with her other foot.

She watches every move I make with a heated stare as she lays propped up so she can watch the show.

Undoing her pants, I see her lacy underwear peeking out and groan. Fuck, she's sexy.

She squirms slightly as I lay my hand on the sweet skin above the line of her lacy underwear. So soft. I run both hands up the plane of her abdomen under her shirt, each grabbing a breast over her bra and giving them a slight squeeze. Such perfection.

As I do, she drops her head back to the mattress and arches her back slightly. I continue to run my hands up to her shoulders, pushing her shirt up as I go. Her skin is warm and so creamy soft. "Hands up."

She wordlessly answers immediately by lifting her arms so I can slip her shirt over her head and toss it over my shoulder.

She moves to unhook her bra behind her back, but I stop her.

"Let me." I reach behind her and unclasp the bra. I kiss her shoulder and neck as I slip the strap off one side.

She holds her breath as I slip the second strap down her shoulder. She flushes and closes her eyes as I slip it off and toss it in the same direction as her discarded top.

I stand, looking down over her. "So fuckin' beautiful."

Her eyes are squeezed shut.

There's a raised circular scar at the top of her right breast near her armpit. Is she embarrassed? She shouldn't be. She's so beautiful, I can't stand not touching her for another moment.

I lean back over her and kiss her nose. "Look at me."

She shakes her head slightly.

"Look at me." I growl it the second time. I need that eye-to-eye connection. I need her to see that she is gorgeous, scar and all. She's so damn beautiful to me.

Her lashes fan open, and those green eyes stare into mine.

"You're so beautiful." I lean in and lay a feather-light kiss on the raised, smooth scar.

She gasps, her hand moving to rest lightly on the back of my head. This close, I see a similar scar further down her right side. I kiss that one, too. And a third one peeking out of her waistband on her hip gets a kiss too. My stomach drops slightly with the realization that they probably are part of what made my Kady silent.

She closes her eyes again, but I don't want her in that dark place. I want here back here.

"Kady, look at me, beautiful."

Her eyes open, and I kiss my way over to her belly button, distracting her from herself. Bringing her back to the here and now, I suck her hard nipple into my mouth, while I tease the other between my forefinger and thumb. Her soft moans urge me on as she arches her back, thrusting her chest up at me. I need inside her. Now.

Kady lets out a disappointed squeak when I finally drag myself away from her breasts and stand again between her legs. "Need these off. Now." Hooking my thumbs into the belt loops of her unbuttoned jeans, I yank them down, her underwear going with them.

She kicks her foot against her opposite knee to help me get her pants off. I discard them and reach up to my nightstand and retrieve a condom from the box in the top drawer.

She sits up suddenly, reaching for the foil package in my hand. I can't give it to her. If she does it, her touch will set me off and this'll be over.

"Not this time, beautiful." I sheath myself quickly as she watches, worrying her lip between her teeth with a bite.

I lean her back onto the bed and place her legs over my hips. I'm right there, so close I can feel the heat from her core.

"I'll try to be gentle, baby." I lock eyes with her, needing to keep tabs on Kady as much as I can. I want this to be good for her. She nods slightly and scoots closer to me, so impatient.

I inch in a little at a time, my eyes glued to hers for any sign of discomfort or regret. She fits me perfectly. I can't help my rumbling groan as I hold back from slamming into her. Just giving her a little. At. A. Time. *Oh, fuck yeah.*

Once I'm completely seated, I hold still. Her eyes hood as she adjusts to me. She swivels her hips as she suddenly sits up. Shit, the way she squeezes me, I almost lose it right there. "Baby, hold on for a second."

She pulls me to her and tries to lie down. She acts like she wants more of me. The contact. Skin on skin.

I move us slowly, with her legs still clasped over my hips until I am laying on top of her, careful to keep my weight on my arms so I don't crush her.

She starts to move under me. Subtle swivels of her hips against me, slow at first. Urging me to move. They get needier, faster. She stares at me, frustrated with my stillness. "I need just a second. You feel so fuckin' good."

I slowly pull back, then thrust into her as she continues to rise to meet me.

Guttural sounds of frustration and rapture erupt from deep within her throat as we work together to find a mutual rhythm. Her nails score my back, pressing me to her as her breasts heave against my chest.

So fucking kinetic. I increase my tempo to keep up with her hip thrusts. I'm not going to last much longer. I squeeze my eyes shut. Football. I don't give a shit about football. Fuck. I need something. Guitar tabs for the new song. She tightens against me. She's fighting it too. Dammit, someone's got to give.

"Kady, I need you to let go, baby." I snake my hand between us and brush against her clit. Her eyes fly open, as does her mouth, in a silent 'O' as her whole body tenses and tightens around me.

"Oh, fuck." I hook my arms under her shoulders and pull her tight to me and that sets her off. She clenches with the first wave of her release at the same time I let go.

"Kady." She arches her back against my hold, then bucks one more time back to me before she bites down hard on my shoulder.

I feel the weightlessness of my release, holding her firmly to me until she relaxes against me. She curls her head into the crook of my neck, and I gently lay her back down on the bed and slip out. I pinch off the condom and take it to the bathroom to toss it in the trash.

I return to Kady with a warm washcloth to clean her. We get under the bedding, and I cover us over. She snuggles into me as I pull her to me, kissing her head and breathing in her tropical shampoo.

"You okay?" She smiles against my chest and nods vigorously with a little giggle.

Chapter 22

Kadence

Feeling smothered makes me wake up. I'm hot, naked, and wrapped completely in Mav.

Mmm... Mav. Last night was... well, there are no words for what last night was, or too many words. Amazing. Hot. Sexy. Desire. Connection.

Connection. Crap, that's the biggest problem. I've fallen hard. Why the hell did I let myself fall for Mav at all? It's reckless to love someone like him. He's a force to be reckoned with on stage. He knows who he is and what he wants out of life, and he'll be leaving soon to go after it.

What the hell am I doing?

He brings things out in me that I thought were dead and gone. He brought back my music. Like right now, I want nothing more than to find my phone and listen to the song he sent me, work it over in my head.

It might be someone else's music right now, but I feel my own creativity effervescing under my skin, trying to break out. My own music. He makes me want to dig out my guitar from the spare bedroom to play and write.

I used to write all kinds of music. Most of it hasn't seen the light of day. It was my way of working through things. Until that night. Until I woke up at the hospital alone. Then again, when Hayleigh was there... I blink away the memories quickly before they suck me in.

Shit! Hayleigh. She probably expected me home, and here I am, wrapped up in Mav. God only knows what time it is. I don't want her to worry. Although apparently, she can just track my phone and see I'm at Mav's, but I should still send her a text. She left me several after the show last night and I didn't even bother to read them, let alone respond.

How do I extract myself from Mav? He's wrapped around me like ivy on a brick wall. I shimmy slightly to see if I can slip out undetected, but he strengthens his grip around me.

"What are you overthinking so early in the morning, Kady?" he mutters into his pillow, not moving a muscle except the ones that clench me to him. He's at an unfair advantage since I can't really answer him.

I wiggle more, and he moans and finally releases me. He rolls onto his back and throws an arm over his eyes. I slide out of the bed and pad off to the bathroom. Even though I'm completely naked, I don't feel shy. If anything, after last night, I feel emboldened.

I use the facilities and notice at some point that Mav put out a new toothbrush for me. I brush my teeth, and walking back through his room, I grab his discarded t-shirt from last night and pull it on so I can go search for my phone downstairs.

I find it on the coffee table in the living room where our make-out session started.

Hayleigh: Holy shit, Kay.

Hayleigh: That was amazing. You! Onstage with the Blind Rebels!!!

Hayleigh: I still can't believe it.

Hayleigh: I assume you're spending the night. Be safe. Text me when you can.

All from last night.

Me: Sorry I didn't respond. Still at Mavs. Be home later.

Hayleigh: I'll be here. See you then.

I return to Mav who's still in bed but is now propped on his side, facing the door.

"There you are. I was just about to start searching for you." He assesses me. "You look good in my shirt." My cheeks heat, but I don't understand why I'm blushing because I feel good in his shirt too.

"Come here." He motions for me to join him back in bed. Slipping between the navy sheets, I lie on my side, facing him. His lips curl in a soft smile as he leans forward and kisses me gently on the lips. "Good morning, beautiful."

I mouth, "Morning" back to him.

"Did you text Hayleigh?" He glances at the phone still in my hand. I nod as I set it on his bedside table.

"Good. I texted her after you drifted off last night. I didn't want her to worry too much." It's a sweet gesture on his part. He understands Hayleigh worries about me, and he wants to make sure that she's okay because he knows she's important to me. I reach up and cup his now stubbly cheek and run my thumb along his jaw. He leans into my hand and kisses my palm.

This is how I want to remember Mav, sweet and tender, not as the guy who is going to break my heart when he returns to his rock star life in L.A. There is no doubt in my mind that my heart will absolutely shatter. It's just a matter of when and into how many pieces.

He takes my hand from his face and uses it to pull me to him. "So beautiful." His brown eyes assess my face before he leans in to kiss me, pushing his tongue into my mouth. Our tongues dance as he pulls me closer and rolls with me until I am on top of him.

I giggle. The sound actually comes out again and echoes off the walls.

His lips curl into a smile, and his eyes sparkle as he looks at me. "I love that sound."

I love it too. Each time he makes me giggle or laugh, makes me hope that maybe I won't be silent forever.

He runs his hand under my shirt. He caresses up my torso, stopping at my breasts. His calloused thumbs rub tight circles over my nipples.

I grab the hem of the shirt and pull it off. He stiffens against my back as I dampen against him.

His shoulder sports the red marks from my bite last night. I can't believe I did that. I run my hand over it softly. He grabs my hand and kisses the back of it. I left a mark. My head shakes.

"Don't." He tucks a finger under my chin and pulls my gaze back to his. "It doesn't hurt. It was sexy as fuck when you bit me." I feel my cheeks heat hot, but I giggle again.

"Mmm... Kady, you're so sexy and that cute fuckin' giggle. I love it." He makes me this way. I've never felt more sexy, more sensual, than I do with Mav.

He reaches and digs through the drawer until he pulls a condom out. "Wanna do the honors this time?"

He lies back, hands behind his head, a relaxed smile on his face.

I shift off him and roll the condom slowly down his length, giving it a squeeze when I reach the base. He lifts his hips off the bed and moans.

I align myself so he's right there at my opening. He lifts his hips, trying to engage. I lower myself on him.

"Oh, fuck, Kaydeee." He draws out my name as I seat myself.

Gripping his muscular shoulders, I lift back up and then slide slowly down again. I can't help but throw my head back as I feel every inch of him.

He grips my hips to steady me and sets our lightning pace as I ride him. One hand slips down my thigh and teases my clit.

I'm closer than I thought. I tilt my hips downward and add a swivel.

"Mmmmm. So good," he groans, the light sheen of sweat on him reflects in the morning sun making him shine.

He quickens the tempo, and it pushes me over the edge. He holds me tight at my hip with one hand as he supports my back with the other.

As I ride the waves of my orgasm, he lets loose with his own.

I am completely sated and limp.

He leans back and holds me to him as we catch our breath, running a hand up and down my back lightly while we are still joined. His heart races in his chest as I lay against him.

He kisses the crown of my head lightly. "Oh, Kady, what are you doing to me?" His whisper is so soft I barely hear it.

R

"I'll see you this afternoon?" Mav walks me to my car that's still in the parking lot at HARD.

I nod. "Good. I'll pick you up at 4:30." He leans in and kisses me first on the lips and then next to my ear.

"Last night, this morning, it was all amazing. Thank you." His words are hushed, quiet in the empty lot. Then he presses another soft kiss next to my ear. He pulls back and watches me slip into the driver's seat of my Scion.

With one arm resting on the open door and the other on the roof of my car, he leans in. "Drive safe. See you tonight." He presses one more sweet kiss to my temple before he shuts the door and watches me leave the parking lot.

When I head upstairs to my apartment, I have only two things on my mind. First, I want to pull my acoustic out and restring it. It's been over two years since I played it and I want to have it handy. I think Mav might be right about my music, and I want it ready when inspiration does hit.

Also, I want to listen to the song that Mav sent to my phone. I have plenty of time to listen to it and work through any suggestions I have, maybe even in time to give him feedback tonight after I play at the studio for them.

Walking through the door, the sweet smells of cinnamon, vanilla, and lots of sugar swirl around me. Hayleigh's baking. She only bakes when she's happy. I wonder if something good happened at work. Shucking my shoes off at the door, I wander into the kitchen.

"Kady!" Hayleigh comes around the kitchen bar and arms spread wide, warning me of the upcoming embrace, flour going everywhere. She hugs me hard and rocks me back and forth. Happiness radiates off her with the megawatt grin she's giving me, although maybe she's just hyped up on sugar.

"You were amazing last night." It almost seems like a lifetime ago that I was on stage playing 'Star Chaser' with the Blind Rebels. I'm sure she can sense the uncertainty in my smile, because just thinking about it makes my stomach flutter with nerves all over again, as if I were about to be dragged out onstage.

"Have you watched the video of your performance?" I shake my head and reach for my phone and text Hayleigh my reply.

Me: I'm not sure I want to. Not yet.

Mav said my stage presence could be improved, so I really don't want to watch it. I was so terrified that I don't remember most of the performance. I remember Mav walking me out onto the stage. I locked eyes with Callum over the keyboard, steadying myself on the bench before the song started. And then Sammy was escorting me to the edge of the stage to bow with the band. Everything in between is a blur of sound and lights.

Hayleigh nods. "Okay. I have it if you want to watch it." She looks at me. "You weren't as bad as you think, Kay. It was awesome. I'm so glad Harden caught it on video. If I'd known, I would have come."

Me: I didn't know either.

Me: I was backstage one minute and Mav was walking me towards the keyboard the next.

Me: It wasn't planned.

"You did look completely mortified when Mav escorted you from the side of the stage," she agrees after reading them. "Anyway, I made your favorite coconut macadamia cupcakes with vanilla icing."

Apparently, I am the good thing that has her baking up a storm. "I also made chocolate chip cookies, and some oatmeal raisin are just about to come out of the oven." I look at her and she giggles and shrugs.

"I was excited to see you, and I wanted to make you your favorite cupcakes. Then I decided to make cookies for Harden, but you can always sneak a couple if you want." She winks at me.

Me: Mav sent me a song he wants my opinion on later tonight.

Me: I'm going to work on that.

Me: I might pull out my acoustic guitar.

She grins the biggest smile I've seen from Hayleigh in years. "Okay. I'll probably be going out in a bit."

Me: I'll be with Mav this evening.

"I figured." She grins, her eyes crinkling up. "So how was last night? And I'm not talking about playing on stage."

My cheeks warm with her insinuation. I understand exactly what she wants to know, and I'm not talking about it.

Me: I don't kiss and tell.

She scoffs at my message. "Since when? And something tells me a hell of a lot more than kissing went on, missy." She's smiling that huge goofy smile again.

I shrug. I really don't want to go there right now with

Hayleigh. My guitar is calling me from down the hall. She's begging me for new strings. I look towards the spare bedroom where she sits in her case.

"Just answer me this. Was it good?" You have to give it to her, Hayleigh doesn't give up easily.

I nod at her.

She squeals, "I knew it!" at a decibel level that could cause deafness in small children. I just walk off, shaking my head as I go. I can't believe she didn't realize I was wearing Mav's shirt. Or maybe she did.

R

MY PHONE'S text alert startles my concentration over my guitar.

Mav: 30-minute warning, beautiful.

Shit, I've been pouring over this new song of Mav's for hours and didn't even realize it. I vaguely remember Hayleigh telling me she was leaving. Time always goes by quickly when I'm concentrating on something.

It didn't help that after I restrung my guitar, I got caught up reacquainting myself with her. It's been ages since I played, back when I used to write songs that I knew would never see the light of day. I wrote them anyway because they gave me a release that nothing else did.

I toss my phone on my bed and go to my closet. I should change out of Mav's shirt if I'm going to the studio. I wonder who'll be there tonight? It could just be me and Mav and whoever they are using to engineer while they are in Vegas. Other tracks could already be laid.

I aim for comfort, picking a loose-fitting purple blouse with a black tank underneath. I swipe some mascara and eye shadow on. Pulling together my notes about the song Mav is calling "Incredible Without Trying," I shove them in my small backpack purse along with my wallet and phone. All ready.

I grab my favorite hoodie just in case I get cold in the studio, then head downstairs.

Mav strolls into the lobby just as the elevator doors open to let me out. He's dressed in full rock star attire and turning the heads of nearly everyone in the lobby. His long bangs are pulled out of his eyes by the mirrored aviator sunglasses he has casually thrown up on his head like an afterthought. His bright red shirt has only the last two buttons done and is semi-tucked into black leather pants. Black boots adorned with silver chains finish off his look. He sees me and smiles, showing all his white shiny teeth. I call it his rock star smile.

"Kady!" He says my name loudly as he throws a bangled, tattooed arm over my shoulder and leans down to press a quick kiss to my head. "Beautiful, as always."

We start toward the door as people in the lobby again stop whatever they were doing to watch us as we stroll out. Mav opens my door to his Corvette that's parked in the red zone right outside the lobby.

He then slides into the driver's seat and grins at me. "Sometimes, Kady, you just have to make an exit." He winks.

He drives us to an industrial complex at the edge of the desert and pulls into a spot next to a Mercedes sedan I haven't seen before. "The lawyer's waiting for us. If you read anything in the contract that makes you uncomfortable, text me and we'll go over it and let the lawyer know. I want this to work for you, Kady, not just for us." I nod and we get out of his car. He offers me his hand as we head inside.

Despite the inconspicuous industrial gray outside of the building, the inside is comfortable in a funky, artsy way. The floors in the lobby are polished concrete. There is a sleek reception desk that is empty. A few red and yellow boxy chairs are arranged in a semicircle around a white shag area carpet with a slick black table. He leads me past the reception area, down a hall to a small room with a table. A short, chubby man in an expensive suit stands up and shoves a hand at Mav. His short dark hair is parted on the side and slicked over.

"Mr. Slater. Nice to see you. I have the label's paperwork here for Ms. Matthews. It's a standard studio-musician contract." I feel Mav stiffen as he releases the hand of the lawyer.

"Ms. Matthews is not a studio musician. She's a songwriter. That should be reflected in the contract." Mav's jaw is clamped so tight, I'm surprised his teeth don't crack.

"I was told she was here to play piano on the rough cuts of a few tracks." The man reaches for a folder in his briefcase on the table. Mav stares him down.

"You heard wrong. It's much more than a studio musician playing on a few songs that may or may not make an album. She's been giving invaluable input into the creation of some of the songs." His voice is steady, and his jaw is set hard. "I told Darren this already. It shouldn't be a surprise."

"Give me a few minutes, Mr. Slater. My assistant is back in L.A. with our standard contracts on file. I'll be right back." He leaves us in the room with his cell phone already to his ear before he closes the door behind him.

"Fucking Darren." Mav shakes his head. "This has his name all over it."

Me: Hey, it's not a big deal.

My message hits his phone, and he reads it over. I squeeze his forearm.

"It's a big fucking deal, Kady." His angry tone makes me jump. "You don't know Darren. He'd take advantage of his own mother if he thought it would net him a few bucks." Mav shakes his head. "I will not let him screw you out of your due credit. You deserve it. You deserve the proper protections and credit on the album."

He doesn't seem to understand that this song is still his

song. I don't know that my text will convince him, but I hit send anyway.

Me: But it's your song. I just tweaked it a little.

His dark brown eyes stare at me, and he shakes his head. "Call it what you want, Kady, it's still developmental. It's song-writing."

I sit in one of the chairs around the small table, but Mav continues to stand, pacing the room. He grabs his phone. "I'll be just outside. Do not sign anything without me." I nod and Mav stalks out of the room in much the same manner the lawyer did.

I'd help without a stupid contract. I'm not doing it for money or fame. I did it because it was helping them. I don't need the contracts and lawyers and record labels. I lived this life once. It's not something I enjoyed.

The lawyer returns, and when his tongue swipes his lip, he reminds me of a snake with his beady little black eyes. "Ms. Matthews, I have the new contract." I grab my phone and type out a message to show him.

M: Mav said to wait until he gets back.

"That's your prerogative, Ms. Matthews, but Mr. Slater is not a lawyer, and I know that this isn't your first recording contract, so you'll understand it." His eyes flash with a familiarity that has me squirming in my seat as he slides the packet towards me.

I start to read the contract over. It seems fairly standard, and the royalty share is more than what I would've asked for. I'm just about to sign it so I can go find Mav when I see a clause about Darren and Monument Records. I stop and read over it a little closer.

What the actual fuck? They think I will give Darren a twenty percent finder's fee on any current or future recordings that I make money from? And give Monument Records first rights of refusal for anything I write over the next seven years?

Fuck that. I grab my phone just as Mav saunters back into the room.

"Ms. Matthews is reading over the new contract. I am sure she will find it agreeable," the suit explains to Mav as he takes his seat next to me.

Me: I'm not signing this.

Mav reads my text, then grabs the contract and starts reading through it.

Me: The second to last clause.

He flips through the contract, looking for the clause from my text. He snorts and throws the contract across the table. "This is bullshit."

The lawyer pales at Mav's raised voice. "Is there a problem?"

"Yes, there's a fuckin' problem. Monument Records is trying to take advantage." I grab Mav's shoulder and point to my phone.

Me: Let me talk for myself.

He takes a deep breath and locks eyes with me. The look in them is almost like he's proud. Of me? He nods and I take my phone back.

Me: I'm not signing this contract without a complete removal of the second to last clause.

Me: I will not be beholden to Monument Records, and I will not pay Darren a finder's fee when he didn't find me.

I slide it across to the lawyer. He reads it and paws at the tie around his neck as if it's suddenly too tight.

"I work for the label. I can't remove those clauses. They are standard," he squeaks as he hands me back my phone.

Me: Then there is no reason for me to be here.

Me: I'm going to have dinner with Mr. Slater before he's due back into the studio.

I slide my phone back across the table. When it reaches the lawyer, I stand and smooth my hands against my pants.

"Big mistake. The Blind Rebels are Monument's biggest act

Bridging the Silence

right now. You don't want to displease us." The lawyer fronts, with his chest puffed out.

Mav snaps up my phone as he stands and reaches for my hand. We are almost through the lobby when the lawyer comes running down the hall after us.

"I have the go ahead to have a new contract written up. It'll be back in an hour or so." He's out of breath and tucking his tie in.

"Don't fuck with us. We'll be back after we've had dinner. Make it right." Mav pulls open the door with his free hand and we exit back to the car.

"I'm sorry. I should have assumed Darren would try to screw you." Mav shakes his head. "It doesn't even surprise me anymore. How sad is that?"

This would have been the perfect time to bring up my past, to tell Mav that the lawyer and probably Darren know exactly who I was, but I let the opportunity slide, because I don't want to bring it up now. It will seem like I've been lying this whole time. I know how that would look.

R

MAV NODS from the engineering room. "Are you comfortable with where the keyboard is at, and the height of the stool?" I nod.

"Okay, give us a second." I nod again.

I haven't been in a recording studio in so long. I was due to go into one a month after I lost my ability to speak. It feels so natural to be here, and my comfort level surprises me. I slip the headset on my ears.

"Can you run through some scales on the piano for me so I can get some levels?" asks Dana, the engineer, his voice gritty in my ear. My hands automatically run through scales as I watch Mav and Dana work the soundboard. Dana's long blonde hair is pulled back in a low ponytail, not unlike how Cal wears his dark hair most of the time. Mav's expression is intense as he tweaks the board before he turns back to Dana. The two of them hold a short conversation that ends with Mav nodding at me and giving me the thumbs up.

"Okay, Kady, we'll do the song all the way through a few times with just your piano. Then I'll come into the booth, and we'll do it together, okay?" I shoot a thumbs up to Mav and Dana through the window. Mav counts me down and I play it. And then, again.

"One more time with just you." I play their song yet again. Then sit and watch Mav and Dana discuss something. I can't hear them. Dana clicks his mic. "It's gonna be a few minutes, Kady."

I relax my posture and take a minute to stretch my back, but keep my earphones on. Sammy waves at me through the glass window that separates us. I wave back. He wasn't here when I went into the booth.

Mav runs his own levels from the vocal booth. He's laser-focused the whole time he's been in the recording studio tonight. He has such a stage presence; it makes sense that he would have that same kind of thing when recording. He's very serious about his music. It's exciting to see recording from another band's perspective. If you had asked me just a few months ago, I would have told you I'd never step foot in a studio again. Yet not only am I here, but I am enjoying watching their creative process.

Cal takes the seat next to Dana at the soundboard and gives me a nod. Dana counts us in, and we start, just Mav and me. It's different playing the song solo compared to playing it with Mav giving it vocals. My pacing is slightly different. When we are done, Mav moves back out to listen to the product while I wait.

"This is great, Kady. I want to do it a few more times. Okay?" I give them another thumbs up. In the background, there's some sort of commotion. Mav swirls around and Cal stands with his back to the window that separates me from the control room.

"What the fuck is she doing here?" The seething words are muffled, but I know the voice belongs to Killian. I straighten up my back to peer through the window into the other room. Kill's chest is puffed out, hands gesturing toward the recording booth I'm in. Toward me. I'm the only 'she' here.

"Just because you're fucking her doesn't make her part of the band. She's riding our coattails. Can't you see she's a fame-whore like all the rest? Except she's even worse than Becka. At least Becka didn't fuck with the music."

In a flash, Mav is in front of Killian, hand fisted in the middle of his black shirt. Dana reaches over and flips off the mic that Mav left keyed open, silencing me from the turmoil on the other side of the glass. But it doesn't matter, I've heard enough.

I slip off my headset and slide out of the booth and make my way down the hall and out the back door of the studio, not bothering to leave the door ajar so I can get back in.

It's dark out here now. I didn't realize how long we'd been in the windowless studio. I slide down the concrete wall until I'm squatting. I'm not going to be the Yoko Ono of this band. They are newly reunited. I will not come between them.

If I hadn't signed that stupid songwriter contract Mav insisted on, it wouldn't be a big deal. I'd just leave. I'm not really a songwriter anyway. Monument didn't even want me to record my own music because I'm not that good. *Stick to what you know, Kandi. These songs aren't what your fan base wants. Not what anyone wants.*

It's uncharacteristically cold out here and, of course, I left my hoodie on the couch in the engineering booth. Shivering, I pull my elbows into my top, trying to keep warm.

The back door squeaks as it opens. Someone steps out,

standing next to me. Sammy's red Chuck Taylors give him away. He squats down next to me and sits there in the silence of the darkened industrial park.

"It's not about you, Kady. As much as it seems like it is, it's not." Sammy reaches out and touches my knee.

I answer him with a shrug, grateful for the dark. He can't see my tears. He's right. It sure seems like it's me. Killian's words seemed pretty fucking personal.

I pull my phone out and type a message.

Me: Can you take me home?

I show it to Sammy, and he blows out a breath, but he doesn't answer. He just continues to fiddle with his phone.

Me: Never mind. I'll see if Hayleigh or Harden will come get me.

"Wait, Kady." This time he grips my knee as if to hold me in place, but he's still messing with his phone.

I should just go. Brushing his hand off me, I stand up. I'm about to head down the dark alley behind the building that comes out on the main thoroughfare. Hayleigh will come get me. Or an Uber. Uber! I launch the ridesharing app. I don't like to rideshare alone at night, but I'll take my chances.

"Shit. Please, Kady. Just wait a minute!" His exacerbated tone is very un-Sammy like. "Let Mav and Cal talk to Kill and iron out their shit. In twenty minutes, they'll all probably be taking shots and toasting the band."

It doesn't mean they'll want me here when they do. Killian's oozed hatred at me since he met me and why would they choose me over their band. They shouldn't. I'm kidding myself if I think that a "talk" will kill the animosity he wields like a weapon. Shaking my head, I start down the alley.

Sammy jumps up behind me. "Ice cream!" He barks it out so forcefully, I turn back to look at him. Has he lost his marbles?

"Come on." He gently takes my elbow and starts walking

with me. "We'll go get an ice cream. Don't they say ice cream makes everything better?"

Minutes later, I'm seated in a small plastic chair glued to the floor of the ice cream shop in a strip mall a few blocks from the studio. Sammy hands me an ice cream cone, complete with rainbow sprinkles. He drops into the chair across from me. He looks comical stuffed into the child-sized chair with his ice cream.

"You can never go wrong with sprinkles." He smiles at me kindly over his matching cone, also with sprinkles. We spend the next several minutes consuming our ice cream in quiet.

"Urg! Brain freeze." Sammy grimaces and moans, looking at me with a pained expression.

"I know, not that I have much of a brain to freeze." He winks to show me he's kidding but something about the look in his eye makes me think he believes that just a little bit. I slide my phone over to him.

Me: Breathe in slowly through your nose, then out your mouth.

Me: It will help warm your soft palate and make the freeze headache go away.

"You're a smart cookie, Kady," he says after taking a few deliberate breaths.

Me: I watch a lot of YouTube when I'm bored.

He laughs. "And funny, too." His light blue eyes watch me intently as I make work of the ice cream he bought me.

"Mav is different with you." He tilts his head slightly when he looks at me. "I've known him for a long time." He takes a bite.

"I mean, yeah, he was engaged to Becka and all that," he rolls his eyes and tosses his head like it's just bullshit. "But he treated her the same way he treated other women. Without attachment. He always held them out here." He mimics holding someone out at arm's length with his ice cream cone.

"But *you* get the real Mav. The Mav we know." Sammy licks

at his wrist to catch the ice cream that's breeched the rim of his cone.

"I think it's why Killian's so anti-Kady. He was in the middle, like me, when shit went down between Mav, Becka, and Cal. He liked Becka. He loves his brother. It was hard on all of us." He gazes into the parking lot.

"I don't think Kill's paying attention. He doesn't see that you're different to Mav. I think he's worried that you'll come between Mav and us like Becka did. He's protective because we're just getting back on solid ground together." He shrugs and licks his cone again.

"I'm just guessing, though." Sammy sounds sage as he ponders his dessert.

I bite the bottom of my pointed cone and suck the melted ice cream out of it, making Sammy giggle.

"You're different, Kady, in the most awesome way." He chuckles and smiles, his eyes crinkling in the corners.

His phone vibrates against the table, and he shoots a text off to whomever. "They're looking for us. We should get back." We clean up our mess and hop in Sammy's Jeep to head back to the studio.

The room is heavy with tension when I walk in behind Sammy. Everyone turns to look at us.

"Okay, let's get to it," Dana says, motioning toward the recording booth.

I text Mav.

Me: *I won't be the Yoko Ono of your band.*

He chuckles as he reads the phone, slinging an arm over my shoulders. "Trust me, you're no Yoko Ono."

He escorts me to the recording booth, but I swear I hear Killian mutter, "No, she's worse."

Two hours later, I'm exhausted. I can't play the song anymore. The first hour, Dana kept calling me out for playing too fast, which frustrated Mav, but we finally got it down. Then

I watched while they worked together on another new song I haven't heard before, but my attention started to fade after a while.

I must have dozed off because I about take flight when Mav leans over and kisses my forehead. "Sorry. I didn't mean to wake you." He looks over at me. "You're beautiful, even when you're asleep on an uncomfortable studio couch." His lips curl slightly, but his face is still intense from the recording session. He reaches out his hand in an offer to take mine. "Let's go."

When he joins me in his Corvette, he looks over at me. "I should probably take you home, but I'd rather take you home with me." Nothing sounds better than being wrapped in Mav tonight.

I mouth, "With you," and nod, so he knows I prefer the second option too.

He smiles at my nod. "Let Hayleigh know." He nods at my phone before gassing the car, tires squealing.

Chapter 23

Mavrick

A desperate keening rouses me from a deep dreamless sleep, then I'm shoved hard towards the edge of the bed. It takes me a minute to realize I'm in the bed here in Vegas and it's Kady. She thrashes her head back and forth, but her eyes remain closed. I murmur softly to her. "You're dreaming, baby. Wake up."

She pushes me hard. "Run!" It's garbled and urgent, but she said it. She's talking, fucking speaking in her sleep, but I don't want to hear it. Not like this. Her face screws up and she starts to cry and gasp.

More thrashing. She gasps and stills. "Angel, wake up." I kiss her forehead.

When she starts kicking her legs, I loosen my grip on her, worried she's about to knee me in the nuts. Then she lets out an uncontrollable cry that makes my heart drop into my stomach.

"Kadence!" My voice is probably firmer than it should be, but I want to help her out of whatever terror she's living in her sleep. I shake her lightly. "Kadence! Wake up, baby!"

"No, no, no, no, no," she whisper-moans. Her hands fly to

cover her face, like she is protecting herself. Hearing her articulate is a momentary shock and I freeze for a moment.

"Kadence." I pant, terrified for her as she continues to fight the demons of her sleep. I shake her again, a little harder this time. She turns her head into the pillow and cries out in pain.

"Come on, Kadence. Wake up. You're okay," I whisper-shout, rising to my knees. I shake her again, trying to oust her from the hell in her head.

Her eyes fly open, wide and unfocused, and she gasps for breath. Her eyes dart around the room like she doesn't remember where she's at.

"You're okay. You're at my place," I say softly and squeeze her shoulders lightly to ground her back here. Tears pour out of her eyes.

"It was just a dream. You're okay." I'm a damn liar, because whatever she's living in her head was very real until she opened her eyes. She pants like she's just run a marathon. Her eyes land on mine finally, and she sags as her body relaxes.

"It was just a dream. You're okay. You're safe." I pull her to me. She shudders against me as she cries. I caress her back and whisper affirmations to her; that she's here and not wherever she was in her head, that I have her. She's okay. Shit, I'd do anything to take these monsters on for her. Whatever they are.

"Want to talk about it?" She shakes her head and burrows into my chest. I don't know how to make this better for her or if I even can. I hold her firmly to my chest and continue giving her quiet reassurances. Her breathing becomes less ragged. Her tense muscles eventually soften and finally her breathing evens out into the long, steady breaths of sleep. I continue to hold her tight, praying I can keep those monsters chasing her at bay, for a little while at least.

R

"YOU SURE YOU'RE OKAY?" I'm skeptical of her nod. Kady picks at her breakfast, the dark marks still evident under her eyes despite sleeping until nearly noon. She fiddles with a strawberry on her plate.

"Still don't want to talk?" She shakes her head. She hasn't been very communicative this morning. No direct eye contact, preferring to answer my questions with simple gestures rather than with her phone. I've quickly learned this is her way of shutting me out. Distancing herself from me. Part of me wants to tell her that she spoke in her sleep, but something tells me that information might not be what she needs to hear right now.

"Feel like working on the song I sent you?" She shrugs and pushes a strawberry around on her plate.

Fuck this. I can only help her if she wants it. I yank my acoustic guitar from its stand and sit in the living room with my notebook. I work on it alone while she sits at the breakfast bar, pretending to be interested in the food I made her.

Humming where I don't yet have lyrics, I play through the song over and over again. Kady eventually abandons her plate and curls up in the chair nearby. She's listening, with her eyes shut and her head bobbing slightly. The next time I run through the song, she starts humming along.

It's fascinating to watch her process the music. It's different for every songwriter. Hell, sometimes it's different for every song, at least it is for me. "Should I play it again?" She nods, her eyes still closed. She hums again with it. She reaches for her phone.

Kady: The time signature is too fast. The lyrics are a ballad. The music isn't soft enough.

"A ballad? We don't do ballads." She shrugs and holds her hands out to me until I relinquish my prized guitar to her. This guitar never gets used on stage, rarely in the studio. It's my first acoustic, a present from my grandmother. No one touches her except me. Until I hand it over to Kady, that is. What is she doing to me?

She turns my notebook on the table so that it faces her. I hit record on the iPad just in case this is more Kady genius, but a ballad? Maybe not so genius after all. The guys will never go for a ballad.

She fingers the fretboard a few times without actually playing. Is she getting used to the guitar? No, she's nervous. She hasn't played guitar in front of me before. She closes her eyes and plays through the song the way I did, then looks at me for approval. She plays it again, this time slowing the time signature and humming along where my lyrics will fit. She stops, scratches some notes in the margin of my page and plays it again, this time more fluidly, but as the ballad she hears. Shit, it's pretty good for a ballad. A ballad will be a hard sell to the guys.

"Play it again. I'm going to sing with you this time, okay?" She nods and I sing. I check her tweaks to my lyrics and as we go, and I make a few of my own.

This shit is gold. No, not gold, platinum.

We run through it a few more times. She smiles at me, slightly smug. It's a new smile from Kady, one brimming with confidence. And I love it.

Kady: Sounds better. Told you it wanted to be a ballad.

I grin at her. "Okay, smarty-pants, run to the studio this afternoon and play this through for the whole group with me. I want to show them what we came up with."

She looks at me uneasily. She doesn't trust Killian, especially after his outburst at the studio last night. I don't either, if I'm being honest. He won't spill about his beef with her, but he promised last night to keep it under wraps.

"Please. For me? I bet Sammy will let you show him the drum parts." Her eyes light up when I mention she might get to play with Sammy's drums.

We stop by her place so she can shower and change. I look through her pictures from the show where she played with us as she does her thing in the bathroom. The one picture of Killian is terrifying, the look he gave her. No wonder she feels so uncomfortable around him. It's something about the look in his eyes. Like she's the enemy. My Kady. I need to figure out how to fix this shit before he scares her away.

When we get to the studio, everyone is already there.

"So, what's up?" Cal asks from the corner of the couch.

"Remember, I told you that Sammy and I had a rough song, but I was still working on it?" Cal and Kill nod.

"You finished it?" Sammy asks, twirling his stick between his fingers.

"Kady and I worked on it most of the morning and early afternoon." I look at the guys. Cal and Sammy both seem interested, but I catch Killian's sneer. I glare at him. He's got to be taught that intimidating my girl isn't going to fly.

"And like she did with 'Star Chaser,' she worked her voodoo magic and turned it into something even better." Sammy bounces with excitement. He's the only member who's even heard it before, but not like this. He has no clue.

"Cal, give Kady your guitar and we'll play it for you."

Cal hands her his guitar, and she fingers the frets like she did back at my place. She's nervous again. Oddly, I am too. I feel naked because usually when I introduce a new song to the group I have a guitar, but it's not just that. It's because this is a departure from our usual sound. We've never done ballads, so I'm going to have to fucking nail it to sell them on this.

I nod to Kady. She starts. I join her.

Kady keeps her eyes closed. I keep mine on her delicate fingers, working their way across the frets. This feels too intimate in front of the guys. I don't want to see the band's reaction as I go. I draw out the last few notes of 'Incredible without Trying.' Kady keeps her head down, looking at the guitar, but I risk taking a look at the rest of the band. It's telling that the usually boisterous group is quiet.

"It's a ballad now." Sammy breaks the silence.

"I love it."

"I hate it."

Of course, the twins feel differently. Kady unstraps Cal's guitar and hands it back to him.

"We don't do ballads," Killian growls. "Why start now? It's not true to our sound."

"This whole album is different, Kill. What's one ballad? Did you hear it? Listen to the words and to how Mav sang it? It'll be freaking awesome live." Cal disagrees with his twin. "The fans will shit themselves."

Meanwhile, Kady slips along the edge of the room and walks into the recording booth. She slips the headphones on and fiddles with the keyboard. I hear the piano from the turned down speakers as she runs through her Bach piece. It's her go to piece. She's giving us the space to be us, to hash this out.

"I like it," Sammy adds in his quiet way. "Yeah, it's different, but good different."

"No, it's sellout different," Killian counters. "This is bullshit. Mav should keep it for his solo album. It's not Rebels material." He tosses his water bottle forcefully at the trashcan in the corner.

"What solo album?!" the three of us answer him simultaneously.

He shrugs and nods to the studio where Kady continues with her concerto. "Aren't you making one with her? That's what all the rags are saying. We've all seen the pictures of you and her playing together." Kill rolls his eyes.

"First, no. Fuck the rags. There is no solo album in the works. You know better than to fall for their shit, Kill. I went to a guitar shop to order a new axe and Kady was there messing around on a piano and some fans started to gather. I gave an impromptu show for the fans. The guitar shop was over the moon, as were the fans. It was good publicity for everyone. All Kady did was play some piano." I shake my head at him.

"Second, Kady's a musician. She's offered some suggestions on this song and on 'Star Chaser.' I'd rather she gets paid per a contract than we take advantage of her kindness, and she sues us later." I level a stare at Killian. "I'm not saying she would, but the songwriting contract is a protection for us as well as her, dumbass."

"And third," Sammy pipes up from his corner of the couch. "Kady is just a cool chick. I really like her."

"Tell you what." Cal stands and stretches before leveling a look at his twin. "Let's cut it. Right now. Give it to the label and see what *they* think." Cal returns his gaze to his twin. Kill shrugs. He knows he's outnumbered.

Sammy stands too. "Heck yeah. Let's cut it."

Kady shows Sammy what she was thinking rhythmically using his studio drum kit. Drum kits are as individual as the drummer. Where what drum is, how high, how tight the head is, where what cymbal is and at what angle. Kady has no trouble behind his drums. She's so adaptable.

Sammy bobs his head along and grins at me widely. "I told you this girl has rhythm. Do you hear this? She's a freakin' drummer too!"

Since Killian was overruled, he's forced to record it with us. It only takes us a few run throughs to get it right. Kady watches from the recording booth, sitting next to Dana, so at home in a studio.

"Mav, Kady and I think that last take is a wrap. Come on in and give it a listen?"

We all take seats around the booth, and I pull Kady onto my lap. We listen to the playback of The Blind Rebel's first ballad ever.

Cal nods, a slow grin pulling across his face the longer he

listens. "That's the shit right there, man." Sammy nods in agreement. Killian, though, remains impassive and blank. He says nothing.

"Remind me why we haven't done a ballad before?" Cal shoots a look over to Killian, knowing he has a sharp retort on his tongue. Even Kady tenses as she sits in my lap, but Kill surprises us all by not saying a thing.

"That track will be the feather in the cap to the label. That's what, twenty-five songs?" I ask Dana.

"Including the ballad, twenty-seven." He nods. "That will give Monument a choice of what to release. You can use the others as teasers on social media or whatnot. It's a good solid slug of stuff." He looks over the rim of his John Lennon styled glasses. "This is great stuff, guys. I'm sure Monument will love it."

"Then that shit is done!" Cal exclaims happily.

"Now we wait for the label to tell us how much it sucks," Killian mutters. I nod. He's not wrong. They always try to change our stuff. We almost never cave. It's our stuff and we're proud. Being with them for nearly ten years and being the most successful artist on the rock side of the label gives us a bit of veto power. This stuff is a little different for us, so they'll probably balk when they hear it. I'm not worried though, we'll win in the end. We always do. This is our growth. We can't sit stagnant, or the music gets old and fans wander.

"Fuck the label. We did it faster than they could have anticipated." I stand. "Let's go to dinner. A celebration. All of us together. Kady too. She's helped with these two songs. She deserves to be part of it." Again, I'm surprised when there's no backlash from Killian. No attempting to bow out, no excuses about having to be somewhere. Color me surprised as hell.

The five of us together will need security at any restaurant we choose. Surprisingly, agreeing on an upper end steakhouse with a private room at one of the casinos is an easy task. Jax arranges to meet us at the restaurant. Fucker is probably already there. He doesn't have a life beyond us.

Jax meets us in the parking garage with Aiden, the newest addition to our personal security team. Aiden's slightly smaller than Jax but is intimidating nonetheless, with his broad shoulders and thick arms. His hair and eyes are dark. And much like Jax, he seems to always be on his toes. They flank us as we walk as a group through the casino and into the steakhouse all the way to the back room.

I sit at the head of the rectangular table, with Kady on one side and Cal on the other. Sammy sits next to Kady and Kill sits next to his brother. We order drinks. Hard ones. Even Kady. She gives me a shy grin as she sips her on-the-rocks margarita. Guess Jax and Aiden will be driving us back tonight. The food is surprisingly good, but what's even better is us. We're together and clicking. Even Killian, who's been the most disconnected from the group lately.

Cal holds his drink up after we finish eating. "To successful reunions, new albums, and"—he pauses to look at Kady—"new friends. May our rough cut be up to snuff and our friendships be lasting ones." He's not sloppy drunk, but I haven't seen Cal this loose since well before the band broke up.

Thank God his Aunt Sandy is in Vegas watching over Gibson. I know having his aunt with Gibson gives Cal peace of mind that his son is being well taken care of.

"Cheers." We clink glasses together as the waitress returns. She's been a star server tonight, perfectly attentive but not overbearingly so. A big tip is in her future. And the way Killian's eye-fucking her, probably more than just a monetary one if she's interested.

I settle the bill. "Who's with who?" I point to Aiden and Jax. "No drunk driving. No buzzed driving." Jax takes Sammy's keys and my keys. Aiden takes the keys from Cal. "Guess that answers that."

"Is it gonna be a problem if I crash with you, Mav?" Sammy asks. He's been rooming with Killian. And Killian's currently passing his number over to our waitress.

"Nah, just stay in the downstairs bedroom, if you get my drift." I waggle my eyebrows, and Kady giggles. He responds by pushing my shoulder, so I put the little shit in a headlock. His arms flail around trying to get to my head and miserably failing in his slightly drunken state. This makes Kady giggle more.

The freer she is with the giggling, the happier I am. I squeeze Sammy a little tighter.

"Fuck, Mav. Uncle." He gasps, and I release Sammy from my hold. "You're a dick sometimes, Mav."

"Stay in the downstairs bedroom and you're golden." I stare at him hard.

"Not a problem. It's not something I want to hear or see anyway. Trust me." He grimaces as I grab Kady's hand.

Our whole group heads out of the steakhouse bordered again by our security.

"Fuck," Jax mutters seconds before we are completely surrounded, cameras flashing, and recorders stuck in our faces.

The paparazzi? We've been here in Vegas for a month, and they are just now figuring it out? Jax moves to step in front of Kady and me. When he makes this move, they crowd around us separates the three of us from the rest of the group. The cameras click non-stop. The crowd swells in even tighter and Kady hides her face in my neck, and I pull her to me instinctively. The closer together we are, the easier time Jax will have fending them off.

"Mav, are you and Kandi together?" Kandi? Who the fuck is Kandi?

"How long have you been together?"

"Kandi, Kandi, look this way! Kandi!"

Are they talking about Kady?

"Kandi, have you been with Mav all this time?"

"Kandi, this way, please!" Kady burrows into my side, so close I can hear her gasp with each call of the name Kandi.

Then the fucking grabbing starts. Someone gets a hand on Kady's arm and pulls her hard away from me. She gasps and grabs my waist to anchor herself to me.

"Hands the fuck off." I slap blindly at the hands reaching for her. They've been known to get a little pushy around me but never this grabby. What the actual fuck do they think they are doing?

"Jax! They're grabbing her."

"What the fuck are you doing? Hands off." Jax roars and thrusts himself between Kady and the person trying to pull her away from me. Someone comes wading through the crowd. Aiden. Thank fuck. The twins and Sammy can fend for themselves, but we're getting fucking overrun and Jax can only do so much.

"I said move aside!" Aiden grabs someone and physically moves them out of his way to get into the small area we are corralled in. Kady's fingers dig into the flesh at my waist, causing me to look at her. Fuck. Those large, terrified eyes are back.

"Jax, get Kady the fuck out of here." I try to release her to him, but her grip on me only tightens.

"Let go of his shirt. I'll get you out of here, sweetheart." His hand grips hers as he gently forces her to release my shirt. "Good girl."

He lifts her off the ground, putting her on his shoulder like a sack of potatoes and pushes back through the group. I don't know where the fuck he's taking her. Aiden steps in front of me, blocking my view of Jax's disappearing head.

"Move aside." Aiden booms and attempts to push us through the crowd in the opposite direction. Split and conquer. It seems most of the group decides to follow Jax. Fuck. Kady.

"I said move the fuck aside." Aiden roars as he pushes

through the last stragglers with his shoulder and heads towards a nondescript door that blends into the wall. He knocks, and it opens slightly, and Aiden pushes me through and follows, making sure the door is firmly shut behind us.

I don't know where the hell we are, but I can breathe a little. Sammy rushes up to me.

"Mav, what the hell was that about?" He looks genuinely frightened. The paparazzi have never been so handsy with us. They purposely divided us, so they could separate Kady and me from the rest of the band, but what the hell do they want with her?

"Where's Kady?" Sammy asks me.

"Kady's with Jax. They went the other way." I turn toward the door and consider going back and following where I thought Jax was going.

"This way, Mr. Slater." Aiden puts a firm hand on my shoulder and guides me farther into what appears to be the working bowels of the casino mall. We pass by back doors, break rooms, and storage areas.

"She's with Jax. Let's get to the designated meeting point," he urges Sammy and me to walk forward.

"To the left, at the fork ahead," Aiden instructs, continuing to guide us through the labyrinth behind the scenes at the casino. How the fuck he knows where to go, I don't have a clue, but that's why we pay him. We turn another corner and they come into view in a dimly lit niche. Cal's arms are wrapped around Kady, holding her tightly to his chest. Even from here, I can see her shoulders violently quaking. Killian's pacing back and forth like a caged jaguar ready to pounce and Jax stands in front of the three of them, arms crossed against his broad puffed out chest.

Kady. She's all I see, all I need. I need to hold her to me. Make sure she's okay. I'm not thrilled that Cal's the one comforting my Kady, but at least someone is comforting her, because even from here I can tell how upset she is. I move around Aiden as we draw closer when Killian jumps in my face.

"I fucking knew it. I *knew* it!" He rants. "She's a fucking liar. A user. She's been using you, brother. I fucking told you. Another famewhore. They're all famewhores, just like Becka."

If he doesn't get the fuck out of my way, I am going to lay him out flat like I did at Sammy's last year, only this time I'll fucking mean it.

But fucking Killian jumps in front of me again. His nostrils are flaring. "How much of a dumbass do you have to be?" I shake my head.

He'd better explain, and fast. My hands ball at my sides. *Come on, Kill, come at me.* I'm wound so fucking tight it won't take much to push me over.

"I thought she looked familiar. She's Kandi fuckin' Matthews!" He says it with such venom, like I should hate her. "She's just riding our coattails, hoping you can get her back in the fucking spotlight."

I lock eyes with him, confused. Who the fuck is Kandi Matthews? He must see my confusion, because I have no idea what the hell he's raving about.

"You know, Kandi Matthews? The precious child star turned pop princess. Disappeared from the spotlight after her ex-boyfriend took a gun to her and her fans at a VIP event at the Monument Records festival."

I vaguely remember hearing about it when we were on tour in Europe at the time. I tip my head and glance over Kill's shoulder at Kady. "Replace the black and purple hair she has now with longer blonde wavy hair, change the way she dresses. I knew she looked familiar."

He shoves his phone in front of my face, a picture of a younger, blonde Kady with a plastic smile plastered on her face, looking directly at the camera.

"It's fucking her, Mav."

What the actual fuck? I snatch the phone from him and scroll through it. Shit. He's right. My Kady is *the* Kandi fuckin' Matthews. Pop princess known around the L.A. pop scene as the diva who tosses anyone aside when she's done with them, even her own fucking family. That's why her brother won't talk to her. She sued her aunt for stealing or some shit and the brother sided with the aunt. She doesn't have many friends in L.A., that's for damn sure.

I look back and forth between my Kady, still wrapped in Cal's arms, and the photos of Kandi Matthews on Killian's phone. Trying to reconcile the girl I know with the infamous star who faded away when her boyfriend went ballistic at the festival. They look so different, but Kady's purposely changed her appearance. Her hair is completely different. She dresses differently. Not that I paid attention to Kandi Matthews at all. I shake my head, not believing what I'm seeing.

Why didn't she tell me outright who she was? Maybe Killian's right about her intent. I take a deep breath and one last look at my Kady, Cal's arm still holding her tight. This has flashes of Becka and him all over it. I don't know what I'm more upset about. Kady lying or Cal taking her side automatically, like he did with Becka, trying to win her over.

Mother. Fucker. She *is* just using us. I can't believe it. Killian's been right this whole fucking time. I believed her. I fucking believed her, and she's just used us to get a recording contract when no one wanted to work with her anymore.

The pain in my chest deepens. I thought she loved me, but she's just stepping on us on her way up the fucking ladder. *My Kady* is an illusion, someone I wanted and needed her to be.

Killian tilts his head at me. "You believe me now, right? Too little, too late. The label will hear her on those tracks and want her to play with us on the album. They probably already know who she is and are going to use us so they can play up the poor traumatized pop princess angle and we'll be left behind. They have an option on her in her contract, right? Of course, they do. Why wouldn't they?"

Sammy's arm on my shoulder pulls me out of Killian's tirade. "Kady's not like that, man."

"Bullshit!" Killian roars so loudly that his vicious echo bounces down the concrete corridor behind me. "She *is* like that, Sammy. Don't you get it? If she wasn't, why didn't we already know who she really is, huh? Why? She had to know that associating with us like this was going to cause a stir, get her recognition."

Sammy is crushed by the weight of Killian's words. "She's a fucking fraud, Sammy." Killian shakes his head. "This is a PR disaster. Just being affiliated with her could ruin us," Kill whispers. "Destroy us, Mav."

Callum holds Kady to him tight. Protective, like he would Gibson, but there is no joy here. She has her head buried in his shoulder, as her sobs rack her whole body. She can't even face us. Face me. She's hiding because she knows what Killian says is fucking true.

Callum's face is as hard as stone as he stares me down over her head. His eyes narrow and he tries to shield her from me. No fucking way. She needs to face her shit. Storming past Sammy and Killian, I go right for the source.

"Mav," Callum's low growl is a warning as I approach. He steps up, chest puffed out as he tries to slide her behind him, but I'm too fast for him. I spin her around to face me, pulling her out of Cal's protective grip. Her reddened eyes immediately avert my hard stare.

"Mav," Cal tries to step up again.

"Stay the fuck out of this, Cal," I roar at my friend.

Kady's trying not to cry, which only makes her body hitch harder. I stare at her, waiting for her to make eye contact, begging her to make that connection. To prove me wrong.

"Is it true? Are you Kandi Matthews?" My voice is ice.

Still not looking at me, she nods one quick short nod.

"So, it's true. You are using us to get back in the spotlight." She immediately starts shaking her head no, denying my words. "I call bullshit, Kadence. Bull. Shit." My voice is steely. She continues to shake her head no.

"If it wasn't bullshit, we'd know who you are. We wouldn't find out when the fucking press practically pushes us out of the way to get to you. Bull. Shit. I can't even."

She leans forward, wrapping her arms around herself in a hug, her face full of anguish. I spin away, turning my back on her.

"I can't even look at you right now."

My phone goes off with a text. It's from Kadence. I don't look any further. Another one pops up.

"Enough. I don't want your excuses, or lame explanations. None of it. I'm done, Kady." I block her number and start down the hall, away from all this bullshit.

The devastation on Sammy's face mirrors the wreckage of my heart as I pass him. Fuck this. No more. I stomp blindly down the hall, picking up speed as I go. I don't even know where the fuck I'm going, and right now, I don't give a shit. Hearing boots following me, I spin around, ready to fight with Callum again, but it's only Jax.

He catches up and walks beside me, matching my brisk clip. "This way." He jerks his head to the right. He leads me out of this crazy maze through the back side of the shops and to the parking garage, out to Sammy's Jeep. He unlocks it and drives me to the lake house, the lake house I almost fucking put an offer in on this morning. Thank fuck I got distracted.

Chapter 24

Kadence

The burning in my chest won't subside as the echo of Mav's brisk steps move down the hall, away from us. He didn't want an explanation. He just accepted Killian's speech verbatim. And while some of what Killian said is true. Hell, most of it; some things need to be explained.

I'm not the complete bitch the media made me out to be. You would think they'd know that, especially Mav. I wasn't looking to ride any coattails. If anything, I was reluctant to be part of the music exactly for this reason, but I should have known this would be the eventual conclusion when the lawyer recognized me yesterday.

I take a huge gasping breath, and the devastated sound I make has my own knees weakening. They finally give, but I don't hit the concrete floor beneath me like I deserve. Cal grasps me around the waist. He doesn't let me fall, but he should. He should leave me here. They all should.

There's no escaping her. I'm always going to be Kandi. I can never get away from her, no matter how hard I try. I thought I could hide out here in Vegas and put Kandi to rest. Life didn't let me.

As I struggle against Cal's grip on me, I catch sight of Sammy. He looks lost, like part of him wants to stay with me, and part of him wants to chase after Mav. He should go with Mav.

I grab my phone and type out a message.

Me: Let me go!

I shove my phone in his face. He shakes his head. "Uh-huh. Not going anywhere." He grunts when I try to elbow him in the guts. It's like trying to elbow a brick wall.

Struggling against his strong arms is fruitless because the more I wiggle, trying to get away, the tighter his freaking grip gets on me.

Giving up, I still.

"You done?" I nod, hoping he'll let me go so that I can get away.

"Why are you protecting that bitch?" Kill spits out, his nostrils flaring at his brother. "She's the fucking enemy, Cal."

Then Killian's face sparks with recognition. "Oh, I get it. You found your new girl. Mav's done with her, so you move in." Kill's words are laced with so much venom they make me nauseous.

"Shut the fuck up, Kill." Cal's words are so icy toward his brother that I shiver. Cal's arm tenses around me. "Kady hasn't given us her side of the shit you so kindly aired on her behalf. I'm betting on Kady having something more to say."

I shake my head no, hoping that he'll let me go, but he just squeezes me a little tighter.

"Let her do her own thing. By herself. We're a family. It's time you recognize that, brother. The Rebels are the Rebels. We are not the Rebels Featuring Kandi." Killian's hot spits lands on my cheek. "I'm going with Mav." Kill takes off in the same direction Mav and Jax went in.

I glance at Sammy. His pale, disappointed face turns from

mine and looks down the hall at Killian. It's then that my heart finally breaks all the way. I go limp against Cal's hold.

I've become the Yoko Ono of the Blind Rebels, only worse.

Me: I'm not worth it, Cal, let me go.

"I beg to differ." His voice is soft.

Me: Please. I wanna go home.

Cal looks at Aiden. "Get us to the car."

He then turns to me. "We'll get you home."

We follow Aiden through the maze of service hallways to the parking garage and to Callum's SUV. Sammy jumps in the front with Aiden and Cal slides into the backseat with me, Gib's empty car seat between us.

I text my address to Cal, who reads it off to Aiden. We aren't far from the apartment, and we are pulling up to the door in minutes. I fling open the door and try to slide out of the large SUV, but Cal grabs my arm.

"I'm walking you up." I shake my head and he shoots me a glare. I slip out the door and he meets me at the hood of the SUV, his expression telling me he won't take no for an answer.

The doorman has the elevator waiting. "Good evening, Ms. Matthews." I don't make eye contact with him or with Cal, instead I just slide into the elevator, praying that Cal will return to his car, but he follows me in and stands as close to me as possible without touching me. He says nothing. We walk through the small foyer to the door, and he invites himself in. I just want to be alone so I can give in to the breakdown that's looming.

"Is your roommate home?" He says it loud, probably hoping Hayleigh will pop out and take over so he can leave.

I shrug my shoes off. Leaving Cal in the living room, I head down the hall and directly through to my bathroom. My head swims with all that has happened in the short amount of time.

I wait for the bathroom to fill with steam so thick I can hardly see the mirror. It burns when I finally step under the cascading water, but I welcome the pain on the outside to match the pain that's scorching my heart on the inside.

I scrub hard, trying to shed Kandi from my skin, but I can't. I'll always be Kandi no matter how hard I work to change. I'll never be free of her and her horrible legacy. It's forever etched into my skin and on to my soul. I'm forever going to be Kandi. By the time I get out, my skin is as raw on the outside as I feel on the inside. I just want to sleep, to turn off the noise in my head, to find the void.

I throw on my oldest sweatpants and blindly pull on a t-shirt. My hair's still soaking wet to the point that I can feel rivulets running down my back under my shirt. I go to my medicine cabinet and grab the bottle that holds the Ativan. I have to make my head stop. I want the numbness. I don't want to deal with the pain that Kandi caused. I open the pill bottle and consider for a single moment taking a handful instead of just one, but it's not fair to Hayleigh, so I carefully select only one.

I head to the kitchen for a glass of water to take my pill when I see that Cal is still here. "Feeling a little better?" His question dies out before he finishes the last word. "Christ, Kady, you're bright fucking red." He sighs. "I know you don't want anything to do with me, but I'm sticking around until Hayleigh comes home."

Why is he still here?

Me: I'm not exactly in the mood to entertain company. I'm going to go to bed. You got me home. You're good.

I walk him to the door. At the door, his face is deeply grooved with concern, but as soon as he's clear of the door, I shut it on him and flip the deadbolt.

Crawling into bed, I pull the comforter up and make sure it's over my eyes but that my mouth and nose still have just enough fresh air.

The hurt grows until it's almost too much. Just another reminder of how I'm unlovable. Unfixable. Broken. My limbs start to feel heavy as I let the Ativan slowly shut everything down and fade away into the heavy numbness that comes with it.

R

"She's still asleep." Hayleigh's hushed voice isn't as quiet as she thinks when she shuts my door behind her. I'm not asleep anymore, but I'd rather stay here in the soft, warm cocoon of my bed than face her, but someone is calling to check on me. Maybe Mav is calling to apologize? Even if he is, I won't accept it. Fuck it. Fuck him. Fuck all of them.

Hayleigh's voice fades as she heads back to the common area of our apartment, but now I'm curious to know who she's talking to. I roll onto my back and stretch my hands over my head. What time is it anyway? My stomach grumbles. My phone tells me it's 12:22 p.m. Shit, how long have I been asleep? Hayleigh's obviously not going in to work today.

I dress and head into my office. Reminders of Mav smack me in the face as soon as I enter. The pictures he wanted framed are propped up against the wall. On the couch is a small photo book of photos I've taken of him. I'll have this shit messengered over so I don't have to deal with him personally. I don't need reminders of him lying around, and I sure as fuck don't want to see him. I don't need any more rejections.

My acoustic guitar lies on the floor by the other end of the couch where I left it yesterday. Now I want to burn her. Break her like I'm broken. Hurt her like I hurt. I'm done with music and anything to do with it. Just done. I imagine the relief I'd feel if I stuck my foot through her. Maybe I need to put my shoes on.

Tomorrow when Hayleigh's at work, I'll go through the bedroom I've been storing stuff in and clear it out. Musical instruments will be donated somewhere. I bet the guy at the guitar shop will know some people who need some guitars, school kids or something. My music may not have died, but I'm going to suffocate it myself.

I can't ignore my stomach grumbles any longer though, as another one reminds me it's been too long since I've eaten. I guess it's time to face Hayleigh.

She's in the kitchen, standing over a pan on the stove. She looks up when I pull a barstool out to take a seat.

"Hey. I was just about to start a grilled cheese for you. I figured you'd be waking up soon and might be hungry." Her voice is woven with concern, but she surprises me by leaving it at that as she slathers butter on the bread before gently placing it in the pan. She puts the cheese on, adds some onion and then slathers more butter on the second slice and places it gently on top.

"You want some water or juice or something?" I shake my head. She assesses me quietly.

"Tea?" I nod. She's in full-on caretaker mode. It makes her feel like she's doing something to help me by making me lunch.

"Peppermint?" I shake my head no.

"Chai?" I nod. I need the caffeine to combat the sluggishness after drugging myself last night. She busies herself making my tea and tending my sandwich.

Me: Thanks, Hayleigh.

After reading my text, she nods back at me.

Me: I'm ok.

"I know." She doesn't believe me either, but she says it when she looks back up at me from her phone. This has to be killing her, wanting to grill me about what happened. I can see it on her face, but she holds herself back, just like she promised she would. "I'm here if you need me."

Me: You're my rock.

Me: One of these days, maybe I'll get to be yours.

She smiles softly when reading my texts, but her eyes are

still sad when she looks up at me. Sad for me. I'm tired of being the poor little broken kid. I'm not sure how to prove to her that I'm not that person anymore, but probably more importantly, how do I prove it to myself? I thought I was doing a good job until last night. It's my own fault. I should have been straightforward with who I used to be from the start.

She slides a perfectly grilled cheese sandwich in front of me. Cheese. My ultimate go-to comfort food.

"Cal called to check on you. He was sitting in the foyer when I came home last night. He gave me the gist of what happened. He just wanted to see if you were okay." So not Mav. As pissed and disappointed as I am in Mav, a small part of me was still hopeful he was the one who was checking up on me. Stupid me to think he might actually fucking care about *me*. Only Hayleigh does. Well, Harden does too. I pull out my phone to reassure her I'll check in with him.

Me: I'll text him I'm ok.

R

"You're sure you don't want me to put these on consignment for you? You have some really nice gear here." The manager of the guitar shop gives me a look as he asks me for the hundredth time while he looks over the last of my guitars. He's already seen all the paperwork on each instrument proving they're mine. He's seen my ID, but for some reason he doesn't believe that I want to give away five electric guitars and an acoustic one. All that I had left of what used to be a music career. I can't stand to look at them. Even just knowing they are in the small room across from mine causes me sleepless nights. Kandi is dead, just like I am on the inside. I slide my phone back to him.

Me: It's important to me they go to students who need an instrument.

Me: I don't need the money.

"Okay. Sign here that you've turned them over to the shop."
I sign the slips, one for each guitar, as requested.

"You don't happen to be interested in giving piano lessons,
do you?" I shake my head. "I just remember you playing when
you were here with the guy from Blind Rebels. I have a couple
of people with kids looking for lessons."

Me: Sorry. I don't teach.

Me: Are we good to go?

I slide my phone back across the counter, and he reads it.

"If you're 100 percent sure." He eyes me again with
suspicion.

I give him a thumbs up and walk out. I spent the entire
morning hauling boxes filled with what Hayleigh had stored of
Kandi Matthew's memories down to the dumpster in behind
the apartments. Any vestige of Kandi I still owned is now gone.

I stopped only to send the framed pictures for Cal's
birthday to Mav via private courier. I'm almost done wiping my
slate.

While I sit in the chair at my favorite salon, waiting for my
new color to process, I send a text to Cal.

*Me: Thank you for calling to check on me yesterday. I'm fine, but
I think it's best if I don't come to your birthday party this weekend.*

*Me: It was a pleasure getting to know you and your beautiful
son. You're such a good father.*

*Me: Give him a kiss from me and tell him I forgive him for
beaning me in the head with a drumstick. Have a happy birthday.*

Me: Please share with everyone that I say goodbye. —Kady

*Me: P.S. Don't take it personally, but I'll be blocking you. Sammy
and Mav too. I need a clean break.*

And as my new hair color processes, I block all their
numbers from my phone.

Chapter 25

Mavrick

My stomach is just starting to feel normal again. Fucking hangover. *Hangover hell, more like a three-day bender.* I should know better than to drink like that. I sip orange juice like a pussy and look across the living room to the stack of framed pictures delivered this morning. Cal's birthday photos. The 11x16 photos are all framed in brushed silver metal with black mats. Simple. Understated yet masculine. She has no way of knowing they're a perfect match to the décor in Cal's Hollywood hills home.

Framed, the photos are more stunning and emotive than they were in the email. Attached to the top of the stack was an invoice stamped, paid in full in red. I didn't pay anything for them. Not one dime for her time or work, the prints, or the framing. Yet still they're marked paid in full. I'm not sure what her game is. Maybe she's trying to get me to contact her. Well, that won't work. I'm done with her.

Since they were couriered over though, I assume it means she isn't coming to the party tomorrow. Just as fucking well.

Tonight's show, tomorrow's birthday party, and then we are back in southern California where we belong. I pray the fucking label doesn't suggest another residency here. I feel the call of the road. This staying in one place, putting down roots? Nah. Not for me.

Sammy: You alive, fucker?

Me: Barely. I don't remember the show last night. How wasted was I?

Sammy: Last night was bad.

Shit. I wonder how bad. His thought bubble disappears and then reappears a few times.

Sammy: Please lay off the booze. You're starting to scare me. Seriously.

I rub a hand over my face, sporting three days' worth of stubble, and I'm pretty sure that this is the same shirt I wore on stage last night and possibly even the night before. I can't remember. I'm a fucking mess. It must have been bad last night for Sammy to say I'm scaring him. I cringe and feel like shit for making Sammy worry. The kid takes everything to heart. I need to teach him it's better to not have a heart. Not to love.

Me: I'll lay off. Tell me I didn't drive home.

Sammy: Fuck no. You couldn't even find your way off stage.

Shit, that's damned fucked up.

Sammy: Aiden drove you home. Jax followed in the 'vette. Didn't want to risk you throwing up in Stella.

A vision of Kady's eyes lighting up when she saw the 'vette and then her bright smile as we drove through town come to mind. Shit, I'm gonna have to garage Stella for a while. Thank goodness I bought the Shelby.

Sammy's text bubble indicating that he's typing is there, but then it disappears, then reappears, then disappears again. He thought better of bringing up Kady. I'm glad. I shake my head. Fuck Kady, Kadence, Kandi, whoever the fuck she is today.

Me: Wanna come over? Jam, eat some tacos or something before the show? Invite Cal and Kill if you want.

Sammy: Sure. Pizza, okay? My treat.

Me: Sure, door's unlocked. No Peppers.

I need to reassure him, hell all the guys, that I'm not boozing it up over here again today. Showing up to three shows drunk off my ass isn't how I roll. I wouldn't put it past them electing Sammy to be the one to suggest drying my ass out. I need to work this Kady shit out of my system somehow, though. A jam session is just the ticket.

I store the pictures in the corner of my bedroom. I don't need Cal seeing his present the day before his party. I shave and shower. As I'm dressing, I hear at least one of them coming through the front door.

As I come downstairs, I see the gang's all here. Good. Full band jams are always the best.

"Ready to work some shit out?" Cal holds up his favorite guitar, his son's carrier in his other hand. He knows just what I need. I nod and he sets Gibs down to slap my shoulder. Probably trying to see if I'm stable on my feet. He doesn't realize I haven't had a thing to drink since before the show last night. If I was as drunk as Sam says I was, Callum has every reason to wonder.

We get two and a half songs out of the jam session and are almost late for the last show at HARD. Part of me wonders if Kady'll show up. I begged her to play two songs with us for the last show. She finally agreed, but that was before everything went down.

I shoot the shit with Harden in his office. He thanks me, us, for taking a chance on his place for the residency. I don't even know how it was picked, but he's decent to be appreciative. That's when I notice Kady's pass on his desk. I can't tear my eyes off it. If she shows up tonight, would I be alright with her being on stage? Fuck. I run a hand through my already messy hair.

I know he caught me eyeballing it, but he says nothing. It's now dawned on me just how overly professional he's been in talking to me today. It's as if he knows what went down and he just wants us out of his hair with minimum damage. Of course, he probably also noticed my inebriation the last several shows, so that could be part of it too.

In the dressing room, the waitress drops my usual whiskey neat at my normal seat.

"Thanks, doll." I throw some cash on her tray as a tip. She's been good to us during our stay here. The other guys follow suit, and she smiles. I don't touch my drink though. I promised Sammy I was going to lay off and I'm keeping my word.

For the first time ever, I'm not looking forward to the show. I've always lived to be onstage. Leading our band through the rigorous give and take with the audience. Usually there is nothing like it for me. It's the best high I've ever found, but tonight, I just want it over with, to be finished and done and back to my Malibu house. Finish cutting the record and get out on the road on a real tour. What's happened in Vegas can definitely stay the fuck here.

R

I NURSE my beer by the pool. It's the only one I'll have today. I'm still keeping my promise to Sammy. Cal, Sammy and Gibs are in the pool. Killian is sucking face with the waitress from the bar over in the corner. I'm trying to stay cool in the shade because it's hot as fuck in Vegas. Darren is around somewhere, but I don't really care. The guys from WatermelonX are here along with some of their chicks. It's a good showing for the twins' birthday. I insisted the chef barbecue so Cal can play with his son and enjoy just being a dad. His Aunt Sandy's around here too, probably in the house with the air conditioning, and I can't say I blame her.

I pull up Kady's contact in my phone. It's times like this that it's hard to resist the urge to reach out to her. My need for answers only she can provide is resilient. I do this several times a day. So is my need to check on her. It's so strong, sometimes I sit with my thumb hovering over the call button, but I never press it. Instead, I re-block it and set my phone down.

Cold water hits the side of my head in a steady stream. Sammy has snuck up on me with a loaded squirt gun full of pool water. He pumps the gun a few times and lets go with another stream, hitting me directly in the face this time. Gibson cackles as he watches from his floatie in the water.

"Fuck, Sammy!" I set my phone on the table and stand. He squats to refill the gun in the pool, and I make my move. My flying tackle of the little shit sends us both splashing into the cool water. When we surface, Gibson's cackling as his floatie rides the waves caused by our combined fall into the pool.

"You think it's funny, do ya?" I pull his floatie to me and tickle him. He throws his head back in another hearty belly laugh, the kind that makes you grin and laugh with him. To be this carefree again.

After a delicious dinner and a rousing version of Happy Birthday to Kill and Cal that scared poor Gibs, the guys from WatermelonX take off with their women in tow.

"Present time," Sammy exclaims with glee when the last guest leaves. It's his favorite part of any birthday celebration and Christmas too. I don't think Sammy got presents much as a kid. Now he loves to give them as much as he loves to get them.

"You guys didn't have to get me anything." Cal drops to the couch, baby monitor in hand.

"Good, since I didn't," Kill says plainly, Sally still wrapped around his arm. Cal shoves at him playfully.

"Mine's first." Sammy goes into the closet for something I didn't even see him stash there. He hands Cal and Kill small identically wrapped boxes. Cal makes a show of rattling his, before tearing into the paper. Kill rips into his simultaneously. They open their boxes to find matching thick pewter BR logo pendants. Cal examines his closely, and then he exchanges with Kill to examine his.

"You made these?" Cal looks up at Sammy. He nods.

"Just the pendant, not the chain. I bought those. I made 'em before we came to Vegas. I made one for each of us. Sorry Mav, it kind of spoils your birthday present. They're each a little different." Kill puts his on right away and Cal holds his out so I can see it. It's our logo hand-carved into the pendant, along with a small gemstone at the end of the R's tail. Cal's gem is a deep forest green. Kill's is black. I wonder what color Sammy picked for me. He pulls out the one around his neck.

"I've been wearing it the whole time we've been here, but you fuckers didn't notice." Sam's stone is a beautiful ocean blue color.

"Wow, these are amazing, Sammy. Something to look forward to." I throw him a wink. "When did you take up doing that kind of thing?"

"I needed something to keep me busy while we were broken up." He shrugs it off. It doesn't surprise me. Sammy always needs to be doing something.

"Okay, my turn. I did not get you guys the same thing. Sammy, come help me. We'll be right back." We return from my bedroom, Cal's gifts in my arms, Kill's gift in Sammy's. It's obvious Kill's is a new bass. I didn't bother to wrap it, just stuck a big ass red bow on it. If it's not square, I can't fucking wrap it.

"Mav! It's the new Fender. I was eyeing one of these. Thanks, man!" He fingers the frets a few times to feel it out, and I immediately think of Kady's nervous habit of doing the same thing. Kill stands to give me a brief hug. "Seriously, man. Thanks." He lifts his chin. I pat his back.

"Happy birthday, dude."

We all turn to Cal to watch him open his present. The pictures are wrapped into one solid block held together with duct tape. Jokes are made about the tape and the shit wrap job.

Cal finally gets the framed pictures free of the paper and each other. He slowly and carefully flips between them, eyeing each one with intense concentration. He goes through them a second time. He's silent in his perusal, so Sammy and Kill move behind him to see what he's looking so hard at.

"Mav." His voice is thick with emotion. He looks up at me, his eyes moist. *Don't cry, dude. Don't fuckin' cry.* I'm hanging on by a hair as it fuckin' is.

"I, uh." I clear my throat because I can't say her name yet. "I asked for photos to show you how we see you. As a loyal brother. A best friend. An awesome father. A musician." He nods. He flips back through them to show Sammy and Kill each framed photo.

"I love them all." His voice is rough. "I wish—" he stops himself and clears his throat.

"These are going to look awesome in my house, Mav. I know just where to put each one. You even framed them to match my decor." He stands and gives me a hard, backslapping hug. I don't tell him that Kady did that herself, sight unseen.

"I just commissioned the pictures, man. Thank her, she did the work." I release him and back off. It's too many feels and not enough alcohol to handle them.

"I wish I could," he mumbles while stacking the photos in a neat pile off to the side.

"Why can't you?" I look over at him. "You have her number."

He shakes his head. "She's blocked us. All of us."

"She didn't block me. She didn't have my number to begin with." Killian snickers and Sammy throws a hunk of wrapping paper at him.

"What time are you all heading out tomorrow?" I'm as desperate to change the subject as I am to get out of this God-forsaken desert.

"Kill and I'll probably head out around noon. You?" Cal looks over at me, his eyes working me over.

"I'm heading out early. I got shit to do in Malibu." I don't. I just need to get the fuck out of here, like yesterday.

He nods. "Beer's tomorrow night at my place?" Cal asks.

"Sure. Text me tomorrow afternoon. Safe travels if I don't see you until then, man." He puts the framed pictures in the back of his SUV and he and Kill take off.

Sammy lingers. "You need help packing or anything?" He picks up the last of the wrapping paper and tosses it in the garbage. "I'm packed and ready to go from my hotel."

"Nah. Cal's got my axe and keyboard. The acoustic will fit in Stella with my clothes and shit. I'm good." Sammy nods.

"Mav, can I stay with you for a few weeks back home?" Sammy kicks at the garbage bag.

"Dude. You know you don't have to ask." He nods and his cheeks redden. "Whatever you need, Sammy, you know that." I pat his shoulder.

Sammy nods, looking down at his shoe. "Thanks, Mav," he mumbles. "Guess I'll see ya tomorrow afternoon."

"You know the gate code. The backdoor will be unlocked if for whatever reason I'm not there."

He nods and leans in and gives me a quick one-armed hug. "Drive safe."

I shoot him a grin. "With Stella and me, there is no chance of that happening. That Vette's made for speed, Sammy." Hopefully she's fast enough to outrun the image of Kady grinning at me from the passenger seat with those damn excited sparks in her moss-green eyes.

"At least wear your fuckin' seatbelt, man." He shakes his head. Throwing an arm up in a half-assed wave, he jumps into his Jeep before I shut the door.

I throw the last of my shit in the empty duffle bag on the floor of the closet. I double check the drawers in the dresser to

271

make sure I didn't leave anything behind. And when I turn to look at the bed, I see the small, wrapped gift on my nightstand.

It was part of the courier delivery that brought the pictures for Cal, but this had my name on it. I didn't feel like opening it yesterday. Didn't think it would be a good idea to open it today. Tonight though, the curiosity has me holding it in my hands. Should I open it or toss it?

Before I know what I'm doing, I've unwrapped a small, bound book. The cover feels like faux leather and my name is in silver lettering in the bottom right corner.

I flip it open and find it's all photos of me. Me on stage, here in the house, at the sand dunes, with the guys, even a few of me with Gibson. There are ones of me laughing, singing, thinking. The last one is one of me looking directly at the camera. I remember Kady taking this picture. I see what Cal was talking about. The way I look at Kady is different. My best me.

I toss it on the bed. It's all a lie. I don't know why she bothered. She's a lie, this book is a lie. It's all a big fucking lie. I toss it in the garbage next to my bedroom door, but then I think better of it. I toss it into my duffle and crawl into bed.

Chapter 26

Kadence

Two months later

"Is that what you're wearing?" Hayleigh asks as I walk into the kitchen. I look down at my outfit. I thought I looked incredibly put together, considering it's the first time in over a week I bothered to put on real pants. I don't go out much since Mav crushed my heart two months ago. Or I crushed my own. I should have told him who I was much earlier. It would have saved me a hell of a lot of heartbreak.

She purses her lips at me. "No, Kady. Come on." She grabs my hand and drags me down the hall to my room. "Give me that shirt." I pull it off and she throws it on the floor and goes into my closet and pulls out a bright pink one. "This one." I look back down at the black shirt on the floor.

"First off, it's black, and with those pants?" She shakes her head. "We aren't going to a funeral, Kay. This is a party." She motions to my black leather pants. I was kind of proud I fit into them. I hadn't in over a year, but it's funny how much weight you lose when all interest in food is gone. It's all bland like the

273

rest of my life and has been since Mav left and went back to his grandiose rock star life in L.A.

"Go on, put it on." I slip on the pink shirt and give her a 'happy now?' look.

"Now we have to fix your hair." I roll my eyes. Really, Hayleigh? My hair is just fine. But she grabs some styling putty from my bathroom and warms it between her hands before she pulls select pieces of my hair through it and then re-fluffs the style. "You spent five hours in the salon. It's so bold, you should show it off."

I roll my eyes and huff at her. I don't care how I look because I don't want to go to this stupid party. It's a work function of Hayleigh's and I'm not sure how or why I let her talk me into this. Oh wait, she threatened to drag me out to the strip in my pajamas if I didn't go. I believe she even used the words 'mopey ass' and then mumbled something about me starting to look like a homeless person.

She gives me a once over and yanks the hairbands off my wrist. "Why do you still put these here when you don't have enough hair to worry about putting it up in a ponytail?" I shrug. I'm not going to describe to her the psychology of it, that it was a suggestion that one of my therapists gave me before I stopped seeing them. In their place, she adds some more bracelets. She tops off my look with a necklace. "There, now you're ready." I follow her out the door and run into her back as she stops abruptly in front of me. Shit. I meant to close the door to the spare bedroom. I didn't expect Hayleigh to come down here and dress me like a paper doll either.

She walks into my spare bedroom and spins to face me, her eyes large at the empty space. "Oh, Kady, what did you do? Where's your stuff? The musical instruments? The awards and clothes?"

I shift my gaze to the side, so I don't have to meet her disappointed look. She walks over to the closet and checks it, only to find my winter jacket and some stupid snow boots I've worn twice. She looks at me again, her eyes wide but her brow knitted.

She whispers, "Oh, Kade, what did you do?"

Me: I need a bigger office.

Me: Especially if I am going to make a go of Photos by Kadence.

Me: I cleaned it out. Donated what I could. Chucked the rest.

She glances at my texts but doesn't say anything. Sure, it's a lie, but Hayleigh doesn't know that. Although it will be a great office, I'll get rid of that awful couch in my sitting room and get a proper matching office set.

"You didn't keep any of your guitars?" She looks around like maybe there is one stashed under an invisible bed.

Me: No.

"But Kady—"

Me: I have no intention of playing anymore, so I donated them to school kids.

I walk out and wait for her out in the foyer. Hayleigh's quiet as she drives us to the party being held at HARD but during the day. It pays to know the owner, I guess. I'm praying Harden will be there, so at least I'll have someone to hang out with. I don't know her work people and she knows that having to explain what is up with me not talking is not something I want to do over and over again.

We get there and head in. The party is already swinging. I seek out the waitress and show her my phone.

Me: Harden here?

"He's in his office, hon. You don't happen to have a way to contact Killian, do you?" I shake my head. "I figured I'd give it a shot." She nods down the hall. "Go on."

I wander down to Harden's office and knock on the door frame. He looks up from his cramped desk, a smile crossing his serious face when he sees me.

"Kady!" He stands and opens his arms at me, waiting for me to walk into his hug. He rocks me slightly as he holds me.

"It's good to see you, kiddo. Short Neon Pink. I like it." He gives one of Hayleigh's carefully coiffed spikes a playful tug. I shrug but don't make a move to leave his hug. He finally releases me.

"You look good. You good?" He looks at me in his Harden way and I feel the stone façade cracking just a little bit as I lift a shoulder.

"You don't want to be here?"

I shake my head.

"But Hayleigh talked you into it?"

I nod.

"Got it."

This is the perfect place to hide out during the party so Hayleigh can be the center of attention that she should be without worrying about what I am up to.

"I'll be right back." Harden gets up and leaves me in his office. I notice my Blind Rebels pass sitting on his desk. I toss it in his garbage can.

When Harden comes back in, he's wearing his bomber jacket. He only wears that when he's riding his motorcycle. "Let's go for a ride. I told Hayleigh." He rifles through a cabinet in the back of his office and hands me a plain white helmet.

Soon, I'm gripping Harden around his waist as he takes us through the streets of Vegas and out of the city up towards Mount Charleston. It's one of Harden's favorite rides. I relax against him as we head up the windy road. I've only been up here a few times to hike with Harden and Hayleigh. I'm not exactly dressed for hiking today, so I hope that isn't what we're up to. We stop off at the visitors' center. I use the restroom and then wait for Harden in the back by the small amphitheater overlooking a wide, rocky gorge. It's pretty here. I walk closer to the cliff's edge, but not too close.

Harden stands next to me. "Those boulders right there are great to sit on and think. Sometimes I come up here to do that. Do you want to ride farther up? Or do you want to have a sit and think?"

We walk toward the boulders, and he climbs up on one and sits. I mimic him on a slightly smaller one. I pull my knees to my chest and rest my chin on my knees. I feel really small all the way up here. The view is awesome. It's cooler by at least ten degrees than down in Vegas. The air smells clean and woodsy, totally different from down on the desert floor.

I wonder for a second if Mav's seen it up here, then I shake my head ever so slightly. Why do I care? He pretty much dumped me without giving me a chance to explain. He erased me from his inner circle. *Expendable.* I shouldn't be thinking of him.

My life now is so far removed from the life I led before Jerrod. I was expendable to him too. I'm still paying for the sins of a young girl forced to grow up way too fast in the show business industry.

Jerrod. I squeeze my eyes shut just thinking his name and just like that, I'm back in the tent at the festival. Talking to two young girls, identical twins dressed exactly the same. Their smiles were wide, and they were a little shy but so excited to meet me that they were trembling. I pushed them through the tightly tied corner of the tent as soon as I saw him enter.

Then it suddenly melts to the confusion on Mav's face when Killian spilled my secret. I see the hurt on his face, and him walking off without even giving me a chance to explain why I kept that part of my life from him. Why didn't I just tell him before it all blew up?

I know exactly why. Because I didn't want to be judged on the mistakes of the empty life I lived when I was Kandi. I shift as my butt complains about the hard rock beneath it. I glance over at Harden's rock, and he's gone. I didn't hear him get up.

He's walked down the ridge a little farther. I hop off my boulder and join him.

"Let's grab a bite." We head up the road to the Lodge.

After ordering our meals, Harden looks across the small wooden table at me. "You know Hayleigh dragged you to the party because she's worried about you."

Me: I get it. It wasn't necessary. I'm done with the pity. I've moved on.

"Good." He nods and fiddles with his straw wrapper. "She mentioned you gave away your instruments and stuff."

Me: It's time to let go of Kandi.

Me: Quit trying to live a dream that's been dead for years.

Harden's lips press into a thin line as he reads my messages. "You seemed pretty happy making music with Mav and the guys. Helping them and playing piano. You were awesome on stage."

I shake my head vigorously, but that seems to upset Harden more.

"I'm just saying maybe you should stick with music. Fuck Mav and do it for you." He looks up from his shredded straw wrapper. "If it makes you feel good, Kade, do it."

Me: It doesn't make me feel good.

Me: It hurts. A lot.

Harden looks up from my text when I clutch my shirt over my heart. Tears threaten to fall. Working with Mav on his songs let me get lost in music for a while. I don't think I've been as free from myself as I was when I was working with him. It was nice to get outside my own head and focus on music, but that was all a façade. Killian was right. I'm just a poser, someone who couldn't hack it in the industry.

I gave myself to someone who threw me away burns even more. My own fucking fiancé used me as a human shield at the festival while he tried to get away. Why would I think Mav would fight to keep me? Everyone's minds are already made up about me, including my own.

I must let it go for good, for my own wellbeing. It's easier to just take pictures and frame people in little boxes, leave them there and pretend I'm good at it.

Me: I'm going to make a go of Photos by Kadence.

Me: Pump up my portfolio so I can make money doing it.

Me: Portraits, engagements, weddings, etc.

He nods at my message. "I just don't want you going backwards. You've gained those wings we talked about. Don't hand them back now. You could also come back to HARD to be the house photographer."

Me: I'll think about it. Right now, I'm leaning away from event photography and thinking more of specializing in portraits.

He pushes his plate away as he reads my last message.

"You want to go back to the party or home?" he asks as we head back to his bike.

Me: Party.

We arrive back at HARD as the party is winding down. I surprise Harden when I hug him before we get back into the club. "Thank you," I mouth. He nods and hugs me back.

R

HAYLEIGH JOINS me in the small bedroom that's now my new office. "Nice. Took long enough to get the new furniture delivered for in here."

It *so* did. Getting it delivered and then put together was a nightmare, but it gave me a chance to repaint the bedroom a soft yet vibrant yellow, and redo the sitting room in a peaceful lavender.

"You put these bookshelves together yourself?" She knocks on the brown shelf while I nod proudly. Not without a lot of frustration and some flipping off of the instruction sheet, but I did it.

Hayleigh sits on my new office couch and nods. "I like the bigger office; it shows you're serious about the photography thing."

She shifts to cross her legs and looks at me like only she can. Shit. Here it comes. "What I don't like is how *you've been*, Kade."

The dressing down that's been brewing for weeks is here. I know how this goes. She tells me how I'm acting, how the way I'm dealing doesn't work for her. Lather, rinse, repeat.

"You're functioning, but you aren't living." She looks me in the eye and leans forward. "This is the Kady from before, the one who lived the way other people thought she should. You keep saying you did away with Kandi, but you're acting just like her. You've turned back into Kandi."

What the actual fuck? I slap at my pockets, looking for my phone.

"It's in the living room, but you don't need to respond, it's best if you just listen right now." She pauses and takes a breath. "You are doing everything you think *we* want to see. That is how Kandi lived. She did what she thought everyone else expected. You've locked your feelings away tight." She looks up at me. "Kandi was not who you are. She was a stage persona that didn't have feelings. That's not you. It wasn't you then, and it's not you now. I don't know how to make you see that." She sighs.

"Kay, it's okay to be sad. It's okay to be mad. It's okay to not know exactly how you feel any given moment, but what's not okay is being fake." She stands up and holds her arms open like Harden does, waiting to make sure I see she's going to pull me in for a hug. "You let yourself love Mav, and now you're hurting. You can talk to me. Or not." She sighs and gives me another quick hug before walking out.

"I'm heading into the office for the afternoon. Text me what you want for dinner, and I'll pick it up on my way back."

I spend the afternoon putting together another bookcase, this one for my sitting room. I deserve tacos for this shit. Between the directions that make me feel like a child trying to put together a Lego creation and my obvious talent for misplacing the stupid little wrench thingy, my frustration almost gets the best of me. Almost. Because I conquered that damn bookcase. I shoot Hayleigh a text asking for pizza because as much as I want tacos, they make me think of Mav and our impromptu dinner on my balcony, and I don't want to go there right now. I want to just enjoy some melted cheese and revel in my triumph over the bookcases.

My sitting room is starting to come together. It'll be nice to have an area to read and relax that isn't also my office. The lavender color of the walls in here eases something in me. I fill one bookcase with my favorite books and tchotchkes and the other gets my to-be-read books, magazines, and a shelf yet to be determined. Maybe I'll fill it with small picture frames filled with my favorite photos.

Hayleigh comes into the apartment, followed by the familiar scent of our favorite pizza from Metro Pizzeria. My stomach grumbles. I skipped lunch, eager to get the bookcases together. I follow my nose out to the kitchen with a grin on my face.

"That smells so good, doesn't it?" I nod, and Hayleigh slides the box on to the bar in the kitchen. "It was all I could do not to grab a piece on the way home. Oh, hey, here's your mail." She hands me a stack of envelopes and a few magazines that I toss on the end table by the couch before grabbing the paper plates because that ooey-gooey cheesy goodness belongs in my belly now.

As we eat, Hayleigh tells me about her meeting and about some new finance law that I don't understand. After dinner, I change into my sweats to go down to the gym downstairs. I've been heading down every night for about three weeks now and I finally notice a difference. I sleep better, but I've also noticed some definition in my calves and arms too, so win-win. Sometimes Hayleigh joins me, but most days I go alone and honestly, I prefer it that way. There's something about it being just me and whatever is on my Spotify that helps me let go of whatever crap is in my head that day.

As I set up the elliptical, another tenant comes in to use the Jacob's ladder. I stay away from that thing; I'm convinced it's a medieval torture device instead of exercise equipment.

I've seen this guy around, unfortunately he seems to be on the same workout schedule as me. At first, he was a little overbearing, trying to hit on me. Luckily, he finally took a hint and now he just smiles and nods before going to his favorite torture device. Maybe I shouldn't have been so quick to shoot him down. He has super muscular calves. His shirt rides up a little and I can see some ink on his side. I absentmindedly wonder what his tattoo is of. I can't see it enough to make out anything distinguishing about it.

"You're toning up well." Oops, he probably felt me staring at him and thought I was ogling, when really, I was just zoning out. I nod and smile. "Seriously, it's really noticeable in your legs especially. Good job."

Apparently, I wasn't the only one checking someone out. Why did I turn him down again? I show him my phone.

Me: Thanks.

He winks and carries on. Maybe next time I'll remember to compliment him on his legs. I'm supposed to do that right? He compliments me and I compliment him. I don't know. Maybe I should ask Hayleigh how this kind of thing works, so I'm not this socially awkward all the damn time. At least I have the non-verbal thing to blame it on. Although I think I'd be just as awkward if I could give voice to what I was thinking.

282

Back upstairs, I grab my mail from the table and throw it on the desk in my office on my way to the shower. One of the envelopes catches my eye. It's obvious by the stamp that it's not the random junk mail I usually get. The envelope is of a different, thicker quality and the return address is Monument Records. What the hell could they want? I rip it open and scan the enclosed document. *Required to re-record the rough cuts of 'Star Chaser' and 'Incredible Without Trying' at the L.A. recording studio next week.* Can they do that?

I rifle through my drawer and pull out my copy of the contract I signed that night at the studio with Mav. Yep, there it is right in the pages. They can require me to play on recordings of any songs I worked on as needed.

I can't go back to L.A. Just the thought of being there makes my chest tighten.

I rush into the common area, looking for Hayleigh. She's on the phone making plans, but when she sees the look on my face, she tells whomever she's talking to that she'll call them right back.

"What is it?"

I shove the letter at her. She reads it. Then reads it again.

"How can they make you do that?" She looks at me for an answer as I hold out the contract I signed at the recording studio. She reads it over.

"Shit. Looks like we're going to L.A." She looks up at me. "I said *we* because I'm going with you. I won't take no for an answer. You're not going back to L.A. without someone." I nod because there is no way that I can get through going back without her. I send her a text.

Me: I can't go back there.

My chest starts tightening the more I think about being in L.A.; the noise, the people, the buildings.

Hayleigh reads my text, then grabs my hands and forces me to look at her. "One step at a time. We'll have Arthur look over the contract to make sure it says what we both think it says. And if you have to go, we'll walk across that bridge together, one step at a time. Okay?"

There is nothing about this that is okay. Nothing at all. I look at Hayleigh.

"Either way, it'll work out. Maybe if we go, it'll be good for you. You can put some things behind you instead of avoiding them," she suggests. I shake my head.

R

A WEEK and several visits to my lawyer later, Hayleigh and I are on the way to L.A. I look out the window of the plane and bite my lip hard. She pats my knee. She knows I don't want to do this, but I signed the stupid fucking contract. I shake my head at myself.

"Instead of this being all about the dread of being in L.A., let's look at this as an opportunity to move past it, Kade." I try to nod. I wish I could convince myself that she's right about this. She squeezes my knee. "We have our game plan, and we'll stick to it. That way, we are in control."

But dread is all I feel. There is nothing good for me in L.A. Nothing. Even with our solid game plan, I don't know if I can do this.

Chapter 27

Mavrick

I 'm not due at the studio until tonight with the rest of the band, but I saw Kadence on the docket to record today. Darren insisted she lay the tracks for 'Star Chaser' and 'Incredible' after two perfectly capable studio musicians screwed it up take after take, wasting the better part of a day of booked studio time. We even attempted to change up the arrangement to accommodate the studio musicians, but that was a terrible idea, and the song turned into a hot, steaming pile of shit.

Once inside the Monument Records lobby, I make a beeline to the right, heading downstairs to the in-house recording studio. As I wait at the elevator bank, I hear a commotion behind me. Outside of the main lobby, there's a sudden cacophony of press shouting demands. Hayleigh strolls to the reception desk, and the shouting from the paparazzi outside dulls when the door swings closed.

The receptionist rises and walks over to the staircase leading to the second level where most of the offices are. When Hayleigh moves to follow the receptionist, it's then that I see Kadence. I almost don't even recognize her.

Gone is the shoulder length black hair with purple tips. Now it's just past her ears and cropped in a brilliant fuchsia shaggy pixie cut with random pieces spiked out. She's dressed like the penultimate star, tight black leather pants with sparkling studs outlining the pockets. She wears a loose-fitting top that swirls purple and pink. She looks like a punk rock barbie doll and she's fucking gorgeous.

Wasn't riding our coattails, my ass. She never dressed so rock 'n' roll in Vegas. Hell, she wouldn't dress like this when she was Kandi. That was all soft colors and her trademark blonde hair. This is her done up all for show. Big dark sunglasses take up most of her face and she walks stiffly, as if she exercised too hard as she follows Hayleigh and the receptionist. She takes my breath away and crumbles my heart at the same time.

I thought she'd be recording, but she heads upstairs instead of my way, so I walk back into the lobby. I shouldn't have come. I can't just hang out in the lobby hoping to catch a glimpse of her again, but fuck if I can leave either. Shit. Now what?

I hide by the coffee bar at the back of the lobby. As I fix myself a coffee, I wonder if I should run upstairs. I could make up some bullshit excuse about needing to see Darren. He'd probably see right through it since he knows I don't like spending time anywhere near him.

The head of the label, Tom, comes downstairs with Hayleigh and Kady in tow. He's in his trademark brown suit and bolo tie. His chiseled face is framed by his short honey colored hair.

"The press conference should be all set up. I'll make sure that they're ready and be right back." He walks the other way towards the smaller of the two press conference rooms. As he walks away, Hayleigh's hand goes to Kadence's shoulder and gives a reassuring squeeze. Her lips move as she talks to Kady, who just nods along like the puppet she's always been.

Tom comes back and escorts them to the press room, his

hand going to the small of Kadence's back in a supportive gesture, but I can see her flinch and stiffen all the way from here. Quick, but not subtle.

I can't help myself. I follow and slip into a chair at the very back. I slouch way down. This should be entertaining.

"Good afternoon, ladies and gentlemen. For those that don't know me, I'm Tom Monument of Monument Records." He stands tall and straight at the podium. "Thank you for coming to today's press conference with Kadence Matthews. Some of you may remember her as Kandi Matthews. She was a child star first known as Kandi from Kangaroo Klub Houze and then she broke out into the pop music scene from there. Most of you probably remember the tragic shooting backstage at the Monument Festival, two years ago. Kadence is here today to talk about some work she's been doing. Kadence will communicate with you via a tele-reader. You'll be able to read her remarks on the screen behind me. Her words will be read out loud for you by Hayleigh Thomas. There will be a limited Q&A after the announcement. Please hold your questions for then."

Kadence types on a keyboard while Hayleigh gives them a voice from the side of the stage. "Thank you all for coming. As a result of the Monument Festival shooting, I have trauma induced mutism, which is just a technical term that means I can't talk any more. Or sing." She pauses, looking up from the keyboard. "As Tom said, I'm here to announce my retirement from entertainment. I'm back in L.A. for a limited time to record some piano tracks for two songs I helped the Blind Rebels with. I met them in Vegas and ended up collaborating on two songs with them a few months ago." She pauses and looks up, gazing around the gathered crowd of press. I slink further down in my seat, so she doesn't see me.

"It was a lot of fun and a great honor to work with the Blind Rebels. While the work I did with them was insignificant in the grand scheme of their album, they insisted I take a songwriter credit, along with Mavrick Slater and the rest of the band on two songs that will be on their upcoming album. I've arranged with Tom and Monument Records to donate any proceeds I would normally get to a foundation that assists children and teens afflicted with mutism."

"We'll take a couple questions," Tom states. "Let's start up front here."

"Kandi, are you romantically linked with any of the Blind Rebels?" All I can see is the back of the guy's head. I cross my arms. This should be entertaining.

"In the few weeks I spent working with The Blind Rebels, I found them to be great guys, a lot of fun to hang out with. All four are very dedicated to their music and sound, but to answer your question directly, no, I'm not involved with any of them, romantically or otherwise. I'm just here to lay some piano tracks. I probably won't even see them." She gives the guy a brief, toothy, and totally fake smile. "And please call me Kadence. I don't like being called Kandi."

"Are you planning to record any music of your own?" A woman, in what looks like the second row, ventures her question.

"No," Hayleigh says for her friend. Kady gives a soft smile to the person who asked the question, but I'm reeling. Why'd she go through all this to give up on her music when she was just starting to get it back? Something's not sitting right with me about that.

"What about more songwriting?" The same woman follows up her question.

"I had a lot of fun working with The Rebels, but no. I don't see myself doing anything music or entertainment related in the future. I'm retiring to live a somewhat normal life, if someone who can't talk can have such a thing."

Tom interjects. "One more question and then we have to get

Kadence down to the studio. We only have her for a limited amount of time."

"How will you be commemorating the upcoming anniversary of the Monument Festival shooting? Will you be at the vigil this year?"

Even from way back here, I can see the blood drain from Kady's face. Her paleness worries me, reminding me of the time outside the hamburger joint when she froze up on me. She grips the lectern she stands behind so hard that her knuckles turn white. Her head hangs from her shoulders and her chest heaves as she gulps for breaths like that day she had the panic attack. I sit up a little taller. As pissed as I am at Kady, I don't want her to suffer a panic attack in front of these vultures. She'd never hear or see the end of it, it'd likely be pushed out to every media service with in the next ten minutes legitimate or not.

Hayleigh mutters something quietly to Kady, who shakes her head. She rests her hand on the small of Kady's back. When Kady lifts her head up, she throws her shoulders back a little bit and sticks out her chin. She doesn't make an effort to try to hide the tears streaming down her face, taking her heavy eye makeup with it. She just concentrates on her fingers on the keyboard.

"Not a day goes by that I don't relive some part of that night." Hayleigh reads as Kady draws in another heaving breath. "I'll spend my life mourning for the lives that were lost, and those that were changed forever. I'll be at the vigil to pay my respects, but know, it's always with me, they're always with me. Right here." Kadence places her hand over her heart. She turns on her high heels and walks from the room.

I WASN'T as incognito as I had hoped. I get caught by the press after Kady leaves. I echo her sentiments about working with her, about it being fun and platonic. By the time I make it out of the press conference and down to the recording studio, Kady's already behind the piano working. I slide into the seat next to the in-house studio's engineer, Terry, ignoring the hard stare from Hayleigh, who sits on the couch with a magazine open on her lap. I slip on the headphones to listen.

Terry's expression is pinched, causing his already large nose to look even longer. He squeezes his eyes shut and shakes his head.

"We can't use this shit," Terry says to me, tossing the paperwork in the air in his frustration. "Why don't you play it? Why her?"

"I can horseshit my way through a live show, but I don't have the technical precision she does for an album quality recording. She wrote the piano parts, so she'll do it until she gets it."

She struggles through 'Star Chaser' a few more times. Ready to throw in the towel, Terry stands up and paces. He shuts down the recording in the middle of taping the song. "This is all wrong. The timing is off. What the fuck, Mav? I can work a lot of magic in the booth, but I can't fix this."

I didn't want her to know I was here, but fuck it, this is our record she's ruining. "Put me in the vocal booth at the same time. It's how we recorded it in Vegas."

Terry stops her in the middle of the song. "We're taking a break to set up with the vocal booth so you can record it with Mav like you did in Vegas." Her back straightens, but she doesn't look up at the window. She hangs her head for a moment and then slips off her headphones. She sends Terry a text that I read over his shoulder.

Kady: Can I have 30? I need air.

"Sure, take thirty, get some air. We'll start fresh when you get back." Kady walks through the engineering booth without looking my way and directly out of the room. Hayleigh stays seated on the couch, staring at me.

Terry scurries to set up the vocal booth for me, and I spin to face Hayleigh. "Aren't you going to follow your friend? Give her a pep talk, maybe?" I spit at her.

Hayleigh shakes her head at me. "She said she needed air. She doesn't need me to breathe." She looks up at me from her magazine. "We purposely worked with Tom to schedule her recording sessions early so you wouldn't be here. So why are you here?"

"This is our record. We oversee everything." I fold my arms across my chest. "Her piano is subpar today." I point at her. "Go tell *your* girl to get her shit together and get back in the studio. Time is money here." Fuck, I sound like Darren. I shake my head.

Hayleigh chuckles at me and crosses her arms across her chest. "She's no more *my* girl than she is *yours*. I don't control her. Kady's her own person. You of all people should know that." She stops and looks me straight in the eye. "She's in the one place she never wanted to come back to, doing the one thing she just told the world that she didn't want to do any more. It's like forcing an eight-year-old to eat broccoli and do math at the same time." She shakes her head. "Of course, it's not going to come out well." She pulls headphones out of her hoodie pouch and tucks them in her ear, shutting me down.

Kady comes back in and sits at the piano forty minutes later. She looks at no one as she pulls on her headphones. She starts by running her fingers up and down the keyboard, doing scales. I give Terry some levels on the microphone in the vocal booth.

"Okay, you two, let's try this. Mav, you count it in." Terry's not convinced that this is the answer. He said as much as we were waiting for Princess Kandi to come back in. I don't want to be here, but I also don't want our album to suck.

"Okay, Kadence?" I breathe, waiting for her to nod or give me a thumbs up or something. She finally nods ever so slightly. "Two, three, and four," I count down and she starts the song. I accompany her. It's sounds a little better. Terry's nodding.

Another forty minutes later, we have a decent number of quality takes to work with.

"Okay, I think we'll call it for today, Kady," Terry says. "We'll work on 'Incredible' the day after tomorrow, same time." She nods and takes off her headset. She gulps from her bottle of water from behind the piano. The band has started filtering into the engineering room.

This could get ugly. The band is pretty raw about Kadence playing on the album. Killian and Sammy almost came to blows over it earlier in the week, and they're fucking best friends. I had to step between them. Me, breaking up fights now instead of being the one to be held back. I step out of the vocal booth and stand over with the guys in case I need to jump in again.

Hayleigh has gathered her things and is already walking out the door. Kady comes out of the recording booth and grabs the bag she stowed under the soundboard. She doesn't make eye contact with any of us. Instead, she heads right to the door, chin tucked to her chest as she breezes by, her pineapple scent lingering as she hurries out.

Sammy goes for the door, looking like someone killed his puppy, but Killian hooks his arm before he gets there. "Don't, Sammy."

Sammy's head drops momentarily, but he stops. "But she's crying," he mumbles. Kill pats him on the back and says something low only Sammy can hear. He nods and flops on the couch. Terry works with the best two mixes and plays back 'Star Chaser' for us.

It's that fucking good.

R

"THIS IS TOTAL BULLSHIT." I slam my fist down on the board. "You said Kady was going to be here today to record 'Incredible.'"

"Don't shoot the messenger, man." Terry throws his hands out in front of him in a semi-shrug. "I got the message this morning that her recording has been pushed back two days."

"Why?" I don't want to fall into her bullshit. She needs to grow the fuck up and act like a professional musician, not a petulant teenager. We can't bend to her every recording whim, or our album will get shelved. That diva shit may have flown for Kandi, but we don't work that way. And this is our album.

"No reason was given. Not to me, anyway." Terry looks at me like I've grown a second head. "Since we have the studio and you're early, let's lay some of your backing vocals." Fuckin' Terry, always all business.

I don't keep track of what time it is as Terry and I work to lay down my own backing vocals. I'm finishing them up on 'Star Chaser' when Callum and Killian walk into the engineering room. My stomach rumbles so loudly that I am sure the mic picked it up. I worked through lunch and possibly dinner.

I join them in the booth, and they look nervous. Sammy's the only one missing.

"I'm starving. Let's go grab something real quick." I grab my leather jacket off the couch. No one moves a muscle. No one says anything. Kill and Cal just look at each other doing that twin nonverbal communication shit that they do.

"Come on, assholes, I'm starving. Let's roll. Sammy can catch up with us if he wants something." I head to the door.

Cal grabs my arm. "Let's order delivery. Eat in."

"I've been here since ten. I could really use some fresh air and a change of scenery, man." I yank my arm back.

"Then we'll eat on the roof," Kill suggests. "My treat." Killian almost never treats.

"Fine. Order burgers. I'll be on the roof." I take the elevator up to the rooftop patio. It doesn't get used much despite being fully decked out. I think they use it for the occasional party. It's the only other time I've been up here. It's warm enough I don't need my jacket, so I remove it and set it on the chair next to me.

Cal joins me after a few minutes. "Kill's downstairs waiting for the delivery." I nod, but my 'something's up' radar is pinging hard.

"What the fuck is going on and where is Sammy anyway?" I shift forward and study Cal's face. There's trepidation in his eyes that has my whole body on edge. Something is not right, but no one is telling me anything which is pissing me off.

"You really don't know, do you?" He leans back. "Fuck. I thought you just weren't talking about it." He scrapes his hands over his face. My stomach drops. No, not fuckin' Sammy.

"Start talking," I bark. "Right the fuck now."

He shakes his head, seeming to sense where my brain went. "It's not Sammy," he states quickly.

"Fuck me, Cal." I finally take a damn breath. "Then what?"

"Kady. Um. Well here." He pulls up something on his phone and shoves it at me. I take it and press play on the TMZ video he pulled up.

Kady and Hayleigh walk briskly down Sunset Blvd, with a group of the usual photographer scum following and shouting at them. An older woman approaches from the opposite direction and grabs Kady by the shoulders. *What the fuck?* I can't tell what the lady's screaming at Kady. Hayleigh tries to jump in between and someone else grabs her from behind and drags her off camera. The woman proceeds to shake Kady and slap her across the face a few times while continuing to scream "murderer" at her.

Kady does nothing. She's frozen in place. From off screen, a shrill scream rings out. "Leave her alone. Let me fucking go. You don't understand." It sounds like it could be Hayleigh. The screen shoots to the left where Hayleigh's being restrained by some guy, kicking and struggling with him behind her. Then it swings back to Kady, where she and her assailant are now rolling on the ground. There is red everywhere. Is that blood? I swallow.

My gut clenches, and I jump to my feet. I shove the phone at Cal, the video still playing. I have to get to Kady. *What the fuck?*

Cal grabs my arm. "Sammy's with them at Cedars."

"Cedars? What the fuck?" All that red *was* blood.

"Sammy says she's okay. It wasn't blood. Not real blood anyway, but he said they ended up sedating Kady in the ambulance, so she was taken for observation. The EMTs oversedated her or some shit. He said that last night she was awake but incoherent. She even threw her phone at the doctor. It freaked Sammy out seeing her like that, so he stayed in the waiting room all night, but this morning she's refusing all visitors except Hayleigh."

Cal's lips continue moving, but I can't hear what he's saying. *Kady. Blood. Hospital.* Those are the only things I heard. I need to see her. Right fucking now. I grab for my jacket.

"Mav, no. Sammy says the paparazzi are out of control at the hospital, even with the security. They are waiting for her to leave. If you show, it'll make it worse."

"But Kady's—"

"Okay. She's okay. She specified no visitors. She won't even let Sammy in. He's stuck in the waiting room, relying on Hayleigh for updates since they kicked him out of her room last night. He says Hayleigh thinks they'll release Kady this afternoon."

"How's Sammy involved in all this anyway?"

"I guess the three of them had lunch together yesterday. They split to go to their respective parking spots. Sammy saw the paparazzi and offered to walk them to their car, but they refused. If you had finished the video, you'd see Sammy wading through the crowd trying to get to them. He's pretty torn up, blaming himself. When I spoke to Hayleigh earlier, she told me that Kady's confusion is a side effect to one of the drugs they gave her in the ambulance." Cal pauses. "Jax is trying to figure out a way to get Sammy out of there without stirring things up, but for now, Jax says it's better if Sammy stays in the private waiting room."

I grab my phone and text Jax.

Me: Forget Sammy. Focus on getting Kady and Hayleigh out safely once Kady's released.

Me: Take them to the Malibu house. It'll be safer for them.

Me: Hayleigh's contact info coming shortly.

Jax: Forget Sammy?

Me: I'll take care of Sammy and a distraction if you need one.

Chapter 28

Kadence

The nurse smiles at me while she slides the needle from my arm and coils up what used to be my IV. I just want to get the fuck out of this hospital. I'm hungry, cantankerous, and I really need a shower. She holds gauze to my arm while she gets a band-aid ready.

"Oh, good." Hayleigh breezes in with a small, brown overnight bag. "This must mean we're getting ready to be discharged?" Hayleigh looks encouragingly at the nurse.

"It's one of the first steps. The doctor will be by soon. He still has to issue the official discharge order. Then we wait for the paperwork." She steps back. "Just ring if you need something." She closes the door behind her.

Hayleigh holds up the bag. "Clothes for the trip home. It was either this or scrubs. I told them to ditch the clothes you were wearing. They're ruined anyway, thanks to the paint."

I nod and grimace. I loved those leather pants.

"You sure you don't want to just say hi to Sammy? Poor guy's still out in the waiting room. I guess Jax is working on a way to get him home because the press are still camped outside."

I shake my head.

Hayleigh puts her hand on mine. "He's worried about you, Kady."

I shake my head again. My phone's gone. I vaguely remember having it in the ER, but Hayleigh can't find it, so I have no way of responding to him anyway. I grab the notebook a nurse gave me on my little tv tray thing and scrawl out a note:

Dear Sammy, I am fine. Thanks for caring. -Kadence.

I rip out the page and hand it to Hayleigh and motion for her to go give it to Sammy. I move my stare back out the window.

"Don't be such a smartass."

She sits on the edge of the bed and pats the top of my hand. "You remember the first time you had a panic attack in front of Harden? How freaked out he was?" I nod. He still gets a little freaked out.

"That's Sammy right now. Only a little worse because he also saw you so drugged up in the ER you didn't know your own name. He watched you throw your phone at the doctor trying to help you. He saw them restrain you to the bed until you finally fell asleep. And then you wake up refusing to see anyone but me. He's worried and a little scared." I continue to stare out the window.

"Kady, he's a guy. They're visual beings. I can tell him you're fine until I'm blue in the face, but he won't feel better until he sees you for himself."

I nod and pull the pad of paper back into my lap. She gets up and a few minutes later she comes back, Sammy in tow. He slips into the room quietly and is oddly sedate from the Sammy I'm used to. He's wearing the same clothes from yesterday, his blonde curls sticking out at odd angles like he's been pulling them. He smiles, but it doesn't reach his eyes, their usual pep extinguished. Dark marks under his eyes are beginning to form, like he's exhausted.

"I'm going to grab a sandwich and some air while you two

visit." She looks at me for permission and when I give her a slight nod, she goes back out the door.

Sammy flashes me an unsteady smile as he drops quietly into the plastic chair next to my bed.

"So, um, you're feeling a little better? More awake?" I nod and he nods back, leaning back in the plastic visitor's chair until it's only on two legs. "Good. This morning Hayleigh said you were still really groggy. I guess that makes sense. They really whacked you out on something. You probably don't remember me being there last night, huh?"

I shake my head and scratch down a note.

I don't remember, sorry. Sorry you had to see me all out of it like that. Hope I wasn't too wacky.

I hand him the notebook. He reads it and hands it back to me.

"I'm just glad to see you acting more like yourself." He pauses and crosses his ankle over his knee. "I should've insisted on walking you to the car. I shouldn't have let you and Hayleigh go by yourselves." He picks at his shoe and looks absolutely gutted.

I scribble.

This is not your fault, Sammy.

I underline not three times.

I probably would have had a panic attack even if you had been there. Sometimes I even have them for no reason. You didn't cause it. If you had intercepted her, it probably would have still set me off. It's not the first one I've had since I've been back in L.A.

He reads it over a few times and hands the pad back to me.

"Still, what she did, it isn't right." He shrugs.

I don't know how to explain to Sammy that I can see it from her point of view. I'm responsible for the death of her loved one. Her son is dead because of me. I more than get it.

Instead of trying to explain, I just shrug as he shakes his head in disagreement.

"It wasn't your fault," he mutters.

We are interrupted by a doctor. I saw him earlier this morning. Sammy stands and shakes the doctor's hand.

"I'll see ya, Kady. Looks like my ride's here." He flashes his lit phone screen at me. I wave.

The doctor checks my chart and looks up at me. "How are you feeling?"

Like a murderer. How about you? I look at the blank notebook pages and contemplate writing it, putting words to how I really feel, but decide against it when I scrawl out my actual message.

A little tired, but that's normal for me when I'm sedated. I'm used to it.

The doctor nods. "Do you have a therapist you work with?"

I haven't seen my therapist in a while. I'll set up an appointment when I get back to Vegas.

More doctor nods. "Good. Do you want a prescription for Ativan?"

I shake my head.

I have a current one. Hayleigh probably has the bottle in her purse, but thanks.

"I'll release you. I'm including the contact information for a local therapist if you need to talk to someone before you get back to Vegas. Just in case." He smiles. "It will probably take another hour or so for your discharge order to process."

Thank you, Doc.

I scrawl at the bottom of the page and show it to him.

He pats my leg and goes.

"Was that the doctor?" Hayleigh comes in with her cup from the cafeteria.

I nod.

"Did he sign the discharge?"

I nod again.

"Good. Are you looking forward to blowing this pop stand?"

I smile at her wording. "There's my girl. Okay, let's start by you getting dressed." She shoves the brown overnight bag at me.

I'm now showered, dressed in my own clothes, and eating a cereal bar Hayleigh dug out of her large hobo bag because she thinks I'm hangry. Maybe I am, but I'm probably just grumpy. I don't like hospitals. I don't care for the sluggishness I feel after I've been sedated. And I probably am a little hungry. It's all a recipe for the curmudgeon Kady to come out.

We both wait impatiently for the discharge to process. Hayleigh's rushed off to figure out how to get the hell out of here without being seen. If I didn't have to finish the stupid recording and go to the vigil, I'd head straight home to Vegas. I'm done with Los Angeles. Nothing good happens here. Ever.

Hayleigh returns with a wheelchair and a floppy hat. "Let's roll. Literally. Come on, I'll push you." She sticks the ridiculous floppy hat on my head.

I don't have it in me to argue about the stupid wheelchair or the absurd hat. I just want out of here, and if she thinks the floppy hat is the way to go, then that's that. We take some sort of service elevator to the basement, accompanied by an orderly. In the basement, we weave through some hallways that are very reminiscent of the back hallways of the casino where Mav told me to kiss off.

Mav. The one person I'd hoped would visit, but didn't. It was sweet of Sammy to stay, though I'm not sure he had much of a choice if what Hayleigh said about the press being all over the hospital was true. I hope he didn't get in trouble because of me and found his way out safely.

We end up in an underground hospital staff parking lot. With a waiting line of three black limousines.

Hayleigh shrugs when I give her my 'what the heck' look. She rolls me up to the first one and the driver standing next to it opens the door with a smile.

"Decoys. It's seriously crazy up there, Kade. I wouldn't put it past any of them to follow us." She jerks her head back to the other two on the ramp. I hop out of the wheelchair and slide across the backseat, removing the stupid hat. I settle in the middle, away from the window. Hayleigh slides in across from me and raids the little fridge, handing me a bottle of cold water.

"You need to keep drinking to help flush that shit they gave you in the ambulance out of your system." Hayleigh purses her lips.

I sip the water to make her happy. The side effects are as disconcerting to her as they were for Sammy, but at least she's seen them before. She knows the most common benzo they stock on ambulances whack me out and then makes me dog tired the next day or two.

I lean my head back and close my eyes as the limo heads up the ramp and out of the parking garage. I refuse to open them until I am damn sure that we've cleared the hospital lot. I don't want to see the press that I know is out there. We've arrived above ground because they rap on the windows and doors. Their shouts are muffled by the windows.

Hayleigh seems concerned about being followed and is on her cell phone texting with someone. When we take the highway, I wonder what the hell we are doing because the hotel is in the other direction. I scribble on a napkin in the car.

Me: Where are we going?

"Not back to the hotel. We're going someplace where the press won't be able to find us for a few days. It's already been arranged with the label. We'll get your next piece recorded and fly back to Vegas as soon as we can."

R

THE HOUSE we pull up to has a massive, dark wooden fence around the property and matching gate. I lived in southern California before moving to Vegas, so I know two things. This is beach front property and whoever owns it is loaded. Probably Tom, or one of the label executives, maybe? The limo waits for the gate to open and then pulls through. The driver instructs us to stay in the car until he opens the door after the gates are completely closed.

The door to the house matches the wood of the gate, but the lock is a keypad on the side of the entryway. Hayleigh enters the secret number, and the door unlocks.

The minute we walk in, all I see is an expanse of blue ocean through the wall of windows in the back. It's beautiful and relaxing and I feel an undeniable pull to go down to the water. If I lived in this house, I'd probably never leave it. I'm drawn forward by the wall of windows and walk into the main room. There is an amazing yard, complete with an infinity pool outside. I must have died in the ambulance and gone to heaven.

"Woah. This place is amazeballs." Hayleigh gives words to my thoughts. I nod my agreement.

"I'm told the fridge is stocked and we're to help ourselves."

I turn to her and motion like I'm scribbling.

"Oh shit, what'd I do with your notebook? Crap." She goes over to our bags by the door, rifles through them, and hands me the notebook. Using the pen I stole from the hospital, I scrawl out a quick message.

Me: Whose place is this?

"Don't kill me." She grimaces and gives me an apologetic look, lifting her shoulders slightly. Her eyes slide to the side and then back to mine. She blows out a breath because she knows the answer is going to be one I won't like.

"It's Mav's. Jax said he insisted we come here."

Me: Mavrick Slater insisted we come here? Jax, the security guard who screamed at me?

I hold my notebook up for her, and she nods hesitantly.

This must be something Sammy has set up. Mav wouldn't willingly have me staying at his house when he doesn't trust me. If I weren't so exhausted, I'd probably balk at staying here, but the truth is, I'm dog tired. Most of it is the aftereffects of the sedation and of staying in a hospital because who can sleep there really with the constant checks from nurses? I'm also tired of being in L.A, tired of being on edge. I'm just tired of it all.

She nods. "He sent Jax to plan our escape from the hospital. I'll show you the texts if you don't believe me." I shake my head. I don't need to see the texts. Hayleigh doesn't make a habit of lying.

I'm not sure why someone so betrayed by me not mentioning who I used to be would go through all of this trouble for me. I don't deserve it. It's probably something to do with the record. I'm confused and bone tired. I sit on the couch and stare out the windows, watching the ocean beyond the patio. I wish I was on the beach, where the sun is starting to slip down beneath the horizon, but I don't have the energy to go down there.

"You look tired. Why don't you take a nap? I'll throw something together for dinner and wake you when it's done?" I nod, not having the energy to even scrawl her a note of thanks.

I wander off to where I assume there are bedrooms and take the first room with a bed that I find. The room is obviously a guest room. It has no personality, but is tastefully and plainly decorated in ocean blues and greens.

I rummage through my suitcase. Everything from my hotel room was packed, and much more neatly than I would've packed it myself. Finding my soft purple blanket that goes everywhere with me, I flop onto the bed and curl up underneath it but on top of the comforter.

"KADE?" I feel a slight pressure on my shoulder. "Kade, wake up or you'll never sleep tonight." Hayleigh is lightly shaking me awake. I blink up at her, taking in the strange room. That's right. We're staying at Mav's place in California.

"I made some stir-fry for dinner, but you were sleeping so soundly when I came in, so I let you sleep a little longer. You need to wake up now though and eat, or you'll never sleep tonight." I nod and sit up and stretch. This bed is super comfortable, and I was just sleeping on top of it.

I follow her to the kitchen where I take a seat on a stool at the white marbled kitchen bar and watch her heat up a plate in the microwave.

"Before I forget, the ER staff found your phone. It somehow ended up under that wheelie cart in the corner. It's all scratched up, and the screen is a little cracked, probably from when you threw it, but it still works." She slides it gently across the bar in my direction.

"Tomorrow we'll see about getting it fixed or replaced." I nod, still not completely awake.

The scratches on my palms throb as I envision getting doused with the red blood-like substance yesterday. The skin on my hands peeled back as they scraped against the rough cement as I propelled myself away from my assailant in a frenzied sort of crab walk.

Hayleigh sighs a heavy breath that makes me look up at her. Whatever she has to say, she doesn't want to bring it up. "The police want you to come in and give a statement about what happened, press charges against the attackers."

I shake my head.

Me: I'll tell them my version of what happened, but I won't press charges.

Disappointment clouds her face as she reads my text, but she doesn't say anything. She knows she won't win this argument. This wasn't the first time I've been confronted about the shooting at the Monument Festival. It won't be the last time.

She sets my plate in front of me, and I eat. I didn't realize how hungry I was. Hayleigh's an amazing cook. Sometimes I forget that. She smiles as she watches me demolish the entire plate of stir-fry.

"More?" I nod as my stomach gives a grumble and I hand her back my plate, my cheeks heating. "Don't be embarrassed; it makes me happy to see you eat. You haven't had much of an appetite lately, even before we came to L.A." She refills my plate and warms it in the microwave.

We watch the massive television over the fireplace, but Hayleigh's exhausted and fading quickly, and of course, I'm wide awake now. I napped too long. It'll be hours before I can go back to sleep. I lead Hayleigh to the bedroom next to mine and we snuggle in her bed and watch stupid sitcoms together until she falls asleep.

Still restless, I explore more of the house. I find a masculine office decorated in rich dark wood and a computer on the desk across from my bedroom. There's a room I've dubbed the memorabilia room with shelves of awards, and framed gold and platinum records. On the other side of the great room, I find a long narrow staircase leading down to a basement area, but the door's locked. I have a feeling it might be a home recording studio. That's what I would put there if it were my house. There's a home gym in a room off the back of the garage, but I don't go in. I don't go upstairs. That would be too intimate, since that's probably where Mav's bedroom is.

On the patio with the lights off, I curl up in a chaise and listen to the waves crash against the shore in the darkened distance. It's comforting and relaxing out here. I've always loved the ocean and sitting out here listening to the perpetual motion of the waves calms my soul just a little.

It's much cooler to be outside this time of night here in L.A.

than it is in Vegas. I pull the hood of my hoodie over my head, hoping to keep off the chill. I may not have lived by the ocean when I was in L.A., but I certainly came to the beach as often as I could back then. If I could live anywhere, it'd be by the ocean.

I hear a commotion in the house and turn around. Mav and Sammy stumble in together, with Jax following. Sammy can barely stand, propping himself up between Mav and the kitchen bar. I freeze, not realizing that Mav is staying here with us, but it's his home, so why wouldn't he stay here. *Stupid, Kady, stupid.*

Mav's breathtaking, even in what I assume is a slightly less inebriated state than Sammy. He rifles through the fridge and pulls out the container of leftover stir fry Hayleigh made. Sammy snatches it from him and inhales it, while Mav makes himself a sandwich. The two carry on a jovial conversation that has Sammy swinging his arms widely, then practically taking a nosedive into the countertop.

Jax heads down the hallway with the bedrooms. Shit, I hope that we didn't take his room. Since he didn't come back, we must not have. Mav and Sammy have an in-depth chat about something. Sammy attempts to wash the stir-fry bowl, but sloshes water all over the counter. Mav takes the bowl from him and sets it down. He escorts Sammy to the stairs and watches him go up them. He returns to clean the counter and the bowl Sammy was struggling with. I can't believe he doesn't feel me watching him. I feel a little creepy just watching him from out here, but it doesn't stop me from taking in his amazing physique. My stomach pangs with regret and yearning at the same time.

When he's done, he moves toward the stairs and stops momentarily, looking down the hall where the bedrooms are. It seems like he's trying to decide what to do, with his head tilted slightly. But then he turns and goes upstairs.

Hushed voices wake me the next morning. It took me a

couple of hours to fall asleep, between my late afternoon nap and the surroundings I am not used to. It was almost too quiet. It didn't help to know Mav was sleeping right upstairs from me.

I gather some clothes and head across the hall to the bathroom. I take a long, hot shower. It feels good to get the sterile hospital smell off. My scraped-up hands sting with the soap as I shower. I probably should have left them bandaged.

When I enter the living area, the only one around is Hayleigh.

"I found a stash of tea. Want some? There is chai, peppermint, lemongrass, and green tea." I grab my phone and shoot her a text.

Me: Chai, but I'll get it if you tell me where?

Hayleigh directs me to Mav's stash of tea, and I make myself a cup of chai with a touch of milk and return to sit with her.

"Mav and Sammy are here, downstairs in the recording studio, I guess? They said Jax is around here somewhere too, but I haven't seen him." I nod. That explains the voices I heard earlier.

Me: Any word about when I can record my part of the last song?

Me: I just want to get this over with and go home.

Hayleigh shakes her head. We watch more television together, but I can only take so much of that, so I go back to my room and get my journal while she checks in with work. I sit out on the patio, choosing a chair closest to the ocean. I write until I run out of things to say and then I just sit and enjoy the fresh, salt-laced breeze. A dog drags a young kid gleefully down the beach. Part of me wants to go stick my toes in the wet sand, but I don't. That's my life right there, wanting to do stuff but never brave enough to actually get over myself and just do it.

I still feel raw, much like the palms of my hands. It's like my soul has a little bit of gravel in it, just enough to remind me that it's not supposed to be there. I'm restless and yet I want to go back home to Vegas and stick my head in the sand.

Listening to my highly conditioned flight response is the last thing I should do. It's always flight with me, never fight, but I need to finish what I started here this time. Maybe it will give me the closure I'm looking for on Kandi. Plus, I have to make good on my commitments to Monument Records and the Blind Rebels. I need to show my face at the memorial gathering this weekend. Those that lost their lives deserve my presence this time.

Chapter 29

Mavrick

I t took the better part of the morning, but I think we have my home studio patched into the studio at Monument. As soon as Kady feels up to recording, we can do it here. It's better than risk going into the Monument recording studio. Jax is getting reports that the sidewalks in front of the label are littered with fucking paparazzi, fans, and other general looky-loos. Tom is probably in hog heaven right now. He's always been the no publicity is bad publicity type of guy.

Kady doesn't need to wade through the sty of press and fans right now. I haven't seen her since the day at the studio. Sammy seems to think she's tender, that her soul is being held together by a thread. Cal said when he talked to Sammy while Kady was in the ER, Sammy was beside himself. It could be that Sammy's the tender one right now, but I'm not taking any chances because all I keep seeing is her covered in red paint. *In blood.*

He hasn't talked to me about the incident specifically, but I know Sammy blames himself. He got lit last night after we finished laying tracks. Hell, we all got a little toasted, but it's not like Sammy to get that shitfaced. I was more than a little worried he'd suffocate in his own vomit last night, so I made him sleep in the upstairs guestroom so I could check on him. Plus, I was pretty sure that Kady and Hayleigh were in the downstairs bedrooms he usually crashes in.

"I'm grabbing something to drink from upstairs. You want anything?"

"Gatorade and Advil." I knew he'd be suffering after last night's indulgences, but he hasn't said a word about feeling like crap. It's just like Sammy to give it his all, despite a massive hangover.

"You got it." I head upstairs. Hayleigh's sitting cross-legged on the floor of the great room with her laptop on the coffee table, discussing things that sound financial in nature. I realize I don't even know what she does for a living. She shoots me a smile but never misses a beat on her call. I wonder if Kady is still sleeping. The house seems especially quiet, with the exception of occasional voices on Hayleigh's video conference.

I lean against the kitchen counter and gulp down some orange juice when I catch sight of Kady standing at the edge of the patio, looking down at the ocean. She has my favorite coffee mug clutched between her hands. A notebook lays on the chair behind her. She's wearing black yoga pants and a dark baggy hoodie. Her short fuchsia hair ruffles with the light ocean breeze.

Even with the underlying layer of anger still humming through me about how things went down between us, my heart aches looking at Kady. The Kady standing on my patio isn't the confident girl that giggled in my bed. I can't see her face, but there is something in the way she stands that is both guarded and heavy.

I jump back when Hayleigh puts a hand on my shoulder, noticing me watching Kady. "Fuck, you scared me."

"She'll be okay." She looks out at her friend. "Being back in L.A. has been really hard for her. She tried to stay here after the shooting but lived under the constant pressure of being recognized. With the lack of a voice, she didn't have a way of communicating when people would swamp her. Even with a bodyguard, it was overwhelming for her. At that time, we didn't even really know what was wrong with her voice. Eventually, she decided it was easier to start fresh by coming to live with me in Vegas."

Kady turns and starts toward the house. When she sees us, she gives a little half-smile as she puts her cup in the dishwasher. She texts Hayleigh.

"Kady says thank you for letting us crash here." I look at Kady and wonder why she's filtering our conversation through Hayleigh, but then I remember that she blocked my number. All of our numbers.

I look directly at Kady. "You're more than welcome here. I have lots of room." She stands there, not moving, not making an attempt to text Hayleigh. "I'm glad you're up. I wanted to talk to you about recording 'Incredible.'"

She starts texting, so I wait for Hayleigh to pass along the message.

"Kady says she'd like to do it as soon as possible. Before Saturday, so she can leave after the vigil." I'm surprised she's still going. It's the second annual memorial vigil of the Monument Festival Shooting. It's nothing formal, just a gathering of fans. They did the same thing last year.

"I have a basement studio. Sammy and I spent the morning setting it up so we can send directly to Monument. So, whenever you feel up for it, I have the keyboard set up in my recording booth downstairs."

She texts her friend again. "Kady says let's do it today. Then we can get out of your hair."

I nod. "Sure. Whatever works. I insist you stay here until you go home. It's safer than going back to the hotel," I call after Kady as she heads down the hall to the bedrooms. In a few minutes, she is back, but missing the hoodie she was wearing. She flashes me the international hand sign for okay.

I lead her downstairs, tossing Sammy his sports drink as I descend the stairs. He smiles as he catches it and then sits up a little straighter when he notices Kady behind me on the narrow stairs.

"Kady wants to record today. She'll run through it a few times and then we'll record together when she's ready. Sound good to you?" I look at Kady and she nods as she makes her way to the keyboard. She changes the seat height and then plays some warm-up scales. She runs through the song a few times, but she's not happy. We go over my notes and my recording on the iPad. Then we run through it together a few times. When we're satisfied, we record it a couple of times for the studio with Sammy playing engineer.

The studio asks for a few more takes and we go through several more times. I'm getting hungry, and poor Kady looks exhausted. Sammy looks rough all around. I think his hangover is catching up with him. We record a couple more takes and send them over. While we wait, Kady winces and holds her left hand to her chest with the right.

I'm calling it a day. She's obviously in pain. I let the studio know that if they need more to call me and we'll work on it tomorrow. I kick Sammy's shoe to wake him up as I wrap up my call to Monument.

"Kady, let's break for today. Your hand cramping up?" She shakes her head and opens her hand, so the palm faces me. Fuck me. Her hand's scraped up and some of the scabs have broken open and have fresh blood seeping out of them.

"Fuck, Kady." I grab a nearby towel and press it against her hand. "Sammy, go get the first aid kit. Upstairs, under the sink."

I check her other hand. It's scraped up but not as severely and it doesn't appear to have anything broken open. "Dammit. I didn't know you'd hurt your hand. You should have said something."

She pulls her hand back to her chest and mouths, "I'm fine."

"Fine? This isn't fine, Kady!" I hold up the towel now with splotches of bright red blood from where I held it against her hand.

Her eyes focus in on the towel and then shift back to me and back to the towel again as her body stiffens in place.

"Kady?" She looks in my direction but isn't focusing on me, and the color slowly drains from her face. I've seen this before. Shit. Panic attack. I need something cold for her to hold. That's what Hayleigh did last time.

"You're okay, Kady. I've got you." I try like hell to keep the fear out of my own voice. "Let's head upstairs to Sammy and Hayleigh." I put my arm around her waist to guide her to the narrow stairs, but her muscles tighten, locking her in place. Dammit, I shouldn't have raised my voice. *Dick move, Slater.*

"I've got you. You're okay. Let's go." I try to keep my voice even. I pick her up and walk sideways up the narrow stairs. "There we go."

I'm almost to the top when Sammy starts down with the first aid kit.

His eyes widen as he takes us in. "Shit, is she okay?"

He's alarmed because I'm carrying her, but he also senses she's not herself. Unfortunately, he's blocking the stairs.

"Kady's okay. Right, Kady? Just a panic attack. Let us upstairs, Sammy." I keep my voice soft and even because I don't want to add to her panic, but Sammy needs to get the fuck out of the way. He goes back the way he came and holds the door open. I carry her into the great room and set her on the couch facing me.

"Hayleigh!" I holler for her desperately. Kady needs her. "Hayleigh!?"

314

"Sammy, get me something frozen. Anything. Quick. From the freezer." He gives me an odd look. "Now, Sammy."

I try to get Kady to focus on me, but her eyes remain glazed over, and her muscles are all tense. She pants instead of breathes. "You're okay, Kady. You're at my house. Sammy's here too." Sammy hands me a pack of frozen vegetables I didn't even know I had.

"Sammy's going to look for Hayleigh, and I'm going to help you hold these veggies. You're okay. You're safe. Just breathe." I wrap my hands over hers and place them on the cold bag. I try to recall the things Hayleigh said that day in her apartment. She did some weird counting breathing thing I don't remember how to do. I should have paid better attention.

Sammy tears down the hallway, then out the back door. Hayleigh must be on the beach. Every minute seems more like twenty, but finally, Kady's eyes finally begin to focus in on my own.

"Hey, you," I reassure, as she smiles unsteadily at me.

"You're okay." She nods a little.

"Your hands cold?" She nods and gives me that shaky smile again. The tightness in her arms slowly releases.

"There you go. Why don't we put these down now?" I gently pull the veggies away from her. I dry her hands, careful not to cause any more cracking. Then I put some antibacterial ointment on her broken scabs and wrap her hand in gauze. "There you go. Good as new."

She nods at my handiwork as Hayleigh comes tearing through the sliding glass door, breathless with Sammy running up behind her.

"Kade—"

"She's okay. Just a panic attack, right, Kady?" Kady nods slowly and Hayleigh pushes me out of the way so she can assess her friend. I return the mixed veggies to the freezer door.

"Do you want me to get you an Ativan?" Hayleigh whispers

loudly to Kady, who shakes her head no. I bring over a glass of water and Kady takes a few sips as Hayleigh pulls her in for a hug.

As much as I want to hover, to hold Kady like Hayleigh is, I hang back and busy myself in the kitchen even though there isn't much to do.

Sammy looks at me with wide eyes from his seat at the bar. "How did you know what to do with the frozen thing?" He speaks in hushed tones.

"It's happened before. I just did what Hayleigh did that day."

He gets up and slaps my back. "Good job, man. Fuck, that was scary. Can you imagine what it's like for her?"

R

I RINSE the last dish from dinner as I follow Hayleigh's return to the kitchen from the patio with an empty glass. She and Kady watched the sunset sipping glasses of wine. I'd be lying if I said I wasn't worried about Kady. She's been distant since the panic attack. She didn't eat much at dinner. She doesn't seem to be her usual self, but then again, what do I know of her normal right now? I don't know pink-haired Kady.

I refill Hayleigh's glass and she smiles at me. "She's okay, you know. Don't treat her like she's glass. She's not breakable. It just takes her a minute after having a panic attack. Can you imagine being fine one minute and then so scared out of your mind that your body stops working rationally for no reason the next? That's what it's like for her. Sometimes there are tears. Sometimes she hyperventilates. She almost always freezes and stiffens." Hayleigh shrugs while looking out at Kady.

"It's my fault. I yelled at her for not telling me that she was playing with injured hands."

"Nope." She shakes her head. "Don't go there. Sometimes

316

they have a trigger, but more often than not, they don't. Unless she tells us what the trigger was, we won't know." I shake my head because this was clearly my fault.

"She thinks it was the blood on the towel this time. It's not something that always has an answer, though, Mav. Sometimes she'll just freeze up in a panic for no reason. It can happen at the oddest times." She looks at her friend curled up on a lounge chair on the patio.

"This one wasn't that bad, but I'm worried. They've been more frequent since we've been in L.A. She's had a couple since we've been here. Maybe the vigil is too much pressure for her. I won't tell her not to go, but I'm beginning to think she should skip it again this year."

Hayleigh shakes her head and looks at me. "Look, even if it was something that you triggered, you're allowed to have reactions and emotions. Shit happens. If I've learned anything the last two years with Kady, it's don't walk around on eggshells. You love her. Just let her be her and accept that sometimes this happens and there isn't a cause. Walking around worried that you'll set one off just makes her more uncomfortable, which tends to set them off at a greater frequency. So does the helicopter hovering I do sometimes. It's not easy to stop, but I'm working hard not to be that person with her anymore. It's my need to reassure myself she's okay, but I'm trying to recognize when I do it and back off unless she lets me know she needs my help." She shrugs.

Hayleigh's right, I love her. My need to comfort her is stronger than anything I've ever felt.

"Speaking of needing, she's asking for you. Go. I got this." Hayleigh takes over cleaning up from dinner.

I sit on the lounge chair next to her, setting down a mixed berry seltzer with a straw on the table next to her, which makes her lips turn up. It's our thing.

"Hey. Need anything else or want something different?"

She shakes her head and fishes my phone out of my pocket, unlocks it and brings up a document and types into it.

Kady: Thank you for taking care of me earlier.

"Always." I want to always take care of her, be there for her, love her. *Love her?* Yeah, I love the shit out of her and realize now I've never told her. Fuck. But first I have to apologize.

"Kady," I blow out a breath. How do you apologize for not pausing to listen to someone? For not giving them a chance to explain themselves? God knows she let me explain myself after the first night I met her.

"I'm sorry." I push my hair out of my face, needing her to see my eyes, and know I'm telling the truth. "I should have let you explain that day at the casino. I didn't let you tell me in your own words. I let Killian's accusations cloud how I reacted. I know better…"

Kady: It hurt. A lot. I don't want that life anymore. I didn't want it when I had it. It took getting shot and losing my voice to realize it.

Kady: You just gave up on me like we weren't something. It proves I'm as expendable as I've always thought I was.

Expendable. And that's exactly how I fucking treated her.

"No, Kady. You are *not* expendable." She shrugs at my words. "I was an idiot. I let Killian's words sway me. That's on me, but you *are not* expendable, to me or anyone else who knows you, knows your heart. And I'm sorry I was careless with it. So fucking sorry."

Her fingers hover over the keyboard on my phone, but don't move. She's thinking.

Kady: Sometimes, I wish Jerrod had killed me at the festival.

Her words take my breath away, make my stomach drop. She's wishing herself dead. My silent, musical, resiliently brave girl wishes she was dead sometimes. I don't want to live in a world without Kady.

"Thank fuck he didn't." I slide up next to her and grip her leg tight.

Kady: *That wish is always much stronger this time of year.*

Kady: *But being here, and then being attacked by that mom and her son on Sunset.*

She stops typing and shakes her head.

Kady: *I don't deserve to be here.*

Kady: *Their child isn't alive anymore because of me.*

"No, no, hon, what happened at the festival wasn't your fault."

She shakes her head vehemently, refusing to accept my words.

Kady: *Kill was right. I wasn't a good person when I was Kandi.*

Kady: *I was shallow and—*

I put my hand over hers, so she'll stop this train of thought.

"You *do* deserve to be here. I'm so glad you are." I pull her as close to me as I can, squeezing her tight, needing her to feel our connection. I don't know how else to show her she deserves to be here, to be loved.

Kady's arms band around my waist and she lays her head on my chest, positioning her ear over my heart. I kiss the crown of her head, breathing in that pineapple scent that is pure Kady.

With a thumb under her chin, I lift her face so she can see mine. I lean in and plant a gentle kiss on the tip of her nose. Her eyelashes flutter and she gives me a soft smile.

"I just realized I've never told you I love you." Her eyes widen slightly. "Yes, love you, love you."

"Me?" she mouths, her eyes still wide. Disbelief clouds her face. She points to her body as if to say, 'all of this?' I nod. She types into my phone.

Kady: *I'm a hot mess.*

I can't help the grin that pulls up on my lips. "You're hot. Yes. But I don't think you're a mess."

Kady: *Trust me, I'm a mess.*

"Then you're my hot mess." I taste the disbelief as I kiss her, taking my time with those soft lips I adore, using our connection to show how much I care for her and need her here.

She snuggles in against me, holding my phone to her chest. Her head rests over my heart again, like she needs its reassurance. My heart that beats wildly for her. Only for her.

She sighs, and this feels like contentment to me. Not restlessness, not fear, but total and complete contentment. Something I only feel with her. It's something I pray I can help her feel on the days she feels disposable or sad.

She shows me my phone. I didn't even notice her tap out the message.

Kady: I want to tell you about that night. Give me a minute?

"Of course. Take all the minutes you need. I'm not going anywhere." I keep a firm hold on her, so she's flush against me while she taps away on my phone. Her minute turns into twenty. She takes a few breaks. During the last one, a sob escapes into the quiet of the patio, and I squeeze her tight to me, ground her to me in the now. Not in the dark shadows of the past that live in her head.

"I can wait if you're not ready. If it's too hard, it's okay. I'm not going anywhere." She shakes her head and pushes through her tears, and eventually hands my phone back to me. She buries her head into my chest, suddenly feeling tiny against me, as I start to read her truth.

Kady: The musician I was? The pop princess. She was not the nicest person. I own that.

Killian was so right about me. I was shallow. I lived in that stereotypical Hollywood self-centered 'everything is about me' world.

Kady: I was taught at a young age that if you didn't take advantage, then you were taken advantage of. My aunt was no exception, and when I found out she was stealing money from my accounts as my 'manager.' I emancipated myself at sixteen.

Kady: It was the best and worst thing I could have done. I had more control over my own life, the jobs I took, the people I associated

320

with, my money, but I also had no family to balance that out. My aunt said I ruined her life when I took her to court.

Kady: She convinced my brother that I was a thankless bitch and maybe I was, but she was skimming off my accounts. My brother still doesn't speak to me. He sided with my aunt at the emancipation trial. They were the only family I had. And then suddenly they hated me. It didn't help that the people that I chose to associate with weren't the best role models.

Kady: Music was always my escape, even as a kid. Monument wouldn't let me make the music I wanted to make as Kandi because it 'wasn't my brand.' So, I was stuck singing pop songs other people wrote. Other people's emotions and stories, not mine. Ironically, it's how I started feeling about my life. I was living it for other people, internalizing their ideas about me and what I should be doing. My life was always for other people. Not for me.

Kady: The night of the festival I didn't want to perform. Shows were tedious, and it was the third night of a back-to-back schedule. My shows were full of costume changes and choreography. They were exhausting, not energizing like your shows. Mine were more of an energy suck.

Kady: I did my media obligations early that afternoon, changed, made my way to the before show meet and greet. They were always my favorite part because there I felt the reciprocation.

Kady: We were in a private hospitality tent. I was signing things, chatting, taking selfies. I remember being happy, remembering why I did what I did. The best part of their night was always the best part of my night too. There were always kids there because Kangaroo Klub Houze was in syndication.

Kady: Jerrod and I weren't together at the time. We had an ugly relationship and an even uglier break up, all very public. You can google it if you want. I had an order of protection against him that had been issued ten days before the festival.

Kady: He was shooting before I saw him. I remember ripping the tent canvas away from the pole and shoving two girls out, yelling at them to run. *I can still hear the screams and smell the coppery blood. I've never been so cold. He grabbed me around the neck. I'm still not sure if it was to take me with him because he thought he loved me or to use me as a shield to get away. I don't remember anything else until I woke up in the hospital. Alone. Cold. Scared.*

Kady: *I've been told the doctor had to sedate me after he told me that Jerrod killed ten people and injured six others. I don't remember being told or being sedated. The next thing I do remember is Hayleigh being there when I woke up the next time. She took charge of everything at that point. And I checked out and let her. It was easier to let her decide for me than to feel.*

Kady: *The days in the hospital blur together. They kept me sedated the first few days. I had three gunshot wounds in my side. I had surgery to repair my hip. At first, they thought my inability to talk was due to vocal cord injury from the breathing tube during surgery.*

Kady: *Turns out it's in my head. My brain short-circuited, and now I can't talk. I've done lots of therapy, speech therapy, psychotherapy, and occupational therapy. Hayleigh found a mutism specialist I saw a few times. Nothing worked. So, I gave up.*

I kiss the top of her head again as I re-read her words. Her story. I save the document she spent so long typing and set my phone down to squeeze her to me.

"Thank you for sharing all of you with me." I squeeze her against me again.

"You're so fuckin' brave," I whisper. Unable to tell if she's hearing my words, I keep steady pressure in my grip on her, holding her to me. Reassuring her and me.

"Everything you feel is okay, you know. Whether it's sad, mad, or panicked. Even receiving or giving love. It's okay to feel it all with me and with Hayleigh." She shakes her head violently at my words and reaches for my phone.

Kady: *It's not.*

Kady: Because of me, there are ten people that can't feel anymore.

She buries her face in my chest and sobs outright. Fuck if I'm not crying with her.

"Not because of you. Because of him. But, Kady, it's okay to allow yourself love and happiness." My voice breaks, betraying the tears that I have rolling down my own fucking cheeks. "It's totally okay to be who you are right now in this moment, to feel what you feel right now. Not the Kady of the past. Not the Kady of the future, but the Kady of right now." I plant another kiss and she fumbles for my phone at my side.

Kady: Sometimes feeling is the hardest part.

"That it is, baby. But sometimes feeling is the best part too. Like how I feel about you. That's the best part for me." We lie together on the lounge chair, me holding her tight.

I never should have left her the way I did in the casino. I should have listened to her.

She stays snuggled into my side until her breathing has evened out and she relaxes on me completely. She's asleep. I remember when Hayleigh told me last time she had a panic attack that they always exhaust her. I carry her to the bedroom she's claimed and set her gently on the bed, covering her over with the soft purple blanket she must have brought with her.

Hayleigh hugs me as I slip out of Kady's room. "Thank you for loving her, for seeing her. All of her. I might not have been your biggest fan at first, but you're right for her. I see it now." How she knows Kady and I just had the most intense conversation of my life, I haven't a clue.

"It's impossible for me not to love her. She fucking owns me."

323

Chapter 30

Kadence

M av just sent the last recording to Monument and now we're waiting for their call, their blessing. I'm pretty sure it'll be the one they're looking for. This one just felt so much better than the first two this morning and definitely better than anything we did yesterday. My hands are still bothering me, but keeping them wrapped helps.

I sit next to Sammy after leaving the recording booth. He hands me a bottle of water and I down half of it in one go, making him chuckle. "You throw water back like a man, Kady!" His laugh is hearty and infectious. I can't help my smile. I throw my empty bottle at him.

Kady: I was thirsty.

He nods at my text just as the studio phone rings and Mav gets it. Sammy leans over to me and talks quietly. "I notice when you play, you mouth the words to the song. Have you ever tried singing what you want to say? Maybe it'd come out that way?"

Kady: I've tried it. Doesn't work.

Kady: If anything comes out, it sounds like pig grunts.

Kady: Not very becoming.

He shrugs in his Sammy way. "It was just a thought. I'm going to hit it. Kill's picking me up and we're going surfing down the coast. Tell Mav I'll see him later." I give him a thumbs up and he bounds up the stairs. I didn't picture Killian as the surfing type.

Mav hangs up and looks up at me. "They said it was perfect. Just like I thought they would."

I smile and pat the seat next to me on the couch. He drops down, and I lay my head on his shoulder and take my phone out to text him now that we've unblocked each other.

Kady: *I never apologized for lying to you and the band.*

He jerks his head up to look at me after reading my text and opens his mouth as if to say something, but I press my finger to his lips and then text.

Kady: *I should have been up front with who I was. Kandi was a bad person, and I tried to leave her behind.*

Kady: *Just so we are completely clear, I wasn't using you or your band to try to restart my own career.*

Kady: *If anything, the fact that you were a musician made me want to steer clear of you, but I couldn't.*

Kady: *I should have told you who I was when we started getting close, and I'm sorry I didn't.*

His expression softens as he finishes the last of my texts, and I can't resist any longer. I lean in and lightly kiss his full lips, not sure how receptive he'll be. He did say he loves me yesterday. I know I love him, even though I'm still not sure I deserve that love or that I can love him back in all the ways he needs, but I want to try.

At the end of my kiss, he pulls my lower lip between his teeth and sucks it. His hands run up my back and mine up his. His tongue attempts to part my lips until I finally relent and let him in.

He lifts me so I'm straddling him, my thighs on the outside of his strong ones. His large hand makes its way under my t-shirt. The feeling of his hand, warm and strong, splayed across my back makes me feel so many things. Loved. Cared for. Desirable. I capture his moan with my mouth. I need to be closer to him, so I run my hands up the back of his shirt, loving the feel of his muscles contracting and releasing under my hands.

He growls my name, and it's the sexiest thing I've ever heard. He pulls away from me to grab the collar of his shirt. He pulls it over his head completely, then he's gripping the hem of my top. He looks deep into my eyes for permission to do the same. Lifting my arms gives the permission he is looking for to pull mine off and toss it towards the soundboard.

His eyes smolder as they rake over me now that I'm topless. I knead his chest and his eyes sparkle as he reaches around with one hand and releases the catch on my bra. He slips it over one arm and then off the other and tosses it in the same direction as the shirt. His lips graze my neck and collarbone as I wrap my arms back around him. His mouth leaves a trail, heating my skin as he goes.

He hardens beneath me. I wiggle against it, and he groans. I tickle my nails lightly down his torso to his belt. I undo the button of his jeans and rub my thumb against the skin there. His hand covers mine, stilling me, and he pulls me away and stands us up.

He runs his thumbs around the waist of my yoga pants and slides them down over my hips. He squats and pulls them and my underwear gently down and off each leg. My hands reach for the band of his jeans, and he shakes his head.

He quickly disposes of his pants, grabbing a condom in the process. He sits back down on the leather couch in his studio and tears open the condom with his teeth and sheaths himself.

He reaches out and takes my hand. Pulling me to him so our legs are touching, he wraps his arms around my waist, pressing his forehead against my stomach. He lays a gentle kiss against my abdomen and kisses a trail lower. His strong hands knead my sides, like he can't get enough of just touching me.

I kneel on the couch hovering over him as he grips my hips and guides me as I seat myself. He leans in and licks the very tip of my pebbled nipple, causing me to clench tight around him and roll my hips. He groans against my chest and takes charge of our movement, but I have no trouble keeping tempo.

The crescendo builds to the point of pleasure-pain. I don't want our connection to end, but I need to let go. It's almost too much and not enough at the same time. He snakes a hand from one of my hips and gently brushes my clit with his thumb. It pushes me over into a free fall that has stars bursting in my vision.

"Kady! Fuck. I love you." He falls over the edge with me but manages to keep me from floating away.

Chapter 31

Mavrick

Fuckin' ties. I hate them. I've been trying to tie it for the last fifteen minutes and I cannot do it to save my life. YouTube can't even help me with this one, I've tried. I leave it hanging loosely around my collar. Cal will be here soon, and he's the only one of us who knows how to tie one.

I check my phone; no word yet from Hayleigh. She promised to text me when they were on the way. She took Kady this morning to get a dress when Kady decided the one she had wasn't quite right. Luckily, the vigil is in the late afternoon. It gave me just enough time to get everyone together.

Cal and Kill stroll in wearing matching black suits. Kill has a red tie, Cal a blue one matching their BR's pendants that I know hang against their chests under their clothes.

"Gibson's good?" It was short notice and I hope I didn't leave him scrambling to find someone to watch him.

"Yeah, Sandy's still in town. He's taken care of." Cal takes the tie around my neck and starts to tie it without me having to ask. "This is a good thing you're doing." He says it quietly and looks me straight in the eye. "I'm proud of you for thinking of this."

I nod and clear my throat. "Thank you for coming." I look over his shoulder at Killian, who stands by the television looking bleak. "Both of you. It means a lot to me. It'll mean a lot to Kadence."

Cal squeezes my shoulders after he finishes tightening the tie. I already can't wait to take the constrictive fucker off.

Sammy comes flying in the door with his suit jacket in a garment bag over his shoulder and a tie in the other hand. "Shit, am I late? I had to find my suit."

I chuckle, knowing Sammy just spent an hour in his storage unit looking for it. He's a good kid, but a bit disorganized. "No, man, you're good. Cal will get your tie squared away."

Hayleigh: *On our way. She doesn't know. Should be there in about 20. Harden's with us too.*

"They are on the way with Harden. They'll be here in about twenty. Anyone want a drink?" I walk behind the wet bar and pull out a glass and look up when no one says anything. The three of them look stricken, morose, like they just realized what the fuck we're about to do. I remember only one other time when we've been so solemn. It was the day we buried Sammy's sister Sevenya.

"Just one." Sammy's not big on the hard stuff, especially since his last drunken escapade the night Kady came here after her stint in the hospital. I'm slightly, but not completely, surprised. I pull out a second glass and consider telling him that we don't have time for more than one, but I don't want to freak him out.

"May as well pour two more." Cal comes over to the bar.

Nodding, I pour out four tumblers of Breckenridge Dark Arts whiskey. It's not my favorite but I feel it fits the melancholy occasion. We quietly sip, no one speaking. It's not often the four of us are subdued for any occasion, but there's a heaviness in the air that calls for it today. As the last sip slides down the back of my throat, the alarm panel indicates the opening of the gate. Must be the limo.

"Ready?" They all nod, still silent, and set their now empty glasses on the bar. I pat Sammy between the shoulders because he already looks like he's going to cry. "She'll be surprised, so it might make her cry. Just to warn you." Tears wreck Sammy, so I figure a heads up might help.

I stroll to the door, opening it as Kady, Hayleigh, and Harden approach.

"Ready?" Hayleigh asks quietly. Kady stands beside her. The black dress she wears is a little bit rock 'n' roll, but conservative enough for the somber occasion. Dark purple lace peeks out of the hem around the bottom of her black skirt. She hides her eyes behind big dark sunglasses, but I can tell Kady's eyeing my suit. I may not like to wear it, but I look damn good in it. I should for as much as it cost.

"Yeah, we're ready." I step to the side and let Kady see the rest of the band behind me in their suits.

A small gasp falls from her lips. A single tear slides down her cheek. I reach out and take her hand. "Let's go."

I hold her hand tight in mine all the way to the festival grounds. The limo pulls up to the crowded front gate. Harden and Hayleigh slide out of the limo first, followed by Sammy, Killian, and Cal. I slide out next, holding my hand out to Kady. She slides to the edge of the seat, swings her legs out the door, but then pauses, head hanging down. The band stands in front of us with their backs to us, creating somewhat of a curtain. We give Kady the minute she needs from the prying eyes of those still making their way into the vigil.

When she's ready, she stands and takes my hand. We move toward the vigil stage as a unit. Sammy and Harden in the front, Hayleigh and I flanking Kady, Kill and Cal behind us. You'd think we practiced it, the way we move as one.

I hold Kady's hand with a steady pressure. She squeezes

hers tight around mine every so often, as if to make sure that I'm still there. A murmur goes through the crowd when we walk to the gazebo and take our places in the seats on the stage. I hold Kady's hand in my lap and gently circle my thumb over the back of her hand. It's a small gesture, but I need her to feel me, to know she's not here alone. I need her to know that we are all here for her, that what she is doing is brave.

Most in attendance wear black rock t-shirts. They stand in groups on the grass in front of the gazebo. Some have real candles that wear what looks like a cupcake holder to catch the wax as they hold them for the vigil. Others have green light sticks. Some hold their cell phones with the flashlights on facing out. They talk quietly. Some cry outright already and the remembrance vigil hasn't even started yet. A few hold home-made signs.

Those of us on the gazebo stage are quiet. Sammy reaches forward and squeezes Kady's shoulder.

Tom Monument stands and gives a speech I don't listen to. I'm more attuned to Kady. She's tensed up a bit, but her hand is still in my lap. I pull it up to my mouth and give it a quick kiss. This distracts her enough to look over at me. "So brave." I say it quietly into the back of her hand, but I know she hears it because she shakes her head so slightly.

Tom calls Kady up. Sammy leans up from behind her and hugs her shoulders quickly before she stands. She goes tight momentarily, but closes her eyes and relaxes. Hayleigh goes up with her. I wanted to be the one up there with her, but she insisted Hayleigh be the one to read the statement.

Two years ago tonight was the worse night of my life. If only I had known what was going to happen, I would have done so many things differently. I can't tell you how many times I've relived that night. How many times I wished it had been me instead of any of the ones that were lost or hurt. So many people's lives were forever changed.

She lets out an audible cry, and I pitch forward to go to her. Cal reaches over and puts his hand on my thigh, but I'm not sure if he's attempting to comfort me or hold me in place. When I look past the gazebo, I can see that the attendees are moved. Many wipe their eyes, including Hayleigh.

But I have to believe that I was left behind for a reason. I'm still working to find that reason, that purpose. We can't give up. We have to remember what happened and also remember to live. If you take anything from this, know that I don't take my life lightly anymore. And I will never forget those who were taken. For those who lost loved ones, and to those who lost their sense of security, I'm sorry and thank you.

She takes another ragged breath before turning and returning to us. We all stand. Sammy hugs her tightly before I can, his face still wet with tears. Harden gives her a quick tight hug, and she gets a similar one from Cal. Killian reaches over and squeezes her shoulder and then mine. We sit and I hold Kady to me, my jacket soaking up her tears.

Cal, Kill, and Sammy rise at the end and head to the front of the stage. I didn't see them bring instruments, they must have brought them earlier because now they sit on the edge of the stage with them. Sammy has the very tambourine he gave Kady at the first firepit jam. They start by playing one of Kady's songs from back when she was Kandi.

Kady and Hayleigh both gasp as they play the song. It's a different version, more our sound, but it's clearly her song. Sammy pats the stage next to him, trying to convince Kady to sit, but she shakes her head. The three of them harmonize well. It starts the wheels in my head spinning.

After they finish 'Dance Tonight,' they start 'Amazing Grace.' I join them, as does the audience. I drop down next to Sammy and pull Kady down and hug her to me as the four of us sing, accompanied by the hundreds in attendance. Kady buries her head in my chest as the song wraps up. I sit there on the edge of the stage, holding her to me, letting her cry.

R

K ADY'S BEEN restless since we returned to the house. She picks at her food, all things that Hayleigh said she loved so I had them catered even though it's just us. She's all raw emotion and unable to be soothed no matter what I or anyone else does. Every time I pull her down on my lap, she gets up a few minutes later. Then she either stares out the window or flitters around the room cleaning up things that don't need cleaning.

I give up trying to console her and busy myself getting the firepit ready down on the beach just past the gate to my back patio. Music soothes the soul, so we all need to play for each other, but especially for Kady. The whole band has stuck around, even Cal. As the fire gets going, everyone migrates out onto the patio. Everyone but Kady. I find her in the kitchen, washing dishes. She scrubs the plates hard and rinses them, like she needs the motion of doing something, anything, to calm her mind.

I wrap my arms around her from behind and pull her to my chest gently. "Leave them." I plant a kiss on to the crook of her neck. She shakes her head and reaches forward into the still-running water.

"Kady, I have a handsomely paid housekeeper. Leave them for her. Come sit outside with us." I plant another kiss on her neck. "We're all here for you, baby."

She turns abruptly in my arms, so she faces me. She clings to my shirt tightly. I hold her and rock her back and forth, pouring all the things I want to say, all the comfort I want to extend to her, into that slight action. It's the only gesture she's to be able to take solace in right now.

The gentle strumming of Cal's guitar filters in from outside.

I'm not sure what he's playing or if he's just making it up as he goes, but whatever it is, it's quiet and moody. Much like the feelings of today.

Kady leans her forehead against my chest and takes a few deep, settling breaths. I keep her wrapped in my arms and place a light kiss on the crown of her head. Leaving my lips there, I murmur the things that I want her to know deep in her soul. That I love her. That I'm here for her. That it's okay to feel sad. That she's so brave by just letting herself feel it, but mostly as we stand here, I repeat how much I love her. Then I kiss the top of her head again, wishing silently I could take even a small part of this hurt on for her.

"I love you too." Her raw, raspy whisper hitches slightly because she's still crying into my shirt.

She looks up at me with her moss green eyes, wide glossy saucers, her lips parting with a gasp that catches in her throat.

Her beautifully audible words both break and heal my heart at the same time.

"Did I? Am I...?" she whispers, stopping as she hears her audible words and gasping again. She holds back a lake of new tears building in her eyes, but her tears are not like the tears she's shed throughout the day. These are different. The other tears were tears of sorrow, of release. And these are tears of disbelief. She raises her hand and touches her lips, her eyes still wide.

It's my turn to be speechless. My beautiful, brave girl has spoken a total of eight words, and I don't know what to do with the pride that swells my chest or the excitement that zips through me. I can't help my reaction, but I have nothing to do with this revelation. I've just witnessed her breaking through her wall of silence. I want to simultaneously hug her and yell with excitement to all of our friends outside, but I do neither because this isn't my breakthrough; it's hers.

I gently squeeze her shoulders and bring my face close to

hers, so close our noses are nearly touching. As much as I want to pick her up and run her outside and share it with our friends, I rub a thumb over her bottom lip before leaning in and leaving a barely there kiss.

"That was all you, Kady. All you, baby. It's so good to hear you, baby."

It wasn't even her full voice, but I can already hear the inflection of her voice in my head. It's just as musical as my heart imagined.

She blinks up at me, her lips parting. She licks them, clears her throat, and makes purposeful and determined eye contact with me.

"I love you, Mav." Her voice wavers but is stronger and louder than the whisper from a few seconds ago. She gasps again, her hand covering her mouth as tears spill down her face.

I clutch her to me tight as she fists her hands in my shirt. We rock back and forth again. "I know you do, baby. I know. I love you too." I whisper into her hair. We stand like this for a while. Not wanting to spoil what we have here in the kitchen, I hold her until she loosens her grip on me and nods into my chest.

She's ready to go outside. She sniffles a few more times, then grabs a napkin and dabs her eyes. I put my arm around her.

"Don't tell." Her voice is quiet, wavering with weariness. "Please. Just in case it's a fluke." Her eyes beg me to go along with her.

"Okay."

We walk out to the firepit, our fingers entwined as we hold hands. She sits on a bench between me and Hayleigh. It starts out slowly, but pretty soon everyone has some sort of instrument and is playing and singing. Sammy outfits Kady and Hayleigh with tambourines and shakers. We all pour ourselves, our hurt, our loneliness, our love, into the music. Because music is what heals, what soothes.

Eventually, though, we stop, and the instruments are put away. Killian is the first to head to the door. When Kady catches on that he's leaving, she walks up to him and hugs him with both arms around his back. The sight catches Cal and me off-guard, but it's caught Killian off-guard even more.

As she hugs him, Killian's already wide eyes widen even farther and his lip's part slightly. She then pulls away from him and looks him in the eye and squeezes his shoulders hard. I didn't hear anything, but somehow, I know. She's spoken to him.

He swallows hard, turns quickly toward the door, and leaves without so much of a goodbye to anyone else.

Not having noticed the majority of their interaction by the door, Sammy shakes his head in frustration with Kill. "I'm sorry he's so rude." He looks out the door after our bass player. "I'll talk to him."

Sammy grabs his duffle from the floor. "It's time I stay with Kill for a while anyway, instead of taking advantage of Mav."

Kady pulls in Sammy for a hug. Cal and I watch as he acts just as surprised as Killian did. Dropping his duffle at his side, Sammy hugs her roughly with both arms, rocking her back and forth. He whispers something back to her. Kady nods and continues to hold on to Sammy until she finally pulls away.

"Uh, I'll call you tomorrow, Mav." Sammy's voice is rough with whatever Kady said to him. He picks up the bag at his feet and heads down the walkway.

Cal walks up to Kady and gives her a big hug. "I'm gonna head out, Kades."

She grips him hard as they hug, and the scene plays out again as she hugs him to her and whispers in his ear. Cal's eyes shut as he listens to whatever Kady is telling him. He nods slightly and whispers something back to her. He squeezes her tight one last time before letting my girl go.

Cal's behavior draws the attention of Hayleigh and Harden, who both stand beside me, watching with curiosity. Hayleigh narrows her eyes, and I put my hand on the small of her back and pat slightly to reassure her that her friend is more than okay.

"Take care. See you soon, Kady. Mav, I'll be in touch for those beers you owe me." He winks his watery eye at me, then flips me off as he heads out the door and home to his son.

Kady turns to Harden and Hayleigh. I extended an offer to them to stay here, since it's not like I don't have plenty of room, but as soon as Harden got into L.A., Hayleigh was off to stay at whatever hotel he's at. She claimed at the time that she did it to give Kady some space, but I'm starting to wonder if they're a couple after all. Or again. Hell, if it was a privacy issue, they could use the freaking pool house if they wanted.

Kady blinks and just stares at them for a few long seconds. I'm wondering if I should back away. Give the three of them privacy.

"Thank you." Her words are slightly less raspy than the ones she gave me, but are still quiet and unsure. Even so, the three of us can hear them clearly. "For everything, Hayleigh. Harden too." She shakes her head as her eyes fill with unshed tears. "I'm as strong as I am because of all you've both done for me. You're the best part of my family, the family I choose. I... I love you both."

Hayleigh stands completely quiet next to me for a few short seconds, as if she is still processing what just happened in front of her. I know the feeling.

"Holy shit, Kady!" She sobs outright while pulling Kady in for a massive hug. She pats her short fuchsia hair while rocking her hard back and forth. "You talked! You freaking talked, Kady!"

Harden says nothing, but his hand is splayed on Kady's back in support and his head is down. He nods slightly, like she sounded just like he figured she would. Because she does. Exactly like I thought. And it's the most beautiful sound.

"Wow, kiddo, just wow," he says quietly into her ear.

When they finally move to leave, Kady hugs Harden tight. Hayleigh narrows her eyes at me. "You're not surprised because she's already spoken to you." The tight line of her lips are slightly jealous, but her voice is also tinged with gratitude.

I nod and confirm her suspicions. "In the kitchen before we came out to the fire pit. She told me she loves me." I shrug, hating that Hayleigh didn't get to see Kady speak to all the band members before her. She loves Hayleigh like a sister and Harden like a brother; it's obvious in the way she looks at them. "She also told each of the guys something as they left. I couldn't tell you what, though."

A big part of me wants to know what she said to the guys, but I'll never ask. Whatever she said surprised and moved Killian so much he wouldn't even make eye contact. She gave both Sammy and Cal a massive case of the feels, as both were teary. That's between them and Kady, and it should stay that way.

Kady hugs Hayleigh and quietly whispers words to her friend. Harden slaps me on the back and says goodbye while we wait for the girls.

"You know I have plenty of room. You two don't need to stay at a hotel." I still can't figure out their reluctance.

Harden nods. "It's not about you, man. It's about us. Hayleigh's always been the one that got away. I'm trying to change that to the one I got back. We've been... reconnecting? Working on us." I slap his back and nod. He's a good guy. I hope it works, but I have the feeling that even if it doesn't, he'll still be in their lives.

Hayleigh pulls away from her friend. "Thanks for ruining

my makeup." She gives Kady one more quick squeeze. "Text me tomorrow."

Kady nods, and Harden puts his arm around Hayleigh as they walk out my front door. I kiss the top of Kady's head as she waves when Harden and Hayleigh pull out past the gate. She looks up at me with those big expressive eyes of hers, and I know she's about to say something, but I kiss her first.

"So. Fucking. Brave." I hold her to me.

Chapter 32

Kadence

I t's been seven weeks since the memorial vigil. Seven weeks since I found my voice. Mostly. It's still tentative. I'm never sure when it will come out and when it won't. If it's just Mav and me, I'm almost always vocal, and not just in a whisper. Same with Hayleigh and me. And Harden. And the band, mostly. Although when we are all together in a big group, sometimes it won't come. It's frustrating that it's never in front of strangers or out in public. I can't order my own food yet. I still can't pick up the phone and call someone, not even Mav or Hayleigh. I still can't sing. I keep trying, though.

I made a speech therapy appointment with Dr. Kennedy. Hopefully, he'll be glad to see me again and have some suggestions now that I can talk some of the time. I see him in a week. Mav wants to come to my appointment with me, support me in everything I do. I love that he does. I can't tell if Hayleigh is relieved that she doesn't have to go with me, or jealous that Mav is going in her stead. I think it might be a little bit of both.

I haven't seen Mav in eight freaking days and it's killing me. He's bought a house here in Vegas. Well, Henderson, technically. It's out by the lake in the same community as the Airbnb he stayed at while doing the residency, but it's even bigger. And more private. He hasn't moved into it yet. He closed on it ten days ago. After that, he immediately had to go first to New York, then Nashville and Florida, with the band for some press things about the new album. I'm so excited for them and a little for me, since I did help with two of the songs.

He's keeping the Malibu house, but he wanted one here too. I'm pretty sure that he's hoping I'll come to L.A. and move in with him when he gets back. I think he's sensed my reluctance to be so far from Hayleigh, especially if he's going to be gone city-hopping doing press for this new release. I don't want to be stuck in L.A. alone. Could I get by? Probably, but I'd miss Hayleigh too much. I haven't decided if I'll move in with him yet, but I kind of want to. But then again, he hasn't asked me outright, so I'm putting the cart before the horse.

Mav: Beautiful. I need a huge favor.

Me: Anything.

Mav: Can you let the delivery guys in the backyard tonight at 7:00? This'll be the last one before I'm back in Vegas. Please?

Me: Sure.

Me: I miss your face.

He sends me a picture of himself making a silly face.

Mav: I miss your everything.

Me: Still coming home tomorrow?

Mav: Yep. I'm trying to move up my flight, but no luck. So as of right now, I land at 6:45pm. I'll let you know if that changes.

Me: You better. I want to pick you up and tell you things.

Mav: And I want to listen to you tell me things. Let me know when the delivery guys get there.

Me: Love you.

Mav: Love you too, beautiful.

I bet it's the outdoor furniture he ordered. I'm excited to see it because he had me help him pick it out. I haven't been to the house since the day before yesterday. I can't wait to see it all put together.

But mostly, I miss Mav. Before he left for New York, we had been together either here at my apartment or at his place in Malibu. We hadn't been apart for more than a day or two. That's why this trip of his to New York is killing me. I should've gone. He offered, and I was tempted, but ultimately decided to stay here. Good thing since I've been his liaison for his Henderson house, letting in movers, interior designers, and painters.

Harden's in the kitchen with Hayleigh, making something for dinner. It smells so damn good in here. He's here a lot more now. I love him and I love Hayleigh. And I love them together. I didn't know them as a couple before, but this seems good for both of them.

"Smells good." I pat him on the back as I pass by.

"You're eating with us, right?" He motions to what looks like spaghetti sauce.

"I have to be at Mav's by 7 for some delivery. I think it might be the patio furniture finally."

Harden looks at me, concerned. "I don't love the idea of you out there alone in the evening with strange delivery men, kiddo. I'll come with."

I pucker my lips. "Mav scheduled them. It'll be fine. I'll text you when I get there and when they get there. Okay?" He's not happy, I can tell by the flex in his jaw.

"Hayleigh and you deserve some you time without me." I lean up and kiss his cheek. "Thank you, though. For caring."

He smiles a soft smile, his eyes suddenly watery.

"What?" I'm horrified. Why is he on the verge of tears?

"It's nice to *hear* you. So fucking nice." He drops his head for a second while he reins himself in, then looks back up at me.

"You know, you thank people, a lot." He pulls me into a hug.

"I'm more thankful than I've ever been," I mutter into his t-shirt.

℞

PULLING through the gate into Mav's new house at 6:50pm, I send a text to Harden, then to Mav. I'm early, so I let myself in and wander around. It's really starting to come together but still smells of fresh paint and new carpet. I set his mail on the counter in the kitchen.

In the great room, I run my fingers along the keys of the piano that was delivered just before Mav left. It's a beautiful, white baby grand piano. It looks so majestic in here, and I envision myself sitting there playing it.

Mav: Are you at the house yet?

I send him a selfie of me sitting at the piano.

Mav: Beautiful as always. Even at my piano.

I roll my eyes.

Mav: Don't roll your eyes.

Shit, he knows me too well.

Mav: Don't forget they'll need to use the side gate, so be sure to turn on the lights in the backyard. I don't want anyone tripping and suing me.

Me: You're bossy tonight.

Mav: You love me anyway.

Me: I do.

I wander over to the light panel and turn on the patio lighting. There is way more light coming through the windows than there should be. Moving toward the patio door, I see the backyard bathed in soft light, faerie lights lining the yard, even though it isn't landscaped yet. Sitting smack in the middle of the dirt yard in a lone lounge chair is Mav.

I drop my bag where I stand and rush out, not bothering to close the door behind me. He smiles and stands when he sees me rushing toward him. He holds his arms out and catches me when I launch myself at him.

"I missed you! I love you!" I kiss his neck and the days' worth of scruff lining his jaw. Then I go in and kiss his lips. It's an urgent, desperate kiss, but I don't care. I missed this man. *My man.* He groans a little when I pull back and look into the depths of his chocolate brown eyes. "Hi. You're early."

Mav gently sets me back on my feet. "Hi yourself, beautiful. I missed you too." He takes my hands in his and pulls me over to the lounge chair. "Sit with me?"

Sit with him? I want to sit *on* him, naked, but he seems reserved, almost nervous, neither of which are attributes I'd usually describe Mav with. Something is wrong. Mav is never nervous or unsure. Not around me. I sit on the side of the lounge chair next to him. He's quiet and stares deep into my eyes, his chocolate to my green.

The quiet is slowly cutting open a wound in my stomach where all my reason is running out into the sandy dirt below. He reaches to the small table and picks up a tumbler of dark liquid. He takes a small sip before setting it back down. I want to grab the glass and down it all myself. Anything to get through this quiet because something is wrong. Really wrong. I feel it in my gut.

Mav takes my hands in each of his and lifts them to his lips and kisses them each tenderly. "Kady, Kadence, I need to talk to you." This is the kiss of death of our relationship; I know it is. *He called me Kadence.* He only calls me by my full name when he's mad at me. I look down at my feet. He's tired of me. Dumping me. Done with me. Turns out Kady is expendable after all. Thank God, I didn't embarrass myself and do something like move some of my clothes into his new house. I won't lie and say I didn't think about it, though. I mistakenly thought he bought this house here because he loved me and wanted to be here with me.

"I'm not doing this right." He shifts on the chair, and I continue to stare at my tennis shoes. "Kadence." His voice is solemn and steady. It's his bad news voice. It has to be.

"Kadence, please look at me." I don't want him to see how devastated I am. After all, he's the one who's been telling me how brave I am. I need to be brave now. I close my eyes for a minute and then give him what he wants. My eyes. When I lift my head, he's no longer sitting on the edge of the chair. He's on his knee in front of me.

"Kady. My brave girl. You wormed your way into my heart the very first time I spoke to you. I was resistant. I didn't want to trust. I didn't think I could trust, but you showed me that first day that sometimes you have to face the unknown with what you have. By just knowing you, I've learned what strength is. What trust is. What love is. And I know one thing. I love you like I've never loved another." He holds out a box and a ring glints in the light. "Kady. My love. Be the music that lights my soul forever. Marry me?"

My eyes are locked on the ring, and I can't tear them away. The ring is a beautiful square-cut diamond with a simple platinum band. Not too big or garish, but then again, not too small. It's perfectly me. I'm sure my mouth is wide open, and I have no words, but not because I can't speak, but because I can't believe that this man wants me. Forever.

"Kady?" He says my name with a nervous laugh, and I look up at him. He's squirming. He's nervous. Mavrick Slater is nervous, and it's because of me. I want to cherish this moment.

"Yes. I'll marry you." I'm careful to annunciate my words completely. His face instantly relaxes, and I lean in and kiss him. He runs his hands up my back and pulls me into a tight embrace and hollers loudly over my shoulder, "She said yes!"

Whoops and hollers rise from the lake just beyond the fenced-in yard. Next thing I know, the gate to the lake's edge opens and in come his bandmates along with Hayleigh and

Harden. Sammy has an open bottle of champagne, and they all already have glasses in various stages of consumption. "We knew she'd say yes, so we started the party a little early." Sammy shrugs and hands me the almost empty bottle of champagne as we all move inside.

I pull Harden aside. "You had to have known. What would you have done if I had taken you up on escorting me?"

He smiles. "I knew you were too stubborn to take me up on it. If I didn't know what he had planned, by the way, I would have become very insistent on coming with you." I hug Harden. He's overprotective and still has a weird thing about insisting on feeding Hayleigh and me, but I love him. He's the brother I wish I had.

That makes me think of my real brother. I wonder where Allen is in the world these days. What he's doing. If he's happy. If he ever wonders about me.

Mav's arms encircle me. "What's got you looking so melancholy all of a sudden, beautiful?"

I turn in his arms. Facing him, I shake my head. He pulls me close. "Talk to me."

I bury my head in his chest and just breathe in Mav. He's my everything. I shouldn't care about Allen. I have the family I chose right here, and it makes me mad that I am wasting my time thinking about him when he threw me away years ago, but it doesn't stop me from wondering. I shake my head at myself.

"Allen." I keep my forehead to his chest when I whisper the name.

"It's his loss, baby. All his loss." He kisses the top of my head and holds me tight. He lifts my chin up so I look at him. "You've got four brothers in this room who'd do anything for you. Give you the shirt off their backs. Protect you. Love you for the woman you are right now." I pull away and survey the four other men in the room. And I definitely feel that unconditional love Mav alludes to. Even from Killian.

346

Epilogue 1: Kadence

A year later

It's the day I've dreaded for almost eight months now. Since the day I started planning the first and hopefully annual memorial concert of the Monument Festival Survivors Organization. It's on the very same grounds as the festival. Although the grounds are set up in a completely different orientation than they were the night of the shooting, I still very much feel the heaviness, the solemnity of these grounds.

Hayleigh and Harden are sticking close to me and have been since they got in Wednesday morning. Part of me expects Hayleigh will try to force anxiety medication down my throat at any moment. She wanted me to take some this morning so it would be in my system by the time we arrived. I refused. I need to feel all of the emotions today, all of them. And other people need to see me feel them, to know that it's okay to feel what they feel. Just like last year. Because that's when I really started healing.

It's no surprise that The Blind Rebels are headlining the memorial scholarship concert today. It was with Mav's support

347

that I went to Tom Monument with the idea of starting a scholarship and grant fund for those affected by the shooting. It's been my pet project of sorts, but the entire band has been very vocal of their support since its inception eight months ago, including fundraising for it through their fan base with a table at every concert on the last tour. I should know, I sat at the MFSO table in the merchandise area at every single show, except for when I was on stage, that is. Yes, on stage. The Blind Rebels bring me out every night to play keyboard on 'Star Chaser' and 'Incredible.' Sammy calls me the fifth Blind Rebel, and he even made me a necklace to match the ones the guys wear. I almost never take it off.

I finally moved all the way in with Mav just over six months ago. We split our time between Malibu and Lake Las Vegas, and I'm starting to feel equally at home in both places.

I haven't seen Mav since he slipped out of bed early this morning. He went for a run down the beach and then headed out with Sammy to the festival grounds. Sammy stays with Mav and me most of the time. He has his own place, a condo somewhere, but as long as I've known him, he's never once stayed there. If he isn't with us, he's with one of the other guys.

I motion to Hayleigh that I'm heading backstage. She nods, and she and Harden veer off. I love that they're still together. She looks at him like he hangs the moon, and he looks at her like she's the sun in his solar system. I should know, since I'm pretty sure I look at Mav the same way.

I duck my head in the dressing room and Gibs squeals, "KayKay!" and launches himself at me in a blur of blonde curls. I swoop him up and snuggle into him as he lays sloppy open-mouth baby kisses all over my cheek. "KayKay, KayKay!" He falls into a fit of full-belly giggles as I blow raspberries on his stomach over his My Daddy Shreds t-shirt. I love this little guy and I haven't seen him in almost a week. Cal's still trying to find a permanent nanny he trusts who'll put up with a touring schedule. Sometimes I get the honor of watching him while the band is rehearsing or recording. Gibs is a full-throttle kid who has a natural love of music. No wonder, since he's surrounded by it.

Sammy comes over and swings an arm around me and kisses me on the temple with a chaste kiss. "You doin' okay?" I nod and he gives me a quick squeeze across the shoulders.

Sammy's the member of the band I worry about the most right now. He's been off lately, and not just to me, but beyond letting him know that he can talk to me whenever about whatever, I'm not sure what to do about Sammy. Neither does Mav, and it's keeping him up at night.

"Mav'll be back in a bit. He had to check on something on stage." I nod and sit with Gibs, who wiggles out of my arms immediately because this boy is all about his independence right now.

"You're playing with us tonight, right?" Sammy asks as he flops down next to me on the couch.

"Yeah. Actually, um, I have a surprise for Mav I've been working on with Cal and Kill. I wanted to fill you in on it because I'll need your help too."

Sammy furrows his brow at me. "Whatever it is, you know I'm in, but why did you just tell me now?"

"Because she knows your dumbass would slip and tell Mav. It's a *surprise*." Killian playfully slaps the back of Sammy's head as he makes his way over to the couch we are on and props a hip on the far arm. I lay out the song I've written while Killian teaches Sammy the beats I'll need as Cal watches out for Mav's return.

The two of them are working on it in the corner when Mav returns. To Mav, it'll just look like they're jamming; it's not an uncommon occurrence in their green rooms. I have captured Gibs again, and he's mostly content with me reading him a story before Cal's aunt comes to take him home.

Mav smiles softly as he drops down beside me. He leans in and kisses me, causing Gibs to look up at me because I've stopped reading.

"No!" Gibs says sternly at Mav and puts his pudgy little hand on his arm. "Mine! No-no!" He waggles his finger at Mav in a way that makes me think that it's something he's been seeing and hearing from Cal lately. I can't help but chuckle.

"Kaykay is mine," Mav says playfully and gives me another kiss in front of the toddler.

"No-no, Mads!! No-no! Kaykay mine." The toddler expresses his displeasure at Mav loudly this time.

"Quit instigating, Mav." Cal pulls his toddler into his arms. "No-no is right, bud." Cal hands Gibs off to his Aunt Sandy with a kiss.

I wrap my arms around Mav, who smiles and kisses me again and gives me that look. He's been giving it to me a lot since we've gotten engaged, especially when we are around Gibson. I think he's picturing us with a child of our own. He hasn't said anything to me about it and I'm glad because that's not a bridge I'm ready to cross quite yet. It's not that I don't want a child. I do. More than one. Just not quite yet. I have priorities. First on the list is getting through my surprise song. My stomach gives a familiar churn when I picture myself singing for the first time. Well, singing in front of more than just Cal and Kill.

The very idea of going from an audience of two to an audience of 7800 makes me want to throw up. It's also another reason I didn't want to take Hayleigh up on the anxiety meds. I need to have all my faculties about me. The song is technical to play, let alone play and sing. I need to be on my best game.

The Blind Rebels go on and I watch from the side of the stage. They work the crowd, and the crowd eats it up like always. Hayleigh and Harden are working the MFSO table for me, so I can catch the whole show and because I don't think I could concentrate with knowing what I'm about to do.

The lights dip down, and Mav invites me out on stage, per normal. He still has no clue. I come out and give the crowd a slight wave as I take my seat. We go through 'Star Chaser' first and then 'Incredible.' Then Killian moves to Mav's mic and grabs it, earning a 'what the hell' look from Mav.

I take a deep breath and look up and Cal is standing in front of me just like the first time I took the stage with The Blind Rebels back at HARD. He gives me a half-smile and holds my eyes, pouring his confidence into me.

"We are going to deviate a little from our usual show tonight. Hope you all don't mind," Killian says into Mav's microphone, and the crowd goes nuts. "You all want to help us with a little surprise?" The crowd goes wild. Sammy runs out onstage with a stool and sets it down for Mav and returns to his drum kit.

"Go ahead and take a seat, Mav." Kill points to the new stool on stage. "You'll be sitting this one out, because this song is *for* you and *about* you, but not *by* you."

Mav looks completely flummoxed as Kill coaxes him to sit on the stool and spins him so he's half facing the audience and half facing me. "Y'all might want to get your phones out for this one." Kill says this as he clips Mav's microphone into the holder attached to my keyboard, then gives me and Cal a nod.

Sammy counts off loud enough for me to hear over my monitor, and Cal and I start. Just like that day on stage in Vegas, I focus on Cal, but this time it's because I know if I chance looking at Mav, I'll lose it.

Steadying my gaze on Cal's, I take a deep breath and start to sing.

Hiding behind my camera.
Shattered beyond recognition.

It wasn't my life I was living.
I was surviving, barely breathin'.
Until you pulled me out of my shell.
I dwelled behind a curtain, replaying visions of hell.

Your love made me whole (whole, whole, whole).
Your touch helped me grow.
Healed my broken soul (soul, soul, soul).
And all I want you to know.
Is it's your love that made me whole (whole, whole, whole).

Your love made me whole.
My silence didn't scare you.
You listened to my heart.
My scars didn't repel you.
You saw the real me.

You awakened my spark.
Helped me see through the dark

I lean in closer to the microphone and close my eyes when I get to my favorite part of the song because I know that Cal will need to move over to his microphone to sing harmony with me.

Your love made me whole (whole, whole, whole).
Your touch helped me grow.
Healed my broken soul (soul, soul, soul).
And I want you to know.
It's your love that made me whole (whole, whole, whole).
It was your love. Your love. That made me whole.

When it's all over, I finally turn to face Mav. "I love you."

He's facing me completely now, audience to his back, because he's crying, full-out tears streaming down his face. This is exactly why I couldn't look at him while I was singing. I stand, pulling out the ear monitors and give a quick bow. The crowd goes crazy.

Mav approaches me and I wrap myself around him in a hug on stage, to give him a slight reprieve to collect himself since he still has about five songs left to perform.

"Give it up for our girl, Kady," Cal shouts into his microphone and the crowd goes wild again. "Come on out here, Kady, and take a proper bow before you scurry off." Mav escorts me to the front of the stage and plants a huge kiss on my temple as I get ready to bow again.

"I love you too, baby," he says into the microphone after I make my way back to the side of the stage. "Wow. That." He takes a breath and glances over at me offstage. I blow him a kiss and grin. "That was quite a surprise. Uh, where were we in the set list, Cal?" He jokes while getting back into his rhythm.

R

After the show and the first scholarship announcement, we attend an after party that goes on and on. It's nearly three in the morning when I finally step out of the shower and make my way into the bedroom of our Malibu house. Mav is lounging on the bed in the gray, low-slung sweatpants that he knows are my favorite. He's watching something on his cell phone.

"Whatchya watching?" I ask as I crawl into the bed with him, but his eyes are not on me. They are still on his phone.

"You." He smiles and finally looks up at me.

"No, I meant on your phone." I lift my chin to the device he sets on the nightstand.

"You!" He grabs me and before I can question it any further, he's over me. "When do I get to marry you again?" His dark eyes sparkle as he leans down and kisses me.

"You know I want to wait. At least a year," I answer when he finally pulls back.

"Won't be soon enough." He kisses me again. "Let's make it six months."

"You've got yourself a deal." I pull him down onto me.

Epilogue 2: Mavrick

Six months later

"Urgh," I moan. "I fuckin' hate ties." I pull at the fabric around my neck because I'm frustrated, then send the fucking thing flying across the bathroom. I just want this over with. I'd rather skip to the part where Kady and I are on a private beach, naked as the day we were born. "Can I just go sans tie?"

"Sans tie? No. Come here, you pussy." Cal grabs it from the floor and expertly loops it around my neck. "Hold still." He ties my bowtie, and I don't look at him. Because I refuse to make eye contact, he holds my shoulders firm and doesn't let go, egging me on to look him in the eye, silent until I finally do.

"This pony show is for her. The after party is for us. The after-the-after-party party is for you two. Got it?" He waits for me to nod and squeezes my shoulder.

Cal's hold and squeeze lingers, as does his stare. "Talk to me. It's just us."

"I just want this over with. I'm ready for the honeymoon." I glance at the door, hoping she's okay. Is she dressed now? Is she nervous? Mad? Will she hate me forever? Did I ruin the wedding she's been planning since she said yes?

"Bullshit, Mav." Cal looks at me, his narrow eyes assessing me coolly. "Talk."

"Her brother's here." I look at Cal. "I didn't think. Told him she was getting married. Suggested it would be a good time to show his face. Maybe walk her down the aisle." I grab the glass of whiskey off the table, gulping down half of it. I wonder if she's seen him yet. "What the fuck was I thinking, Cal? Letting her meet her brother without me? Stupid."

Cal's eyes widen at my confession, and he grabs his phone and his jacket and heads for the door as Sammy strolls in.

"You alive, fuckers?" Sammy smiles his usual carefree smile. "Look, I tied my tie myself!" he says, his chest puffed out towards Cal and me, his green tie a mess of loose loops against his neck.

"Um, no." Cal sets his jacket down and undoes the mess that Sammy was so proud of. "This looks worse than when Mav tries to wrap a present himself and uses that weird ribbon to tie a bow."

Sammy's smile drops when he catches that Cal isn't happy and I'm in a shit mood. "What's goin' on, guys?"

Cal barks at Sammy. "Stay with him. Keep him here until it's time. Gonna go check on Kady." He storms out with his jacket over his shoulder.

Sammy turns to me. "What's goin' on, Mav?"

R

Kadence

Hayleigh sighs as she curls my last blonde and lavender ringlet. "You look so beautiful, Kade. The dress is perfect." She hugs me to her, then pulls me away quickly. "Don't you cry and mess up my masterpiece."

I nod and try not to sniffle. There's a lot more going on here than just pre-wedding nerves, but I haven't told anyone yet. I wanted to tell Mav first tonight, but I can't hold out that long.

"Hayleigh," I start. I have to tell her. I have to, or I will bust. I'm a little worried about what Mav will say, but I think he'll be okay with it. "I'm pregnant," I blurt out.

She drops the tissue she was holding and turns, her pink lips in a perfect 'O'. "Pregnant?" she repeats. "Pregnant, pregnant, or I think I might be pregnant because my stomach is upset, but really, I am just nervous and not pregnant?"

"Blood test at the doctor's office pregnant. I found out the day before yesterday."

She grabs me and hugs me tight. "Oh my God. I'm gonna be an aunt! I'm so excited..." Her voice trails off when she notices my apprehension.

"I haven't told Mav. We haven't really talked about babies. I wasn't trying. I don't know what I'm—" We're interrupted by a sharp knock on the door.

Hayleigh turns to answer the door but stops and turns back to me. "You'll tell him tonight after the reception when it's just the two of you, and he'll love you even more than he already does." She puts her hand on the doorknob. "And if he doesn't, you'll come back home."

She flings the door open, ending our discussion. Cal starts into the room, his jacket slung over his shoulder.

"Hey, just wanted to come by and see how things are going over here. Wow." He stops just inside the door when he sees me in my dress. "Kady. You look ..."

"Pregnant!" I exclaim and burst into tears, unable to stop either my words or the rivers running down my face.

Cal's eyes grow huge, and he swallows loud enough to hear over my sobs. "Uh," he starts. "No?" His answer is unsure, his eyes as huge as saucers as Hayleigh grabs the tissue box.

"She just found out. They weren't trying and haven't talked kids yet. Oh, and Mav doesn't know." Hayleigh catches Cal up on our conversation from a few minutes ago. "Welcome to the bridal party." She winks at Cal.

He takes the box from Hayleigh, pulls out a couple of tissues, and hands them to me. "Dab under your eyes quick, before the makeup runs," Cal instructs me. "Mav'll be excited, Kady. I promise you." He pulls me in for a hug.

"But, but we haven't even talked kids yet." I swallow and look at Mav's best friend and best man. I can't believe I just unloaded all this on him, minutes before I'm scheduled to walk down the aisle at my wedding.

Cal whispers in my ear. "He's always wanted to be a dad. Trust me. I'd never lie to you, Kady. He wants babies with you, I promise." His hug and his words instantly soothe me, and I nod, even though I'm still locked in his embrace. "Tell him tonight, so it's just between the two of you. Don't let him know I know. I'll act surprised when he springs it on me, I promise."

"Okay." I nod and dab the napkin under my eyes as another knock on the door sounds.

Cal looks instantly nauseated. "I'll get it." He rushes to the door and slips out before we can see who's there.

I shrug and turn to Hayleigh. "Is my makeup still okay?"

"Let me see." She holds me out at arm's length and inspects her work. "Yep. Beautiful as ever."

Loud voices and scuffling come from just outside the door. Cal's voice is the only one I can pick out. "Now's not the time, man. Later." There is scuffling and angry-sounding voices I can't make out. "Maybe after the wedding. Kill! Some help?"

"What in the hell?" I march over to the door, fling it open and almost instantly fall to my knees in my white dress.

Luckily, Cal turns my way just before my knees give out

completely and grabs me under my arms and walks me backward toward the couch. "Sit."

"You!" He points to Allen. "In here. Shut the fucking door." Allen has no choice but to comply as Killian stands behind him, blocking his getaway route. Killian's face is stoic and slightly menacing.

"Hayleigh, get juice for Kady." He looks at Hayleigh, the only one who hasn't complied with his demands. "Hayleigh. Juice. Now."

She walks toward the door but turns before she gets to it. "You have some nerve showing up here, today of all days." Her voice is low and tight, and as she seethes, her nostrils flare with each word. "You fucker!" She screeches and lurches for Allen, but Killian catches her around the waist and pulls her out the door behind him. Her screeching echoes as she's dragged down the walkway up to the main house by Killian.

When the door shuts and all is quiet, Cal thrusts a hand through his hair and mutters, "shit."

Meanwhile, I just stare at Allen. He looks older than I remember, but then again, I haven't seen him in nearly a decade.

Cal turns to me. He drops down beside me and takes my hand. "Kade, Mav screwed up and realized it. It's why I came down here."

I look at Cal because he's not making sense. "Mav?"

Cal squeezes my hand. "He was being an ornery asshole this morning, even more than normal. When I finally got him to tell me what was bothering him, he told me he'd contacted Allen, expecting to be blown off. He didn't expect your brother to actually show up."

"I—" Allen starts when Cal cuts a deadly gaze at him.

"You shut the fuck up. It's not about you. Today is about Kady. Only Kady." His voice is cold and even, but the tension in his jaw tells me Cal is not above using his fists if his words aren't clear enough.

Allen swallows whatever he was going to say. In this moment, I love Cal. He's more of a brother to me after knowing him a little over a year than my own flesh and blood has ever been.

"Allen, here, may be under the impression that he's going to walk you down the aisle, but that's not going to happen unless you say so. Harden's ready to walk you as planned. This is your day. It's up to you." Cal squeezes my hand.

"Kadence." Allen's voice sounds exactly as I remember, and I close my eyes. "I, I'm sorry I haven't been around. I, uh, there's no excuse, but—"

"No. You're totally right. There is no excuse. You wouldn't even come when Hayleigh called when I was in the hospital, when I needed you." I look at him hard, wanting him to see not just how his actions affected me then, but also to see how strong I am now. "I'll listen to what you have to say. I will, but you're not welcome to be part of my wedding. This is MY wedding. You're welcome to stay for the ceremony, enjoy the reception and open bar. I might talk to you after I get back from my honeymoon. Maybe. Maybe not. We'll have to see when I'm ready."

I turn to Cal. "It's time." I rise and hold out my hand to Cal. "Will you escort me to Harden, so I can go get married?" Cal tucks my hand under his as I grip his arm and leave to go find my almost-husband.

R

Mavrick

Kady glows as she throws her head back in laughter at something Sammy says as they dance on the hardwood dance floor that's set up under the tent on the beach next to where we got married, just behind our Malibu home. She's so fucking beautiful, and she is so fucking mine.

She seemed a little off yesterday. I attributed that to jitters about our upcoming wedding, but she also seemed unsettled at the beginning of the reception. Maybe it's because Allen chose to stick around for the first time ever. Why, I don't know.

I'm not sure why I even bothered to invite him. Killian pulled me aside as we were getting some pictures done between the ceremony and the reception. He explained that Cal went off on Allen and then Kady told Allen that this was her day and that she'd decide if she wanted to talk to him after the honeymoon.

I wish I had been there to see that. Nothing makes me happier than when Kady is pissed off and standing up for herself. It's a sight to behold, even when it's directed at me occasionally.

"Stella's out front and ready when you are, man." Cal drops my keys on the table in front of me. He pulls out the chair next to me, sitting in it backwards and following my gaze over to Kady. She, Hayleigh, and Sammy are now holding hands in some sort of nursery-school-like circle and jumping around to the song playing. It's comical, but my girl's happy and that's all that matters.

"She's happy, huh?" Cal takes a slow sip of whatever he's drinking tonight and watches me.

I nod, having trouble tearing away my gaze from my beautiful wife. "Seems like it. Mostly. She's been acting a little, I dunno, off, the last few days." I look over at him. "Nerves, I guess?"

"She seemed pretty damn sure when I was with her before the wedding, man." He slaps my back. "I don't know much, but I know three things for damn certain. One, that girl loves you, asshole and all. Two, you love her back just as much with all of your assholey self. Remember that. Always. She's different." I wait, but he seems done.

I tilt my head and look at Cal. "How much have you had to drink? You forgot number three." I chuckle at him.

"I'm probably the second most sober man in the room, Mav." He leans forward. "Three; this band and Gibson are my life. I'm glad you found love, but I've got my hands full." He downs the rest of his drink and slams the glass on the table. "That's it. The three things Cal Donogue knows. Write 'em down." He winks at me and stands. "I'm gonna dance with that bride of yours before you whisk her off to do God knows what with her."

I let him take her for a spin or two around the dance floor. While they do their thing, I make my way over to Allen. "Nice to meet you. I'm Mav, your sister's husband, but you probably figured that out by now." I stick my hand out and he takes it with a firm handshake back.

"Nice to meet you, man."

"Part of me feels bad because I kind of fucked up the reunion. I probably should have started it earlier, but I've heard, pretty much, what went down between you and her in the pool house while she was getting ready. We'll be leaving tomorrow morning for fourteen days in Fiji. We'll be stopping in Hawaii on the way back for another three, and then we'll be back stateside. I just texted you her number. I suggest you make the effort when we return."

I return my gaze to the dance floor where my wife now dances with my best friend. "You may be her blood, but Kady chose her family, and I think she's chosen pretty well. If you're interested in really knowing the amazing and brave woman your sister is, make the effort, because she's worth it, but make no mistake, Allen. She already has four brothers and a husband to call family. So, if you hurt her again, you'll answer to all of us this time." He looks at me, shock on his face.

"Now if you'll excuse me, I'm going to remove my wife from the clutches of my best friend and get her out of that amazing dress she's wearing. Nice to meet you."

R

Mavrick

"Tell me again why we're staying at this hotel instead of in our own bed?" A very naked and well-sexed Kady snuggles up to me in the honeymoon suite at the Hyatt House.

"Because it's closer to the airport and we have an early flight." My hand caresses circles absentmindedly on her arm as she uses my shoulder as a pillow. She gives a happy, contented sigh and kisses the underside of my jaw, my favorite place for her kisses.

I hold her to me and revel in us. This is truly the happiest I've ever been.

I think she's fallen asleep, but then she whispers, "Mav?"

"Hmm?" I answer.

"I need to tell you something." I can hear the hesitation in her voice.

"What is it, beautiful?" I kiss the top of her head to reassure her.

"A few days ago, I went to the doctor. Mav, she told me I'm pregnant." She's holding her breath. I can feel her holding it in. Wait? Did she just say pregnant? As in a baby?

"Pregnant? Really?" Even I can hear the disbelief in my voice. We haven't gotten to that conversation. The one about babies. I look down at her and she's still holding that breath. If she doesn't breathe soon, she'll turn blue. "Baby, breathe." I kiss her lips and she finally expels the breath.

"I didn't do it on purpose. I just went to get blood work for my physical. It wasn't expected. I never missed my pill, I swear. I'm—" I hush her with another kiss.

"Maybe I did it on purpose." I look into those green eyes of hers, wet at the bottom like she might cry.

She's confused. "Did you mess with my pills?"

I kiss her again.

"No, silly girl. I just mean, our baby isn't a mistake, it's an on purpose. Might not have been expected, but—" I place my hand on her abdomen under her belly button. "It's much wanted and loved. Just like you are."

The Playlist

I'm a playlist junkie. I decided to recreate my writing playlists for these books from Apple Music to Spotify because more people have access to that then they do Apple Music (not to mention my Apple Music account is not under my pen name).

This is a small sampling of the music on the Spotify playlist for 'Bridging the Silence' (BTS):

1. Saints of Los Angeles- Motley Crue
2. Let Me Go To The Show- Poison
3. What Can I Say?- Jet Black Romance
4. Hollywood (so far, so good)- Warrant
5. Desperately- Slaughter
6. I Wanna Rock- Twisted Sister
7. Rise and Fall- Jet Black Romance
8. Rhythm From A Red Car- Hardline
9. House of the Rising Sun- Five Finger Death Punch
10. Rebel Love Song- Black Veil Brides

The full Spotify playlist for BTS is 56 songs and plays for nearly 4 hours and is perfect for long stints writing/editing or when you're procrastinating by cleaning.

Bridging The Silence Playlist on Spotify. (Spotify: https://open.spotify.com/playlist/1oFNyID9JgFgSPEiHoJIoZ)

You can also this find this list on my website: amykaybach.com (it's under Books and then Bridging the Silence) .

Or in my FaceBook Reader's Group: Backstage with Amy Kaybach under the Guides tab.

What's Next

Want to know which of the Blind Rebels boys is up next? That'd would be Rebels guitarist and single father Callum Donogue.

Blending Chords

Callum

Guitarist. Rockstar. Blind Rebels bandmate. My public persona embodies all of these titles fans have gifted upon me. But none of them matter as much as the role bestowed on me two years ago: father.

My son is my world, yet juggling being a single father with everything else hasn't been easy. I know I need help, but how can I trust a stranger with the one thing my entire world revolves around?

Arista

I must get out of my sister's house. As much as I love her, I can't tolerate her handsy husband. Armed with a degree in early childhood education, I'm determined to find a live-in nanny position that will allow me to truly make a difference in a child's life.

Being a nanny for Callum Donogue looked like the opportunity of a lifetime. Unfortunately, he seems to resent me being there, spending time with his son. Can we find a way to make this work? Or will our constant clashing prompt him to hang up his guitar and abandon the Blind Rebels mid-tour?

Want to know which of the Blind Rebels boys is up next? That'd would be Rebels guitarist and single father Callum Donogue.

Blending Chords, Coming June 2022

Acknowledgments

I read a quote somewhere that writing is a lonely pursuit, and while I guess that is somewhat the case during the writing part, it also takes a village for an indie writer like me to create a book out of the stories that live in her head. Here's a small glimpse into my village:

Misty: You may not have been in on it from the beginning but that's only because I wanted to make sure I'd actually follow through with it. I know you'll be cheering me on anyway because that's what you do. Always. No matter what crazy antics I've gotten us into. Here's to many more years of me getting us into crazy situations.

Jamie Morgan: I wouldn't have pursued writing and publishing these rockin' characters in my head if it weren't for your stalwart encouragement and support. You've read the rawest of first drafts, sometimes when the books weren't even done and given me the most honest, helpful feedback. The Blind Rebels exist because of you!

Tricia: Thank you for lending your eagle and legal eye to my book and for your cheerleading and unending support!

Shayna Astor and Sherry Bessette: Thank you for your willingness to not just critique my words but provide honest feedback and encouragement in general. This includes the gentle nudges Sherry gives me about when the books are coming out or where I'm at in the next story and Shayna answering my million and three questions about the entire process. I promise to pass along the help if/when someone comes to me.

Hayleigh of Editing Fox: Hiring an editor was the scariest part of the process for me. The very idea of handing my precious characters and stories to a virtual stranger whose job is to find the problems within them was terrifying. I knew in my gut I wanted to work with you after just a couple of quick email exchanges because you were just as enthused with my characters and their stories as I was. You saw my boys for who they were and helped me develop them until they reached their potential. I've learned and continue to learn so much from you in this process. I'm pleased to call you not just my editor but my friend.

Charli: For answering my call for help with the creation of my website (and mailing list and online shop) all last minute. And putting up with my limited design knowledge. She even fixed the webpage after I broke it before it went live. Then agreeing to help me get the shop going too! She rocks!

Emily: For making me awesome covers befitting of the Rebels that didn't have people on them. My Blind Rebel boys have very specific looks, and I couldn't imagine a cover model that could possibly match what I see in my head (especially for Sammy and Killian). And for putting up with all my newbie questions!

My parents: They supported my crazy idea without having read a word and were proud just because I was daring to doing it. They even gave me ISBN numbers for my birthday.

This was all because of you and I appreciate it!

About amy kaybach

Amy Kaybach has been writing since she learned to hold a pencil at three. When she's not daydreaming about sexy rock stars and how to put them into print, she's working in IT or planning her next great adventure with her best friend since junior high. She lives on the central coast of California with her two obnoxious, but well-loved beagles.

She's loved both music and motorsports since she was teeny tiny. As a motorsports fan she loves her cars loud and fast and her drivers a little brash. As a music lover she her music hard and loud.

She loves to connect with her readers. You can find her on Instagram, Facebook and AmyKaybach.com or you can email her at authoramykaybach@yahoo.com.

facebook.com/RockinAuthorAmyKaybach

instagram.com/authoramykaybach